# KITCHEN WITCH

## LIBERTY VALLEY LOVE: BOOK 7

## JOSIE MALONE

*Kitchen Witch is dedicated to my sister writers of the Evergreen Writer's Group who helped make this book better. I'm grateful to them for the critiques of various chapters, and the suggestions to improve the story. As the saying goes, "Friends are the sisters we choose for ourselves." Thanks again. I couldn't have written this book without you.*

# KITCHEN WITCH – TRILUNON GLOSSARY

_Amalodia_ —The largest continent in _Trilunon_ with a matriarchal society, its witch queen rules the entire realm with the support of the Mage Priests from _Ethlestia_ and the soldier-wizards of Warpathia.

_Banexorting_ — A spell that transports someone or something thousands of miles including through Time.

_Capostrol_ — The wizard-partner to a witch who serves as a _Vaslattel_, who is a secondary mate, subordinate to the other wives and any female servants in the household. Her children also reflect this lesser status.

_Ceroymatand_ — Man in an arranged, marital match, but there isn't a soul-bond and in the higher classes, any children return to the woman's family if something happens to her. If she holds a higher rank, like that of a queen, he's considered a consort, not her equal.

_Chapalmatand_ —— a wizard who sacrifices his heart, mind and soul in an ancient rite binding himself to a witch – no, this doesn't kill him, but he swears to love and protect her beyond death in an eternal soul-matching ceremony.

_Dracklegons_ — A cross between humans and dragons, these Mage-Priests are the dreaded enforcers of Trilunon laws burning criminals alive in the _Fires of Eternity_ since they prefer their "meat" roasted. This fatal punishment keeps convicted criminals from reincarnating.

_Ethlestia_ — The smallest continent in _Trilunon_ where the Mage-Priests, _dracklegons_ rule and create the laws that the people of Trilunon follow.

_Garungap_ — Foul, muddy sludge at the bottom of a sewer.

_Hisprinarch_ — Oldest son and heir to the throne of _Warpathia_.

_Hisprinling_ — The title for a second royal son who might ascend the throne of _Warpathia_.

_Huspowner_ — How a woman refers to her chosen soul-match in _Warpathia_.

_Laspowima_ — A female, eternal mate, or partner, usually a _Trilunon_ witch who accepts a soul-bound wizard for an eternal life match where he agrees to "know all, accept all and love her unconditionally." She must be worthy of such a noble sacrifice.

_Liminfovia_ — A _magick_ place, between Time, Life and Death. People end up there when they anger witches. It may take days, weeks or even years to escape, or cross from one realm to another.

_Majeenler_ — Title for the High Queen or Regent of _Trilunon_.

_Relkinam_ — All members of an extended family.

_Siblerbro_ — New brother after a soul-matching ceremony with a female relative, often a sister or cousin.

_Stalenary_ — Hereditary, powerful alpha, either male or female, who controls all the shapeshifter packs in a region. Trained by the Mage-Priests or Mage-Priestesses to rule equitably, there is usually one for each were-species. They work with the _Trilunon_ royal family but consider themselves subservient to no one.

_Talipenlace_ — An enchanted set of jewels created by a wizard and then he seals them with his heart, mind, blood, and soul in an eternal spell-casting before giving them to his mated witch.

_Trecesalty_ — Three royal witch-queens born at the same time – (triplets), a rare occurrence in _Trilunon_, and one that unites all three continents since it's seen as a sign of immense favor by the _Goddess_ and her consort, the _Horned God_. The three witch babies are blessed by the Mage-Priests and marriages are arranged for them while they are still in the nursery to gain support from everyone who lives on the three continents.

_Triholath_ — A religious, holy day when the Sabbats or Fire Festivals fall on days when all three moons are present, and the three rings of the sun show in _Trilunon_. It often includes the Fires of Eternity.

_Trilunon_ — A distant realm with three moons and a three-ringed sun, destroyed by the treachery of a demon prince who unleashed a _magick_ curse that affected the air, soil, and water killing many of the inhabitants. The survivors managed to escape through a portal to this realm (Earth).

_Vaslattel_ — A secondary mate, subordinate to the other wives and any female servants in the household. Her children also reflect this lesser status.

_Vow-Shredders or Oath-breakers_ — Those who break their promises and dishonor their families, a heinous offense to the people of _Trilunon_. Punishment is a death sentence, one that prevents reincarnation.

_Warpathia_ — One of the three continents in _Trilunon_, with a patriarchal society based on a military structure. All male citizens must serve in the armed forces.

# KITCHEN WITCH CHARACTERS

## Corbettstown, Washington – 2018:

(Most inhabitants left their home of *Trilunon* when it was destroyed in a plague 300 years ago and came to this realm. When reincarnated, they don't have their memories of the past until they turn 30 or find their soul-matched mates).

**Gunnolf Marvin (Jarvesel)** — 355-year-old sorcerer - demon prince who serves as police chief, and enforcer, second in command of the official shape-shifter (wolf) pack. Father of Meteor, Astra & Venus.

**Corrine Corbett (Corrinadora)** — 350-year-old female primal alpha, life-mate to Gunnolf. Reborn 23 years ago, she is still coming to terms with her past and her abilities. Leader of Shadow Pack – resistance in Corbettstown.

**Latham Sellers (Lavarutesel)** — Gunnolf's demon apprentice, pack executioner.

**Frank Corbett (Frejakenscar)** — Corbettstown pack alpha, director of Corbett Logging.

**Lorena Corbett (Orrensakamor)** — Corrine's adoptive mother.

**Hester Corbett (Halinester)** — Treyton's mother and Corrine's mentor at the police department.

**Andrel Corbett** — 23-year-old alpha shifter, police officer, Corrine's best friend, Second in command of the Shadow Pack.

**Treyton Corbett** — 23-year-old beta wolf shifter, police officer, Corrine's previous boyfriend.

## Eagleville, Washington – 2018:

(Most inhabitants left their home of *Trilunon* when it was destroyed in a plague 300 years ago and came to this realm. When reincarnated, they don't have their memories of the past until they turn 30 or find their soul-matched mates).

**Meteor Jamison (Matiranika)** — 28, Hereditary Kitchen Witch, Entrepreneur, Shapeshifter. Soul-Matched to Jed Corbett. Mother of two sons, one daughter.

**Jed Corbett (Thojedescar)** — 35, Soul-bound Wizard to Meteor, Logger, Shapeshifter, Father of two sons, and one daughter.

**Astra Jamison (Satiranika)** — 28, Hereditary Witch, Meteor's sister, Criminal defense lawyer.

**Rowdy Tall Deer (Rowindache)** — 38, Soul-Bound Wizard to Astra, High Healer. From 1888.

**Venus Jamison (Katiranika)** — 28, Hereditary War Witch, Meteor's and Astra's sister, Rancher.

**Hugh (Holt) O'Connell (Hughondear)** — 35, Soul-Bound Wizard to Venus. From 1888.

**Gard Devlin (Gardersolter)** — 38, Bodyguard, Private Detective, Friend to Jed Corbett.

**Rebekah Corbett (Robinaranika)** — 24, Half-Sister to Astra, Meteor, & Venus, and Trina Corbett. Astra's Apprentice. High Healer in training, Potential *Guardian,* Member of Shadow Pack in Corbettstown.

**Brigid Dawson (Brijudbekif)** — 32, Pastry Chef, Apprentice Witch to Meteor.

**Junior Corbett (Frajunescar)** — 33, Jed's cousin, Frank Corbett's son, wolf shifter.

**Cherry Corbett (Ruchalmanex)** — 31, Junior's mate, wolf shifter.

**Trina Corbett (Palwhimara)** — 26, Half-Sister to Rebekah (same father, different mothers), wolf shifter.

**Estelle Jamison (Clympetranika)** — 52, Foster mother to Astra, Meteor & Venus, Regent-Queen of Trilunon who arranged soul matches for them to their wizards. Co-leader of largest coven in Washington State. Spiritual sister to Diana Yarbro.

**Diana Yarbro (Dianaranika)** — 52, Mother to Astra, Meteor, Venus, & Rebekah, Former High Queen of Trilunon, Co-leader of largest coven in Washington State. Spiritual sister to Estelle Jamison.

## Liberty Valley – 1888:

**Grayson Mallery (Jarvesel)** — 255-year-old sorcerer - demon prince who serves as Corbett's Town Marshal and enforcer, second in command of the official shape-shifter (wolf) pack. Father of Meteor, Astra & Venus and twin sons with Korinna.

**Korinna Corbett (Corrinadora)** — 250-year-old female primal alpha, life-mate to Grayson. School-teacher in Corbett's Town. Mother to twin sons.

**Leander Selby (Lavarutesel)** — Grayson's demon apprentice, pack executioner.

**Frederick Corbett (Frejakenscar)** — Corbettstown pack alpha, owner of Corbett Logging.

**Mary Corbett (Matiranika)** — 31, Hereditary witch, Shapeshifter. Soul-Matched to Tom Corbett. Mother of one son. Murdered by Frederick Corbett.

**Tom Corbett (Thojedescar)** — 35, Soul-bound Wizard to Mary Corbett, Logger, Shapeshifter, Father of one son. Murdered by Frederick Corbett.

**Astrid Hunter (Satiranika)** — 31, Hereditary Witch, Mary's & Kallisto's sister.

**Kallisto Hunter (Katiranika)** — 31, Hereditary Witch, Mary's and Astrid's sister.

**Bethany Rose Chambers-Morgan** — 35, Former Eagleville Homicide Detective, now a Junction City Detective and *Guardian*. Married to Marshal Rad Morgan. Mother of two adopted daughters.

**Rad Morgan** — 42, Liberty Valley Marshal, based in Junction City. Married to Beth Morgan, time-traveler from 2018. Father of two adopted daughters.

**Kyle Morgan** — 31, Writer, Cowboy, married to Nina Armstrong, new *Seer,* a time-traveler from 2018 who sees the dead.

**Nina Armstrong-Morgan** — 32, Photographer, new *Seer,* a time-traveler from 2018 who sees the dead. Married to Kyle Morgan.

## PART I

---

# "LET GO AND ALLOW THE GODDESS TO DECIDE."

— Meteor Jamison, shape-shifter, entrepreneur,
and hereditary witch

# PROLOGUE

## "MAGICK, MARRIAGE AND MONSTERS!"

*Trilunon*

*10 days before the New Year Triholath festivals*

A TEAR TRICKLED DOWN MATIRANIKA'S PALE, WASTED CHEEK AS SHE leaned against the pillows of the giant bed she shared with her sisters in their tower prison. Several blankets covered her, but she still shivered in one of the high-necked, long-sleeved nightgowns she always wore. Struggling to breathe, she stared across the stone-walled chamber at her older sister, Satiranika. "You can't be serious."

"I always am." Born in the same hour nearly thirty years before, the trio were the *Trecesalty* and considered favored by the *Goddess*. She was the oldest, a former High Judge in the courts of *Amalodia*, their country. Satiranika glanced at their youngest sister. "Well, say something."

"What is there to say?" Katiranika, the war-queen of their family, favored armor over the dark blue tunic, leggings, and riding boots she customarily wore. She pulled a decorative dagger from its sheath on her slender hip. "Our aunt, the regent of our land, steals

3

the thrones left us by our mother instead of turning them over to us at the Winter Festivals this year. Now, we're denied the privilege of royal deaths at the sacred fires. Instead, our aunt orders us wed, gives us away like sex slaves from the marketplace, as if we really are the treasonous criminals, she labeled us. Who does that witch think she is?"

"The new High Queen of our realm." Matiranika drew another ragged breath. "Who would match with us? My *ceroymatand* died in the first wave of the plague. Yours would have taken you, but his *relkinam* refused you, Sati, saying you're too much like our sire who slew our mother. Our aunt delayed Kat's binding to Prince Hughondear of Warpathia."

"She claimed to fear my death from the disease that killed the women and girls in that region." Katiranika ran a careful finger along the edge of the blade, testing its sharpness. "Even she can't mean to give us to strangers from other worlds. It'd lead to more wars."

"It's not strangers." Satiranika picked up the goblet of wine on the table near the door, crossed the thickly carpeted floor, and carried the glass to her middle sister. "Drink your tonic or you won't live to the New Year. You'll be on a *Journey to Rebirth*, rather than joining us in the sacred fires or at a soul-binding ceremony or traveling with us since she's banished us to a distant realm."

Matiranika nodded agreement before sipping the restorative beverage. Her links to *Trilunon* poisoned her as much as the fire rain that fell from the smoky, gray skies. She barely managed to breathe the soot-laden air and rarely tasted the food delivered from the palace kitchens. "So, who are the men?"

"The *Warpathians* I sentenced to death before my arrest." Satiranika sat on the edge of the bed, holding the golden cup for her sister. "After the *Priest-Mages* of *Ethlestial* demanded we serve our sire's sentence when he fled the fires and our aunt refused to send us to die when we were baby witches playing with our first wands, there aren't any other males for her to choose."

"What else did you learn?" Katiranika joined them on the bed, glaring across the room at the elaborate painting of their aunt on the wall. "Giving us to the felons in the dungeons couldn't have taken that long. How does she know they won't kill us when we're sent to this new world?"

"At first, she only said what I told you." Satiranika placed the goblet on the table next to the bed. "We talked of the *Healers*, Kat. They still don't have a way to cleanse the waters, air, or soil of this realm. The creatures here in *Amalodia* continue to die as do the people. Our aunt intends to have the *Healers* strip our powers before the soul-binding rites. Those in your army are to go with us to a new land far from our home here. She asked after Mati and wanted to know you controlled your temper."

"My temper!" Katiranika leaped to her feet. "I'll show that witch my temper." Whirling, she hurled a fireball at the painting. Ashes scattered on the carpet as the picture burned. "So much for her spying!"

Shaking her head, Satiranika waved her hand and put out the fire. "Cease, Kat. This chamber is smaller than either of our palaces, but at least we're together where she had us jailed. As for your other question about our mates, our aunt has decided they will serve as our *chapalmatands*."

"What does that mean?"

"Using a set of jewelry as tokens, they sacrifice their hearts, minds, souls along with their *magick* and powers. It doesn't kill them." Satiranika continued describing the ancient rite that would bind them and their newly matched mates. "We will wear the ornaments, the *talipenlace* sets for the rest of our lives and we will be bonded forever, through *Time*, *Death* and *Rebirth*."

"I won't." Katiranika lifted her chin, narrowing violet eyes. "I'll only be pushed so far. I will not be degraded or some man's property."

"Our aunt says that all three of us must wed on the same day, at the same hour or we lose our *magick*," Matiranika said. "She claims it's the law decreed by the *Goddess*."

"That isn't true. Our aunt doesn't know as much as she thinks."

Satiranika gestured for her sisters to draw closer. "I'm the one who has always studied every canon and *Book of Shadows* in all of the libraries here, in *Warpathia* and in *Ethlestial*. We are supposed to choose the *talipenlace* sets that we wish to wear. We can refuse and insist our newly *Chosen* mates place the jewels on us. They will believe us obedient, as women were in their land before dying in the plague."

Katiranika rested a hand on the dagger hilt. "If I set myself afire at the ceremony, it will start a war. I'd rather be dead than linked to Hughondear."

"No, Kat." Matiranika held up her palm. "If harm comes to you, I feel it. Your death will bring about mine."

"And I will die without both of you." Satiranika caught both their hands and gripped tight. "Listen to me. Our aunt doesn't have to win. For the *talipenlace* jewels to affect us, we must wear them of our own free will. Otherwise, they become tokens of *Power*. They focus our *magick* but give us the talents of our new mates too."

Matiranika ran a hand through her thinning hair. "I might regain my health."

"That alone would make it worthwhile." Katiranika frowned thoughtfully. "Could we really trick them so easily? Afterwards, we'll escape. I'll rally my soldiers and take back our thrones. Let our aunt go to the fires she loves so much."

"One problem at a time." Satiranika relaxed her grip. "I've never trusted our aunt with her love of the throne. Think. Who'd be forced to do the evil ritual to strip our *magick* and return all our powers to the High Queen?"

"Our oldest half-sib, the leader of the *Healers* who serve with Kat," Matiranika mused. "It'd slay Robin's heart. She cries when she comes to heal me now. She'll pretend to take our powers and lie to our aunt. We act as if we're without *magick* until we evade our enemies."

"A simple ploy," Katiranika said, "but those tend to be best in wars."

"Exactly." Satiranika stood and went to the table on the far side of the room to fill three glasses with wine. "Thanks be to the *Goddess* that we've always treated our older sister with respect and kindness. She serves us willingly and with much love. She knows we are the royal *Three*."

"And the *Three* are the *Trecesalty*," Katiranika and Matiranika joined on in the chant. "*Trilunon* is ours. We have the powers of the *Three*."

———

Matiranika half dozed in the large bed. Dimly, she heard her half-sister's healing chants, but the words barely made sense or provided any surcease from the unending pain. She hadn't even taken time to notice the decorative tapestries or blankets or candles when she was carried into this new chamber. At some point, the wizard who was her new soul-match would arrive and she hoped he wouldn't suffer too much when she died. Yes, he was a convicted felon, but that didn't mean he deserved to perish when she did. Before her death, she had to save him.

She heard the door open and then footsteps as he approached. "What's wrong? What's happened? Why are you ill?"

The question almost made her giggle. "I die, *Warpath*—" A spasm of coughing broke off the words. She looked down at the elaborate, enchanted gold necklace he'd created for her to wear, one that bound them, mind, heart, and soul. She touched the spoked sun festooned with tiny, jeweled creatures. "I'd hoped this would help me. It hasn't."

"Give it time." Robinaranika, the *High Healer* held out the goblet with the tonic. "You've only worn it a few hours. His energy is strong. Let it cure you."

"I have no time." Matiranika sipped the wine. "My aunt didn't tell—"

"She told him nothing. If she had, your condition wouldn't surprise this man."

Matiranika eyed Thojedescar, the tall, dark-haired wizard who

7

knelt beside the bed. "Call the priests, Robinaranika. The life-bonds must be broken. I will not do evil in my remaining hours, nor will I allow an innocent to suffer."

"I'm not that innocent." He covered her hands with his. "I'm satisfied with our match, *Trecesalty*. How do I help her live, *High Healer*?"

"By not offering food, water, or wine from *Trilunon*. As our realm dies, so does she. When the *dracklegons* open the portal and we leave here, I believe she will flourish in our new home."

"I wish the two of you would listen to me." Matiranika glared at the pair.

"We will when you say something worth hearing, *Chosen*." He raised her fingers to his lips. "Now rest and let me talk with your *healer* about how best I can serve and save you."

———

*In the Very Beginning...*

Official Ethlestial Scroll given to the Bard for safekeeping.

So, it came to pass the three moons of Trilunon aligned. The thrice-ringed sun shone bright on the *Triholath* when the *Trecesalty* were given away in soul-matching rites by their regent. Yet, their *chapalmatands* culled from the prisons of *Amalodia* were an insult to the three young queens, the long lineage of the Ranika *relkinam* and the *Mother Goddess*.

Following the ceremony, the *Trecesalty* were exiled from the realm which gave them life. Stripped of their magic, they were sent with their *chapalmatands* to die ignoble deaths in a world that denied sorcery and the true *Mother Goddess*. Thus did the usurper, Clympetranika declare herself to be High Queen, and steal the thrones of her own sister's daughters.

This was a plan long in the making for Clympetranika. It all began when she murdered her own sister. Afterwards, Clympetranika cast the blame on the innocent *ceroymatand*, Jarvesel. His only crime was to love the Most Serene, Most Gracious, Most Beautiful, Most Powerful of all Witches, Mother of the *Trecesalty*, the true High Queen, Dianaranika.

With her sister's death, Clympetranika stole the three royal babies from their nursery and spirited them away, declaring herself the Regent of *Trilunon*. When the innocent *ceroymatand*, Jarvesel attempted to reclaim his children so he could serve as their rightful Regent, the usurper had him jailed.

In a mock trial, he was sentenced to death, doomed to die in the fires of the next holy day. However, he managed to escape this punishment. Determined to save his daughters from those who would enslave them, he followed them in their disgrace to a new realm...

Enscribed by the Bard, Destynee LaFleur, for Jarvesel, Rightful King of *Ethlestial* and True Ruler of all of *Trilunon*.

# 1

*Eagleville, Washington*
*Wednesday, November 28th, 2018*

AT 4:00 A.M., IT WAS STILL DARK WHEN METEOR JAMISON PARKED her red Ford Explorer behind the two-story duplex she and her partners remodeled for their business. The building stood on the corner of one of the main streets in town. She'd painted a huge mural of fantastic creatures that included unicorns, centaurs, and winged horses frolicking as well as large letters spelling out Captivating Catering when they bought the structure. She'd started the company with three of her college friends five years before. At long last, the enterprise supported them, and they could quit their proverbial 'day jobs'. While they worked hard, it was worth it.

Her day usually started before dawn. Mentally, she began running through the list of tasks she needed to accomplish before the first customers arrived to order pastries and their breakfast espressos. She'd start by checking the walk-in refrigerator where she'd find loaves of bread, homemade bagels, croissants, and doughnuts waiting to be baked. Lizzie Drake, the head chef would have prepped the items on the lunch menu but sandwiches, quiches and two large tureens of soup always required finishing.

Still tallying the waiting work, Meteor unlocked the back door and entered the large commercial kitchen. She headed to the main bank of switches and turned on the fluorescent lights and then her favorite classic country music station before glancing around the room. The steel counters gleamed and so did the tile floor. Obviously, Daphne Hollister had finished her day by meticulously cleaning the establishment when she closed up yesterday. Meteor walked through the kitchen into the small restaurant area, admiring the pristine tables, chairs, and booths. Pictures of elves, fairies, satyrs and other fanciful creatures courtesy of Lizzie Blake and her friends brightened the cream walls.

Most visitors saw the long strands of small quartz stones hung like garlands around the room and windows as decorations. Few realized they were part of an early warning system intended to protect the bakery and its owners. Her sister's soul-matched mate had installed them a few weeks before, shortly after his arrival from 1888 when he explained they were in mortal jeopardy from their father, a demon prince.

*I'm lucky to have such wonderful partners*, Meteor thought, not for the first time as she returned to the kitchen. *Most people would think I've gone around the bend, not accept me as a sole practitioner of magick or kitchen witch. Of course, it helps that all of them aren't a hundred-percent human.* Lizzie was a fairy, Daphne, a frost elf and Tolliver Woods, part satyr. The four of them met at Washington State University ten years ago as freshmen and immediately recognized each other as 'something more.'

Meteor turned on the commercial ovens, and the giant coffee pot on the way to look at the whiteboard outside the office. She hummed along with the song on the radio, enjoying the opportunity to harmonize with it and was grateful Tolliver wasn't there to complain about her being off-key. He always said he didn't get paid enough to listen to her howl and that a wolf should have better pitch.

While she read the list of upcoming events, she put on a long white apron, tying the strings around her waist, then added a hairnet over the coronet of braids on her head. Two birthday parties, a wedding and a baby shower this weekend. *Everyone covered for me big-time while we waited for Astra to heal from her injuries and then return from that walk among the stars.*

For a moment, she recalled the witchy work she and her sisters needed to perform before *Yule*, the winter solstice. They had to deal with the evil that still stalked the streets of Corbettstown in eastern Liberty Valley, but the shape-shifting pack had run rampant during the twenty-four-plus years Frank Corbett served as alpha. No, he didn't *serve* the members. He ruled like a despot, and he needed to be stopped before there was more bloodshed.

As three hereditary witches destined to lead their people, the triplets had a duty to protect the innocents who'd followed them to this realm from their home in *Trilunon* so long ago. She remembered what Venus, their youngest sister, the war-queen proclaimed a few days before. "We're the *Trecesalty*, the sacred three who stand together. As it was once, as it will be now and forever."

"I'm the matriarch who protects the land, the sea and the air, along with their inhabitants," Meteor whispered softly, "and those include my children and my sisters."

She took a deep breath, dreading the upcoming battle. In four days, she and her soul-matched mate, Jed Corbett, would confront Frank Corbett, the older shapeshifter and let him know things were about to change in Liberty Valley. For a moment, she wondered if Jed feared the fight as much as she did. Probably not. He'd been a soldier-warrior long before they went through the soul-binding rite and male shapeshifters enjoyed wrestling with one another even in mock, rough and tumble battles. She'd certainly seen enough of that with their two sons during the past month after Edwin's arrival from 1888 with the two wizards soul-matched to her sisters.

When she opened the walk-in refrigerator, she spotted six tall, upright carts with trays of cookies waiting to be baked. Obviously, Brigid Dawson, her apprentice, a younger kitchen witch had spent the weekend here instead of shopping holiday sales, or celebrating with her family, or saving a federal agent from angry shifters, the way Meteor had with her sisters. What happened? How had Brigid's family put the fun back in 'dysfunctional'? Would her cousin share any of the pain she'd experienced or continue to suppress it?

Meteor heaved a sigh. *Sooner or later, I'm going to have to breach those walls and convince her it's safe to let me help, but today may not be the day.* Breakfast rolls baking and the baguettes for sandwiches in the other oven, she brought out the first cart of sugar cookies. The doorbell sounded at the front of the building, and she glanced at her watch. She didn't open for another two and a half hours, but someone might not recall that since the schedule had undoubtedly been erratic for the past two days while she stayed at the ranch nursing Astra.

She saw the two F.B.I. agents from last Friday night standing on the sidewalk outside and unlocked the front door to speak to them. The older one, a tall, stocky man, stepped forward, opening a black billfold, and revealing a badge. "Ms. Jamison, I don't know if you remember me or not. I'm Wardrow Roberts." He gestured to his companion, a handsome, young African-American, Native-American, mixed-race man with close-cropped black hair. "This is Agent Fletcher Gaines."

"I know. I remember you." Meteor wouldn't tell Gaines that he was a hell of a marksman, especially when it came to shooting from a moving helicopter. He'd only wounded the wolves she fought on Saturday morning. If he'd been armed with silver rounds, he'd have killed them. "Did you find your missing agent?"

"Yes." Concern swept into Wardrow Roberts' face. "I don't know who your sister's client was, but the information she received was correct. She died trying to save Special Agent Newsome. He and Agent Endicott are still in the hospital, but they're both expected to fully recover. Your brother-in-law—"

"Your info is incorrect." Meteor glanced swiftly at the younger agent. "Astra's fine. She'll be back in court this afternoon."

"That's not true. She had a sword in her back and was bleeding out." Fletcher Gaines took a step forward, a concerned frown on his face, dark brown eyes narrowed. "I've seen people die in combat. She couldn't have survived an injury like that, not when she was taken away before receiving medical treatment. Your brother-in-law should have waited. We'd have helped her."

Meteor shrugged and glanced over her shoulder at the wall clock. The smell of freshly baked bread wafted through the air. She had things to do, and these men were taking up way too much of her time. "I don't know what you saw, but both my sisters are fine. So are my cousins. So are all the women I know." She deliberately looked at her watch. "I have cookies to bake, and I need to get back to work. There's a lot of prep to do before the breakfast rush. So, if that's all—"

"We'd like to speak to your brother-in-law about the incident Saturday morning and find out who assaulted your sister," Wardrow Roberts said. "Where do we find him?"

"I have no idea, and I still need to finish the bagels. But I do know what my sister would tell you."

"What's that?" Fletcher Gaines asked eagerly.

"Get a warrant." Meteor closed the door, locked it, and hurried back to the kitchen in time to hear the timers on the ovens buzz.

A short time later, while she created gourmet breakfast sandwiches on the bread Brigid baked, the doorbell at the front door of the store jangled. Meteor went to greet what must be a new delivery person. Not everyone knew where to park or where she accepted supplies. It wasn't a truck driver or a customer wanting cookies, or to order a cake, or to arrange an event. This time it was Hilda and Erik Armstrong.

Meteor took a deep breath, hoping her dread didn't show. She hated hurting others, but Kyle Morgan and Nina Armstrong simply weren't safe in this day and time, not when the Corbett wolves saw them as prey. The couple had a better chance of survival in Liberty Valley of 1888. It was why she and her witchy sisters sent them through a *Time Portal* to the days of yesteryear. She certainly couldn't admit that, so she opted to hide the truth when she opened the door. "Hi. Have you heard anything from Nina or Kyle?"

"Not from law enforcement or the detectives we've hired." Erik stood six foot, six in his socks. A giant blond, he always dressed in cowboy style like the Hollywood stuntman he'd been in his younger days. He carried a medium-sized, wooden, steamer trunk with metal trim. "Hilda found this in the museum at the Bar M. She says that Nina left it for you and your sisters. Where do you want it?"

"Upstairs in my apartment." Meteor hugged the taller blonde woman. "I'm so sorry. I know you miss them. I wish there was something I could do to help you."

"It's all right." Hilda smiled, faint amusement slipping into her face. "I know this will sound absolutely strange and my big brother thinks I'm ready for the looney-bin—"

"I haven't said that."

"I see it in your eyes when I talk about them." Hilda lifted her chin. "Nina came to the Bar M for weeks to take photography classes with Will Dawson. He taught her to use the antique cameras in the museum. She never was in the storage area where I keep vintage clothes."

"Just because you didn't see her doesn't mean she wasn't there."

"She wasn't." Hilda gestured to the steamer trunk on his broad shoulder. "I know that even if no one in my family ever believes me. If they have me locked up in an insane asylum, I expect you and your sisters to rescue me, Meteor Jamison."

"We will." Meteor looked at the trunk. "What did you find?"

"I didn't remember seeing it before, but I must have. When I opened it, I found a red walking dress, button-up shoes, and a 'fascinator' style hat. They were very carefully wrapped with a tag addressed to Astra. There's an ornate dagger in a sheath for Venus and for you, an assortment of recipes in a bundle of sheet music for a spinet piano."

"How did she know I had one?" Meteor glanced at Erik. "I hate to agree with a man about anything, but your cousin was never upstairs in my apartment, and I don't recall mentioning it to her."

"I don't know." Hilda's smile widened. "I think I'll opt for Shakespeare and Nina's favorite quote, 'There are more things in heaven and earth, Horatio, than are dreamt of in your philosophy.' She left that in a note for me in another place she never went to when she came to the Bar M."

"Really?" Erik glowered at his sister. "Where was that?"

"The closed off wing of the house where the original Kyle Morgan, his wife, Antonina, and their children lived. Nobody ever called her that here, but it was Nina's full name." While Erik and Hilda squabbled about their cousin, Meteor led the way to the door that hid the staircase to her apartment. They might not entirely believe it, but now she knew she and her sisters had been right to save the young couple who'd obviously lived a full life in Liberty Valley.

Nina had left them a message letting them know *magick* worked, and they'd used it appropriately, at least this time. Who was to know what would happen in the days, months, and years to come? Foretelling the future wasn't one of their talents although Venus still spoke of an upcoming war, and Astra *Saw* the outcomes when people tried to harm innocents.

An hour later, Meteor was packing the neatly assembled holiday turkey sandwiches into individual cardboard cartons, so they'd be ready for the lunch crowd. She'd turned up the radio, allowing the music to break the silence that made the hairs on the back of her neck rise. As a shifter, she had a keener sense of smell and hearing than most humans. She was a natural hunter, but it didn't mean she enjoyed the dread that haunted her as she worked alone in the huge kitchen.

She heard the buzzer at the back door and the jangle of the warning wind chimes when it opened to reveal Lizzie Blake, the chef who created their unique and amazing menus. She opted for tattoos that covered nearly every inch of her small body, most of which had something to do with dragons. She'd dyed her light blonde hair in varying shades of crimson and green, decorated with multi-colored ribbons. Purple, pink and electric blue makeup used as a fantastic fairy mask emphasized her large eyes, forehead, and the top of her cheeks, matching the wings on her back. Few would realize they were real, not an affectation.

As usual, she'd dressed for attention and to make tips when she worked the front counter, choosing a steam punk outfit, a skirt and fitted vest in rich, embroidered pewter gray taffeta. A cream stretch blouse with full sleeves matched the ivory and cream attached petticoat with layers of different ruffled lace. The skirt had a slight 'V' line shape in the front and dipped down longer at the back. The hem had been decorated with a pleated ruffled row of more taffeta. Gray tights ended in lace-up, stacked, low-heeled boots.

"Wow, you're styling today. What's the occasion?" Meteor laid out more slices of bread on the counter. "Hot date?"

"A major party tonight and I don't have time to go home and change before I meet the others in the woods for our annual frolic of fairies. I asked Brigid to bake an assortment of tea cakes for us and I'll take along some cookies too. We do like our sweets at festivals." Lizzie paused at the end of the counter to check the two soup containers. Steam rose when she removed the first lid to stir the contents, and the rich aroma of chicken and spices filled the air. "Jed Corbett is already here to pick up lunch for the logging crew."

"That doesn't make sense." Meteor spread a thin layer of cranberry sauce on the bread. "Those guys burn a lot of calories, and they prefer the he-man burgers, onion rings and fries from the Crosscut Tavern to what they call our 'hipster' fare. Are you sure you saw him?"

"Yes. He parked in front of my car and was getting out of the Corbett Logging truck when he saw me." Lizzie replaced the lid and proceeded to check the Cabbage Patch Soup in the next tureen. More spices and another enticing smell, this one of fresh vegetables simmering together. "Time to open up. I'll let him in the front door. I'll call back his order when I have it."

"Sounds good." It still didn't make a lot of sense, Meteor thought. She didn't know why he'd come to visit or why Lizzie hadn't mentioned his companion, Gard Devlin, the private detective who always rode along with him. "I'll touch base with Jed later. Maybe he wanted to talk to me about the kids."

"Could be." Lizzie kept walking, bootheels clicking on the tiled floor. "When Tolliver gets here, have him help set up the showcases before he begins making mochas."

"You've got it." Meteor glanced toward the back entrance when the stocky, short man in jeans and a sweatshirt entered, taking a moment to lock the door behind him.

He gestured to the string of quartz amulets hanging from the line over the doorframe. The stones shone, reflecting white light and she shuddered, fear sweeping through her. Slowly, she turned and looked at the next set of rocks outlining the windows. More shimmering from the small fragments of star-shaped stones, but they didn't rattle on their lines like they would when danger entered the room. "What set them off?"

"I don't know," Tolliver rumbled, his deep voice oddly comforting. "Did they react to anything before?"

Meteor shook her head. The *magick* alarms hadn't gone off when the F.B.I. agents or the Armstrongs were here, and it meant they didn't intend to harm her. So, who did? She remembered what Lizzie had mentioned a few moments before, but she didn't see Jed or the truck from Corbett Logging outside. Would he know? When she was on break, she'd call him and ask if he'd seen any strangers around the bakery.

After one more careful glance at the amulets, Tolliver picked up the first tray of thickly frosted maple bars, carrying them toward the dining area. Half satyr, he'd enjoyed October when he didn't have to disguise his pointed ears, or horns, or furry legs and hooves. Now, he suppressed his true nature when strangers were around.

A steady flow of customers kept them busy all day and Meteor didn't have time to think about anything except work. When they closed, she helped Daphne clean the dining room. Lizzie and Brigid prepped for the next morning, scouring the kitchen between mixing new batches of cookies, setting bread to rise, and stirring up cake batter.

Just before sunset, while she washed the glass front door, Meteor spotted the older blue pickup taking a premier spot adjacent to the building. Jed Corbett slid out of the driver's seat. At six foot six, he was a foot taller than she was. Thick coal black hair curled around his ruggedly handsome face. A nose broken in one of his many brawls saved him from looking insipid. He could have been a cover model or an actor if a director wanted a rugged, he-man type.

Today, he wore heavy work jeans, as usual without a hem, cut-off about halfway between the knee and ankle so they wouldn't hang up on brush and limbs in the woods. For safety, he didn't wear a belt, but orange suspenders over a zip-up striped hickory shirt and spiked boots known as 'caulks', which strangely enough was pronounced as "corks." He definitely wasn't a fashion statement, but his visits always sent excitement racing through her.

Gard Devlin, a brawny, brown-haired private investigator hired to protect him followed Jed. Luckily, the other man had grown up in a logging town in Oregon, so he knew what to do with a bulldozer, part of the reason Jed was able to get him a job at Corbett Logging. Gard had dressed for cat-skinning success. His unbuttoned blue flannel shirt revealed a green tee that clung to muscled arms, wide shoulders, and a broad chest. Faded jeans encased long legs and he wore battered boots.

The two men sauntered around the building to the back door and buzzed for entry. Meteor went to meet them. When she opened the door, Jed's slow smile warmed her to the heart, but she hoped that didn't show. She tilted her head and met his night-dark gaze. "We're closed."

"Good." He feathered a thumb over her lips. "Then, you can come look at that cottage your mom intends to rent to my cousin, Junior and his wife, Cherry."

"I'm busy and Diana's real estate shenanigans aren't my concern."

"Yes, they are, sweetheart." Jed chuckled, a deep dark sound. "Bring your witchling to help you cleanse and ward the place while your aunt and Rowdy sever Junior and Cherry's ties to my uncle's pack and connect them to us. Cherry wants to help guard you and our younglings, so they don't end up as a feast for the Corbettstown shifters."

## 2

---

*Everett, Washington*
*Five days before*
*Black Friday, November 23rd, 2018*

ASTRA JAMISON GLANCED AROUND THE FOOD COURT, SEEING several shoppers who had the same idea of taking a break from the stores, but didn't spot her father waiting at any of the spindly-legged tables. She strolled toward a large one in a corner surrounded by greenery. Before she pulled out a chair, her mate, Rowdy Tall Deer did, waiting until she seated herself and then took a chair next to hers, facing the courtyard. She eyed him warily. "I can't believe you're adjusting so quickly to this time."

"What choice do I have when it's where you are?" Faint amusement filled his voice and lines crinkled around his dark eyes. "I never did see much use in complaining. It doesn't cure anything and generally only makes matters worse."

Astra looked at a laughing group of people passing by on their way to another sale. Some wore blue jeans and casual tops. One of the girls in a short, tight black dress sported several tattoos on her arms and legs. "What do you find most unusual?"

"How fast things happen." He followed her gaze. "Depending on the weather and the horses, it took days for Holt and me to travel to places unless we created a wizard's portal and that used too much *magick*. If we hadn't been in Washington Territory when Mary sent for us, we wouldn't have arrived in Corbett's Town before she died."

Astra nodded. "And the fact I'm a criminal attorney isn't a problem for you? It took until well into the nineteenth century for women to be able to practice law in America, and even more time to run for political office."

"I'm a *High Healer*. We've always had trouble finding enough folks with talent and keeping those who have different shapes from fulfilling their destinies makes no sense. I'd like it better if you protected only the innocents, not those who hunt them. It diminishes your soul when you send the wicked to die at the hands of your father or his minions."

She stiffened, trying to read his intent, but his face suddenly seemed impassive and calm, too calm. "Are you ordering me to do that?"

"No, it has to be your decision." He leaned forward, his fingers touching the bracelet she always wore now, the one that linked them forever. "As I told you before, you'll treat witches, wizards, and healers with the respect due them. You'll allow your sisters and their *Chosen* to decide their paths without your interference. And finally, you won't stray off any trail I set for you, which also means not manufacturing evidence. Let others have the outcomes they deserve."

"I always have." She started to pull free, but his hold tightened on her wrist, and she stopped. "You may not like it but my guilty clients either end up in jail or I send them to Corbettstown to serve my father and the pack as prey to be slain and eaten. That in turn protects many of 'your innocents' from becoming sacrifices, which is what Trina faced when my father tired of her, so it was lucky she managed to escape from him."

"Not just 'tired', he'd have taken all of her shifter magick before killing her or giving her to someone else who'd let him keep that *Power*."

Astra didn't disagree with the assessment. She glimpsed the distinctive light brown of her father's cop uniform and watched him approach, a powerful, muscular man in his early fifties. When he started balding years ago, he shaved his head. A thin, gray-haired man in a tired, black suit accompanied the police chief.

The two were close to the same age, but not a wisp of his dead victims trailed her sire, unlike his companion. She didn't see the actual victims, but enough of their residue remained to let her know that once again, she faced evil in a human form. She forced herself to remain still and not reveal she recognized Gary Smith.

Someone placed a white cardboard cup in front of her and she smelled peppermint in the rising steam. She flicked a quick look over her shoulder and saw her sisters, Meteor, holding another cup while Venus stood sentinel beside her. For once, Meteor had abandoned her favorite lemon-yellow wig. In faded, tight blue jeans, a gray and scarlet, Washington State University sweatshirt, and with her red hair braided back from her face, she bore an even stronger resemblance to Venus.

Their younger sister opted for black pants tucked into black boots and a dark navy-blue blazer over an ebony tank top. She'd coiled her hair in a bun on the back of her head, difficult for a foe to grab. Astra wasn't fooled by her sister's innocent appearance. Venus wouldn't enter any battle unarmed. She hid matching daggers under the full sleeves of her coat and undoubtedly had another pair sheathed in her low-heeled boots. Her favorite sword would be in a scabbard on her back, and a pink Glock in the shoulder harness barely disguised by the cut of the jacket.

Astra eyed the pair. "What are you two doing here?"

"We're the *Trecesalty*, the three queens destined to rule our realm and all our people," Venus said. "*The Three* stand together. As it was once, as it will be now and forever, you pronounce judgement and I'll render it."

"It's not safe for you to be here."

"I'm not a child you need to protect any longer, Satiranika. I'm the war-queen and I choose my battles."

"And I'm the matriarch who protects the land, the sea and the air, along with their inhabitants," Meteor said. "One of those is my elder sister."

"But your children?"

"Are safe with their father and his guards along with my *Chosen*," Venus said, her violet-blue gaze holding a lethal purpose. "Now, let's get this done so we can shop for *Yule*. Rebekah's holding our place in line at the toy store. We promised to bring lattes and mochas for the people near her."

Astra took a deep breath and met her father's dark brown eyes when he joined them. "As you asked, I'm here. What made you decide one of your followers needs a defense attorney?"

"You're not introducing me to your companions?" He raised an eyebrow, obviously amused. "Afraid I might go after them?"

"You?" She mirrored the look, letting just enough contempt fill her tone. "You don't recognize my sisters? Your other two daughters?"

"I haven't seen them in years. You and your mother kept them away from me." Gunnolf Marvin drew out a chair and sat down, gesturing for his companion to do the same. "I didn't expect a family reunion tonight."

"Good, because this isn't one. What do you want?" Astra barely flicked a glance at Gary Smith. "Why haven't you arrested him?"

"My jurisdiction stops at the town limits, and he hasn't committed any crimes in Corbettstown. You will turn him in at the county courthouse and represent him in the legal brouhaha."

"No. He's a killer."

"Alleged." Gary Smith spoke for the first time. "Never convicted."

"Not yet," Astra said, "but I *See* your doom coming. You defied the restraining order and attacked my client, Nina Armstrong and her fiancé, Kyle Morgan last month."

"I'm only one of several suspects." His tone smug, Gary Smith smirked at her. "Law enforcement doesn't have any proof, or any bodies after the fire at my cabin on All Hallows Eve."

"Evil surrounds you, an odorous miasma, and the wraiths of those you've tortured, maimed, and murdered follow you. As a handmaiden of *Hecate, the Goddess of Death and the Crossroads* she allows me to *See* what remains of their spirits, even if others can't." She returned her attention to her father. "Why haven't you ordered your executioner or Frank Corbett to take him as prey? If anyone deserves to be butchered and fed to rogue shifters, he does."

"Again, he hasn't done anything in my town, or harmed the pack."

She narrowed her gaze on him, recognizing a truth he hadn't yet shared. "He serves you and harms those you want injured. So, you allow him to hunt as he pleases and take out his rage on any females who fight you, plus women and girls who can't defend themselves, even the ones I serve as a lawyer. He doesn't observe my boundaries or yours."

Gary Smith stirred in the chair. "Speak to him with respect."

"Watch your words and attitude." Rowdy spoke for the first time. "If you wish anything from my mate, you owe her civility."

Gunnolf froze, his dark gaze narrowing. "I thought he was just your latest toy. You've taken him?"

"He's mine to do with as I please." Astra met her father's eyes, glare for glare. "I choose what happens to him, how long I keep him until I finish with him. You don't have a say. If you send your disciples, or any of your favored minions to attack him in this life before I'm done playing with him, I will end them."

"And you say you're not mine." A slow smile creased Gunnolf's face. "You'll always be more mine than your mother's with her silly, weak, white *magick*. I took your heart years ago." He leaned back in his chair. "So, you won't speak for my servant. Open the portal and I'll send him to safety in Liberty Valley of yesterday."

"I didn't close it, so I can't open it." Astra rested her arms on the table, closing a hand around the cup of tea, letting it warm her fingers. "It won't do you any good to perform a blood ceremony there. Try to force me and I will end you."

"If Smith hadn't already tried a sacrifice, we wouldn't be here." Gunnolf stood. "However, you don't control all the doorways to the past, my dark enchantress. He's served me well, so I'll take him to a different gate, the one near the Canadian border."

"I'm training a new Dawson witchling," Meteor said, her tone icy and calm. "Don't use her blood for your rites, or your home in Corbettstown will be smoke and ashes when you return."

"Another threat." Gunnolf's smile widened. "Does your mother know two of you are more mine than hers?"

"You truly are an idiot." Venus took a step forward, closer to the table. "Fair warnings and refusals to do your bidding don't darken my sisters' hearts or souls, *Jarvesel, Soul-Eating, Demon-Prince of Transgressions and Untruths.* Ward yourself. Light conquers darkness, as it was and ever will be—"

"You can try to stop me." Gunnolf Marvin gestured to Gary Smith, who rose, ready to follow. "You're not the only ones who issue warnings, my darling daughters. Thwart me and you die after I take your loved ones and skin them alive for my pleasure. As it was before, I'll enjoy eating their hearts again."

———

From the time Corrine Corbett was a little wolfling and learned shifters lived, died and were reborn again and again, she knew she was different. Her playmates talked about having their memories of past lives return when they were thirty or when they met their soul-matched loves. Instead, Corrine had always heard a woman's voice deep inside guiding her. The hidden stranger taught her how to survive in the dysfunctional Corbettstown pack with two ultra-controlling men.

The alpha, Frank Corbett insisted everyone in town use his last name whether they were related to him or not, down to the smallest adopted child like Corrine. Violence was a daily occurrence in the pack. Fights broke out between shifters in taverns, restaurants and even the local grocery stores for the most inconsequential reasons.

It wasn't uncommon to see the Corbettstown Police Chief, Gunnolf Marvin, the enforcer and second in command of the pack striding into the area businesses with his patrol of vicious deputies right behind him. All of them were ready to bust the heads and tails of those they perceived as rulebreakers. It was lucky shifters healed quickly from broken bones, and bloody injuries when they changed into their wolf forms. Otherwise, everyone would be on crutches or in wheelchairs all the time, males and females alike.

Even as a child, Corrine hated seeing the more serious offenders belly crawl to the enforcer and hearing them call Gunnolf their owner and master. Their punishments continued for at least a year until they'd served their sentences. On rare occasions the alpha granted clemency, or the pack executioner eliminated unrepentant lawbreakers. Her foster mother always told her that nobody truly owned a shifter, something Corrine kept to herself. She didn't want to see her mom punished for that opinion.

Most of the she-wolves were strict with their pups. Lorena told Corrine she was at school to receive an education, not to tussle with her classmates like she did during play time. Even young wolves weren't exempt from the enforcer's rules. He walked into the middle school one day, dragged a snooty cheerleader, Quincy Corbett, to the front of their English class and spanked her for almost killing a human resident's cat. Although she didn't like the girl, Corrine still felt sorry for her, but her attempts to befriend Quincy were repeatedly rejected.

Corrine stood on the back seat of the classic Crown Victoria and looked out the windows. Fog swirled around the police chief's car, and she almost tasted the *magick* he'd used to shield it from holiday shoppers in the mall parking lot. If anyone saw her, they'd be sure she was a K-9 officer waiting for a human partner, perhaps a Belgian Malinois in a service harness. Nobody would see her, a hundred-pound, gray timber wolf wearing a jeweled collar that changed into an antique gold and silver necklace when she was in her human form.

*I'm on his shit list again, and the stupid bastard doesn't realize it's all a game. My game! He's been hunting the members of my shadow pack for the past five years. He hasn't found any of them and the alpha is getting more and more pissed at him, even though they still claim to be best friends. At least my bestie isn't a complete and utter idiot like him. She covers my tail all the time. Nobody knows I'm the leader of the resistance and she's my second in command.*

Corrine stretched out on the bench seat again, contemplating her latest scheme. She intended to help two more members of her pack, Frank's son, Junior Corbett and his mate, Cherry escape before the alpha assaulted the other woman. The pair were soon to be off to Eagleville, living under the protection of the witches and wizards who resided there. The shadow pack would sanitize their house, so it reeked of bleach. No trace of the shifters who'd lived in it for years would linger and the pungent odor of the strong cleaning agents meant they couldn't be tracked by the enforcer or his minions.

Recognizing the approaching footsteps nearing the car, Corrine heaved a sigh. Time to adopt the persona of a brainless, twenty-something who screamed her head off during her orgasms when the enforcer fucked her. After she lost her temper and nearly succeeded in killing Frank Corbett, the alpha when he raped her almost a year ago, Gunnolf told the shifters in town she was his mate, commuting her death sentence. Corrine chose not to flee judgement. She stayed, deciding it was a good way to hide her true purpose, saving as many innocent shifters as she could in their small town.

*Goddess bless me. Gunnolf's such a freaking dumb-ass. At least, he's good in bed. Of course, he should be after almost three hundred and thirty damned years as a sex demon. He doesn't realize he only gets the shifter magick I choose to give him when he fucks me and of course, he also hasn't got a clue that I know more about him than he thinks.*

*Granted, his decision saved my life last Yule, but if I have to call him my owner and master one more time — Suck it up, Corrine. It's part of staying undercover and doing what you need to do! Keep playing the game and when you defeat the alpha, you can kill his enforcer too! Like you tell your pack, nobody owns a shifter.*

She glanced at the metal screen between the front and rear seat as he opened the door. He slid behind the steering wheel. The smelly serial killer who reeked of death sat in the passenger seat. She ignored him, sending a mental message to Gunnolf although he'd answer aloud, rather than in the same manner. She didn't know if it was stupidity, or pride, or arrogance on his part and never bothered to ask, careful to block her private thoughts from him.

*'Where's my waffle cone with a double scoop of Yesteryear butter pecan ice-cream?'*

"Sorry, my pet. Next time."

*'I should have known. Liar, liar, liar!'* She made a big show of burying her muzzle on her paws and closing her eyes. *'Hate you, hate you, hate you!'*

He slid the key in the ignition and started the car. "We'll stop somewhere else, and I'll get you a pup cone. Those have less calories and you don't get enough exercise in the winter."

*'Whose fault is that when you don't let me run off-leash? Call me fat again, you lying human scum and I'll kill you.'* She turned her head away from him. *'Not eating a shit cone. Wanted a good one for a change.'*

"No potty mouth. You know I don't like it."

*'Fuck you, asshat.'* She snarled, revealing her gleaming white teeth. *'And that's not an invitation. Wanted my real ice-cream. Hate you, hate you, hate you! Never speaking to you again.'*

He laughed, driving out of the lot toward the exit. "I don't know why you always say that when we both know it's not true."

There was more than one way to share her opinion of the two killers in the front seat of the car. She lifted her tail and farted loudly three times. She wagged her tail afterwards. *Smell my shit.*

Smith started coughing and cursing her. Gunnolf opened his window and told the other human to shut his mouth.

Since the enforcer thought she was annoyed about the broken promise when she truly didn't care about the ice-cream, he'd have no idea she wasn't ignoring him. She was taking advantage of the respite offered by their road trip. And she had plenty of her favorite flavors of ice-cream in the freezer at home buried underneath packages of his disgusting, organic vegetables. She'd dig into one once he fell asleep tonight. He thought he'd trapped her in the wolf form as a punishment after she wrecked his car last week. She was only supposed to be able to shift when he ordered it.

*Hah! I'm a primal alpha, a dominatrix and I do as I please. I can shift whenever and wherever I want. Let him believe what he likes. He's such an imbecile. He doesn't know I used stealing the car as a way to distract him and his minions so I could get Trina Corbett, the shifter the alpha gave him at Samhain away to safety with the witches in Eagleville.*

Enjoying the cool night breeze from the driver's window, Corrine blocked Gunnolf and Smith from her mind. They'd decide she dozed. Meanwhile, she'd plot new strategies for the youngest members of her shadow pack to avoid being judged and killed at the upcoming Yule celebrations by Frank and the pack executioner if they couldn't change from their human shapes to their wolf forms.

*I have to save my innocents. It's my job. It always has been. Now, why do I know that?*

# 3

---

AS HE DROVE THROUGH THE NIGHT, NORTH TOWARD THE CANADIAN border a short time later, Gunnolf Marvin thought about his daughters. He hadn't seen the three of them together in years. They'd been gone when he returned to Corbettstown twenty-two years ago with baby Corrine after a hiatus. Some fathers would be proud of their obvious beauty like their mother's. He preferred their undoubted intelligence, the danger and lethal threat they emanated.

*My princesses* and he smiled. Of course, he'd threatened to destroy what they loved before killing them, but they wouldn't make the upcoming battle an easy one. And it'd been more than a hundred years since two of them attacked him with their allies after their middle sister died. They severely wounded him and burned Corbettstown to the ground. He didn't doubt they'd try to do it again.

Gary shifted in the right bucket seat of the Crown Victoria.

"Wish I was going to be around a while longer. I hate missing a bloodbath."

"You should have thought of the consequences before you took that woman to your cabin," Gunnolf said. "I told you there'd be time to deal with her, but you've always been too impulsive. You ought to have counted on her man following, since he already knew what you intended to do to her. They may not have been a mated pair like the shifters in the pack, but it didn't mean there wasn't a bond between them."

"I didn't expect them to escape while I established an alibi elsewhere, or to burn down my place."

"Good story, but nobody here will believe you didn't kill them and dispose of the bodies before setting that fire." Gunnolf signaled for a lane change. He'd take the next exit and drive as close as possible to the *Time Portal*. "My girl, Astra, couldn't get a jury to buy it and she's pulled off some damned fine work in the courtroom, freed a lot of real scum because this alpha prefers to feed humans to the pack."

"I'm telling the truth. I didn't finish them."

Gunnolf glanced into the rearview mirror to check on his pet wolf lying on the back seat behind the barrier. She didn't shift her position, but her golden-brown eyes opened for an instant, before closing again, ostentatiously ignoring him. So, she was still sulking because she had to wait in the Crown Victoria at the mall and he hadn't brought the gourmet ice cream cone he promised if she was good.

Well, he'd stop at a grocery on the way home and get one for her. Otherwise, she really would try to kill him in the next day or two. He'd fended off enough of her attacks in the past to learn she wouldn't tolerate him lying to *her*. As his youngest daughter called him, he was indeed *Jarvesel, Soul-Eating, Demon-Prince of Transgressions and Untruths*. He'd become a demon more than three centuries ago, but his transformation hadn't come with a warning about not angering a primal alpha female shifter.

Did Smith have any idea what really happened to his supposed victims and where they truly were? *My girls do good work*, Gunnolf thought again. Of course, they didn't suspect he knew about their antics on *Samhain*. He certainly wasn't telling them, and he suspected their mother didn't know either. They hadn't spoken in years, so he wasn't sharing what he'd learned with her. He still couldn't believe Diana had been able to make family court judges believe he'd tortured and abused her, much less convinced his oldest daughter to swear he molested her.

Diana's lies and deceit would infuriate human males, but he was a demon. He admired her tactics. She'd defeated him, uncommon for a witch with a strict moral code who was supposed to serve the *Goddess* and *The Light*. Astra confronted him eleven years before when she graduated from high school. He would never do such a thing, not even to his witchy child. When he told her so, she'd called him a liar.

She hadn't forgiven him, not when he gave her an apprentice, not when he paid for college and law school, not when he tolerated her sexual antics with various shifters during her visits to Corbettstown. She was a dark enchantress and his true heir, even if she didn't acknowledge it. Still, she always sent the worst criminal offenders she met as prey for the pack.

"Why hasn't anyone seen them?" Gunnolf turned his attention back to Smith. "The Armstrongs are raising all sorts of hell, and their political cronies are keeping the search alive for their missing chick and her fiancé. Do you think they'd hide the two of them and throw fits to distract everyone?"

"Wouldn't be the first time somebody's done that."

The road narrowed, winding up into the forest and Gunnolf concentrated on the highway, pleased there weren't many oncoming vehicles, which meant he wouldn't have to be concerned about witnesses. He'd close the portal once he sent Smith through, but there wasn't any point in telling the man no escape route existed.

Let him live and die in nineteenth century Liberty Valley while the Corbetts cleaned up the messes he'd made. The new *Guardian*, who could heal people and animals from lethal injuries and her ally, the *Seer* who talked to the dead would undoubtedly try to kill him. Not for the first time Gunnolf considered letting him know about the potential threats and then decided against it. The women from the twenty-first century could fend for themselves in the nineteenth.

"Will anyone find the one you sacrificed?"

"If they do, they'll think he fell off the cliff in a drunken stupor, but the wildlife should take care of what's left of him."

Huge cedars crowded close to the two-lane highway. "Who was it? Someone you picked up in a bar or a prostitute from a street corner in Seattle?"

"No, I got tired of the feds snooping around and following me everywhere, so I eliminated them."

Gunnolf's hands tightened on the steering wheel, his knuckles whitening. "You killed a FBI agent? Did you even consider what happens to the rest of us?"

"He wasn't quite dead when I left after I couldn't open the portal. The bears and the other predators will take care of him."

"You're lucky this is one of the few mistakes you've made." Gunnolf pulled into a darkened parking lot at the trail head. "We walk from here. Let's go."

"Won't we need a blood sacrifice? Isn't that why you brought the wolf?"

*'Let me kill him, Master. He's bad.'* The wolf licked her lips. *'And I'm hungry!'*

"No, my pet. You don't eat humans. They'll poison you. They're too toxic." Gunnolf wouldn't say he'd collected sufficient *Power* punishing his crew of minions, okay deputies when they allowed Trina, Gideon Corbett's daughter, the shapeshifter female the alpha rewarded him with at *Samhain* to escape.

Gunnolf hadn't given up hope of finding her. When he did, he'd keep her in the *magick* kennel in the basement of his home until she accepted him as her owner and master, just like Corrine eventually had during the early days of her death sentence. "You may need the extra boost of *Power* from a blood sacrifice, Smith, but I don't."

Outside the car, he opened the back door and hooked a leash on the large gray wolf's collar. She jumped out and stood sniffing the cold night air. Switching on his flashlight, Gunnolf started toward the trail. "Heel."

*'No. Let me hunt, Master. There's elk.'* She yanked on the lead, trying to pull free. *"Deer. Master, a deer!'* She wriggled, whirled around, leaping in the air, fighting his hold as she smelled the wind and wildlife. *'A bear. I haven't had a bear forever.'*

"Stop!" Gunnolf jerked hard on the leash. "Heel."

When she balked, he snapped his fingers. Once, twice, three times to get her attention. *Sex Magick* was his special *Power*. After she was particularly rebellious at the harvest festival in September, he taught her to have an orgasm when he used that signal.

She froze, shook for a moment, and whimpered. *'No more. Please, Master.'*

"Are we going or not?" Gary Smith demanded. "If you aren't sacrificing the animal, leave her behind."

"Don't tempt me. She wants to kill you." Gunnolf stroked the wolf's head. She closed her eyes in pleasure. "Now, come. After we finish our business, I may let you run."

*'You won't. You're lying. You always lie. You kept your witch daughters and Astra's healer for yourself tonight.'* Corrine growled. *'And no ice-cream. They have good cones at the mall, not the icky, nasty, low-cal kind like the frozen yogurt ones you buy me at the burger places. I should have barked and howled, not been good and quiet. It's not fair.'*

"There'd be consequences if you ignored the rules again, Corrine." He didn't doubt she'd have broken out of the vehicle if she could but there was more than one way to ensure she remained the way he wanted and where he left her. Not for the first time, he'd shrouded the Crown Victoria in a web of silence so if she caused a scene, nobody would see or hear her.

He kept petting her thick gray fur. "Bad puppies get in trouble when they don't mind, and you don't like that."

*'I'm not a puppy. I'm a she-wolf.'* She continued complaining,

*"You hardly ever let me off leash in the woods and there's deer. You didn't let me run with the pack at the last full moon.'*

"Because you were very naughty. You crapped all over the house when I was punishing my deputies for letting Trina run away. You tore up my couch and recliner again. And it's not as if you like the minions."

*'You hurt them, and you spanked me with a newspaper where they could see. They're wolves too.'* She nudged him with her nose, nipped lightly at his leg. *'And they hunted an elk. I wanted some.'*

"It wasn't a real elk." He ruffled her fur. "I've never let you eat humans, not even when you were a puppy on your first hunt."

She sighed, leaning against his leg. *'Let me kill the bad man then. I won't eat him. Payback for the good dogs he's slain. They try to help people and he executes them for doing their jobs.'*

He rested his hand on her back and glared through the darkness at the waiting killer. "You murder service dogs, Smith?"

"Only those who get in my way." Gary Smith shrugged. "The last one was the partner of that homicide cop, Beth Chambers. She kept harassing me for killing those sluts when I should have gotten a reward for cleaning up the streets."

Gunnolf tensed. He could take care of himself, but he wouldn't risk his pet. He bent slightly, caught her head in his hands, looking into her eyes intently. "Listen. No rabbits. Last time you ate one, you were very sick. Doc had to give you shots."

*'Those hurt. And you spanked me for biting him, Master.'*

"Don't chase coyotes. They're tricky and will gang up on you."

*'I like fighting them.'*

"Are you hearing me? Will you be a good puppy? Or do I have to lock you in the car?"

She gave an odd moan. *'I'll be good, Master.'*

"That's my girl." He relaxed his hold and petted her. "Stay where you can hear me."

He touched the jacket pocket where he kept his conjuring stick. He'd converted it to look like an old-time, gold song whistle for most of his spells. When he used it with her, it took the form of an antique dog whistle, tuned to her and emitting a high-pitched sound only she could hear. "Don't make me use this or I'll be annoyed. Tell me what happens to bad puppies."

*'Spankings, being locked in the kennel in the basement and having to chase stupid balls with stupid humans at the stupid dog park. I'm a wolf, not a dog'*

"That's right." Gunnolf unsnapped the leash and turned her loose. She licked his hand in a quick kiss before racing into the darkness.

Her excited call echoed in the night. *'A deer, Master! A real deer. Not a human changed into one.'*

While he and Gary Smith hiked into the forest, Gunnolf heard her reporting back. The deer got away. It wasn't much of a surprise because his wolf actually hated raw meat. She preferred the T-bone steaks he grilled for her on the barbecue at home. Then, she found coyotes. She remembered the warning and only drove them further into the hills, holding off from a battle.

She was a fierce fighter especially if the shifters in Corbettstown were what she considered disrespectful. When his deputies tried coming into his office without permission, she attacked them. And she wouldn't tolerate those same minions in anything she considered her personal space. Gunnolf had his share of clashes with her since he'd taken her home last December.

*I should have expected it. I've spoiled her too much.*

---

It didn't take long to open the portal into the 19<sup>th</sup> century and send Smith into the past. Afterwards, Gunnolf headed back to the patrol car. The Crown Victoria was still the only one in the parking lot. His wolf hadn't returned, and she'd stopped sending reports. He wasn't surprised.

She was very young and often took advantage when she decided he was distracted. He opened the trunk, removed a towel and the blanket he used when they went on picnics.

He unbuckled his gunbelt, stored his gear in the trunk. He shrugged out of his jacket and took the whistle from the pocket before dropping the coat inside. He sent a mental message. "Where are you? Come back now!"

No answer. All right, he'd give her a few more minutes before he really called her. He walked toward the grassy area, spread out the blanket and began to undress. The original Corrine always made him promise to let her go to *Summerland* when she died of old age, but it was a lie. He had no intention of losing her. He discovered her long ago in their former home in *Trilunon*. Few realized how rare a treasure a primal-alpha female was, especially one being educated, trained to rule a shifter pack.

He always took what he wanted so he romanced Corrine until she fell in love with him and agreed to elope. They'd been together ever since. More than three centuries weren't long enough. She always insisted on living what she called a 'normal human' lifespan in this realm. Whenever she was about to go to *Summerland*, he transplanted her spirit into a new body.

Twenty-five years ago, he thought he had more time to find a new one for her essence, but she died before he did. All he could do was store her soul in his conjuring stick and then roam the country searching for another dominant female alpha. Three years of traveling hadn't produced a suitable vessel for his mate when Frank Corbett, the Corbettstown leader of the shifter pack demanded Gunnolf meet him in California for a ceremonial visit to a wolf pack with a new alpha.

Deciding to humor Frank, Gunnolf agreed. A few days after his arrival, he toured the nursery where he saw an orphaned wolfling playing with the other children, none of whom could shift yet. The alpha explained the little girl managed to change forms and escape after a car accident killed her parents before the vehicle tumbled down an ocean cliff. Her power frightened most of the adults in that pack and they wanted her dead. It solved many problems when Gunnolf asked for her.

The alpha promptly gave him the little girl as a gift. It infuriated Frank when he learned Gunnolf had his own plans for the child. She wouldn't be harmed, molested or eaten as dessert at one of the alpha's ceremonial feasts. Worse, the wolfling had a strong sense of independence and refused to swear fealty to the pack leader. Although, she wasn't very verbal yet, she repeated again and again he smelled *bad* and telepathically ordered Gunnolf to keep the bad wolf away.

Amused by her spunk, he did. On the drive home to Washington State, he used his sorcerer's song-stick to transfer his former lover's soul into the child. He'd have to wait for her to grow up but eventually, in about twenty or so years when she remembered him and their lives together, she'd be his mate again.

He changed his original wand hundreds of years ago, when he began his foray into the darker side of *magick*. His song-stick had a built-in compass. It guided him to those who didn't have much morality and he chose one of them when he was ready to move on to a younger, stronger form. Many of those who'd come from their old realm accepted limited life-spans. He didn't. Granted, human bodies wore out sooner than he liked, so he found a new form when he was close to dying.

This particular one was a crooked cop thirty years ago in Seattle who decided he could rob what he thought was a rich, helpless old man who'd been mugged and lay dying in an alley. The lawman didn't realize Gunnolf had lured him close enough to trade places. He was the one who'd been robbed. Gunnolf didn't think of it that way. He needed a new body, and the cop's was an appropriate one.

Nude, he sat on the blanket enjoying the cold, November night and the way the winter breeze washed over him. He demanded incubus talents when he turned to what some considered the dark side. Much of his power was derived from *Sex Magick*. He absorbed life energies from his partners when he had them, especially Corrine. Another bonus was his endurance. He could and did fuck for hours, but it meant he often ended up with an excessive amount of *magickal* residue that he stored to use later.

She'd had enough time to romp and play. He picked up the dog whistle and blew. She knew better than to ignore the high-pitched sound. "Now. Come to me. Now!"

He heard joyous splashing. So, she was at the river.

*'A duck, Master.'* Delight filled her contralto voice. *"There's a duck! A real one! It's too stupid to live.'*

Corrine always loved testing the rules, he thought, while he waited. Thrilled with the opportunity to be a mother after she'd miscarried yet another child, it delighted the local midwife, Lorena Corbett when he brought her a living souvenir. She named the little girl after his long-lost lover and offered to let him visit on a regular basis. He did, but he spent his time with Lorena, not the new Corrine. She needed a mother, not a man who wanted the woman she'd been before and would be again.

He made a few ground rules and Lorena adhered to those. In middle school, Corrine's friends started self-defense classes and learned to handle knives, swords, pistols, and rifles. She went to ballet and gymnastics. Lorena asked about archery lessons after Corrine read the *Hunger Games* books and Gunnolf refused. The young teen stormed into his office and demanded to know the reason for his antediluvian attitude.

Yes, she was grateful he'd found her a loving mom, but that didn't make him the boss of her. He said he still admired her spunk and drove her home. On the way his former Corrine called him all sorts of names telepathically and vowed to kill him. Gunnolf already knew she would and could, another reason to keep weapons away from her. The years passed and he waited for her to see him, for his Corrine to return to him.

On her twenty-third birthday last year in December, he threw a large party for all the adult shifters in the entire pack. There'd been meat from a butcher in Eagleville because he didn't allow her to eat humans and nobody else could that night. He gave her the *magickal* gold and silver necklace he'd created for her centuries ago. She kissed his cheek, called him her favorite grandpa, and ran off to play with her latest young love.

The alpha mocked him for thinking she'd come to him. Gunnolf smiled and said she'd accepted his mate-bond gift. He was going out of town to renew an alliance with a pack in Idaho the next week. He didn't share that he and Corrine had been together three hundred and thirty years. Sooner or later, she'd remember him, and he could wait although he was certain she'd come to him when he returned from Boise.

Then, he learned Frank arranged for two of his undercover police officers to frame her while Gunnolf was gone. She didn't know the pack leader was behind the accusations she was gay. Of course, the misogynistic, homophobic, crazed alpha decided to punish her. His Corrine fought back and almost killed Frank, so he told the three cops who arrested her to slay her. They hadn't gone that far. Gunnolf found her in one of the special jail cells that prevented shifters from changing forms to heal as wolves.

Once he helped Corrine into her wolf shape and arranged for medical treatment, he visited the alpha. He didn't knock. He stalked inside where he found a frightened, young female serving Frank's dinner. Gunnolf ordered her to leave, and she fled from the room. He knew she lingered in the hallway to listen, but he didn't care. Let the pack hear what a degenerate alpha they had.

"My mate. You took my mate. How dare you?"

"She wasn't yours yet and she's a shifter. She belongs to me."

"The hell she does! You've wanted to kill her since she was an infant. She's a lone alpha. She never accepted you as *her* pack leader, not when she was a baby wolfling, not when she came of age and not now. She always has been a solitary wolf."

He grabbed Frank by the shirt collar, slammed him against the wall. "Hear my words. I've served this wolf pack for more than a hundred years, your pack now, even if you don't admit how long I've been here. I've killed for it. I've died for it—"

"I know that, Gunnolf. I made a mistake. She's a freak. Destroy her and we go on from here."

"No, she's my mate. She's with me now. Touch her again. You die. If she doesn't kill you, I will."

"She broke the code of the pack. I had to order her death for attacking me."

"Declare a moratorium. Nobody harms my mate."

When he left, he saw the girl cowering in the hall by the front door. Gunnolf looked at the shifter. "Tell everyone. If he tries to hurt you like he did my mate, come to me. I will protect you."

# 4

Sumas, Washington
Saturday, November 24th, 2018

HE STARTED TO RAISE THE WHISTLE TO HIS LIPS, TO CALL HER AGAIN, but then he saw her loping across the field toward him. He put the device aside, neatly tucking it under his clothes. She ran to him, paused, and shook, spraying him with cool water from her swim.

He wiped off his face with the towel. "You're late."

*'I told you. It was a stupid duck, a real one. I caught it and ate it.'* She licked her lips, and he smelled fresh meat on her breath. *'Delicious. Would have been better if you grilled it.'*

"You're a naughty puppy." He gave her a slow onceover. *"Change."*

*'Not if you're going to spank me.'* She bared her teeth and growled. *'I won't. I'll stay like this and rip out your throat.'*

He folded his arms. *"Change* now or I'll *change* you."

She glared at him, narrowing those amazing golden-brown eyes. Then, she did it the same way she always had. Most shifters had trouble going from human to wolf and back again. Not her. She shimmered in the moonlight, streams of color, pink, yellow, blue, purple, orange and red around her as if she danced in a rainbow.

Moments later, she was in front of him. Long golden hair fell to her hips because he restored it after she had it cut a few weeks ago. He smiled at her. She was such a pretty shifter. At five feet, five inches, she was tall enough for her head to reach his shoulder. A lovely face with high cheekbones, angled dark brown eyebrows, a pointed chin, full lips. Her breasts rose and fell, the perfect size to fill his hands. His necklace, the mate-gift he'd given to her last year on her twenty-third birthday glimmered in the winter moonlight.

He beckoned to her. "Come here, my pet!"

She caught her breath, a furious blush rising in her cheeks. "I'm not a dog. Don't talk to me like one."

"You're my puppy." He caught her hand, drew her down on the blanket next to him. "Be very good or I'll make you howl loud enough for people on the freeway to hear you when you climax."

She gasped when he kissed her, his tongue laying claim to her mouth. She kissed him back, her body pushing into his. She moaned when he cupped her breasts, thumbs tormenting her nipples. "Don't stop."

"I won't." He bent his head, his mouth roving toward one pink nipple. "You're going to make up for keeping me waiting for so long."

While he sucked her nipples, two of his fingers speared inside her. He slid them in and out of her in a series of strokes. She moved with them, rising and falling until she came. After the first orgasm, she squirmed eagerly, arching toward him. "Please."

"Who owns you, my favorite little puppy?"

She glared at him, but her head fell back when he kissed the hollow of her throat. His lips trailed toward her breast. He cupped the beautiful, golden mound between her legs, stroking through the curls. "You want me, don't you? Who's your owner and master, my pet?"

"You are." She wriggled closer. Her hips moved toward him, her breasts, and nipples nearer. "Please."

His fingers slipped into her wet heat again, his thumb finding her clitoris. He sucked one of those aching, pink nipples, then lifted his head. "Beg me, puppy."

She buried her lips against his neck, kissing his ear. "Do it, Master. Have me."

"That's my good girl. Now, howl for me."

A moment later, he was buried deep inside her. She wrapped her arms around him, moving back and forth on the blanket. Her hips met his as he fucked her, long, deep strokes. She wanted to kiss him, but he didn't let her. He enjoyed her cries far too much when she climaxed numerous times.

Very few in the pack realized how much *Power* he drew during sex when he drained his partners of their life energies and their *magick*, especially a young woman destined to be a female, primal alpha in the future. She always provided him with more of her shifter power. Oh yes, she was his perfect puppy. Granted, she was still fighting their bond, but they had time. Years and years of it. And sooner or later, she'd stop trying to kill him.

———

Two hours later, she lay next to him, her head pillowed in the hollow of his shoulder. Stars still dotted the sky. The moon teetered on the edge of the horizon. A cool winter night wind teased her body, and she relished the warmth of his, another bonus of him being a demon. He tended to be warmer than a human.

Corrine nipped his ear. "Your daughters? How are they?"

He smoothed her hair down her back. "As beautiful as their mother. Jealous?"

"Of them? Their mother, Diana? No. You fuck a lot of women. I'm just one of many—"

"No. I've told you before. You're the only one I fuck. They're my job." His hand curved over her hip. "You're my mate."

"It'd mean something if you were a shifter." She lifted her head, gazed into his dark eyes. "You're only a human who lives with them. Are they evil like you? Your daughters?"

"No." Faint pride trickled into his deep voice. "They're fierce. Strong. Brave." He considered it for a moment. "Dangerous."

"Good. They'll need to be. Did you warn them? Will they be watching for you?" She felt the tension increase in his body and rolled on top of him. She propped her elbows on his wide chest, rested her chin on top of them and gazed at him. "Tell me what bad thing you said, Gunnolf."

"That I'd kill their loved ones first and eat their hearts in front of them before I slew the three of them."

"Very good." She rarely kissed him first, but he'd earned a treat tonight. She lowered her head and their lips met for a moment. "I won't let you harm any of them."

"You can't stop me."

She smiled. She could and she would but let him have his delusions. Slowly, she trailed a line of kisses across his chest to his nipples. "You did something good."

"Not on purpose."

"You prepared your daughters for war." Corrine eased down and felt his eager response as she neared her goal. "You deserve a reward."

"Really? What did you have in mind?"

"I'm going to fuck you until dawn." She positioned herself and eased onto him, catching her breath when he slipped inside her. She rose, then slid down again, repeating the motion. "You'll like it."

"Yes." He caught her hips, guiding her movements. "Do a good job and you won't be in trouble for using my name."

"Get over it." She leaned forward to kiss him. "You've claimed me as your mate for damn near a year and I'm tired of calling you, my master. The hell with the alpha's death sentence! Gunnolf, Gunnolf, Gunnolf!"

———

When he took over the pack after his older brother's death twenty-five years before, Frank Corbett made it clear shifter females were to fulfill traditional roles—they were only allowed to cook, clean, breed and bring forth more male children. Girls were to leave school after eighth grade and be trained as future mates if they could shift into wolves. If they couldn't, they were sacrificed to feed the pack at their celebrations. Of course, any youngsters who showed signs of being healers, priests, priestesses, witches, or wizards definitely went to their deaths at early ages.

While she didn't share anything about the secret friend who shared her body and mind, her adopted mother seemed to understand how restrictive Corrine found the rules. Lorena often said, nobody owned a shifter. She explained Gunnolf was from a different generation and thought girls should be 'sugar and spice and everything nice.' He didn't need to know all the details of their lives. Lorena let Corrine see the same movies her friends did from the *Hunger Games* to *Divergent* to *Wonder Woman*, anything with powerful heroines.

After she confronted Gunnolf in his office and he laughed at her, he drove her home. She was furious when Lorena smiled sweetly and agreed he was the enforcer. Once he left, she explained Corrine needed to learn to be discreet, not rub his nose in her defiance. He'd arranged a dispensation for her to attend high school in Eagleville while her mother worked there as a midwife.

Lorena took gifts to the Elder Witches of the local coven and asked them to have their sword-mistress teach her daughter to fence. It took some finagling to arrange times so visiting shifters never learned what Corrine was doing and didn't report back to the enforcer or the alpha. After Corrine attended a few classes, she discovered her new teacher was one of Gunnolf's witchy daughters.

Another secret. As far as he knew, Corrine happily enjoyed her experiences at high school from earning a spot on the cheerleading squad to playing softball to writing articles for the paper. She was popular with her peers and didn't limit herself to shifters for friends. She liked everyone, witches, healers, wizards, actual fairies, and elves. They returned the favor. They partied together on weekends, and she dated extensively. She didn't neglect her academics. She took AP classes and college courses. She not only graduated with honors, but also her associate degree and high school diploma.

As a reward, Gunnolf bought her a sturdy, mid-size Subaru SUV with the caveat she drive it responsibly, not the way she treated the patrol cars like bumper cars at the carnival. She agreed to be careful with her new vehicle. When the alpha reminded Gunnolf that female shifters were restricted to Corbettstown, he used his position as pack enforcer to demand another exemption.

He helped them move back to Corbettstown and Corrine became a full-fledged, adult shifter. She attended the pack activities like the rest of the wolves, sleeping with other single shifters who weren't ready to find mates. She worked as a waitress, circulating through the various restaurants, switching jobs if she was bored or wanted higher pay. With a different alpha, she might have been able to follow her dream of becoming a schoolteacher. Since it wasn't possible, she volunteered at the day-care and tutored younglings at the elementary.

She loved her life in Corbettstown but stayed in contact with the friends she made in Eagleville, using her rig to visit whenever she had time. Only the shifters could come to the twenty-third birthday party that Gunnolf threw for her shortly before *Yule* last year. He'd given her a lovely, antique gold and silver necklace. She'd hugged him, kissed his cheek, calling him 'grandpa' when she thanked him.

Then, she darted away to dance with her latest guy, a shifter, Treyton Corbett. He was so charming and sweet, she'd begun to think of him as a possible mate even though he was a 'beta', and she was an 'alpha'. They'd been necking at the campfire when Gunnolf interrupted them, reminding her to be a good hostess. She apologized, teased him by saying he was a typical, stodgy old man and ran off to fulfill her duties.

However, when she rejected A.J. Corbett, an aggressive deputy's advances a few days later, he told the alpha she was gay. It wasn't true but then Frank Corbett claimed he'd heard the same story from another cop, a female shifter, Quincy, who rebuffed her. Corrine denied the accusations and requested a trial by combat with both officers. Frank refused. She demanded to have the enforcer speak for her when he returned from Idaho as was her right. Another veto. Instead, the alpha insisted she live with him as his latest shifter female. Given no choice, she didn't cook or clean and constantly criticized his lack of skill in the bedroom.

In the next week, the situation worsened. He beat and raped her. She fought back, using the skills she learned from the warrior witch to throw him down the stairs. The alpha managed to send a psychic call for help to the police before she slit his throat. After a thorough thrashing by the responding officers, she was dragged into one of the special cells at the jail. She couldn't change to her wolf which meant she wouldn't heal quickly.

Disrespecting the alpha was a heinous offense, a death sentence in the pack for anyone, especially a lone wolf who hadn't bonded to the pack. Females had little status and she was doomed. On his return, Gunnolf visited her. Infuriated by her condition, he helped her shift into her wolf form to heal her broken ribs, shattered legs and internal injuries. After hearing the town doctor denied the jail matron's and a different officer, her best friend, Andrel Corbett's requests to treat her, Gunnolf arranged for Lorena, her foster mother and a midwife, to come.

That night, Corrine woke up in his bed screaming. She saw him sitting in a rocking chair in the corner of the bedroom. He comforted her and promised she was safe. She wasn't sure how she'd shifted back to her human shape since the last thing she remembered was sleeping as a wolf. Over the next three days, he fed her, helped her to the toilet, held her while she cried, gave her the tonics Lorena made for her and promised everything would be all right.

The fourth night, he wasn't there when Corrine awakened. She went to the ensuite by herself, surprised to find her favorite toiletries in the vanity. She showered, washed and dried her hair. In the bedroom, she discovered some of her clothes in the bureau. She dressed in jeans and a T-shirt, before she went out to the back deck.

She sat down at the table and watched Gunnolf grill huge steaks for them.

He was a large man well over six feet, big and bronzed. Wide shoulders and a broad chest filled out his light brown, uniform shirt. A gunbelt and all the police paraphernalia emphasized his narrow hips. His ironed slacks always had military creases and his lace-up boots sported a mirror shine. He was human, the only enforcer in their world who wasn't a shifter, but he moved like one, light on his feet. He'd shaved his head for years, but he had dark eyebrows above his brown eyes. His rugged features attracted interest from some of the older female shifters in town.

Healing took a great deal of energy and her wolf craved meat. He poured her a glass of the red wine she preferred to beer. Dessert was her favorite strawberry cheesecake.

"Thank you for taking such good care of me." Corrine pushed away her empty plate when she finished her third steak. "I'll be ready to return to my apartment tomorrow. I hope I can get back my job. Frank made me quit."

"I'm sorry, my little wolf." Gunnolf kept his steady gaze on her. "I've told your landlord and your boss, you won't be back. Most of your belongings are at your mother's. You're not leaving here or me."

"Why not? Between your nursing and my wolf, I'm fine."

"You attacked the alpha of the Corbettstown pack." Gunnolf shook his head ruefully. "My pet, when you try to slay someone, make sure you send him or her all the way to *Summerland*."

"I would have, but he called for help before I could."

"A bad mistake. Don't make it again." Gunnolf slid her silver blade in its sheath across the table. "Put that away. You may need it." He paused. "Don't try using it on me. Silver works on shifters, not on humans."

She returned the scabbard to its usual place on her belt. "Why doesn't silver work on me? I'm a shifter."

"Because you're a special female alpha. If you weren't a lone wolf, you wouldn't have been able to attack a pack leader."

"That's weird, but it actually makes sense." She tilted her head to one side. "He frightens everybody else in town, but I'm not afraid of him, Gunnolf."

"So young and silly. You should be." He stood, walked around the table, refilled her glass, then kissed her forehead. "You're staying with me because you failed, and you're being punished by the enforcer. FYI, I've told Frank and everyone in Corbettstown you're my mate."

She frowned thoughtfully, fingering the silver and gold chain necklace with its delicate engraved wolves and their diamond chip eyes. She'd loved it from the moment she opened the velvet box at her birthday party two weeks before and hadn't removed it. Unlike other jewelry she'd had over the years, it changed with her when she shifted to a wolf, so she didn't lose it.

"Do they think this is like a wedding ring is for humans? I'll return it."

"It's yours." He lifted his glass in what was almost a salute. "It has been since —" He stopped. "I'll tell you someday."

"But I'm not ready to be your mate. To be anyone's mate."

"Do you want to live? Since everyone knows you belong to me, I won't have to enforce the death sentence for attacking the alpha."

"How long do I have to pretend we're married?"

He shrugged. "Probably until Frank dies in a shifter battle and another alpha takes over the pack and you create an alliance with him. At least four or five years."

"That's forever!" She gaped at him. "How do I get out of it?"
"You don't."

"What if I make you mad enough to throw me out? Reject me and it'll be a shifter's divorce. Then I'll go back to my life."

"And someone else will kill you and collect the bounty the alpha is offering for your head." He narrowed his dark eyes. "I've been the enforcer longer than you've been alive this time, my puppy. Grown wolves have tried fighting me and lost. You're my new mate. Get used to it. Now, finish your wine. It has more of your healing tonic in it. Go back to bed. You need sleep to finish mending."

"No, I'm going to watch a horror movie on your flatscreen." Grabbing her wine, she sulked her way into the living-room. She fell asleep on the couch and woke up in his arms, in his bed. She didn't tell him how much she appreciated his attempts to keep away the nightmares. He didn't have a need to know.

Through the next two weeks while she continued to recover, he reminded her she was an adult member of the pack. Her mother encouraged Corrine to humor her new mate and to perform traditional female activities like cleaning his house, doing his laundry as well as her own, going with him to buy groceries and cooking meals.

She refused. She plugged her ears when he lectured her constantly, including on their daily five mile runs. Gunnolf laughed at what he called her silly ways and repeated she had choices. It was past time to act like a full grown she-wolf. Until she adhered to the community's expectations, she would have to stay with him twenty-four, seven, and he took away the keys to her beloved SUV.

She accompanied him to the police department and did office work, discovering he'd assigned A.J. and Quincy to the pack executioner, Latham Sellers, for special duties. The deputies who answered the alpha's call and abused her were still recovering from their own injuries. Gunnolf said he'd made it plain for years that nobody was allowed to touch her except him, and they deserved the battering he gave them. However, the jail matron and Corrine's best friend received bonuses and promotions for trying to protect her.

One Friday afternoon in late January, bored with Judge Judy wreaking justice, Corrine went to find him. He was in the bedroom packing. "What's happening?"

"I'm speaking at a law enforcement conference tomorrow in Seattle. If I could get out of it, I would, but this has been scheduled for months." He zipped a garment bag around two immaculate uniforms. "I'll be back Sunday night in time for dinner."

She trembled in sudden fear. "Take me with you. I'll be ready to go when you are."

"I would if I could, my pet." He glanced at her. "It's not possible."

"Why not? I'll hang out in the hotel. None of your friends need to see me if you're concerned, they'll think you're some kind of perv because your so-called wife is younger than your daughters."

"Not quite." He shook his head. "You know we're from *Trilunon* and came here three hundred years ago. I'll be glad when your memories return, and you remember who and what you are to me. You're much older than you look."

"I feel that way a lot." She went across the room, clung to him. "Don't leave me alone here. Not again."

"Listen." He hugged her tight. "I'd take you with me if I could. I don't care what anyone thinks. But you *'Change'* if you have a nightmare, and you scream constantly when I keep you human. The best way we get along with the citizens in this realm is by not showing how different we are. So, you're staying in Corbettstown where shifters are safer than in the big city. Nobody here will freak if they see your wolf. If you want, I'll have the deputies cruise by."

"Don't threaten me." She broke free, glaring up at him. "Give me my keys and I'll go to Eagleville where it's safer for a lone wolf."

"You're being punished for attacking the alpha. You don't leave my property without me for at least two months. No driving anywhere. Not your SUV or my car. If you don't want to think of it as being my new mate, then consider it being grounded like a youngling."

"I'm not a child. Don't treat me like one."

He flicked her chin. "Be grateful I haven't treated you like a grown shifter. Right now, you're benefiting from your age as a young wolf who's still maturing, not in *Summerland*, as a dead one, waiting for a new life. If anyone else attacked the alpha the way you did, I would have had to kill her. I couldn't have saved her by claiming her as my mate, but luckily, I'd already given you a mate-gift for your birthday. You need to learn to control your temper."

"Blah, blah, blah! I'm not listening to another of your damned lectures. If I'm stuck here, you'll be sorry when you return. I'll see to that."

"There's my girl. Your turn to heat up supper." He chuckled and patted her butt. "When I get home, plan to show me that my new mate is a grown-up shifter. Don't embarrass me or yourself. If you're naughty, I'll have to punish you. You've seen what happens to serious rulebreakers here and your sentence will be at least a year. The next step is begging for the opportunity to please me and calling me your owner and master."

"You wish, Gunnolf Marvin. You wish. Nobody owns a shifter."

# 5

*Corbettstown, Washington*
*January 2018*

AFTER HE LEFT TOWN WITH SOME DEPUTIES ON SATURDAY MORNING, Corrine sent out a psychic message for her shadow pack to join her at his house. Most of them hadn't seen her since Frank attacked her. The shifters she'd claimed during the last five years needed to know she was still their leader, still strong and in charge.

She refused to think about the vulnerability she'd shown to Gunnolf the night before. It was mortifying. How could she have pleaded to accompany him? And he'd been kind, but he obviously pitied her. He might say she was his mate, but he didn't view her as one. Instead, he still saw her as a child, desperate to be saved. She was an alpha, not a mean or insane one like Frank, but still a pack leader. And pay-back was in her nature.

The first to arrive for the meeting was Andrel Corbett, her best friend since they had played together at day-care. She showed up with a trash bag filled with foul smelling, rotting garbage from a local restaurant.

"What is that?" Corrine wrinkled her nose in disgust. "Why is it here?"

"The price of admission for the party you're throwing." Petite and dark-haired, Andrel had the 'chameleon gift' from her witchy ancestors. If she'd seen any female before, she could change into that woman's shape, albeit human, or witch or shifter as well as a tawny gold wolf. "I told everyone it's a celebration since you've taken over the enforcer's place."

"That's bogus, but I know you're the strategist. What's the plan?"

"A big drinking, eating, dancing, loud music, game-playing orgy like any college kid would throw when the 'rents are away. Nobody will think it's our shadow pack having a meet, especially after we trash the place tomorrow before the enforcer returns."

"He'll lose it. He's a total control freak."

"Yes, but he'll never think you're sabotaging the town and the pack. He'll decide you're an utter and complete brat, not old enough to be the mate he's bragging about choosing."

Corrine nodded slowly. "Brilliant. But you're one of his deputies. What if he learns you were here?" She paused. "Of course. The neighbors called and pitched a fit because of the music and the noise. You came to tell us to turn it down and we did when you were here. As soon as you left, we cranked it up again."

"I like it."

"So do I." Corrine hugged her bestie. "With any luck at all, you're right. He'll kick my sorry tail to the curb. So much for him declaring I'm his mate."

"And if he doesn't, we'll know exactly what he, the alpha and the executioner are doing. Then, you'll be able to short-circuit their plans."

"Our pack is different. We are a team," Corrine said. "Working together, we'll defeat them."

Other shifters showed up with more bags of trash which she stored on the back deck. People from Corbettstown brought food and her friends from Eagleville arrived with their *magick*. Drinking, dancing to loud old-time rock music all night long, eating, games on their computers – everyone had a great time. She told her friends she was being a 'good hostess' and snickered. Sunday before he was due to return, they trashed the place.

Some of the guys broke out the windows and slashed the tires on his classic Crown Victoria cop car. Others festooned the trees with toilet paper. A few more destroyed the flowerbeds and left tire tracks on the pristine lawns. Her witchy pals made it look like those came from the patrol cars at the Corbettstown precinct.

Meanwhile, Corrine and her shifter girlfriends went berserk in the kitchen, dining room, and living room. They couldn't get into his study or the basement. They busted up the furniture, covered the floors with the restaurant garbage, smashed all the dishes and glass-ware. The stainless-steel appliances even had deep scratches from her wolf claws. When they finished, she sent the members of her shadow pack away, intending to take total responsibility for their actions. Then she headed into his bedroom, turned into a wolf, and continued to wreak havoc.

She tore his uniforms into rags, chewed up his boots, crapped on the king-size bed and new plush carpet. It was surprisingly fun to act childish and destructive after being a victim for the past month. She'd changed back into a human and was breaking the antique dresser into firewood when Gunnolf arrived. He looked at her, then slowly turned and scanned the mess she made.

"Well, Grandpa. Are we done now?" She lifted her chin and met his dark brown gaze. "I'm more than ready to move out of here, to have my life back."

"Oh no, my pet. We haven't even started yet." He walked further into the room, put his small, duffle bag on the nightstand. "Who helped you?"

"I had two full days to entertain myself, so I did." She sneered at him. "Why would I need help, old man? I'm not a puny human. I'm a shifter. You never even asked if I wanted to be your mate. You just decided, made a public announcement all over town and created a fait accompli. Well, how do you like your choice now?"

"You are a very, very bad puppy." Collecting a rolled-up newspaper that appeared on the nightstand, he sauntered toward her. He carefully avoided stepping in the piles of steaming shit ruining the plush cream rug. "Are you sure you want to take credit for all of this, my little wolf?"

"Why wouldn't I?"

"Because I'm the enforcer. It's my job to punish wolves who break the rules, even my new mate who acted like a naughty youngling all weekend." He shook his head, eying the destruction again when he reached her. "Come here."

"Go to hell, Grandpa."

"I've already been there and it's too damned hot." He snagged her wrist and towed her toward the rocking chair in the corner. He sat down, spun her around and pulled her across his lap. The first blow from the newspaper landed on her butt. She yelled and tried to wrench free.

Despite her shifter strength, she couldn't break away. He ignored her punches and kicks. He paddled her until she stopped fighting. Then, he pushed her off him and she collapsed in a heap at his feet. Sobbing in a combination of fear and pain from her sore backside, she tried to crawl away, stopping when he fisted his hand in her hair. "What?"

"You were a bad puppy who earned a spanking for wrecking my house and car. Others have received worse for lesser offenses. I've told you more than once you're on the pack's equivalent of Death Row. Being dismembered, ripped to shreds and hearing the hunting party quarrel over your bones before you die is much worse than becoming my mate." He reached down, caught her chin and feathered his thumb over her lips. "Go wash up. You're a naughty wolf pup, not a raccoon."

Gulping back her tears, she hurried into the ensuite when he released her. He was right about her so-called, waterproof mascara. It streaked down her face, running into the blush on her cheeks. She flicked a glance through the partially open door and saw him standing in the middle of the room.

He reached into his shirt pocket and removed a vintage, gold slide whistle. He blew softly and a tune started. He played for a few moments, then paused, "Make everything the same as it was before —as perfect as it was yesterday when I walked out the door..."

A cool breeze swirled through the room, although the windows were closed. The strange song continued, and a wave of exhaustion swept over her. Dimly she recalled, she was asleep when he left. She'd barely awakened when he kissed her forehead, promised to bring her a present and quietly closed the bedroom door behind him. She swayed, felt her knees buckle and she slid onto the floor. Sleep claimed her.

The sound of the bathroom door opening awakened her. Opening her eyes, she stared up at him. It puzzled her that she was naked and then she remembered she slept that way so she could shift into her wolf form when she dreamed. She'd seen him without a shirt while she lived with him, so his wide shoulders, broad chest, muscled arms didn't come as a shock. A flat belly—he had the body of a younger man in his prime. Narrow hips and she glanced lower. He was bigger than the shifters she'd been with, and he wanted her.

She backed a step, but he caught her arm. He picked her up and carried her to the bed. "Gunnolf—"

"Oh no, my pet." He shook his head, his face an expressionless mask. "You're in trouble now. I warned you before I left. You're a serious rule-breaker. For the next year, you call me, your owner and master."

"I won't."

"Oh, you will by the time I finish with you."

He lowered her onto the crisp, ironed sheets. He kissed her until she responded. He explored her body first with his hands, and then his mouth. She'd found herself returning the favor, sliding her hands over his broad chest, clutching at his muscled arms while he sucked her nipples, one at a time while he rolled the other one between his fingers.

She gasped, moaned, and wriggled closer, their legs tangling together. He caressed her. His hand found the curls between her legs. He kissed her, his tongue mimicking the motion of his fingers sliding in and out of her, while his thumb tormented her clitoris. It shocked her when she climaxed.

But he didn't stop there. He spread her legs further apart and took her with his mouth, his tongue expertly delving deep until she had one orgasm after another. They were fucking, when his deputies came to find him and report on the status of the house repairs. She didn't care if they had an audience — she just wanted more of what he provided. And he'd given it to her, ignoring the shifters who stood and watched while she convulsed again and again.

They laughed when she screamed in pleasure. Humiliated, tears streamed down her face. She hated him and them. "Do it again. Please!"

"Oh, I've barely started, my pet." He kissed away her tears. "Next time, I have to go somewhere, you'll be a very good puppy while you wait for me at home, won't you?"

She pushed him off her, sat up on the edge of the bed. "I'm not a puppy."

"You'll always be my puppy." He laughed, drew her back, pulled her up on her hands and knees. He slid into her from behind. He began fucking her in what he called, 'doggie style' while his minions walked away, laughing and betting on how many orgasms she would have and how long it'd take their police chief to train his new mate.

*'Don't worry. It's all right, sweetheart.'* Her secret voice promised. *'We'll kill him and them. Together!'*

––––––––

She did her best to drive him crazy enough to throw her out, but nothing she did worked. If she piled garbage on the table or in his favorite recliner or the refrigerator, he made her clean it up and then fucked her. He took her shopping, bought her short skirts, tight dresses that barely skimmed her bottom, low-cut tops sans bras although she was full-figured.

Most mornings he prepared breakfast, so she had time to style her hair and apply cosmetics after her shower. She wore the perfume he'd given her when he returned from Seattle. Of course, she pointed out it wasn't much of a gift because he'd chosen his favorite classic scent, one with violet, rose, jasmine and lily. He escorted her to the nail salon in town and read a *Louis L'Amour* paperback while she had a manicure and pedicure. She complained it wasn't customary for shifters to have fake fingernails. He reminded her she was under a death sentence which meant his 'pretty puppy' would look the way he wanted. It was a mild punishment compared to that of other serious lawbreakers.

He liked her boobs, saying he preferred a decent handful. Her panties went in the trash since they got in the way when he wanted her. Thigh-high stockings were sexy and so were the stiletto heels he bought for her. It took her ages to learn how to walk in those. Surprisingly, he didn't laugh at her when she fell down, although he often took advantage of the situation and fucked her while she was on the floor. He said she'd have to earn the privilege to wear the jeans, T-shirts and boots she preferred.

He came after her whenever she ran away and brought her back to his house. He posted a female deputy to stay all day with her, and she wasn't allowed to shut the bathroom door if she used the toilet. She escaped two more times and jumped off bridges into flooding rivers determined to fake her death. She shifted into her wolf and swam to safety. He met her on the river shores. He ordered her to change to human form and spanked her with a rolled-up newspaper.

When he had business in town, she stayed in a kennel in the basement. He waited in the same room while she cooked supper, cleaned the kitchen, and then took her with him to the living room. In the evenings, he enjoyed drinking beer and streaming old games of the Seattle Mariners playing baseball. He'd pull her down on the couch next to him and fondle her, stroking her hair, cupping her breasts, toying with her nipples.

She removed his shirt and caressed him, exploring his chest, kissing his throat and ears. If there was a stream of commercials, he'd push up her skirt or dress and slide his fingers inside her, driving her from one climax to another. When the game ended, he'd fuck her for at least another hour or two.

She never understood how or why he had so much stamina. From her few experiences, it seemed like an aberration and her girlfriends had often complained about their male partners who were too quick in bed. One afternoon when she was lying under him on the sofa, she asked why he lasted so long. He told her it was the difference between being with a man, not a boy.

Corrine deliberately rocked into him, her hands resting on his broad chest. She kissed his throat, debating if she could bite hard enough to kill him. Reluctantly, she decided she'd have to wait. "You're a liar."

"Why are you saying that?" He kept moving, long, deep strokes. "Who says so?"

"Me." She gripped his shoulders. "Nobody fucks as long as you do."

"You do, my puppy." He chuckled. "You're insatiable." He shifted his hips, varying his thrusts, slow and easy, then fast and hard. "Howl for me, my pet. Let's entertain my deputies who are cleaning up the branches after the last windstorm and setting up the barbeque."

———

In mid-February, she stormed around the house, stomping through the chores he assigned. Most of the housework was done by the cleaning service that came once a week while she supervised them.

He sauntered into the laundry room and watched when she hurled his uniform shirts into the washer. "You're scum, Grandpa. I hate you and someday soon, I'm going to kill you."

"Not again. That sassy mouth of yours gets old, my pet." He strolled to her, wrapped her braid around his hand. "*Change.*"

"Don't want to."

He lowered his head, kissed her fiercely. "I said, '*change*'. You do it or I will."

She did, snapping at him as she shifted into her wolf. Her skirt and blouse landed on the floor. The vintage necklace he'd given her for her birthday turned into an elaborate jeweled dog collar, one he told her was from Liberty Valley of yesteryear. It had enough silver that she couldn't remove it, but it didn't burn her. The embossed gold in the chain links made sure of that.

He attached a leash to the collar. "You need a walk and it's time for me to go to the office. I'm a good owner and I know how to take care of my pet wolf."

His car was still at the body shop for repairs, so they walked from the outskirts of town to the town hall and police department. Of course, his neighbors recognized her as a wolf. When he stopped to speak to them, he ordered her to sit next to him as if she were a dog. Mortified, she snarled at him. He ordered her to behave, or he'd put a muzzle on her.

In his office, he pointed to the large dog bed behind the desk, telling her to lie there while he worked. He didn't allow her to shift into human form to use the adjoining bathroom. No, she had to wait for him to take her outside so she could pee like the pet he called her. After that, he decided he wanted to check on the local businesses and day-to-day activities in town. He strolled down the sidewalk treating her like an animal in front of everyone.

When she balked, snarled, or tried to bite him, he jerked on the leash. The chain collar bit into her neck. She leaped up, determined to rip out his throat. He knocked her down and she landed on her paws in front of him. Somehow, he found a rolled-up newspaper and smacked her butt several times in front of shifters, and humans alike. Everyone laughed at her.

Next, he conjured a basket-style muzzle out of thin air and strapped it on her head. It covered her mouth and prevented biting. He told her she'd still be able to eat and drink like a dog while she wore it. When she acted like his good puppy, he'd remove it. For now, she needed to heel beside him, to sit at his side when he lingered to talk to people, to lie at his feet when he stopped for a meal at a local restaurant. She had to eat the pieces of meat he gave her from his plate and accept a dog treat if he offered one.

After she'd been embarrassed in front of the entire town, they returned to his office. He removed the leash and muzzle but put them on the desk for future use. He ordered her to shift into her human form. She hadn't wanted to because the door was still open to the rest of the building. She abhorred the idea of the deputies and town employees seeing her naked. However, she did it when he threatened to '*change*' her himself. She didn't know if he really could, but he was the enforcer, and she didn't want to find out the hard way.

When she was human, he pulled her into his arms and kissed her.

Furious, she bit his tongue. Using shifter strength, she punched him in the face. She blackened both his eyes, bruised his jaw, bloodied his nose. When he grabbed her wrists, she kicked him as hard as she could, although her bare feet didn't make much of an impression on his boots before she managed to knee him in the groin.

Hearing the struggle, three of his deputies rushed into the room to help him. He ordered them to leave. He had a wolf puppy to train. Ignoring his injuries and the blood running down his face, he dragged her over to a visitor chair. He sat down, pulled her across his knees and spanked her with a rolled-up newspaper from his desk. He called her a 'bad puppy', more than once and reminded her that he was her owner, her master.

After that, he pushed her off his lap onto the floor long enough to open his pants. Then, he pulled her back on top of him, slid inside her and proceeded to fuck her until she climaxed repeatedly. She'd screamed his name again and again, only it wasn't really his name. She called him, her 'master' and begged for more. She heard his minions laughing at her from the hallway, but she tried to ignore them. She wasn't sure how Gunnolf managed to use her shifter magick to heal all his injuries by the time he finished with her.

He was the enforcer and now she knew why he'd been chosen to discipline the wolf pack. He had more *magick* power than anyone else in town. During the next few weeks, they went for car rides with her in her wolf form in the back seat of his restored classic patrol car behind a metal screen. That lasted until he found somewhere secluded. Then, he'd demand she shift into human form again. She didn't have any clothes with her. He'd start touching her, exploring her body first with those calloused, strong hands, fingers slipping inside her.

Next, he'd have his mouth on her. He'd use his tongue lapping, licking, and driving deep into her until she climaxed. Eventually she'd be lying under him on the trunk of the car while he fucked her to a fare-thee-well. On the way back to Corbettstown, he'd stop and buy her a 'doggie' ice cream cone at a burger place, because she'd been such a very, very good puppy and pleased him. He'd hold it and she ate it like a wolf, adding another reason to hate him.

Much to her disgust, Corrine found herself initiating sex with him, not merely waiting until he reached for her. She couldn't get enough of the climaxes that rocketed through her, leaving her clinging to him, and howling for more. And he always obliged. His stamina was incredible. He could and did fuck her for hours at a time.

On snowy days, they stayed home in bed. Determined to play the role of a lifetime, she acted, okay over-acted, what she called the part of a typical pack woman, a real 'Stepford' female wolf. She tried to make him crazy by asking his permission to do anything and everything. She cooked meals and cleaned up afterwards. She ironed creases into his uniform shirt and pants, using way too much spray starch. She polished his shoes and boots until they gleamed.

She told him she'd be a good prisoner, serve her sentence and hope for parole at some point before the year ended. He laughed and packed her off to bed, saying he'd enjoy the reprieve. Meanwhile, the two months were almost up, and she could leave home alone as long as she returned in time to cook supper. He gave back the keys to the SUV and Corrine promptly seized the opportunity to escape to Eagleville and her classes with his daughter, the war witch.

*The more I learn, the easier it will be to kill Frank Corbett,* Corrine told herself. *Once he's dead, nobody will be around to pay the bounty on me, and I'll have my life back. Gunnolf Marvin can find another fool to be his mate. When he's not paying attention, I'll kill him!*

# 6

*Corbettstown, Washington*
*March 2018*

ONE RAINY MARCH AFTERNOON, SHE WAS HALFWAY LYING ON HIM while he sat in the recliner, streaming an early baseball game. He'd pushed up her skirt and his long fingers were inside her, sliding back and forth, thumb teasing the bud buried in the curls between her thighs. She rocked with his strokes, moaning. "Please. Take me now. Please."

"Soon, my puppy, soon. Wait until a commercial." He paused. "We have to talk. The alpha wants you to live with him again. He's promising to pardon you, to take the price off your head. You'd have to swear fealty to him, agree he's the pack leader and pretend to like what he does to you."

"I won't. I'm not going there." She froze in Gunnolf's arms, no longer enjoying his touch. She buried her face on his shoulder and burst into tears. "Don't make me. Don't make me. Don't make me!"

"Hush, my puppy." He cuddled her against him, stroking her hair. "It's going to be all right."

"He's the alpha. You do what he says. Everyone does." Sobs wracked her body. "Kill me. Please. You do it, not the executioner. It'll be quick that way. You've killed shifters before."

"Only bad ones." He rested his chin on top of her head. "And you're not—"

"Yes, I am. I'm bad to the bone." She clung tighter to him, nails digging into his back. "I almost killed Frank after he raped me. I would have if he hadn't called for help and got it."

"Almost doesn't count. He deserved it."

"I'm never becoming part of his pack. He's not my alpha."

"No, he's not. You're my lone wolf, not his."

"Females aren't supposed to leave Corbettstown. Ever! I break the rules and do it all the time."

"I'm the one who gave you a SUV. I know you go where you want, but you always come home on time to me. Not a killing offense, my pet."

She sniffled, kissed his neck. "When we fight, I hurt you. Bad. Someday, I'm going to kill you."

"You've been trying to do that more than a hundred years." He tipped up her chin, brushed her lips with his. "And you always make up for it when I fuck you. I take your shifter magick to heal."

She heaved a sigh. She hadn't shared her bigger crimes with him, and she wouldn't. If the crazed alpha learned about the shadow pack of shifters she'd created with young women, progressive men, and the children in town, or the way she passed out birth control pills to fertile females so there wouldn't be any babies, or how she tutored teen girls and arranged for them to graduate from high school, he'd have no choice. Frank would insist Gunnolf kill her.

She laced her arms around his neck and looked up into his rugged features. "I am a very bad she-wolf. I'm not a good mate. If you were a smart enforcer, you would kill me before I kill you."

"I'm not that smart." He chuckled. "I like it when you're bad and I'm not hurting my puppy. Never my puppy."

"Then, what are we going to do?" She lifted her head, kissed the fierce line of his jaw. "I'm not going to him. I'm staying here in your house with you."

He outlined her lips with his thumb. "It will be dangerous."

"I'm an alpha, a shifter, not a human. I can do it. I will do it."

"Good girl." He adjusted her position, unzipped his pants. He gripped her hips, drove into her. "I need to think. You're mine. You've always been mine. We'll make plans later."

"Much, much later." She kissed him. "Hours and hours later."

———

The plan began with him delivering her to the alpha's house. In front of half the town, she clung to the enforcer. She begged and pleaded to stay with him. She cried, howled and made what the shifters considered a terrible scene. It was highly entertaining since TV reception in Corbettstown could be erratic in the winter. Those who didn't see it, heard about it from friends and neighbors. When Gunnolf tried to leave, she dropped onto her knees in the snow. She clung to his legs and pleaded for him to take her home to his house.

It mortified Frank. When he pulled her away, she screamed and promised to do whatever he wanted, begging him not to beat or rape her again. More public humiliation. Embarrassed, he released her and stormed into the house. She ran after Gunnolf's car. He stopped at the corner, and she hopped inside. They went to the cop shop. He carried her into his office, claiming she needed to be punished because she'd been so disobedient. They had a fucking good time.

When Frank called, Gunnolf agreed to bring her back three days later. He offered to wait until she realized she was safe there. The alpha didn't like that condition and vowed he would control his temper if she behaved herself. All of the neighbors were watching when the enforcer brought her back. She was apparently a credit to her last lesson. She walked up to the alpha, greeted him with an appropriately bowed head and quietly, docilely went into his house.

As far as the town was concerned, the Corrine who lived with the alpha was a perfect pack female. She kept a clean house, cooked his favorite meals, asked permission to go grocery shopping and do needed errands. She wore whatever he liked and when there were visitors, she attempted to be a good hostess. Granted, if he frowned, she immediately burst into tears and begged him not to beat or rape her again.

Two weeks after her arrival, the alpha stalked into the enforcer's office, Corrine supposedly beside him. When he sat down, he had to give her permission to do the same. He glared at Gunnolf. "Do something with her."

"Why does she need to be punished?" Gunnolf petted the gray wolf beside him. "What has she done wrong?"

"I don't know." The Corrine in the chair began to cry. "I do whatever he says. I cook. I clean. I wash clothes. I fuck whenever and wherever he wants. I give him blow jobs at meals. I never tell him I spit his stuff on the floor because it's so disgusting. It's not my fault my owner — you won't let me eat humans and it's the only kind of meat he has in his house. What does he want? I'll do it. I'll do anything so he won't hurt me again."

Gunnolf looked at Frank. "What do you want her to do? Tell her and she'll obey."

"I've heard about her screaming in delight when you have her. Hell, the whole town has. She never does that for me."

"Really?" Gunnolf eyed the woman and the tears running down her cheeks. "Why not?"

"I didn't mean to fall asleep last night while he was doing it." She sniffled. "I thought he was done. He's so little, not big like you and he can't go for a long time like you do, and I never have an orgasm. But I always obey him like you said I had to do because he's the alpha, the Corbettstown pack leader. I lay perfectly still, so he won't get mad and hurt me again." She heaved a dramatic sigh. "I let him fuck as much as he wants, and I wait until he falls asleep before I take a shower because I hate his smell on me. When can I come home, Master? Haven't I been punished enough? I'd really like a good fucking for a change."

"That's what I mean." Frank threw his hands up in disgust.

The Corrine next to him immediately quailed, shrieked and begged loudly for him not to beat her, not to hurt her. She didn't mean to make him mad. More screams and wailing brought a half dozen deputies rushing into the office to defend her. Gunnolf gestured for his wolf to take her to the restroom to compose herself and waved for the other officers to leave him alone with the alpha.

Inside the bathroom, Corrine went into a stall, shifted into her human form and pulled on the dress she'd secreted. She stepped out into the main room. "Really, Andrel. Please don't make me laugh so hard when I'm a wolf. I almost peed on the floor."

Her dark-haired bestie jumped down from the counter and hugged Corrine. "I'm so sorry he hurt you. I couldn't believe it when that bastard A.J. and that bitch, Quincy told the alpha you were gay and then both of them started lying about me and telling him I knew. I'd never say anything like that about anyone here and we both know shifters who are hiding it, staying deep in their proverbial wolf-dens. The chief is still pissed about what happened to you, and Frank is such a —"

"I know. I lived with him for a week." Corrine kept her arm around her friend. "This is above and beyond. Pretending to be me and living there. How did you know about Gunnolf's abilities? You've never had —"

"Oh, honey. Women talk. I haven't been with him, but the stories have gone around for years. He's supposed to be huge, and men are always super sensitive about their sizes. And a guy who can make a woman have *beaucoup* orgasms? I'm so ready for that especially after the alpha who is horrible in bed."

"You know I won't share the enforcer." Corrine laughed. "Anything else?"

"Hmm, maybe." Andrel pursed her lips, blue eyes narrowing. "You marked me as yours years ago when we were pups playing in a sandbox at your mom's house. You're my alpha, and I'm part of your shadow pack. Of course, he doesn't know about us. But he keeps saying there isn't any place for a lone wolf in Corbettstown and I need to pledge allegiance to him. I can't. I won't. Of course, he thinks I'm you."

"What do you tell him?" Corrine glanced anxiously at the door, hoping nobody interrupted them. "You're my wolf, my second in command and I depend on you."

"Because you always have and will. Frank doesn't need to know what we're doing, so I tell him I can't because the enforcer is my owner and master."

"Nice. Good job sowing dissension between them." Corrine high-fived her best friend. "Let that come back and bite both of them in their tails. It really surprised me when Gunnolf agreed to protect me from Frank and went along with this scheme. I didn't expect it. How else can I help you?"

"When I come back to the office, give me a heads up when you're going to fuck the chief. I'd love to win the pool on how many climaxes you have. We'll split the pot when I take all the money these bastards bet. And is there any way you can cover for me one day next week? I want to take my mama out for lunch on her birthday."

"I'll talk to Gunnolf and try to make it happen."

The next week, Frank sent Andrel to the office for discipline. She arrived in jeans and a T-shirt. She deliberately slammed the office door behind her which roused attention. Gunnolf gestured to her to leave through the window. When she did, he signaled Corrine. She shifted and within ten minutes, he was fucking her.

Andrel returned hours later. She left in a borrowed skimpy red dress and stilettos for Frank's, a sight bound to offend the alpha. He preferred shifters to wear comfortable attire so they could fight like wolves, twenty-four, seven. A week later, the enforcer showed up on Frank's doorstep shortly after Corrine and Andrel switched places. Corrine treated him like a guest. She took ice-cold beers and snacks to the Great Room where he and Frank watched TV.

When the alpha told her that the enforcer was there to continue her schooling, she threw a major fit. She demanded to know why. She wore what he liked, kept the house clean, did whatever he wanted in bed. She even laid down for him whenever he wanted — well, actually Andrel did — but neither of them pretended to have orgasms for an inept fool who had the world's smallest dick.

Frank said he didn't like her attitude. Corrine hurled the tray of meat and crackers at him and told him to get over himself. She was a shifter, not a slave even if she was under a death sentence and had to call the enforcer her owner and master for at least a year. She told Frank he was a liar and a horrible alpha because he hadn't kept his word about granting her clemency.

When Gunnolf came at her, she threatened him with one of the beer bottles. She anticipated him ducking so she still connected, striking him in the face. Blood running down his cheek, he grabbed the broken bottle before she could cut him a second time. Then, he picked her up, slung her over his shoulder. He reminded Frank that he'd been warned she wasn't fully 'trained' and needed constant discipline. Without it, she'd act out instead of being a credit to her handler, adhering to his requirements and pack rules for females.

Pretending to be enraged by his assessment, Corrine began struggling. Gunnolf carried her into the study. He tore off her T-shirt and used it to wipe his face. He ripped her sports bra in half, and it landed in the garbage. Boots, jeans, and panties went next. By the time he started fondling and running his hands all over her, she was wild with excitement. She climaxed as soon as his fingers slipped inside her. She was squirming, bucking against him, and pleading for him to have her even though she knew Frank was just outside the door listening.

It didn't matter when she and Gunnolf were together. He fucked her for more than an hour, a short time for them but she had several orgasms. Afterwards, he sent her upstairs and told her to come back in a dress and heels. No underwear because he didn't want to deal with it. He stayed for dinner and then came into the kitchen while she was cleaning. He had her again.

Frank started sending Andrel to the enforcer two or three times a week, which gave her plenty of days off, so she and Corrine hung out together at the cop shop. If Andrel wanted to visit her mother at the grocery she owned, Corrine covered for her best friend. Gunnolf always came to the alpha's house a short time later, claiming he needed to reinforce her training. She practically jumped him as soon as he walked in the door the next time he visited. He picked her up and held her against the wall in the hallway while he fucked her. Truthfully, he'd had her all over the house, in the study, the kitchen, the Great Room, the laundry, the pantry, the basement and on the back deck.

Eventually, hearing her scream so often during her frequent climaxes frustrated Frank even more. He told Gunnolf to take her upstairs to one of the guestrooms, to have normal sex with her in a bed. The alpha hated hearing her call the enforcer, her owner or master, but she'd say whatever he wanted to get him to fuck her and provide those amazing orgasms.

At Beltane in the first part of May, Trina, the town doctor's daughter, took her place with the alpha. Still believing she was Corrine, Frank returned Andrel to the police department. She continued working as an undercover detective. Meanwhile, Corrine remained there since the alpha and enforcer agreed she'd become a part-time deputy instead of returning to work as a waitress.

Because she hadn't agreed to accept Frank as the pack leader, he refused to remove the bounty on her. Gunnolf warned the deputies if his mate was harmed in any way, he'd kill the perp, and then the officers who didn't protect her. The word spread throughout Corbettstown and even the pack executioner knew he was expected to guard her, not honor the alpha's commands. Nobody argued with the police chief because his rage was legendary.

Corrine actually didn't know anything about law enforcement, but Gunnolf Marvin wasn't concerned. He liked having her in the office so he could fuck her regularly, not just at home. Hester Corbett, an older shifter female who served as the manager taught her how to handle the phones, answer called-in complaints, dispatch the deputies, file paperwork, and greet visitors who came to town which was slightly different than waiting on them in restaurants.

Corrine wasn't paid as much as the deputies, but the enforcer said she still needed walking-around money. Of course, he didn't know the fix was in when she screamed during her climaxes or about the way most of the officers bet on how many she'd have when he had her. And none of the men knew she and Andrel continued to split the bucks the other woman won when she joined in on the bets.

Gunnolf agreed she could volunteer at the day-care and tutor at the elementary school a few days a week. When she was bored, she headed out to Eagleville and Liberty Valley to visit friends. Often, she used her trips to smuggle endangered other world creatures like fairies, elves, witches, and brownies out of town and birth control pills back to her mother who would pass them onto fertile females. Corrine also continued her self-defense classes with the war witch.

She asked the leaders of the coven about removing the *magick* necklace he'd given her because it tracked her whereabouts. They couldn't. However, they were able to block Gunnolf from learning about her activities when she wasn't in Corbettstown and Corrine had to be satisfied with that. She arrived home in time to change from her favorite clothes to one of the dresses he liked and cook supper.

After school ended in June, she spent more days working at the precinct. Hester warned her to be careful. The alpha hated rebellious females and eventually found ways to slay them. If the police chief decided she was too much of a challenge, he'd kill her when he got tired of fucking her. The fact everyone thought she was his mate wouldn't save her. Many of the male shifters including the town doctor had either killed their partners or sent them to be executed by the alpha when they showed unacceptable talents such as *magickal* healing or witchcraft.

It was good advice and Corrine kept it in mind through the rest of the summer and into the fall. She discreetly met with her shadow pack who continued their subversive activities, helping those in danger, especially the younger men leave town. Most of his minions saw Gunnolf screwing her before her supposed time with the alpha and they weren't surprised it happened again now that *she* was back with the enforcer fulltime after May.

They laughed if she called him, 'Master,' and screamed during her multiple orgasms. She refused to show how much it embarrassed her when they came in the room and saw their boss fucking her. Instead, she mentally counted up how much money she and Andrel would share later. Gunnolf seemed to relish an audience. He'd finish, step back and zip his pants while she lay where he left her on the couch, scrabbling for her clothes or the blanket he kept on the back of the sofa.

Once he'd given them instructions, they'd leave. He'd either unzip his pants, not bothering to remove them before he drove into her, or else he'd go down on her, taking her with his mouth until she was yelling loud enough for everyone in the town hall to hear. More degradation as if she needed that!

She continued plotting how to kill him! And the other woman inside her encouraged her to think outside the puppy kennel. She promised she'd killed him before and together they could do it again. *Soon, very soon!*

# 7

*Bar M Ranch,*
*Washington Territory, November 1888*

THEY LEFT JUNCTION CITY IMMEDIATELY AFTER BREAKFAST ON
Wednesday since it'd take most of the day to reach the Bar M.
Leading the packhorse he'd rented from the livery, Kyle looked at
the three women riding down the wagon road in front of him. Like
Nina, Kallisto Hunter had opted for a divided skirt, but her older
sister, Astrid rode side-saddle in a dark blue habit. He didn't hear
their conversation, just the rise and fall of their low, feminine voices,
but it didn't matter.

They were undoubtedly discussing topics his wife would share
with him later. His wife. He marveled at the concept once more. It'd
taken too long, but at last, he had a family. He watched Pooka guide
the way to the Bar M. The pup seemed to love their new home as
much as his owner. Kyle gazed ahead at Nina's straight back under
the heavy duster. He couldn't see her short dark brown hair covered
by a knit cap, but perhaps she'd let it grow as long as his when she
felt safe.

He remembered the warning she said she'd received from Astra Jamison yesterday before the witch left for the future. Gary Smith might show up in this time and they'd have to deal with the man if he did. Granted, they probably wouldn't be able to kill him, but at least they could see Smith stood trial and was imprisoned for his crimes.

As the hours passed, the temperature dropped, and snowflakes brushed his face. It was late afternoon when they arrived at the ranch. Nina stopped her horse in front of the house. Before she dismounted, the door opened, and Señora Ortiz rushed out on the wide porch. "Did you find them?"

"Find who?" Kyle urged his Appaloosa gelding, S.O.B. closer. "What's happened?"

"I sent the children to collect eggs for me this morning and they disappeared. Everyone's looking for them."

———

Nina turned her horse further into the yard and rode closer to the dark-haired woman standing on the porch. "When did you realize they were gone?"

"After dinner." Hannah Ortiz pulled a shawl closer around her shoulders. "The girls helped me with the dishes and Michael filled the wood-box. They've spent so much time around the house these past few days. They were stir-crazy and I didn't see the harm in letting the three of them go to the henhouse near the barn."

"How old are they?" Kallisto and Astrid shared a glance. "Did any of them have a rifle or pistol?"

"Of course not." Hannah twisted her hands. "I know Michael learned to shoot when he lived at the Lazy B, but there isn't any need for that here, not when I keep him close."

"Becky's eight and Michael turned eleven a couple of months ago. Sorrel's almost twelve." Nina frowned thoughtfully, glancing around the snow-covered buildings, but she didn't see any unusual tracks, just boot-prints of varying sizes. "Kyle, why don't you put the packhorse in the barn? Hannah, do you have something that belongs to one of the kids? A shirt or a dress or a nightgown?"

"What are you thinking?" Kyle reined his strawberry roan close for a moment. "I know you have an idea."

"When you first came to work at my place, we taught Pooka to find you and I'm betting he can find the girls. He plays with them often enough."

"Brilliant notion. I'll be right back."

When he'd ridden off toward the barn and Hannah Ortiz hurried into the house, Nina eyed Astrid. "I'm betting if something or someone killed any of the children, I'd see their spirits. Is that right?"

"You're right. As the *Seer*, it's your job to send the dead where they need to go."

"That's what I thought." Nina swung out of the saddle and passed the reins to Astrid. "Kallisto, you'll need to reload our rifles with silver ammo. I don't know where the children are, but I suspect they haven't returned home because they're trapped by some of those wolves."

"That makes sense." It was the other woman's turn to dismount. She removed the rifle from the scabbard on the saddle. "I'll do mine first, then yours and Astrid's. Mister Morgan can take care of his when he rejoins us."

The front door opened, and Hannah hustled toward Nina, holding out two garments and a dirty sock. "I did laundry on Monday, so these are the ones the girls were wearing this week. Michael changes his socks every day."

"Fair enough." Nina called the dog and petted him when he came to stand in front of her, tail wagging. "Okay, Pooka. Time to play." She held out the smallest nightie to him and he sniffed it. "Find Becky."

Pooka cocked his tri-colored head, and she repeated her action, letting him smell the article of clothing. "Find Becky."

The young dog scurried around the yard, tracking a scent, then trotted off toward the barns. She tucked the other nightshirt and Michael's sock in the saddlebags. Picking up Missouri's reins, Nina followed her pet. He moseyed around the henhouse by the barn, then by the cabin Hannah shared with her husband and son.

When Pooka paused to scratch an itch, Nina approached him. She held out the small nightgown again. "Find Becky."

The dog yipped, then tore off toward the pastures. Nina put her left foot in the stirrup and vaulted back into the saddle. Collecting on the reins, she squeezed her legs and sent the retired show-horse into a slow canter after the collie. She heard hoofbeats and glanced over her shoulder, not surprised to see Kyle riding behind her, followed by the Hunter women.

He caught up within a few strides. "Where do you think they went?"

"I'm not sure, but Pooka seems to know." They passed the field where her horses had originally grazed with other stock kept close in for riding. Pooka kept going down the track and they followed the dog. Nina eyed Kyle. "I think he's taking us to the pasture where Rad keeps the Appaloosas. He planned to put Georgia and Minnesota in with them while we were gone."

"I hadn't recalled that, but you're right." They neared the next paddock and Pooka advanced on the gate, barking wildly. Nina pushed her Arabian to a gallop. She saw the herd of horses running toward them, several wolves behind the brightly colored Appys.

She vaulted out of the saddle, quickly sliding her rifle out of the scabbard. She dropped the reins on the ground and Missouri froze, a credit to Kyle's training. She steadied the rifle on the fence rail, picked her target, a large male wolf streaking toward Georgia, and pulled the trigger.

The bullet struck the animal in the chest, and he tumbled into the snow. The small bay filly whinnied and raced in her direction, followed by her former stablemate, then the rest of the horses. Nina aimed at another wolf, fired, and watched it fall. She suddenly grew aware that Kyle stood next to her, shooting at the pack. A third wolf stumbled into a fourth, each wounded and barely able to walk. Kallisto didn't hesitate to shoot at them and neither did her sister.

"Enough." Astrid lowered her Winchester as the remaining wolves turned and bolted into the evergreens. "Let them go for the time being. We'll hunt the rest later."

"Works for me." Nina leaned down to pet her pup who sat next to her. "Now, where are those children? Pooka, find Becky."

The dog whined, then ducked under the bottom rail. Nina passed her carbine to Kyle while she went between the middle and lowest poles. She took his rifle and held both of them when he followed her. Meantime, Astrid collected the reins of the waiting horses and held them so her sister could join the quest.

Several of the horses came to greet them and Nina paused to pet her two mares before she went after the collie. He headed toward the pond before he swerved to the left and three giant logs in a pile, obviously left to dry, prior to being split into posts and more rails. He stopped, tail between his legs, and whimpered.

Nina caught up with her pup and rumpled his white ruff. "Becky, Sorrel, Michael, where are you?"

"Here." Michael stood up behind the logs, holding a hefty wooden club. "We're here, Miss Nina."

She advanced on him, then saw the two girls behind him, petite, blonde Becky hugging a white wolf. Blood dripped from several bite marks on the animal's body. "What on earth are you doing, child?"

"She ran off to visit Georgia." Michael sounded disgusted. "And Sorry and I came to find her, only there were a bunch of mean wolves. These two drove us in here and they fought the rest."

"Where's the other one?"

"Here." Red-haired, green-eyed Sorrel waved to Nina from the wooden sanctuary. "And she's hurt bad. I think she's gonna die."

"Okay." Nina took a deep breath and went into the makeshift fort. She saw the smaller black and gray wolf lying in the snow, blood pooling from the injury in the throat, more gashes in the animal's chest and legs. "Sorrel, go with Kallisto and get my saddlebags. We'll do our best to bandage them up and take them to your mama. She told me she can heal people. I'll bet she can heal these two wolves as well."

"Detective Morgan healed Trace's stallion when he was hurt bad," Michael said. "If anyone can make that wolf better, she can."

"Astrid has the healing touch too." Kallisto urged the girls from behind the logs toward the pasture. "I'll send her your way. Mister Morgan, keep an eye out in case those others return. They're not going to be happy because these two betrayed the orders of the pack leader."

Kyle nodded agreement, then passed Nina's rifle to Michael. "Your ma said that Trace taught you to shoot. I figure you can help me stand guard."

The boy checked the weapon, heaving a sigh of relief. "I'd really like it if you'd tell her I'm eleven now and not a baby."

"I'll do my best, but I'm not losing out on Señora Ortiz's biscuits. My horse would never speak to me again."

Nina suppressed a smile, then turned to the darker wolf and stroked her head. "Thank you for saving them."

*'I don't hunt or eat children, not my own, or those of witches, or humans.'* A woman's shape drifted in and out of the animal's body. *'You sent my mate to Summerland, Seer. If I die, send me to join him.'*

"I will." Nina smoothed the black fur. "Like your husband, you have to promise to help Jed Corbett in the future when you come around again. He was known as Tom Corbett here."

*'I promise.'* Breath rattled in her throat. *'So will my pack sister when her time comes.'*

"Good to know." Nina glanced at the white wolf who limped toward them. "We owe you too. You're welcome at the Bar M for as long as you want to stay."

————

Kyle closed the bedroom door behind Beth. "How are they?"

"Sleeping. I've done my best with Ruby. She was a mess, but Petrina only had a few serious injuries. Astrid and Kallisto are looking after them tonight." Beth started for the stairs. "Any idea about what I do with my girls? Becky shouldn't have run off like that, but Sorrel and Michael should have come to get us."

"Most folks would wallop them."

"I'm not most folks." Beth led the way toward the kitchen and Kyle followed his sister by marriage. "I had too many beatings growing up and I didn't learn a damned thing from them except to run and hide from sons of bitches. When I couldn't escape, I fought back. Rad said you and I have a lot in common because you were raised by strangers too."

"That's true," Kyle agreed. "Rad told me once that Trace Burdette-Prescott's grandpa used to say if 'you give a child or a critter a lesson in meanness, don't be surprised when they learn it.' I won't whip any of my sons or daughters. Nina had her share of poundings from her stepfather before she went off to boarding school. She won't strike a child either."

Kyle saw the entire family gathering around the table in the kitchen, Señora Ortiz washing up after supper. He went to join his new wife, putting an arm around her waist, and glanced at his older brother. "Reckon this is your business and Bethany's, so Nina and I are going to leave you to it."

"Any suggestions?" Rad studied the three children sitting at the table. "Been the marshal around and about Junction City for years, but I'll admit to being plumb out of my depth with young lawbreakers."

"Beth said Trace Burdette-Prescott raised Becky and Michael." Nina pressed close to Kyle's side. "What would she do if you broke the rules at the Lazy B?"

"Lots of extra chores," Michael said immediately. "And if she was really mad, she'd take away your horse, like she took Frog away from me until she decided I was old enough to handle him, but at least she didn't sell him. Not like her grandpa did to her horse in Arizona when she was bad."

"Don't take Georgia." Tears filled Becky's light blue eyes and rained down her cheeks. "I'm sorry I was naughty. Really, I am. I just missed her so much."

"She'd have missed you more if Ruby and Petrina hadn't risked their lives to save you." Pausing to pick up an oil lamp from the counter, Kyle turned Nina toward his room, Pooka following them. "We'll see you in the morning and you can tell us what you and Bethany decided, Rad."

"Sounds fair to us."

Once in their room, Kyle stepped away from Nina and went to add wood to the blaze in the fireplace. "Well, that was an adventure. I'm glad Gabe took the ranch hands to bring back the bodies. None of them spoke to you, did they?"

She shook her head. "Their spirits must have followed the pack home to Corbett's Town. We need to go there as soon as we have enough ammunition. We've been lucky so far, but they're not going to stop, are they? They'll keep coming after our children, won't they? And Beth and I are both pregnant. Our babies won't be safe from them, will they?"

"No, they're not. So, we'll hunt them down and kill them before they get the chance to do us harm." He unbuttoned his shirt and hung it in the wardrobe. "Let's call it a night, Missus Morgan."

———

Nina eased out of Kyle's embrace and the four-poster bed. She lingered to cover him up, before sliding into her robe. Pooka snoozed by the fireplace, and she left them to sleep. The large room was a mirror image of the one that Beth shared with her husband, easily big enough for a married couple. Like other rooms in the house, the plank walls glistened a soft gray under a coat of whitewash.

A hooked rug stretched across the wooden floor. A large wooden wardrobe stood in one corner with a matching bureau and a washstand along the same wall. When she walked through the dark house, she saw light shining from the kitchen and heard low voices. She headed there to put on her boots for the late-night trip to the outhouse.

Beth sat at the long table with Kallisto and Astrid Hunter. The three of them enjoyed tea and toast while a tall, slender woman with ash-blonde hair had joined them. She wasn't having a light snack but ate a thick roast beef sandwich.

Nina eyed the stranger. "Who are you? When did you get here?"

"I'm Petrina Corbett and your husband carried me here on his horse, *Seer*."

"He brought a wolf—" Nina stopped speaking. "Well, that was stupid. You're a shifter, aren't you? How's your friend?"

"Sleeping and healing. Thanks to the *Guardian*, she'll live."

"And thanks to both of you, so will my daughters." Beth rose to her feet. "Do you want a cup of tea, Nina?"

"I'd love one, but first I need to take the proverbial walk. When is your husband installing indoor plumbing?"

"Soon, very soon." When she returned to the house, she found Petrina drawing a diagram of Corbett's Town, describing the inhabitants and the pack structure. Kallisto asked questions about who'd lead the attack against them and which of the wolves would be most formidable.

Petrina shuddered, clenching her fists until her knuckles whitened. Blue eyes filled with terror. "Frederick Corbett is the alpha, and he thinks he's tough, but the most dangerous in the pack is the enforcer, Grayson Mallory and the third in command, the executioner does what Grayson says."

"Which one will come after you and Ruby when the others report what you did?" Nina leaned forward to cover Petrina's hands with hers in an attempt to offer comfort. "The alpha or the enforcer?"

"Grayson." A tear slid down the pale cheek. "He'll order Leander Selby, the executioner to kill us for betraying him, but he didn't know I overheard him relay the alpha's orders to take the Guardian's children and bring them to him for meat."

"So, he dies too." Beth refilled their cups. "The only question is which of you gets him first, ladies."

"Me." Astrid shared a look with her younger sister. "We've been hunting them for a long time, *Guardian*. If we don't take them in this life, the witches we become will destroy them in the next."

# 8

*Corbettstown, Washington*
*November 2018*

MOST OF THE OFFICERS AND EMPLOYEES AT THE TOWN HALL DIDN'T hide their contempt when Gunnolf insisted she wear her special uniform, a low-cut blouse sans bra, a short pencil skirt that barely reached her knees, thigh-high stockings, no underwear, and stilettos because he liked how her legs looked.

He told his deputies not to let her have a loaded gun because she'd shoot them or him. She always carried her silver dagger either on her hip or in the special scabbard under her skirt. After she almost gutted A.J. Corbett last March and it took him three days to heal as a wolf, the other male deputies learned the enforcer was the only one allowed to touch her.

Then came *Samhain*. She hadn't been allowed to attend the New Year celebration because she disgraced herself at *Mabon*, a harvest festival in September. The enforcer commanded her to shift into her wolf form to accompany him. When she refused, he fucked her. Then, while she was naked and recovering from that, he forced the shift. The next thing she knew she was in the shape of her wolf.

Furious, she attacked him. He could order her to become a wolf. He didn't have the right to make her. She almost tore out his throat, but he managed to block that with his arm. She still ripped it down to bone, loving the taste of his blood. He knocked her down, threw her halfway across the room. He turned around to grab the newspaper off his desk.

She launched into the air. As a gray wolf, she weighed a little over a hundred pounds and it was all muscle. When she hit the middle of his back, he fell forward, striking his head on the desk. The blow knocked him out. She bit into his ankle and dragged him over by the visitor chairs. He was still face down and she used her paws to shove him onto his back. Blood ran from his forehead toward his closed eyes.

A little guilt formed, but she listened to the woman's voice inside her. He'd hurt them so many times. He always lied. He cheated. He shamed her in front of his minions. He tried to control everything she did. He claimed her as his mate without consulting her. He told everyone in town he owned her. Well, he didn't. She was a free shifter. She went for his throat. Her teeth ripped into his skin.

Before she managed more than one bite, he caught her collar.

Surprising her with a sudden burst of strength, he pushed her off. "Bad girl."

He struck her with the rolled-up newspaper, once, twice, three times.

Because he was seriously injured, the blows barely landed. They didn't even disturb her fur. Remorse swept through her. She could have killed him today. Ignoring the voice inside telling her to finish him, she crawled to him on her belly. She rested her head on his boots, whimpering. Her surrender pleased him, and he told her to change into a human. The sex lasted longer while she had multiple orgasms. Dimly, she was aware he used her shifter *magick* to heal his injuries.

Once they showered and he had on a fresh uniform, he told her to shift on her own or he'd *change* her. Angry tears sliding down her face, she obeyed. She wore the jeweled silver collar, and he leashed her. He tucked the dog treats in his jacket pocket and warned her to be a good puppy or he'd conjure up a newspaper and paddle her in front of everyone. And then, he'd fuck her in front of the entire pack while she screamed encouragement.

Terrified by the threats, she intended to behave the way he wanted. She tolerated Frank Corbett's praise and allowed him to pet her like she was a dog, not one of his shifters. Gunnolf sat on the deck, drinking ice-cold beer with some of his deputies, the alpha and the pack executioner. Most of the men laughed while they watched her play 'fetch' with the pack children in the yard. She chased tennis balls until she was exhausted. She was lying on the patio, panting when Trina approached with a bowl of cool ice water.

The other shifter said it was time for dinner. She appreciated Corrine humoring the pups and entertaining them, so they didn't get into trouble. Trina told Gunnolf that Corrine should change into her human self now for the meal. There were clothes in the guest-room, she could borrow since she hadn't brought her own. The enforcer refused to let her. He said she'd had lunch at the office, and they'd have dinner when they got home. She didn't need to eat at the alpha's with the pack. Human food was bad for his pet wolf.

The pity on the tall, graceful blonde's face incensed Corrine. She stood up and proceeded to pee all over the woman's designer shoes and the hem of her vintage black gown. Unfortunately, Frank saw it. The infuriated alpha demanded the enforcer punish her. Gunnolf said Corrine knew the consequences, so he'd do it immediately. The only reason he didn't was because Trina intervened. She claimed it was all her fault for patronizing Corrine and apologized for being rude to a guest.

She couldn't stand more sympathy, so she promptly crapped on Frank's shoes. It was his fault. He was the one who attacked her in the first place. That got her kicked out and the alpha told the enforcer she couldn't return to any of the festivals until she apologized. Fair being fair, she did it again on the way through the house, taking two more huge dumps on the way to the front door. The alpha's entire place reeked of her poop.

Frank started baying like a coyote, screaming for Gunnolf to do something about her right now. He followed them to the patrol car, still raging. Annoyed by his high-pitched howling, Corrine snapped at him. Nearly biting him shut him up for the moment. Of course, it also earned a quick scruff shake like she really was a disobedient puppy from the enforcer before he locked her in the back of the patrol car.

Gunnolf Marvin did something so she couldn't hear any more of what Frank said. When the alpha stormed back into the house, the enforcer drove up the mountain to one of his favorite picnic places. When he let her out, he told her she'd embarrassed him for the last time. Still in her wolf form, she sat and looked at him, wondering if he intended to kill her. Then, he smiled and told her to change shape.

She hesitated and finally did it. Was she going to die as a human? He spread out the picnic blanket and called her to come to him. She wasn't sure what he had in mind since he still wore his uniform but decided to play it safe and humor him. When she stood naked in front of him, he framed her face with his hands and said they were having a basic 'obedience' class. He put the leash on her necklace.

For the next two hours, she had to come, sit, stay, heel, lie down, fetch a tennis ball, drop it, and pick it up again. If she didn't do it fast enough, he smacked her butt with the rolled-up newspaper he created out of thin air. If he was happy with her, she earned kisses and what he called, 'good puppy rewards'—times when he ran his hands over her, licked her breasts and sucked her nipples until she climaxed.

"Now, you're going to learn something new."

"What?" She kissed his throat, sliding her arms around his neck. "Are you going to have me now, Master?"

"Oh no, my pet." He smiled, stroking her back, smoothing her hair. "I'm going to train you to 'come' whenever I snap my fingers."

"I don't understand." She tipped back her head, staring into his face. "Haven't I already come when you called during this stupid 'obedience' class?"

"Not that kind of coming." He eased a finger inside her, followed it with a second. His thumb rocked against the small bud nested in the curls between her legs. "Time to move for me, my pet."

She did, rising and falling with the strokes of his hand. She moaned, gasped, and kissed him, finally crying out when the orgasm claimed her. She looked into his eyes when he snapped the fingers of his free hand.

"What are you—" She stopped, realizing what he intended. He meant for her to have an orgasm whenever he signaled her. "No."

"Oh yes, my pet. You may call me your owner and master, but after today, you'll mean it. You won't be rolling your eyes, sighing, and acting like you're placating me. You'll be sincere." He began to move the fingers still inside her, sliding them in and out of her. "Whenever you want to make a scene and shame me in front of others, I'll snap my fingers. You'll come like you do when I fuck you. Remember that next time you decide to shit on someone. Who owns you, my pet?"

"You do!" She couldn't help it. She met the motion of his skilled fingers and heard herself begging for more. This time when she came in a long climax, she saw him snap his fingers. Soon, she was under him on the blanket while he fucked her, really fucked her and she came again and again whenever he gave the new signal. She hated him even more and silently contemplated how she'd kill him.

On the way home, she sat in the passenger seat, wrapped in the blanket while he repeated the action. And of course, he laughed at her while he snapped those damned fingers again and again. Someday, she'd cut them off and shove them down his throat!

She was shaking from the repeated orgasms when they walked in the house. She followed him to his den and saw him stop in front of the shelves that held more rows of decanters like the ones at the police department. During one of his absences, she'd inspected them and found most were empty. She wasn't sure why he kept them because he really wasn't a drinker. Exhausted from the extended afternoon of sex and constant orgasms, she swayed and nearly closed her eyes.

Then, she saw it. What looked like a *magickal* stream poured from his hand into the first bottle. He sealed it with a cap, and filled a second one, then a third. She yawned. Her knees buckled and she collapsed onto the hallway floor. She woke a few moments later to find him carrying her toward the bedroom.

He kissed her forehead. "I'm installing a doghouse and a kennel in the back yard for you, my pet."

"Why? I've lived with you nine months and shifters mate for life." Tears filled her eyes and one trickled down her cheek. "Don't you want me anymore?"

"You're mine. Even when you raise hell, I want you. I'm keeping you, but I saw too much at the alpha's today." He lowered her onto the king-size bed. "Trina has started boring Frank. He has a short attention span. Soon, he'll decide she needs training and send her to me. I can't have two women in the house, especially a jealous, little she-wolf-bitch like you."

"Then let me go. I'll move back in with my mother and come to the office every day."

"Oh no, my sweet pet. I claimed you as my mate last *Yule*." He covered her with the rest of the blankets. "I'm not letting you romp around town off leash, especially when I'm finally getting you trained."

She knew she ought to be angry about his arrogance and the name he called her, but she was too tired. She drifted into slumber and woke hours later when he joined her. He parted her legs and his mouth found her. She longed to ask what he'd been doing, why he needed sex again so soon, but didn't quite dare.

She rose and fell against the intimate kiss, gasping and crying out when his tongue drove deep. Soon he slid inside her and she was moving under him while he took her with those amazing thrusts that lasted forever. She came again and again, every time he snapped his fingers. She wasn't surprised to see a six-pack of empty wolf-shaped bottles on the nightstand or him adding energy to them when he thought she was dozing between sexual rounds. Why had he stock-piled so much *magick* lately? What was he planning? Had Frank enraged him too often? Did Gunnolf intend to get rid of the alpha and take over the pack like he had before?

———

Gunnolf was right about Frank being ready to dispose of Trina. It happened at *Samhain*. Corrine was perfectly happy to miss the cele-bration this year, but the enforcer had to attend. She'd sent him off in a perfectly ironed uniform and brilliantly shined boots. He'd been absent most of the day and she happily enjoyed having the house to herself. Since he was gone, she loved wearing her pajamas and bathrobe the majority of the time. She ordered pizzas, drank wine, streamed romantic movies and laughed at the saccharine dialogue.

He wasn't home when she went to bed on Friday, but she'd always slept naked in case she needed to shift to her wolf form in the middle of the night. He arrived while she was sleeping. When she woke in his arms, she smelled Trina on him and knew he'd fucked the other shifter. It infuriated her. The least he could have done was take a shower. It didn't take much strength to kick him out of the king-size bed and he landed on the carpet. He rolled to his feet and yanked the blankets off her. When she stormed toward the bedroom door, he caught her and dragged her back to face him.

She glared up into his rugged features. "You're scum and I won't share."

"You'll do as you're told, my pet." He pinned her wrists behind her back and lowered his head to kiss her. "Bite me and you'll wish you hadn't. It's my job, Corrine, only my job."

Tears filled her eyes at the sound of her name, her real name. He never used it, not after the first time he took her almost a year ago.

He always called her, his pet, or his wolf or even his puppy and occasionally his mate. "You're throwing me away, aren't you, Gunnolf? Who are you giving me to this time? The alpha? One of your deputies? Not A.J. Please, not him. I'll die before he kills me."

"You're not dying." He pulled her close, locked her body against his strong one. "And nobody else can have my bitchy she-wolf."

His mouth seized hers and she surrendered, kissing him back. His large hands cupped her bottom, his finger sliding into her. She started to move with the rhythmic strokes, then remembered her anger and hurt. She stopped, forcing herself to stand perfectly still.

Their gazes met, clashed and she lifted her chin. "I really am a wolf. I won't share you."

"And I'm the enforcer. I have to provide discipline, or the pack will fail. It's already in jeopardy with a weak alpha." His thumb found her clitoris and rocked against it. A second finger joined the first. He kissed her forehead. ""You're still being punished as a rule-breaker under a death sentence. You're not allowed to use my name, are you, my pet? I'll let it go this time, but don't do it again."

She struggled to remain still, but couldn't when he moved those long, skilled fingers. She met his strokes, rising and falling. After a few more kisses, he worked his way toward her breasts and nipples. She hadn't climaxed yet when she landed on the bed beneath him, and he deliberately snapped his fingers. She came all at once. Retribution was hers. She punched him in the ribs with all her shifter strength, happy when she heard the bones crack.

He groaned in sudden pain. "After this, it's 'doggie style' for you all weekend, my angry little puppy. And we'll see what it takes for you to go into heat and give me a litter of sons."

"I won't." She gasped when he thrust deep inside her, barely supporting his weight on his elbows. Her hips met his as he fucked her. The long, deep strokes went on and on until she climaxed twice, and he'd used enough of her *magick* to heal. They hadn't finished when he shifted positions. He guided her onto her hands and knees and took her from behind, holding her butt firmly against him. Despite hating what he called 'doggie style', she came again and again, barely aware he only snapped his fingers twice.

———

Before he left for the alpha's house later that day, Gunnolf moved Corrine into what he referred to as the 'doghouse' in the huge five-acre backyard. It was what most humans would have called a grand-parent's cottage, bigger than a tiny home or she-shed. It had a covered porch, perfect when she wanted to sit outside on rainy days, common in the western Washington winters.

When she walked in the front door, there was a combination living-dining room and kitchen with a small pantry, already fully stocked with canned goods and staples. He'd furnished the place. A sofa, new recliner and big flatscreen on the wall. Books by her favorite authors, along with a selection of classic fiction filled the shelves. A table and four chairs were close to the kitchen. Dishes in the cupboards, pots, and pans by the stove along with a teakettle because he didn't like coffee. He hadn't let her have it for almost a year, saying caffeine was toxic for shifters and it could kill her.

He'd installed a back door in the utility room which would come in handy when she was dirty from working in the garden. She loved flowers and fully intended to buy more rose bushes and plant them around the house. She'd be able to throw her dirty clothes in the new washer on her way to shower in her own bathroom. Her clothes went in the walk-in closet off the good-sized bedroom. She had her own king-size bed.

While she was putting on flannel sheets, he stood in the door-way. "I don't like those. They're too hot."

"I don't care. You'll be sleeping in your house with Trina. This is my place." Corrine tossed her head. "I'm going to totally enjoy you 'training' her and do as I please for however long she's living here."

"She hasn't arrived yet." He chuckled. "Come here, my jealous puppy."

Corrine spread a thick comforter on the bed. "Go to hell!"

"I was there before and it's too damned hot." He folded his arms, still slightly amused. "I said, come!"

She ignored him and ripped off the plastic wrappers on the new pillowcases. She was a dominant alpha female like Hester had told her last summer. He could teach Trina to be at his beck and call. After all, she was the one the alpha decided needed to be trained.

Gunnolf laughed and snapped his fingers. "You are a stubborn little thing. Come!"

Corrine shuddered as the first orgasm rolled through her, followed by a second, then a third. By the fourth, she managed to walk toward him. By the fifth, she was on the floor in front of him. "I swear I'll kill you someday soon."

"That's my puppy. Thanks for the warning. I know you will. You've done it before." He dropped to his knees behind her, pushed her skirt up to her waist. "Now, let's celebrate your 'doghouse' properly." And he drove inside her.

He fucked her over an hour, and she climaxed several more times. Exhausted, she fell asleep on the floor clutching the pillow that still smelled like him. He was gone when she woke up. He didn't return until Sunday night and he brought Trina with him. She was firmly ensconced in his house and bed.

Corrine reminded herself that she didn't care. He was the enforcer. He'd had plenty of women before her. His adult daughters certainly proved that. One of them had three children so the enforcer was a grandfather even if he didn't act like it.

She heard the voice of the woman inside. *'He'll have more female shifters after us. It's not the first time he brought Trina to live with us. He did it before when we were in Corbett's Town in 1888.'*

*'Why does sharing him with her hurt so bad? I don't love him.'* Corrine thought. *'And I never will!'*

The woman inside her responded. *'We got rid of her once and we will again!'*

**9**

---

*Corbettstown, Washington*
*Sunday, November 4th, 2018*

TRINA CORBETT FLICKED A SIDEWAYS GLANCE AT THE ENFORCER AS he drove toward his home on the outskirts of town. Despite carrying her from the alpha's house over his shoulder like a conquering hero, he'd been oddly courteous once she was in the passenger seat of the classic Crown Victoria. He reminded her to buckle her seatbelt. Behind the wheel, he didn't speak to her. He listened to the radio calls and interrupted the dispatcher a few times, changing who went to deal with various complaints around town.

A neatly mowed front yard and lovely flowerbeds filled with autumn blooms showcased an older ranch style house. "Do you have a landscaper? Whoever it is does an amazing job. The place has wonderful curb appeal."

"Thank you." He didn't answer for a moment and parked near a detached garage. He looked out toward moonlit rose bushes. "Corrine takes care of it."

Trina recognized the regret in his deep voice and knew he

missed the younger woman. The alpha said he'd ordered Gunnolf to kill the rebellious shifter after *Mabon* in September. The enforcer never refused an order. "Do you want me to maintain it as her legacy? I'd be happy to do so."

"No." He managed a low chuckle. "My little wolf is the jealous type. Leave her flowers alone or I'll come home and find you dead."

"What?" Trina gaped at him, stunned. "But the alpha said for you to —"

"He's a fool." Gunnolf Marvin shifted, and their gazes met. "He's afraid of her because she could take over the pack and run it better than he does."

"Especially with your support." Trina opened the patrol car door. "She was well loved by the children and that made many of the parents her allies."

"Someday, she will come into her own." Gunnolf carefully removed his keys. He locked the vehicle, then looked toward the back yard. His gaze narrowed on a cottage with a six-foot cyclone fence around it. "It's been a long weekend. You must be tired. Let's go inside."

The inside of the house wasn't what she expected either. The living room was comfortably furnished with an assortment of antiques and classic furniture. The huge flatscreen provided a jarring note as did an over-sized recliner. He showed her the dining room and said it was where he wanted all meals served despite the fact that he had an updated eat-in kitchen with brand-new, gleaming stainless-steel appliances. A combination pantry and utility room held a massive freezer as well as the washer and dryer. He checked the French doors to the rear deck and told her to make sure they were locked if she went anywhere.

"I help my father at his clinic. He likes me there when he treats the women and children."

"Wait until Wednesday. The alpha thinks we're having a few days together. Let him." Gunnolf pointed out the door to the basement where he punished or tortured those who needed it. "Don't go there."

She nodded and agreed to stay out of his den as well. He led the way down the hall. He paused, gestured toward an open door. "There's your room. It has an ensuite. Goodnight, Trina."

She stared after him when he walked into the room across the hall. Beyond him, she saw the main or master bedroom. "I thought you wanted me in your—"

"Not tonight. There will be plenty of time for that. Get some rest." He closed the door after him.

She looked up and down the hall. She could leave. His place was within walking distance of most of the town and she had friends who'd let her couch surf. She yawned. If she did go, someone was bound to report it to the alpha and Frank Corbett would have a major meltdown. No, best to remain where she'd been sent so she didn't pay the cost and the enforcer didn't have to punish her.

He obviously believed she hadn't done anything to deserve it, or he'd have already taken her to his torture chamber. Plus, he made sure every time they had sex this weekend, it was consensual, and she totally enjoyed it. Far different than anything with the alpha during the last five months.

When she walked into the bedroom, she saw a flannel night-gown lying on the full-size bed. A bowl of fresh fruit sat on the nightstand. She spotted a note next to it and walked across the room. A chill ran along her spine when she saw her name.

*'Trina, be comfortable in my home. There's fresh towels, sham-poo, and soap in the bathroom. Bottled water and real meat, not the alpha's prey in the fridge. Stop eating humans. It's against every law the dracks gave us back in the day and ruins your soul. Candy and junk food in the top drawer of the bureau. Don't tell the master. He doesn't allow it. No chocolate. You should know by your age, it's toxic for us and too addictive like heroin or meth. Enjoy, Corrine. P.S. If you fuck my owner, I'll know and I'll kill you.'*

Trina sat down on the edge of the bed. The younger woman wasn't here. The alpha demanded she be murdered a month ago. The enforcer followed those orders despite speaking of her in the present tense.

Ergo, Corrine must be gone. He's still grieving for her. Corbettstown breaks the other rules. Do we have ghosts? Is she haunting this house instead of going to *Summerland* to wait and be born again?

*Will I see her? Why does she call the enforcer, her owner or master? We're shifters. Nobody owns us!*

The next morning, she followed her nose to the kitchen where she found the enforcer scrambling eggs and frying bacon. She jumped in to help, making breakfast tea which he preferred to coffee. She pulled a tray of biscuits out of the oven, eyeing him under her lashes. Tanned, buff and looking surprisingly handsome in freshly ironed clothes, jeans, and a plaid shirt. She hadn't heard his shower, but he must have taken one even if she didn't hear the water running across the hall.

She'd enjoyed having the privacy of her own bathroom. She'd found a fleecy, red robe hanging on a hook, along with a pair of perfectly fitting slippers on the floor. She wore them over the nightgown this morning because she wasn't going to wear an evening dress in the daytime. Too tacky!

He dished up the food, carrying the plates to the long table in the dining room. "Did you sleep well?"

"Yes. Thank you for the nightgown and treats last night. They were very nice since my things haven't arrived yet."

"Not me." He sat down in the biggest captain's chair and began to eat a large helping of eggs. "Corrine doesn't blame you for any of this, but I'm on her shit list."

Trina nodded and put a cup of tea in front of him. She sat down across from him, picking up her own fork. She remembered the note and carefully avoided the bacon, unsure if it came from a real pig or a human turned into one.

On *Samhain*, the veil between the living and the dead, the old and the new was much thinner when *magick* ruled. It was a time to celebrate the lives of those who'd gone to *Summerland*. It was when they paid respect to ancestors, family members, elders and all other loved ones who'd died.

"I didn't see a white candle in any of the windows to guide Corrine to her final rest. I think it'd be all right to do it today."

"What?" Gunnolf sputtered into his tea, dropping his fork, and laughing so hard, his broad shoulders shook. "I wasn't killing my little pet on an inept alpha's say-so. Yes, she was very naughty at the *Mabon* festivities last month, but you protected her after she pissed on your dress. Most women would have demanded her head."

"It was only a dress." Trina felt a smile trembling to life and giggled. "I sent it to the dry cleaners, and it was fine. It's the one I wore yesterday. Where is she?"

"Out back in her 'doghouse'." He pointed out the glass doors toward a cottage inside a fenced area in the back yard. "She likes to sleep late so I'd wait to visit." He paused. "I've cloaked her presence in town. The alpha doesn't see her even if she's standing in front of him. Nobody can tell him about her either. Remember that."

Trina nodded. She knew she ought to be afraid of the large man who enforced all the laws, but somehow, she wasn't. He'd protected the new alpha destined to take over their pack and so would she. "Well, this makes me feel better about the note on the nightstand. I was freaking out about a ghost haunting me here."

"If you want to see ghosts, go to Baker City. My oldest daughter serves *Hecate, the Goddess of the Crossroads and Death*. She doesn't tolerate them in Liberty Valley." He reached for another biscuit, slathered it with butter. "What note? Get it."

Something in his voice and the narrowed gaze told her that he wouldn't wait. She rose to her feet and hurried into the bedroom. The white lace curtains blew in the breeze, although she hadn't opened the windows. It was too cold in November. She hastily closed them. Of course, the note was gone. Would he believe that she hadn't destroyed it? Well, lying to the enforcer wasn't a wise decision.

She returned to the dining room. "I'm sorry, but it's not there now. My room is freezing. I had to shut the windows."

"It's okay. My little pet must have retrieved it." His tone softened and he gestured to her plate. "Do you want to warm it up or is it all right?"

"It's fine." She sat down again.

"Do you remember what the note said? Tell me."

Leaving out the part about the names Corrine called him, Trina reviewed the basic elements of the hospitality the younger shifter offered. "And she said if I fuck you, she'll kill me."

"That's not going to happen." He took another biscuit. "I'll have you, Trina, like I did this past weekend, but I'm not fucking you. Like you said, you haven't done anything to deserve to be punished. Keep it that way. Any other questions?"

She looked at the crisp rashers on her plate. "The bacon?"

He shrugged. "Corrine buys it at the grocery here in town. You'll have to do the shopping now. She won't."

"I will later this week." Trina cut into the rasher on her plate.

After breakfast, she cleaned up. Mid-morning, there was a knock on the door. When she answered, she found the alpha's son, Junior with her suitcases. She greeted him with a quick hug. Unlike most of the Corbetts, he had dark brown hair, and gray eyes, but Junior barely topped six feet. "How are you? How's Cherry?"

"We're fine. She insisted on packing for you so nothing would happen to your belongings." He glanced past her toward the enforcer. "I couldn't tell my cousin, Jed about you coming here. He'd have been on the doorstep raising hell. He has issues with my dad treating female shifters like they're interchangeable."

"It's all right," Trina looked over her shoulder at the older man. "I'm much happier now. If Jed asks, let him know. Tell Cherry I'll meet her for lunch on Thursday like usual."

"No worries. I will." Junior hesitated. "In my last life, I remember dying when I attacked the *Seer's* mate during a raid on the marshal's horses. She bound me to take care of Jed, but you and Cherry didn't wait until you were on your deathbeds to do the right thing—"

Trina frowned, staring at the enforcer. A dim memory came of overhearing him relay the alpha's orders to take the *Guardian's* children and bring them to him for meat more than a hundred years before. She and Cherry had fled their hometown to protect the youngsters. Their mother could open *Time Portals*, save people and animals from lethal injuries, and allied with the *Seer* who spoke to the dead.

"Who is the *Seer?*" Gunnolf asked. "The *Guardian* in this time hasn't come into her powers yet, so I haven't destroyed her. When she does —"

"I have no idea." Junior shrugged. "The *Seer* I met back then was Nina Armstrong in this time. By the time I got there, she was engaged to the marshal's brother, Kyle Morgan."

Gunnolf smiled, rubbing his jaw. "And I will bet my daughters are the ones who sent them to safety in Liberty Valley of yesteryear." His deep voice took on a menacing edge. "You *will* stay silent about their destination, not reveal it to those who search for them and not tell the witches we know where they are. We'll let them be for now."

Junior nodded. "Of course. What do you want me to do with the roses, shrubs, and fruit trees the hardware store sent? Corrine ordered them, but I don't see anywhere to plant them."

"Leave them on the porch and I'll take care of them." Trina reached for the handle of her suitcase, but Gunnolf picked it up before she could. He carried the luggage into her room, told her to unpack and get dressed. He'd see her at lunch.

That afternoon when it stopped raining, Trina went out to the cottage. She moved the trees to one sunny corner to create a grove. She lined up the rose bushes on either side of the cement walkway. The shrubs would disguise the six-foot cyclone fence, so the place didn't look like a prison.

"What are you doing out here?" Corrine demanded behind her, fury in her voice. "This is my place. Did he send —?"

Trina turned and saw the slender blonde, twenty-something behind her. Long golden hair fell down her back. She wore jeans, boots, and a snarky sweatshirt with a wolf on it, and not a speck of cosmetics. Her fingernails were short and natural, not the artificial polished claws she normally sported. She carried a carton of what smelled like homemade cookies and several shopping bags.

"I wanted to thank you for letting me stay so I thought I'd help with the new plants Junior delivered today." Trina recalled what the enforcer said about her being a potential pack leader and opted for elaborate courtesy. "Did I do them correctly? Would you like me to move anything?"

Tilting her head to one side and then the other, Corrine considered the layout. Then, she smiled, warmth filling her golden-brown gaze. "Better than what I planned. You definitely have an eye for color. My yard will be beautiful in the spring, and I like the way you use the evergreen Arborvitae bushes for a hedgerow to block that disgusting fence. Come inside and have coffee with me." She held up the box. "Mama and I went shopping at the outlet mall. We stopped at the bakery in Eagleville, and I brought home an assortment. Peanut butter, snickerdoodles, oatmeal raisin, shortbread, and sugar cookies. Those kitchen witches can really bake. Better than me."

"We're only allowed to go there on special occasions." Trina took the bags from her. "I can't believe the alpha gave you permission to leave Corbettstown."

"Screw him." Corrine shrugged and headed for the porch. "Whoops, already did that and it totally sucked. Is he still as awful in the sack as he was when I lived with him?"

Slightly shocked, Trina followed her up the steps. Finally, she laughed and admitted, "I don't know about you, but I kept using up the batteries on my dildo."

"Nice. I just acted out until I was sent back for more training." Corrine led the way inside toward the kitchen table. "And Gunnolf can fuck better than a mechanical appliance."

Trina stopped and stared. "That's not what you called him in your note."

"Nope." Corrine put the box of cookies on the table, then headed toward the coffee machine on the counter. "He makes me call him, my owner or master because I'm under a death sentence for trying to kill Frank. I'm on hiatus while he's training you. I already told Gunnolf I'm going to come and go as I please and do whatever I want."

Awestruck and amazed, Trina gaped at her. "I don't believe you. You really are an alpha, a stronger one than me. No wonder he says you're destined to lead a pack."

Corrine paused for a moment, then continued pouring water into the canister. "Hester told me that I'm a dominatrix and it's why I can attack Frank while the rest of the pack can't. Do you want to see my new clothes?"

"Definitely! Where did you go?"

While they drank decaf coffee and ate most of the cookies, Trina admired the colorful array of panties, bras, camisoles, and bustiers. After that, there were two more pairs of jeans, tank tops, bodysuits, crop tops and even more lace-trimmed camisoles with spaghetti straps. "You have great taste. Next time I have permission to go shopping in Seattle, come with me."

"Love to." Corrine opened a little refrigerator and drew out a bottle of wine. "As the song goes, it's five o'clock somewhere. Ready for something stronger?"

"You know it!"

## 10

*Corbettstown, Washington*
*Monday, November 6th, 2018*

THEY CARRIED THE GLASSES OF WINE WITH THEM INTO THE BEDROOM and Trina helped remove the tags and hang up the new tops in the walk-in closet. They were totally different from the low-cut blouses pushed to one side. She saw one pair of runners and another pair of boots, but all the other shoes were stilettos in a rainbow of colors.

She heard footsteps and recognized them as the enforcer's. Was he looking for her?

"Have you had a good time misbehaving today, my puppy?"

Trina gasped. How dare he speak to a premier alpha female so disrespectfully? Who did he think he was?

She started to charge out of the closet to confront him, but the door closed in her face and locked. Corrine was obviously determined to protect her. The girl was a true alpha leader who looked out for the members of her pack whether it was an official one or not.

"I told you already, Gunnolf Marvin. You're not the boss of me while you have another woman."

"Such a naughty puppy." He sounded more amused than angry. "She won't be staying for long and when I find her a new home, you'll still be here. Now, explain why you have cookies from my daughter's bakery. You don't have my permission to visit witches."

"I like your daughters and I'll see them whenever I wish, Gunnolf. I ordered a broadsword from your youngest, the war witch today. When it arrives—"

"You'll use it to try and kill me." The good humor faded. "You'll fail, my pet. Thanks for the warning. It gives me time to think up a special punishment for you. Maybe I'll take my wolf to a dog show and see how many ribbons she wins in obedience or agility."

Trina twisted the doorknob again, but it still didn't work. She heard him whistling as he walked out of the cottage, snapping his fingers at least a half-dozen times. When he was gone, she escaped to discover Corrine lying on the carpet, shaking in her boots.

"Oh, my *Lady and Lord*. What did he do to you?" Trina grabbed the young alpha pack leader and hugged her. "Are you all right? How can I help?"

"You are just too kind and sweet." Corrine heaved a sigh and managed to sit up, leaning against her. "I'm okay. After *Mabon,* he trained me to have an orgasm whenever he wants. The signal is—"

"Not the whistle. It's when he snaps his—"

"Precisely." In a few moments, Corrine stood up. "Well, if you think he's pissed off tonight, wait until tomorrow. I'm skipping work at the police department and going for a haircut in Eagleville. Now, let's eat. I have leftover Chinese food to go with the wine."

———

After they ate, Trina left, and Corrine washed the dishes. Despite his annoyance because she visited his daughter's bakery, he hadn't thrown away the rest of the cookies. Corrine stored them in the new wolf-shaped jar, along with a slice of bread like the baker suggested, saying it'd keep them soft. Then it was time to turn on the flatscreen, find a good movie and pretend to watch it.

Halfway through it, he limped in the door. "You are a very bad puppy. You've turned Trina against me. She attacked me with your marble rolling pin."

"I knew I liked her." Corrine smiled, as sweetly as possible. She swept her gaze over him, eyed the bruised cheek, jagged torn ear, and swollen shoulder. "Why didn't you fuck her and use her shifter *magick* to heal?"

"Because she's not to blame. She's fighting for her new alpha." He crossed the room, picked up the remote and turned off the TV. "I should have dragged her out of your closet, but I was too angry about you creating a connection with my daughters. Don't do it again."

"I already told you. I'm doing as I please, Gunnolf." Corrine lifted her chin in defiance. "Tomorrow, I'm getting a haircut."

"It won't last beyond the full moon. Shifter women always complain about their hair not listening to them and it being naturally long." He leaned down and kissed her. "Now, remove your new clothes or I will."

"Go to your new woman."

"So stubborn." He snapped his fingers, and she felt a wave of pleasure rocket through her. "I can do this all night, my pet. Strip."

She debated fighting him, but she really didn't want him destroying her jeans, sweatshirt, and T-shirt. Heaving a dramatic sigh, she slowly unlaced her boots, kicked them off and followed that with her socks. When she stood to unbutton her jeans, pushing them off her hips he took her place on the couch.

Before they hit the floor, her panties followed. He kissed the golden curls between her legs and licked the small bud buried there. "Who am I?"

"Gun—"

"No." He pointed to a rolled-up newspaper that suddenly appeared on the end table. "Be a good girl. Don't make me use that."

She glared into his eyes. The bruise on his cheek had already started to fade. "What if I don't?"

"Oh, you will." He cupped her rear end, brought her closer and his mouth claimed her, lapping, licking and then his tongue found her. She writhed, responding to the intimate kiss while he drove her higher and higher. A second climax followed the first. Soon, they were together on the couch, kissing and caressing each other. When he finally took her, he was back to normal. It lasted a long time, and she came again and again.

After that, he carried her off to the bedroom. She slept in his arms until he woke her up for a second, then a third round. When he left before dawn, he told her to stay away from Trina. The woman was his, not hers. Both of them needed to remember he was the enforcer. They were to obey his dictates, not stir up trouble so he had to discipline them.

———

After breakfast on Tuesday, Trina cleaned the house before she went to plant the roses, bushes, and trees in Corrine's yard. The younger shifter was gone all day and half the night. Trina wasn't the only one who noticed. The enforcer spent a lot of time pacing from room to room, glaring out the windows.

"You deserve whatever she does to you." Trina informed him, barely suppressing the urge to laugh at him. "You were so rude and mean to her yesterday."

"Where is she?"

"I'm not sure. She said she was going shopping and getting a haircut."

"That still makes no sense. It's natural for shifter females to have long hair. It's usually down to their backsides. That's why it grows back so quick."

"It's why we see stylists every month."

"Well, I forbid it."

"Good luck with that, Gunnolf. As Dr. Phil says on TV, how's that working for you?"

The enforcer turned around. He frowned at her. "I'm never going to be able to get a new owner for you until you learn to be respectful to males."

"I'm a shifter. Nobody owns me."

"Wrong. For now, I do." He strode toward her. He snagged her wrist, picked her up and carried her down the hall. "Let's see how long it takes you to scream and beg like Corrine does."

Rage still swept through Trina on Wednesday morning while she loaded the dishwasher after breakfast. She couldn't believe he'd been able to take her to bed and reduce her to a quivering, begging husk of a person who had multiple orgasms. She was a shifter, damn it. Nobody owned her and he thought he could give her away as if she were a mere possession.

She glared over her shoulder at him when he walked up behind her and slid his arms around her waist, drawing her back against him. "No wonder Corrine plans to kill you. Next time, I see her, I'll ask if she needs help."

Gunnolf laughed, patted her butt. "She doesn't. Behave yourself."

Before she responded, she heard the doorbell and went to answer it. A young, male dark-haired shifter in a cop uniform stood on the porch. He removed his hat respectfully. "Excuse me, ma'am. I'm here to speak to the chief."

"What is it, Treyton?" Gunnolf approached and eyed him. "Is something wrong at the office? Why didn't your mother call?"

"Your cell phone barely works here, sir. It's why you have a land-line. Something or someone tore up that underground line and chewed it in half." Treyton paused. "Nobody knew it until I got here. We just knew we couldn't reach you. And I'm sorry, sir, but I think the same wolf, maybe Miss Corrine, vandalized your car. Broke the windows, crapped all over the inside, flattened the tires. Excuse my language, ma'am."

Gunnolf folded his arms, a muscle twitching in his tight jaw.

"You didn't come here to tell me that. Why did your mother send you?"

"She was worried about Miss Corrine, sir. Nobody's seen her at work in three days and then this morning, there was a letter of resignation pasted on the front door."

"Pasted?" Trina struggled to suppress laughter. "With what?"

"More poop, ma'am. I'm sorry. I don't mean to be offensive."

"Stop apologizing, Treyton. Nobody blames you." Gunnolf scowled. "Call your mother. Tell her to send out a patrol and find Corrine. Bring her here."

"She won't come willingly, sir."

"I said bring her!"

"Yes, sir!"

————

Being part incubus meant he craved a great deal of sex. He'd had Trina twice today and still wanted more when he left her sleeping in the guest room. Finally, he heard vehicles pulling into the driveway, long after the telephone company finished the needed repairs. Gunnolf glanced at his watch. Damn near five o'clock. It was about time. He stalked into the hallway in time to see the front door open and his long-ago novice, Latham Sellers, stagger inside, Corrine in front of him. The politician wore his usual dark suit, a white shirt, and tie. Blood covered his shoes, definitely not hers, so it must be his.

In jeans, boots, and a lacy tank top under a denim jacket, she looked fine, in better condition than the four walking-wounded deputies behind her. She had gotten that damned haircut. Her long golden hair was gone, trimmed into a very short, cap style. He'd been around more than three hundred and fifty years, and he preferred long hair on his woman even though she bitched about how much care it took. He liked brightly colored, feminine nails and often took her to the salon in town. She'd had the artificial nails removed and one hand gripped a broadsword. She was a little too comfortable carrying it.

Judging by the cuts that his minions sported, she hadn't hesitated to use it on them. One man, Jasper Alan Corbett gripped his right arm, blood dripping between his fingers. His brother, A.J., could barely walk. He'd obviously been hamstrung, dragging one leg behind him. Another held his head, unable to speak through the blood seeping from his mouth. Even poor young Treyton sported black eyes, a broken nose and a hand that dangled helplessly from his broken right wrist.

Gunnolf eyed the band of shifters. "Why aren't you '*changing*' and healing?"

"Because I won't let them." Corrine sauntered toward him. "I'm tired of them laughing and howling like banshees when you fuck me. They can heal like humans and start acting like true wolves."

"She won't let Doc Corbett help us either." A.J. limped closer. "I stopped there, and he couldn't see or hear me. Neither could his nurses."

Gunnolf folded his arms. "You're not a pack leader yet. You can't do this."

"Too bad, too sad. I'm an alpha, a bitch-queen." She glanced over her shoulder at the uniformed men. "I get respect, or they suffer the consequences until they learn manners."

Trina came down the hall, freshly showered, wearing a clean set of blue scrubs that matched her eyes. She barely suppressed a smile when she saw the injured men. She bowed her head in a sign of respect for Corrine. "What would you like me to do, ma'am? Shall I fetch bandages? Wine to soothe their pain? I don't have any of the sedatives my father uses for his human patients."

"Thank you for your concern," Corrine told her. "You can do that in few more minutes. For now, they suffer. Then, they'll be courteous when you patch them up, Trina."

Treyton whimpered. "It'll take months to heal that way. I'm sorry."

"What about me?" Latham demanded. "Why are you punishing me? I just helped the cops. They needed it."

Corrine pointed her sword at him. "Do you honestly believe I haven't heard what you did to Astra Jamison time and again, life after life? Women talk, you brainless lizard. You're lucky I didn't castrate you when you put your hands on me."

Latham reeled against the wall, blood pooling on the hallway floor. His jacket parted. Gunnolf saw the torn shirt, the long cut across his abdomen, the exposed tissue revealing his intestines. If he didn't get help soon, he'd bleed out and die.

Utter silence as the deputies gazed hopefully at Gunnolf. He couldn't let them suffer the wrath of Corrine, not when he'd sent them to find her. He strode to meet her, ignoring the blade when she pressed the tip into his chest. "I'm the one who likes fucking you with an audience. Try to punish me, not the innocents."

"Latham isn't innocent."

"All right. Kill him, but let the others shift."

"When they apologize and promise to do better."

"I'm sorry, Miss Corrine." Treyton dropped to his knees in front of her. He lowered his head, gazing at the floor. "I shouldn't have tried to handcuff you when A.J. told me to, but he's the senior officer. I was disrespectful. I should have asked you to accompany me to the enforcer."

"Like that would have worked." A.J. glowered at the younger male. "Be a shifter, you coward."

"Yes." Corrine nodded at the youngest deputy. "Go be a wolf. Shift and heal. Your mother raised a fine son."

Treyton gazed at her gratefully. After a quick salute, he hurried out the door. A moment later, Jasper followed his example. He apologized and she forgave him. He was gone, promising never to embarrass her in private moments again.

The distraction provided by their departure allowed Gunnolf to grasp Corrine's lower arms. He pulled her closer and stared down into her face. "*Change.*"

She tried to pull free, but he wasn't releasing her. "*Change* or I'll *change* you."

He knew the other men expected a drawn-out process as she went from woman to wolf, but it didn't work that way with true primal alphas, not like other shifters. The sword clattered to the floor. She shimmered in the usual rainbow of colors. In a moment, the large gray wolf stood where she had. He caught a strong odor of rotting fish but kept his attention on her. She contemplated an attack, and he pointed toward the basement.

The locked door opened without him touching it. "Go!"

She whined and he swatted her backside once with a rolled-up newspaper. "Go, bad puppy."

He saw Trina looking at him, then her. Awe and wonder filled the woman's lovely face. He gestured toward the clothing and sword. "Take her things to the doghouse. Then, come back and fix supper. Salad, baked potatoes with all the fixings and cheesecake. There's steak in the freezer. Marinate six T-bones and Latham will grill them when he wakes."

It was one of Corrine's favorite meals and she gazed at him hopefully. He shook his head, gestured toward the basement and she obeyed. It always amused him that her wolf could sulk with each step the same way the woman did.

It only took a few minutes to force the shift on A.J. and his buddy. Once they were wolves, the pair could heal themselves. Gunnolf opened the door and A.J. limped onto the porch, dragging his leg, followed by his friend still unable to speak.

Gunnolf helped Latham into his study. "When a woman originally trained by the *dracklegons* holds a sword, don't be so quick to attack her."

"I thought I could take it away from her. And she wasn't a woman then. She was a wolf rolling in dead fish by the river."

"Sometimes, you're a fool, Latham. Shifters move lightning fast and Corrine's a vicious fighter as a wolf or a woman. I'd have thought you'd learned better with your hellhound this past year."

Gunnolf opened a decanter of the *magick* he'd stored and used the power to heal his apprentice.

Once he helped Latham into his recliner in the living room to sleep an hour or two, Gunnolf secured the door to the study and headed downstairs. He found her wolf pacing the floor of the central area, avoiding the three locked doors to the chambers he allowed Latham to use to torture witches, wizards, healers and other *magick* folk in the past. However, they had vanished from the environs of Corbettstown especially in the last five years. He suspected it was the work of the shadow wolf pack he hadn't been able to locate.

The room was the equivalent of a man's cave if he didn't count the large black kennel, he'd bought at a feedstore. He'd reinforced it with silver and other warding spells so it could hold any shifter in both their forms, although he usually made them remain human during the imprisonment. Corrine hated being locked in the cage, forced to sleep on the dog bed, drink water out of a bucket and eat dry kibble although he dressed it up with canned meat. She had to wait for him to let her out to use the toilet in the downstairs bathroom. After she did, it was time to fuck her. That renewed his supply of energy, so he had it ready when he wanted to use it.

When he approached her, the stench of dead salmon grew even stronger. He snapped the chain on her collar. "Bath time for you, my smelly pet."

'*No! I'll take a shower. Gunnolf, don't!*' She pulled on the lead, trying to get to the bathroom. '*Let me go! Please!*'

"Oh no, you should have remembered this before you decided to play in the rotting salmon on the beach. A shower won't work. Your wolf needs to bathe and that means I get the pleasure of washing my stinky pet."

He guided her over to the wet bar, hooked the chain to the strong post while he prepared. She howled when she saw him put down the tarp to cover the tile floor. He centered a wading pool on it. He kept it close enough that he didn't have to unhook her from the post. She'd run for it if she could, and he didn't feel like chasing her through the neighborhood.

Next came the hose and sprayer. More vocal protests. Barking, howling and growling when she saw the bottle of dog shampoo, conditioner and hair blower. He stacked large towels on the counter. "I'm taking you to the salon tomorrow. I want back my pretty puppy."

*'No, no, no! I'm not going anywhere with you, not when she's here.'*

"Is that why you wrecked my car, tore up the phone line and made a scene at the office?"

*'Told you already. Won't share. I won't, won't, won't! You'll be sorry whenever you have her!'*

"Such a jealous, naughty wolf." He shrugged into the raincoat he kept for this activity. He added rubber gloves because he didn't want to end up smelling rank, like dead fish. It wasn't the first time he'd given her a 'doggie' bath. Her wolf loved rolling in disgusting, decaying animals. She never seemed to learn to leave skunks alone.

"Perfect. Not too hot but not cold."

She struggled when he forced her into the pool, trying to bite him. He rapped her nose. "Be good or I'll get your muzzle."

*'I'm not a dog. I'm a wolf. Want to wash myself, not have you do it!'*

She yelped and ki-yied when he sprayed her with warm water. The howling continued as he worked the shampoo into her fur. He always enjoyed having his hands on her. He washed her from head to tail, rinsed her and did it a second time before he switched to the conditioner. Yes, she smelled like a wet wolf, but her silver fur was soft.

She continued barking, growling and yowling. *'Hate you, hate you, hate you. Going to kill you, kill you, kill you!'*

Bathtime over, he rubbed her all over with the towels, then used the hair blower to dry her fur. She wriggled and howled more, trying to avoid the blasts of hot air. *'Don't! Don't! Don't!'*

When he turned her loose, she bolted over to the daybed he used instead of a couch when he slept down here. She crawled under it, whimpering as she hid from him.

Humming, he dumped the tub and put away the supplies. He peeled off the gloves, the coat and finished undressing. He folded his clothes, went to her, snapped his fingers. "Come. Time to *Change.*"

She crawled out, stood in front of him and shifted. She glared at him. "I hate those kind of baths. I could have taken one on my own."

"You never get your wolf clean unless I help and they're always fun for me." He bent his head, his mouth roving toward one pink nipple. "Now, we'll make up for lost time."

Two of his fingers slipped inside her. He slid them in and out in a series of strokes and she moved with them while his thumb rocked into her clitoris. She kissed him, mouth buried against his neck when she came.

That wasn't satisfactory. He preferred the loud noises she made most of the time. "Arms around my neck. Spread your legs for me."

When she did, he lifted her, hands cupping her round bottom and drove into her. She shuddered, pressing tightly against him, locking her legs around him. He began to move, slow thrusts this time. In and out, long and deep, short and shallow, one stroke after another.

She arched against him, trying to encourage him into faster motions. Being a demon-prince, he had unbelievable stamina, so he kept going. Deliberate, unhurried, steady thrusts. She met each one, moaning his name, louder now. She climaxed and he continued driving her further and further. This time when she spasmed around him, she screamed. "Master, please."

"That's my very good puppy." He teased her with little movements of his hips while he carried her to the daybed. "Who am I? Say it now."

"Master! You're my master." She came again when he lowered her onto the mattress. He kept sliding in and out of her with leisurely, measured strokes, sucking her nipples. She had three more orgasms before he finally let himself finish.

Afterwards, still buried inside her, he kissed her forehead, her brows, her lashes, her ears, and her lips. He felt himself stiffen inside her. He barely had to move his hips and she rewarded him with more orgasms. Good. He'd need the *Sex Magick* to restore his car after she trashed it.

# 11

*Corbettstown, Washington*
*Wednesday, November 8th, 2018*

TRINA FORCED HERSELF TO FOCUS ON THE SUPPER MENU HE'D ordered. She already had the steaks marinated, large potatoes in the oven and the cheesecake chilling in the refrigerator. Now, she tore lettuce for salad. She shuddered, remembering Corrine's cries from the basement. He must have done something terrible to her at first. The later ones sounded like they were having sex.

Boots sounded on the basement stairs. She spun around to face him. "Dinner will be ready as soon as the steaks are grilled, but Latham isn't awake."

"He will be in a moment." Gunnolf strode down the hall. He returned, shoving the younger man ahead of him. "While we do our part, go to the doghouse and fetch Corrine's red dress and the candy-cane stilettos. Hurry, so you can finish the salad."

Latham picked up the pan of steaks and went out the back door to the deck. Before Gunnolf followed, he added. "Find her red stockings and she goes commando."

*I don't think so,* Trina thought, remembering the stockpile of lingerie Corrine bought a few days ago.

When Trina returned with the clothing neatly in a bag, the enforcer was adding toppings to the potatoes. "Shall I take these to her?"

"Yes." He glanced quickly at her. "She has ten minutes to dress. I'll be down to let her out to do her hair and makeup before we eat."

Trina nodded and followed directions. The basement was fully furnished but her gaze went past the couch, recliner, wet bar and daybed to the dog kennel on the far side. Corrine lay sleeping on a large thick pad, covered by her hip-length gold hair. Yes, it would have grown back more quickly than a human's, but not in an hour or so. This was *magick*! The enforcer had as much power as a witch. Did Frank Corbett know who and what he'd angered?

Trina shuddered, a whimper rising in her throat, and she struggled to control it. She hoped she sounded calm. "Corrine, I brought you clothes."

"Thank you." The girl sat up, the mane of thick golden hair falling around her. "Damn it. I spent over a hundred dollars for that haircut yesterday. I'm killing him."

"Did you know he could restore your hair?" Trina went to the cage and eased the department store bag she held through the bars. "He's coming to let you out in a few minutes."

"Good." Corrine opened the sack. Her eyes widened when she saw the contents. "Trina, you are amazing. And considering the other things I've seen him do, my hair is minor."

"Like what?"

"Later. We'll talk later." Corrine started dressing, silk panties, a matching bustier, then the short, tight dress that clung to her curves. "Are you happy in Corbettstown?"

"No real she-wolf could be." Trina glanced anxiously over her shoulder. "I want to be in a progressive pack, one where the alpha allows women to go to college. Maybe in California."

"Eagleville is closer." Corrine drew on the first thigh-high stocking. "Let's plan on getting you out of here."

"He took me to bed yesterday. I didn't try to seduce him, but—" Trina clenched her fists. "How do I stay away when he— He's much bigger than anyone I've been with before. And I had so many orgasms."

"I told you." Corrine glanced at the staircase and Trina followed her gaze, seeing Gunnulf coming toward them. "He's a fucking machine. You won't need your dildo while you're here."

"No potty mouth." He unlocked the cage door and waited while she finished putting on her shoes. "Hair and makeup. Dinner's ready."

Corrine almost elbowed him as she walked by, heels tapping. He patted her butt. "Behave. No broken bones tonight. Or you'll be in the kennel again."

"Don't count on it."

Smiling, Trina started toward the staircase. She stopped when his hands dropped onto her shoulders. She glanced up at him but didn't speak when he turned her to face him.

"When I give an order, you obey." He tipped up her chin. "Did you misunderstand me when I sent you for her clothing?"

"I don't do tacky." Trina met his gaze. "And I'm not starting now."

"I consider it convenience." He brushed her lips with his, lightly at first. Then, the kiss intensified.

She tried to wrench free, but his hold tightened. He kept kissing her while he pulled her against him. She felt his hands sliding under her loose shirt, caressing her back. Then, he cupped her breasts, thumbs teasing her nipples. She moaned under the pressure of his lips, twisting against him. When he lifted his head and stepped away, she saw her bra in his hands.

She reached for it, but he ripped it in half before he threw the pieces in the trash. "No underwear for you either while you live with me. Now, I'll get Corrine and let's have dinner."

After they ate, he sent Latham home. He ordered Corrine to clean the kitchen. Trina jumped up to help the other woman. She'd barely carried two plates out of the dining room when Gunnolf caught up with her. He put the dishes on the counter. Then, he swung her up in his arms and carried her to the guest room.

"We can't do this— I won't take my alpha's man."

"I'm not her man." Gunnolf dropped her on the bed. "You're here for discipline. And it starts with sex." He pulled off her scrubs and then her panties. Kisses, caresses and his mouth on her until she came again and again. Then, he took her, and the climaxes continued. She found herself clinging to him, begging for more and he didn't stop.

After they finished, she fell asleep in his arms. He didn't stay. When she woke up, she took a shower and decided another piece of cheesecake would be perfect. Wrapped up in the new robe, she tiptoed past his door. How could Corrine ever forgive her?

Light spilled from the living room, and she heard the murmur of a ball game on TV. Trina glanced in the door and saw him sitting in the oversize recliner drinking a beer. He wasn't alone. Corrine lay half on top of him, arms wrapped around his neck, dress bunched around her hips, panties on the floor, along with his shirt. One of his large hands rested on her butt, under the long, gold curtain of her hair.

She nipped his neck. "Do it, Master. Fuck me again."

"Wait for a commercial, my puppy." He paused, laughed and put the bottle on the table, then his hands were on her. "Here, you like this just as much."

Embarrassed, Trina walked away, forgetting about the damned cheesecake. She'd never been so mortified in her life. She thought it meant something when he had her, but it didn't. Behind her, she heard Corrine panting and moaning, then crying out as she came.

*What's wrong with me? Why did I let him have me when I knew he belonged to a strong alpha female? I've got to get out of here.*

---

For the next few days, Gunnolf enjoyed the luxury of having two women in his house. He could have as much sex at home as he wanted. Corrine also went to work with him and that meant he had her in the office too. Life was good. He suspected the two of them plotted against him, but he didn't mind. They could do whatever they liked as long as each of them provided him with their shifter *magick* when he had them and their schemes were very entertaining.

After she and Corrinne became allies, Trina definitely waged war. He had to watch for poison in his food and beverages, physical attacks when he entered the same room, and the battles didn't end even after sex. Once when the two of them were in bed after a particularly wild bout, she said she loved him. He laughed at her, and she damn near smothered him with a pillow. So, he took her again and again that night. When he'd drained her enough, she went to sleep.

After a shower, he headed out to the doghouse. He slid into bed with Corrine. She cuddled next to him, her head pillowed on his chest. He smoothed her hair. "You gave Trina rat poison to put in my tea this morning. You're so naughty."

"Want her gone," Corrine murmured sleepily. "Stop fucking her, Gunnolf."

"I've had her, but you're the only female I fuck. Wake up. I'm taking you now."

She rolled on top of him, mischief in her eyes. "Fooled you. You thought I was going to miss out on you." She kissed him, her tongue teasing his.

Kisses led to more touches. He explored her body and sucked her nipples. She squirmed against him, gasping. She moaned when he spread her legs and took her with his mouth. Sighing, moaning, she arched into the intimate kiss. When she was ready, he slid inside her. He began to move, and she matched him, meeting his thrusts.

He remembered her calling his first name more than once the first week he'd had her in his bed. After he made her wait to climax when he fucked her, she learned better. Tonight, she was deliberately holding back, not letting herself finish because she was still pissed about the other woman. He snapped his fingers. The orgasm rocked through her. That was more like it.

He kept sliding in and out of her with leisurely, measured strokes, sucking her nipples. She had three more orgasms before he finally let himself finish.

Afterwards, still buried inside her, he kissed her forehead, her brows, her lashes, her ears, and her lips. "You should say you love me."

She shook her head. "How can I love a man who constantly reminds me I'm under a death sentence and makes me call him my owner and master when he fucks me? One who refers to me as his puppy in public and private? One who gives me a cottage and garden and then calls them a doghouse and kennel?"

He grinned appreciatively, smoothed her hair, and stared into the golden-brown eyes. He shifted his hips, feeling himself stiffen inside her. "Anything else you hate?"

"The way you fuck me until I scream even though you know everyone at the cop shop can hear me although you don't make much noise." She lifted her chin in defiance. "And how you like to do it with an audience."

"Don't stop yet, my sweet, hot, little puppy. One day soon, I'll catch you in heat and give you a son or two."

"I'm a wolf, not a dog."

He chuckled, kissed her, his tongue claiming her mouth before he lifted his head. "And you're my favorite wolf-bitch. Move for me now."

She shrieked in rage, slamming her fists into his back. "You bastard!"

"Oh, you're so looking for another spanking. You know better than to call me anything but your owner and master." He began a steady set of thrusts, and she met them, rising and falling, their hips meeting. When she was in the throes of an intense climax, all she wanted was him to fuck her. And those orgasms were what gave him that wonderful primal-alpha female *Power*.

———

## Corbettstown, Washington
### Sunday, November 18<sup>th</sup>, 2018

Corrine hit the gas pedal and the Crown Victoria increased its speed. She loved driving this car although Gunnolf never let her touch his four-wheel baby. Today, she hadn't asked permission. She and Trina had concocted a good story for her to use when she got to Eagleville and sought asylum from the witches. An added bonus was that she'd have her tie to the Corbettstown pack severed and would be able to go wherever she wanted and do whatever she wished.

Meantime, Corrine would play distract by stealing, okay borrowing the car. She heard sirens behind her and increased her speed. Suddenly, she hit a patch of ice and the huge car fishtailed. Damn it! She wasn't ready. She took a deep breath, wrenched the wheel to the right and the vehicle slammed into the guardrail. The seatbelt jerked. The airbag deployed and darkness claimed her.

She roused when A.J. Corbett pulled her out of the broken vehicle. "The chief's gonna be pissed this time. Fuck me like you do him and I'll tell him it was an accident."

"He sees through lies. It won't work. You don't want to end up in his kennel in the basement for days while he tortures you. And then he'll kill you for having me. He's human but he's been with the shifters too long."

"Good points." A.J. helped her into the passenger seat of his cruiser and headed for town.

When they were in his office, he told Gunnolf about where he'd found her. The enforcer sent him away and told her to *change* and heal. She dreaded what would happen next but couldn't disobey. Once her bruises, cuts and broken arm was healed, she shifted back in time to see him conjure a rolled-up newspaper.

The spanking wasn't as bad as the ones last spring. Granted, she still cried and pleaded for him to stop. Because he didn't use full strength, her backside was sore, but she only had a few bruises. Then, he unfastened his pants, sat down, and demanded a blowjob, something he knew she hated more than anything else. After that, he made her bend over the desk and took her in what he called, 'doggie' style.

The only thing worse was exploding in one orgasm after another, begging him not to stop and knowing everyone in the building heard her when she climaxed. Eventually, they wound up on the couch with him taking her again and again. When a couple of his deputies came to check on them, he reminded the officers she'd she'd been forbidden to drive the department vehicles after she destroyed a second patrol car months ago. If he discovered who didn't report it when she left in the Crown Victoria, he or she would be dead. They were sent to pass the word to the others.

Mid-afternoon, he ordered her to shift into her wolf. Once she had, he leashed her, then took her with him to meet the tow truck. Exhausted by the rounds of sex, she collapsed on the sidewalk in front of the police department and fell asleep. When she woke two hours later, she saw him using *magick* to restore the badly damaged patrol car.

She quickly realized he was shielding the scene so none of the other shifters would know he had more *Power* than the alpha. She kept her head down on her paws and continued to play possum. Once he completed the repairs, he crossed to her and toed her with his boot. She pretended to wake up, slowly stood and yawned.

Still in wolf form, she accompanied him to a restaurant where he ate a large meal to recharge his energies. He ordered a take-out dinner for her. At home, she shifted into human form, dressed, and had her own supper. She was eating when he discovered the broken window, the trails of blood and realized Trina was gone. He raged around the house, calling the deputies assigned to watch her. His fury increased after he realized it was his fault.

He'd pulled them off the surveillance to look for Corrine and his car. Once it was located, they returned only to find Trina gone. They'd been looking for her ever since. Luckily, Gunnolf didn't realize it was a 'put-up' job, that Corrine was the one who helped the woman escape.

Before she and her mother had connived with Trina and Cherry to keep children from being born. When they were old enough, the kids would be tested and killed if they couldn't shift. Granted, the two younger women didn't know she was part of that conspiracy. And Corrine hadn't marked Trina as part of her shadow pack until the woman planned to flee.

Gunnolf joined the hunt for Trina that night, but she successfully vanished. By morning, her tie to Frank's pack was severed and Corrine knew she was safe with the witches. While the enforcer was gone, she finished the cleaning Trina started, did his laundry, and polished his boots. When he returned, her attempts to placate him pleased him. He took her to bed. and they had two long, slow bouts of sex to renew his *magickal* resources.

The next morning after breakfast, he'd ordered her to switch to her wolf shape and they went to work. He said she'd remain in it, and he'd treat her like his pet for the next two weeks. The only time she'd be allowed to be human was at night when they went to bed or if he wanted sex during the day. Corrine didn't tell him she was actually grateful for the reprieve. Now, he wouldn't know who was working behind the scenes to destroy his efforts to control Frank's group of rogue shifters while she continued to strengthen her own shadow pack. She'd wait a little longer to kill Gunnolf Marvin.

## PART II

---

# "TURN YOUR TROUBLES OVER TO THE GODDESS AND TRUST HER TO HELP."

— Rebekah Corbett, Healer-Mage, Potential Guardian, and hereditary witch

## 12

*Eagleville, Washington*
*Wednesday, November 28<sup>th</sup>, 2018*

BRIGID DAWSON SLID AN OBLONG CAKE PAN INTO THE OVEN. SHE still had two chocolate cakes to prepare. Wow, she enjoyed this job as a baker at Captivating Catering. She'd feared there wouldn't be many chances to create the elaborate cakes she loved after the bakery where she worked for so many years had closed, and she'd be stuck working on the family homestead or managing the Silver Lake Pony Ranch forever. Yes, she still taught lessons on the pony farm and looked after the livestock there, but when she had time off from those responsibilities, she raced to Eagleville and her cousin, Meteor's place.

Before she began mixing the ingredients, she saw Meteor return followed by Jed Corbett, tall, muscular, dark-haired, and super-hot. Gard Devlin, equally sexy in a brown-haired, brawny kind of way trailed behind the pair. Both men reminded Brigid that celibacy was overrated but she wasn't ready to go man-hunting at Billy-Bob's

Cowboy Bar and Grill, the local watering-hole owned by her aunt and uncle.

She flicked another glance at her cousin who was slightly shorter than Brigid's five foot, eight. The triplets bore a strong resemblance to her and four of her five sisters with their red hair and varying shades of blue eyes. *Mom says I'm disloyal to my family when I'd rather hang out with the Jamisons, but they don't take pleasure in dealing brown stamps or hurting my feelings. Meteor hasn't said anything about me coming here after Thanksgiving with my family and I don't know if she will. I'm sure she saw how many cookies I prepared over the weekend. After all, she baked them.*

Meteor flashed a quick look over her shoulder at Jed, then turned her attention to the other cook. "Lizzie, I need to borrow Brigid for a bit. We'll be gone a couple of hours. I'll help her finish up when we get back. Don't wait for us. Go to your party."

"Works for me." Lizzie continued dicing fresh vegetables with the food processor. "Anything you want to share?"

"Not really." Meteor gestured toward the pantry. "Fetch the cleansing herbs and distilled water, Brighty. Then, we'll hit the road."

Nodding, Brigid followed directions, heading into the pantry, before crossing to the adjacent room where they kept herbs, spices along with the various syrups, elixirs and powders derived from plants, grasses, and flowers. She didn't know all the uses for the remedies yet, but allowed what Meteor referred to as her 'third', or 'soul' eye and what Brigid considered her intuition to guide her to the appropriate shelves and the jars she needed.

Odd, she thought, not for the first time. Meteor claimed to being a witch, but she spent more time cooking and cleaning than she ever did casting spells. Back in the large, commercial kitchen, she heard Jed telling Lizzie that this was the first time he'd been to the bakery that day. The petite woman in the fairy costume obviously didn't believe him, repeating she'd seen him in a white company truck early that morning before they opened. Gard agreed with Jed, saying they'd hit the woods at dawn in his older four-wheel-drive rig. The late model company rigs were built for highway driving, not for backwoods, off-road work.

"That's your story," Lizzie said, "but I know what I saw."

When she and Meteor were ensconced in the other woman's SUV following Jed's pickup through town, Brigid asked, "What's going on? Why don't Jed and Gard admit they stopped by earlier? It's not a big deal."

"He says he wasn't there." Meteor kept her gaze on the road in front of them. "We'll believe him for now, but I'll still mention it to Rowdy and Aunt Diana."

"And that's another thing," Brigid said. "According to my mom, your aunt isn't related to the family."

Meteor's hands tightened on the steering wheel. "Aunt Diana and my mother met years ago in the same commune and became best friends. When they left, they claimed to be the sisters they've chosen to be and that's what makes her my aunt."

"Makes sense to me." Brigid relaxed in the heated passenger seat, wondering what the older woman or Astra's latest lover would have to say about Jed's early morning visit to the bakery, his subsequent denial and why it mattered.

A short time later, Meteor parked in the driveway facing a small blue house with white trim. Brigid slid out of her seat and opened the right, rear door. When she lifted the cardboard box out of the back seat, Rowdy Tall-Deer, a lean, wiry man arrived and took it from her. Long black hair speckled with gray tied in a ponytail with a leather thong, he wore the same kind of work clothes she often saw him in, a suede shirt, brown pants, and low-heeled boots.

Meteor kissed his cheek. "Blessed be. Have you heard from Astra? How is she?"

"Fine." A quick smile lightened dark eyes. "At least I haven't heard or felt anything otherwise. When we finish here, I'll go to her." He carried the box toward the front porch and open door where a tall, stately woman with bright red hair wearing a brilliant blue caftan waited.

"I don't understand," Brigid said. "Why are we cleaning this house? Shouldn't it already be done if your aunt intends to rent it?"

"Cleansing means warding to keep out evil," Meteor explained. "It's a protective ritual like the one Rowdy did around the bakery a few weeks ago."

"And what you wanted Daphne and me to do to Jed's truck back then."

"Exactly." Meteor waved toward the one-story rambler. "At least, this house is much smaller than the ones at the Rocking J, so it won't take as long. Let's get started."

Brigid nodded agreement and followed her cousin. Inside, they found Diana Yarbro ushering Cherry Corbett, a petite, curvaceous brunette through the various rooms. An open space living room flowed into a dining area, and country style kitchen with granite countertops and stainless-steel appliances. At the far end of the hall was the master bedroom with an ensuite, but there was also a full bath for company and a second bedroom that could serve as an office or nursery.

Rowdy stood at the center island in the kitchen, pouring bottled water into a clear glass bowl. "I've already sealed the basement doors and posted windchimes there, as well as amulets around the windows."

"Fair enough." Meteor reached in the carton. "I'll set up the candles."

Through the next hour, Brigid watched, listened, and helped carry different items as they circulated through the small house. White sage from the bundle Meteor used to smudge the rooms combined with the smell of the vanilla candle Rowdy carried. They chanted a simple rhyme and Brigid found herself joining them. "Nothing evil may enter here and the new family will live in this home without fear…"

Once Rowdy proclaimed the entire building was cleansed, safe and ready, they joined the others in the basement. Diana had already drawn a chalk pentacle in the middle of the tile floor. She removed a necklace with a gold sun-shaped disk and curling golden spokes from her pocket. Tiny animals were carved into the center, jeweled ruby, or sapphire, or emerald, or diamond eyes gleaming.

Diana turned to Meteor, offering her the pendant. "I'm glad you're here. I told Fallyn you needed this today—"

Meteor's hands clenched into fists, and she narrowed sky-blue eyes. "I never want or need that *garungap*."

Brigid didn't know what the word meant but by the way her cousin spit the term, it must be some sort of insult. "It's lovely."

Meteor eyed the vintage necklace as if it was poisonous. She paled as dread crept across her face. She shook her head. "I didn't wear it when we severed Trina's ties to the Corbettstown pack and I'm not wearing it today."

"But it's so beautiful." Brigid tried to smooth over the situation before it erupted into chaos. With four diva, younger sisters and a wanta-be superstar mother who could and did give them lessons in emotional tantrums, this wasn't her first ticket to the show. "I've never seen anything like it."

"Thank you." Jed smiled down at her, oozing practiced charm. "It took me more than a month to make it for Meteor."

"And like I've said before, you can have it back and shove it where the sun—"

Brushing past his cousin, a shorter dark-haired man in logging attire, Jed advanced on Meteor.

"Enough!" Stepping between them, Rowdy held up his hand, aiming a censorious gaze at the pair. "We all know you have concerns to sort, but this isn't the time or place. Sister, we need all the strength and power you can muster, so please wear the *amunec-dant* for this ritual."

"And what about him?" Meteor tossed her head, shooting a furious glare at Jed. "Why aren't you lecturing him?"

"Because it rarely does any good. My words don't change Thojedescar's actions." Rowdy folded his arms, focusing his atten-tion on the younger man, giving him a slow, steady onceover. "How-ever, I will add that attempting to lure a fledgling witch ill becomes a true alpha, especially a mated one."

Brigid blinked, unsure of the meaning behind the measured scold. Yet, it did mean something to Jed Corbett. Faint red edged his high cheekbones, and he took a step back to stand next to his smaller cousin, creating distance between himself and the women.

Putting on the old necklace, Meteor laughed, a sharp-edged sound that held little amusement. "Okay, let's get this party started."

———

When they completed the ceremony separating Junior and Cherry Corbett from their previous pack and tying them to his new one, Meteor invited them upstairs for food and drink. Jed sent Gard ahead and waited for Rowdy. "I'm faithful to my mate, but I've never claimed to be a saint."

"Obviously." Rowdy stalked toward the stairs, anger edging his gravelly tones. "With three younglings and a pack to lead, don't you think it's past time to grow up, Thojedescar? How will you defeat your uncle by continuing to play the wolf pup?"

Jed winced. "You're right, but her contempt doesn't make it easier."

"Nor does regularly blaming others for your actions." Finished with the discussion, Rowdy climbed the stairs.

After the ritual meal, the group slowly proceeded toward the driveway and vehicles. Jed caught up with Meteor near the SUV, where she lingered waiting for her apprentice. "Edwin invited me to the holiday concert his class will have in two weeks. I'd like to attend if you don't mind."

"You're his father." She paused by the driver's door, the gold necklace glinting in the afternoon sunlight. "You should come if it fits into your schedule. However, I'll warn you they're not on key and barely manage to sing the same words at the same time."

"That probably bothers you more than it does me." He chuckled. "You love music so much."

She tilted her head, eying him speculatively. "You remember that?"

"I'm trying to remember everything, *Chosen*." He smoothed a strand of flyaway red-gold hair away from her lovely face. "It's not easy to avoid those *magick* blocks you created to stop me."

"Maybe not." She lifted her chin. "And I'm trying to forget everything about you."

"Why aren't I surprised?" He traced her pouting mouth with his thumb, then yielded to temptation. He kissed her, a quick soft touch of his lips on hers.

She growled and stepped back, but not before kicking him as hard as she could in the shin. "Don't do that again."

"I'll wait a while, my shape-shifting queen." He grinned down at her, grateful for the protection of his logging boot. "I still owe you a *Trilunon Nine-Time Kiss* from *Samhain* and you owe me more than one of those from that celebration a month ago."

———

While she waited in the SUV for Brigid, Meteor watched him stride away, a long, tall muscular 'drink of water' as her uncle used to say. She trembled, remembering the sexy promise. Just recalling the *Sex-Magick Kiss* brought back far too many memories of hours in bed with him. Not that it had to be a bed, of course. They were shifters and she'd mated with him in so many forms during their past four lives.

But they reserved the *"Kiss"* for their human shapes. He'd start by kissing her ankles, then onto her knees, working his way to her thighs and bypassing the place most craving the touch of his lips and tongue before teasing her navel. She shuddered and slid the key into the ignition. She struggled to ignore the sudden dampness of her panties. "Damn him! I'm not falling into his arms, not in this life, not ever!"

Two hours later, they'd finished cleaning the commercial kitchen at the bakery and everybody else left. Meteor debated what to do with her evening. Of course, she could go to her apartment upstairs, but that meant a long, lonely night. She spent enough time bartending when they catered parties and never had enjoyed the bar scene unless she had a specific purpose in mind. Three plus years ago, it'd been stopping Jed Corbett from pursuing her baby sister.

Borrowing Venus' shape to seduce him had consequences, a baby girl. Meteor glanced at the clock. If she left now for the Rocking J, she'd arrive in time to tuck Fallyn into bed and return the *magick* necklace to her daughter. For a moment, Meteor remembered what Jed told her when he saw the child wearing it.

"I traded all of me, my heart, mind, and soul to make the *talipenlace* set for you, my shape-shifting queen, not one of our wolflings. Meantime, I'll have to create another necklace to trade for the one you're letting our baby girl wear, or it will break her heart when you take it away."

Meteor didn't shift into one of her animal shapes to visit the Jamison ranch, opting to drive the Ford Explorer instead. She still had issues with her mother and aunt who hadn't done as much as they could to protect Meteor and her sisters from their father who would have had them tortured and killed in a blood sacrifice when they were children.

*I don't trust Estelle Jamison or Diana Yarbro despite the fact they are the Elder Witches of one of the most powerful covens in the region. Astra doesn't either. We were expendable when we were children and as far as the two of them were concerned, we still are. I'm not Venus, my baby sister who allows her heart to lead her. I've made that mistake too many times in too many lives and learned better.*

When she parked the SUV near her younger sister's door, Meteor spotted Jed's pickup. She grimaced. She wasn't in the mood to put up with her mate's antics or demands. They might be matched with eternal bonds because of their *magickal* abilities. It didn't mean she wanted to reconcile with the wizard who could send her screaming through the rafters with his touch, his kiss, and his muscular body.

She shook her head, dismissing the memories. Collecting a box of beautifully decorated holiday cookies, she headed for the side porch. Childish yelping and growls from the back yard attracted her attention. She glanced in that direction and saw a large male wolf romping with two young pups, allowing them to attack him. Even as juvenile wolves, her sons had sharp teeth and claws they happily used on their patient father who taught them how to fight in mock battles.

Smiling, Meteor tapped on the kitchen door before she entered the room. She found her younger sister standing at the stove. Like her, Venus had red hair, but she was taller, almost 5'10 in low-heeled, riding boots. She wore black pants tucked into the black boots and a navy-blue, plaid flannel shirt over an ebony tank top. She'd coiled her hair into a bun on the back of her head, difficult for a foe to grab.

"What are you making?" Meteor put the carton on the counter and crossed to the stove. "I thought you ate dinner with our half-brother and Estelle."

"Not since last week when I learned she sent our oldest sister to serve our demon-father, his executioner, the alpha and their minions as a virgin sacrifice in each and every one of her lives when she reached puberty, as punishment for writing the *banexort* spell when we arrived in this realm. No matter what crimes they claimed she committed, no witchling deserves to be gang-raped and have her throat slit."

"You're singing my song." Meteor glanced at the pot. "Tomato sauce? Are you making noodles to go with it?"

"Yes, but I'm not as good a cook as you are." Venus stirred the sauce. "I went with a jar of commercial spaghetti sauce, added a can of diced tomatoes and one of mushrooms. I fried the diced onions and sweet peppers with hamburger before I added them to the sauce, since the younglings prefer that."

"Good start. Let me help. I am the kitchen witch. I saw my sons. Where's my daughter?"

"Hughondear took her with him to feed the horses. She was upset because the boys shifted without her when Jed Corbett arrived. She needs to learn how to do it and it's not something I can show her. I'm the war-queen, not the shifter-queen in this family."

"You train her how to use a sword and I'll teach her to change her shape. I taught her brothers. It's my job as her mama."

"Works for me." Venus passed her the large spoon. "We'll start tonight after supper. You'll come with us to my salon."

Meteor blinked at the reference to the war-room Venus used in the basement. "What? Why?"

"You're going to Corbettstown and kick some tails soon. You need to know how to use real weapons to kill before you get there, not just how to poison food and I'll make sure you do."

# 13

*Corbettstown, Washington*
*Wednesday, November 28th, 2018*

THE STREETS STILL HAD TOO MANY COUNTY, STATE AND FEDERAL law enforcement vehicles taking up the parking slots when Frank Corbett drove to the Corbettstown City Hall in the late afternoon. Inwardly, he raged about the alarm system warning the witch when he tried to invade the bakery that morning. How had she known his nephew wasn't a threat? He'd used Jed's shape before to kill her and she'd never seen the difference between them.

Gray clouds piled up on the horizon and he smelled rain. He hadn't needed the talking heads on television to tell him what was in the forecast. If the temperature dropped, it'd change to snow. If the weather grew fierce enough, it'd keep the loggers out of the woods and that would cost him and the company money.

Frank Corbett glared at the closest black and white sedan. Luckily, he had enough space to park the white Corbett Logging pickup next to it. When would these unwelcome visitors learn he had nothing to do with the disappearance of the supposed victims they sought? He'd talked to all of his shifters. None claimed responsibility or knew anything about Nina Armstrong's or Kyle Morgan's deaths. As if that wasn't irritating enough, now his son and daughter-in-law had disappeared.

He stormed up the sidewalk to the brick one-story building that housed the town administration. Inside the cop shop, he found an older female officer, Hester Corbett sitting at the reception desk, ready to greet visitors.

In her late forties, the slender woman with curling brown hair wore a well-fitting beige blouse, matching slacks, and polished, lace-up boots. She rose to her feet. Even equipped with a pistol belt, radio, and other police paraphernalia, she approached him cautiously, lowering her head so their gazes didn't meet and waited for him to speak.

The show of respect slightly eased his temper. "Where is Chief Marvin?"

"In his office. Do you want me to tell him you're here?"

"I will." Frank stalked around the counter and down the hall. He knocked and then opened the door without waiting for an answer. Inside, he glared across the room at Gunnolf Marvin, the large man who sat behind a huge, oak desk. He hadn't removed the oversized dog bed where he used to make Corrine stay when she joined him at the office in her wolf form. "Junior and Cherry are gone."

"What?" In his tan uniform, with a shaved head, Gunnolf was more muscled than many of his shifter deputies. "Last Sunday, you told me Junior called and said Cherry had the flu so she wouldn't be at your house to be the hostess for the meal. I thought perhaps she was pregnant, but you hadn't said—"

"I hadn't had her yet." Frank folded his arms. "I went to their house to check on her. It's empty. Not a stick of furniture, no clothes, no food. The place reeks of bleach—"

Gunnolf narrowed his dark gaze. "When Trina fled ten days ago, she took what clothing she had at my house and ensured there wasn't a trace of her. My place smelled the same way. She used cleaners and bleach, so my deputies wouldn't be able to track her. Who are Cherry's friends?"

"Other than Trina and her younger sister, I don't know. And you insisted I give Rebekah to your daughter as a minion when she graduated from high school. We knew she couldn't shift. We should have eaten her years ago. We haven't seen her since. Her father hasn't heard from her either. She doesn't even send him a card on his birthdays or visit on holidays."

"Astra wanted her for a present and I've served this pack longer than you admit. It didn't hurt you to humor me. My daughter demands obedience and deference, not mere courtesy. Rebekah must serve her well or she'd have been given back for meat at one of your rites." Gunnolf glanced at the old-style, black landline phone on his desk. "Astra should be home from court by now. I'll call her, but I'll also send my deputies to ask the younger women what they've heard. Someone must know something."

Frank nodded. "Good. Let me know what you learn."

"I will." Gunnolf rested his hands on the desk, his face still, his gaze calm, too calm. "Anything else?"

Frank glanced at the jar of dog treats, the neatly coiled leash, a basket style muzzle, and a handmade cowhide whip nobody ever saw him use on his spoiled rotten mate. He always opted for a rolled-up newspaper which obviously didn't do anything to teach Corrine manners.

"Isn't it time to get rid of those things, Marvin? She's gone."

"Not to me." Gunnolf's jaw tightened. "I arranged for Lorena to raise her from a pup. You knew Corrine was destined to be my mate and you assaulted her after you sent me out of town."

"It was my right to have her first. I'm the pack leader. And I told you to leave her when that stupid California alpha offered to give her to you. He thought you were bringing her home for us to eat her."

"She'd have died there, and I wasn't letting her be a sweet dessert for us or them. She was only a baby, barely two years old.

She needed someone to take care of her and they didn't want to do it."

"She should have died with her parents." Frustrated, Frank glowered at his long-time friend. "Think, Gunnolf. Have you ever seen a toddler shift before? It doesn't happen. Our younglings don't *Change* before puberty. The girl wasn't normal."

"A very special wolfling." A faint smile creased Gunnolf's rugged features but didn't touch his dark eyes. "She shifted, escaped from her car-seat, and climbed out the window before the car went over a cliff. Then, she managed to heal herself and survive for three days on her own, hunting mice and drinking rainwater on the wild California coast before her alpha and pack found her."

Frank took an angry step forward. "She pissed on Trina's dress when my woman offered hospitality at *Mabon* in September. She shit all over my shoes and my house."

"It aggravated her when she was the only wolf at a pack festival." Gunnolf leaned toward him. "Why wouldn't you let her come in human form? She was learning to be a good she-wolf, a good mate to me. She could have been a loyal pack member."

"Not when she refused to accept me as her alpha." Frank glared at his second in command. "I'm glad I told you to execute her. You should have brought back her body for the feast, not buried her on the mountain. It was a waste of good meat."

"Nobody in this pack deserved to eat her." Gunnolf rose and pointed toward the door. "Go, Frank. At some point, I'll be able to forgive you, but it won't happen today. You ordered me to kill my mate. She'd served nine months of her rule-breaker sentence and as part of her punishment, acted as my pet."

"I never liked her." Frank snarled. "Not from the start."

"I just heard from the new leader, the former second of that California pack. Your friend, the old alpha faced *drack* justice for murdering her parents. The lawgivers are coming for you. When they arrive, I'll say you don't honor mate-bonds—"

A chill went through Frank's body, and he shuddered. "It's your job as the enforcer to protect your pack leader from all adversaries, even the *dracklegons*."

"I always do my job. I have for the past three hundred years since we came from *Trilunon*." Gunnolf eyed him, expressionless. "I'll consider what you say."

They'd been friends a long time, but for once Frank couldn't tell what Gunnolf Marvin was going to do. When it came to Corrine, all bets were off.

Frank stomped out of the office. A few other deputies came out of the breakroom, heading toward the hallway and the front door. Two of the cops nodded respectfully, but the other shifters turned their backs on him and walked away as if he didn't exist. The blatant shunning shocked him.

Did they think he hadn't heard the stories about them laughing when their chief fucked Corrine in front of them? He was the alpha. He knew everything and they'd pay for this insult to their pack leader.

———

*'He didn't see me, and I was right here.'* Baffled, Corrine placed her head on Gunnolf's knee when he sat down again. *'I am a wolf. I'm not invisible. And he doesn't know when you lie to him. You still say I'm your mate. I've never agreed to it.'*

"You were my mate in our past lives, and you're my mate now, even if you're too stubborn to admit it." Gunnolf stroked her fur. "You're invisible to him. I've made sure of that. You were a very good puppy. Nice and quiet so he didn't realize you're still here."

*'Won't your minions tell him the truth?'*

"No, I've blocked them from saying anything about you."

*'I have friends in Eagleville. I can stay with them and then you won't have to worry about them talking and the alpha learning I'm alive.'*

Gunnolf shook his head. "Oh no, my pet. You were good right

now, but you were very naughty and wrecked my car ten days ago."
He stared at her for a moment, considering that fact. "*Change.*"

*'Why? You said I had to be a wolf until next Sunday because I stole your keys and took the car for a joy ride.'* She grinned at him, baring her white teeth and wagging her tail. *'It was fun! I got to drive it. Ride in the front seat instead of being locked in that awful dog cage in the back. You weren't there so I wasn't fucked on top of the trunk and best of all, I didn't have to eat one of those stupid 'doggie' cones at a fast-food place. They're terrible!'*

He leaned forward, gripped her collar. "*Change* or I'll *change* you and you don't like that."

She sighed, shimmered into her human form. He pulled on the necklace, and she landed on his lap. She laced her arms around his neck, wriggled and felt his instant response. She pressed her breasts against him. "Are you going to fuck me, Master?"

"Not yet." He framed her face with his hands, tipping up her chin with his thumbs. "Why did you steal my car? You knew I'd come after you. Either I'd find you or my deputies would."

"It was fun. I was bored. You had Trina. You didn't want me anymore." She nipped his ear. "Fuck me. I need you."

"I've already had you three times today here at the office." He glanced toward the desk. A rolled-up newspaper formed on the blotter. "And if you keep stalling, I'll know what you did and why. You knew Trina intended to run away, didn't you? You took the car to distract us, so she'd have an opportunity to flee. She told you—" He paused. "Why didn't you tell me? I was supposed to train her."

"Why should I?" Corrine shrugged. "You're my owner, not hers. And she didn't tell me anything. I didn't want her there. So, I got rid of her."

"You're a very bad puppy. I have to do my job." He smoothed her long, golden hair. "You deserve a spanking."

"No." She reached for the zipper on his pants. "You already did that when you saw the car. Now, fuck me."

"No." He caught her wrist. "*Change* back."

"What? Why?

"*Change.*"

"Don't want to." She kissed him. "I'm tired of watching you work."

"Such a naughty girl." He outlined her lips with his thumb. "Are you going to mind me? Or do I have to force you?"

She heaved a sigh. Reluctantly, she eased off his lap and stood. She took a deep breath and a moment later, she was a silvery gray wolf. When he picked up the leash, she bit him, careful not to draw blood. It earned her a smack on the butt before he snapped the leash on her collar, collected some treats out of the jar.

"All right, my bad puppy. Let's go for a car ride. We'll do everything we always do."

'*Will you turn me loose to chase a deer? An elk?*' She pulled on the leash '*I'm ready to have a different adventure, not lie around and wait while you shuffle papers. It's boring here except when you fuck me.*'

He chuckled. "Oh no, my very bad girl. We're going to do what you said. Ride, fuck and get you a puppy cone. Heel!"

———

*Seattle, Washington*
*Wednesday, November 28th, 2018*

After a visit to the bakery to pick up fresh bread, Astra's favorite baked red potatoes and small, iced cakes for dessert, Rowdy returned to the ranch and helped Holt stretch a last roll of fence wire on the boundary. Once they finished work, he used *magick* to travel to Seattle to spend the night with his mate. When he arrived at her home, he found her brewing tea in the kitchen. She still wore a cream shirtwaist and knee-length dark skirt. A matching black jacket lay across a stool with her briefcase nearby.

She turned to face him, a fierce frown settling around her mouth and landing in the deep, sunset blue eyes. "You did this!"

"Did what?" He petted Ivor, the large, ebony dog that came to greet him before returning to the parlor where the other two hell-hounds, his mother and younger brother kept watch, but didn't move from where they lay on giant, padded beds. "Should I wait to ask what bothers you, my own?"

"After the day I've had in court, I want at least one or two glasses of wine." She glared at him, scooping the raspberry teabag out of the cup with a spoon. "I can't have it without pickling my daughter's brains in alcohol before she's born. I had my life planned and having a baby next June wasn't on my schedule."

He chuckled, crossed to her, and put an arm around her waist. "It will get worse before it's better. Are you nauseous in the morning?"

"Not yet and when I am, I'll castrate you. I don't have time for that. I need to take the dogs for a run first thing, not spend time puking my guts out."

He tipped up her dimpled chin, caught her mouth in a long, slow kiss. "I've missed you today. Take your tea and we'll sit down. You can tell me why you're really angry with me and later, I'll fix supper for us."

"I told you already. I'm pregnant and I can't drink." Carrying the cup, she allowed him to guide her toward the wood table on the far side of the room. Large windows provided a view of the city lights in the distance. "And the attorney my aunt chose to assist me is a fool. I want my clients acquitted, not imprisoned."

Rowdy hooked a foot around a chair, pulled it out and sat down. He took the cup, put it on the table, then drew her onto his lap. "What else bothers you?"

"Are you even listening?" She gasped when he stroked her knee, slipping a hand under the skirt. "Rowind—"

"Keep talking, *Chosen*." He kissed the side of her neck. "What did that lawyer do to annoy you?"

She turned her head and their lips met for a moment. Then, she said, "He let the doctor describe the victim's injuries in too much detail."

"But I'm sure you salvaged the situation." Rowdy allowed his fingers to trail a new path up her leg. "Have I told you how much I like these stockings of yours?"

She wriggled closer. "Please, Rowindache."

"I'm going to, but only if you keep telling me about your day, my own. What did you tell the jury?"

More gasping when he worked his way past the thigh-high stockings to the fine silk drawers barely covering the soft hair between her legs. She squirmed beneath his touch, moaning softly when he gently cupped her. Pushing aside the cloth, he slid a finger inside her. "Tell me what you want."

"This." She arched up to meet his hand. "I want this. I want you. Everything else can wait."

Sitting on a barstool at the counter a half-hour later, Astra sipped cold raspberry tea and watched Rowdy putter around the kitchen while he prepared a meal for them. "I've shared what happened in court today. What did you and Holt do on the ranch?"

"We scrapped and patched the hog-wire we scavenged from around the spread and then put it on the back fence. He'll ask the war-queen to go to town tomorrow to buy more. We finished that shortly after dinner, so I joined your mother, and we did a warding on one of her houses in Eagleville." Rowdy added sliced tomatoes to the bowl of salad. "We bound two more shifters to Thojedescar and your sister."

"Who are they?" Astra eyed him cautiously. "How do you know they can be trusted and aren't sent as spies by my demon father, the pack executioner and Frank Corbett?"

"Because they fled to protect the woman from the alpha's attack." Rowdy turned toward her, narrowing his dark eyes. "Did you know none of them honor mate-bonds? It's not just those of the *Trecesalty*, but others as well."

She stiffened. Her mind raced as she recollected her sire occasionally mentioning he'd disciplined some of the female shifters, claiming they insulted the alpha of the pack. When Trina escaped from the group, she'd said their relationship started that way but once she realized he intended to give her to one of the male shifters as a mate, she fled not only from his house, but her hometown.

Astra hadn't considered the ramifications, dismissing it as idle gossip when he had a new woman staying with him during her occasional visits. Had it been a way for her father to let her know the boundaries he crossed?

She frowned. "I thought the *dracklegons* created laws that forbade assaulting others, and they insisted on consensual relationships."

"They do, but it seems your father, the alpha, and the pack executioner don't respect anyone's choices but their own." Rowdy crossed to the stove, his attention drawn by the smell of the chicken and potatoes baking in the oven. "Cherry informed us the alpha had killed her mate more than once in hopes of having her. She fled to the *Seer* and *Guardian* in her last life. Did she say anything to you when you visited Liberty Valley and the *Land of the Dead*?"

Astra shook her head. "No, I helped with the service when we buried her mate, after Nina Armstrong, the *Seer* sent Junior to *Summerland.* He'd attacked her and her soon-to-be husband Kyle Morgan, so she shot him, using the silver bullets Venus gave her. Cherry told me that she'd wanted him to ally with Meteor's mate in their last lives and Junior wouldn't risk offending his father, the alpha. The pack had its suspicions when Thojedescar was murdered but their leader didn't admit killing him. Of course, everyone is supposed to have free will. Junior could have chosen differently in those days."

"Yet, he opted to change things this time and ask his cousin for help."

"More members will leave and join the new pack in Eagleville." Astra finished her tea. "After the *Samhain* festivities last month, Rebekah told me several of the younger women decided not to have children until it was safer. My demon-father's executioner and the alpha still sacrifice younglings who cannot shift. In yesteryear Liberty Valley, the *Guardian* sent her mate, the *Seer,* her husband, me, and my sister to burn Corbettstown to the ground around their wolfish ears."

"Hopefully, that won't be needful on Sunday night."

"If it is, we'll do what we've done before and save as many of the children and any other innocents as possible." He kept his back to her, but she saw tension in his shoulders and knew the *healer* in him dreaded the potential loss of life. She eased off the stool and went to stand behind him, wrapping her arms around his narrow waist.

She nipped his ear. "How long until dinner? If it can wait, I won't."

He chuckled and turned slightly so their lips met. "You always have demands, my own."

"If they're too much for you, let me know." She tilted her head and their gazes clashed. "You're the one who chose me as your *vaslattel*, Rowindache. I've been re-reading the *Warpathian* laws. It seems part of that is the *geas* you quoted on our soul-matching night, ensuring only you can satisfy me for the rest of eternity. Now, honor your choice."

He grinned appreciatively. "Always."

She gasped when he turned, lifted her into his arms and carried her toward the bedroom. "I thought we'd have sex here—"

"You think of too many ways to torment me, my sweet. Tonight, before supper think of me, only me and what I do to you in our bed."

## 14

*Eagleville, Washington*
*Thursday, November 29<sup>th</sup>, 2018*

THE INCESSANT BUZZING OF THE RADIO-CLOCK ROUSED METEOR from a troubled sleep. She pushed the covers aside and slowly sat up on the edge of the bed. Shower, she thought. Dress, go downstairs to the bakery and prep for the day. She glanced at the nightstand and the bright red numbers. Three-thirty in the damned morning. *Lady and Lord, help me. I'm so late!*

As a skilled witch she had a great many powers, but none of them included freezing time. She rose and headed toward the bathroom, her aching body screaming in protest. Why had she ever agreed to join her younger sister, the war-queen in what Venus referred to as her salon last night after supper? Stretches, tumbling on the mats, hand to hand combat first with a knife and then with a sword and finally without any weapons.

*What made me decide to even try that? Because it's Thursday. In three days, I'm facing a pack of rabid shifters and I already know their alpha won't hesitate to kill me or order them to do it.*

*According to Astra, he's done it several times before. I need to be able to protect myself, not die like I did in my past four lives.*

Under the boiling hot spray, she remembered fragments of her dream. It'd started with her mate initiating her in what the *Trilunons* referred to as the ceremonial and very carnal series known as their *'Nine-Time Kiss'* on their first mating night. Prior to beginning, he'd described where each kiss would land, from foot to ankle to knee and onward to her thighs, navel, breasts, throat, ears and lastly her lips. It could be very innocent and sweet or extremely intense and sensual. He'd opted for the second option rather than the first.

She'd agreed to the eternal match with Thojedescar because she faced a lingering death, when her demon-father poisoned their realm's air, water, and food sources. As the matriarch of the land, her *magick* was linked to the land and what destroyed it would kill her. Surprisingly, the *Sex Magick* spells cast by her new mate healed her enough to pass through the portal to a new world.

Turning off the water, she stepped out of the shower, wrapped her long red hair in a towel before drying off. While she dressed, she recalled how happy she'd been with him. He'd been so thrilled when he learned they were expecting their first child. She combed and braided her still damp hair, added a minimal amount of makeup to disguise the shadows under her eyes. In the kitchen, she filled a travel mug with coffee from the waiting pot, grateful she'd preset the timer, so it brewed without her.

The clock on the microwave revealed she still had five minutes when she sauntered toward the front door of her apartment. She breathed a sigh of relief. As soon as she baked them, she'd snag an almond-poppyseed muffin top. Downstairs, she walked through the dining room, as usual immaculately clean due to Daphne's efforts.

Meteor glimpsed a large silhouette standing outside the door. She didn't have a clear view of the visitor, but somehow, she knew he was a threat. When he tapped on the glass, the string of quartz amulets hanging from the line above the frame shone. They blasted rays of white light. She spun and looked at the next set of rocks outlining the row of four windows beside the door. The small fragments of star-shaped stones rattled on their lines delivering another warning.

She lifted her hands, calling on the energy of the node below her home. *"Lady and Lord, all Powers above and below, guide, guard, protect me and mine from each and every foe. Any enemy disarm and keep us safe from those who would do us harm—"*

A bolt of light energy speared through the door, and she heard the stranger yelp in pain before he staggered away in the direction of a white pickup parked at the curb. *I hadn't finished,* she thought. *Apparently, I didn't need to.* Who was that? Why did he look so much like her mate, Jed Corbett?

It wasn't him. He didn't want to interrupt customers waiting for service, so he never came through the dining room. Instead, he usually used the back door and he always waited for one of them to open it. *And he doesn't come alone, not since Samhain. He always has Gard Devlin with him for protection.* Another stray wisp of memory, a dream from their first life together taunted her.

Because of the coming babe, she'd been sick morning after morning. He'd held a basin for her while she retched, something his *healer* friend told her would pass with time. Afterwards, he'd tucked her back into bed that particular day, encouraging her to sleep a few more hours. He'd left their chamber and returned a short while later, with a jewel encrusted cup of spiced wine to settle her stomach.

But it didn't, Meteor thought. Although she really didn't want the brew, she'd swallowed a few mouthfuls to please him, touched by his loving concern. Agony ripped through her, burning pain—

*He killed me. While I died, I heard him laughing and I saw the evil gold of his slitted eyes—*

*Wait a minute! Thojedescar's eyes are black. They've always been black. Even when he shifts to wolf or bird or stallion, they're obsidian black! Who is it? Who stalks me? Or could it be him? Could his eyes change like that?*

She took a deep breath, began the incantation once more, determined to protect herself, her friends, her apprentice, and their clientele. Later, she'd call and warn her sisters about the wanta-be intruder. Keeping the idea in mind, she entered the large commercial kitchen. She headed for the main bank of switches and turned on the fluorescent lights and then her favorite classic country music station before she went to the row of ovens, setting them to preheat before switching on the giant coffee urn.

Next, she brought out the huge carts with loaves of bread, croissants, muffin tops, bagels and doughnuts waiting to be baked from the walk-in refrigerator. Then, it was the sandwiches, quiches and two large tureens of soup that required finishing. Meteor left the sheet cakes on the shelves in the cooler.

Brigid must have baked those for birthday parties. She'd decorate them today and they'd be ready for the customers who'd ordered them. She'd already started on the groom's red velvet cake and probably intended to work on the formal one for the wedding today. The woman had many gifts, but still wasn't in touch with how many or how different they truly were.

———

Ponies and chickens fed, Brigid Dawson headed into the house to hit the shower. She found her sister, Kate, sitting at the kitchen table hunched over a cup of peppermint tea. Like Brigid, she was tall, voluptuous with a mane of red hair flowing down the back of her purple bathrobe. She'd moved from the Lazy B, the family's ancestral home to live with Brigid at the Silver Lake Pony Ranch when their mother and younger sisters discovered she was pregnant and World War Three erupted at Thanksgiving.

Kate had made her intentions clear. She was a grown woman, damn near thirty-one years old and she was keeping her baby. It'd caused several arguments among the immediate family who weren't ready for her to have different priorities, rather than training horses and students at their riding stable. Brigid hadn't made any points when she refused to take part in the family wars. Instead, she offered one guestroom to Kate and said they could turn the second into a nursery.

Meanwhile, the baby's father, Gavin Killian remained in the picture and continually proposed marriage. Kate had agreed to renew their engagement but said the wedding would wait until the Dawson family accepted him and treated him with respect. Personally, Brigid thought it was a stupid hill to die on, but like her aunt said, pregnant women sometimes had strange notions. Once Kate realized their dysfunctional family would never change, she'd hopefully move forward into a happier future.

Brigid picked up the tea kettle from the stove and topped her sister's cup with hot water. "How are you today? Want breakfast?"

Kate dunked the teabag, narrowed blue-green eyes, and considered the question for a moment. "Scrambled eggs and toast might work. No seasoning. This kid is fussy."

"Got the idea after cooking for the pair of you this past week. I'm good, Katy." Brigid washed her hands and prepared a light meal for the two of them. While they ate, she discussed the lesson schedule with her sister. Two college girls, Sandy and Marcie would be in to teach the afternoon classes and do evening critter chores. All Kate had to do was provide 'adult supervision', collect fees, and encourage the parents to sign up their little darlings for more lessons next week.

"No worries." Kate scooped eggs onto her dry toast. "You need to stop at the feedstore on the way home from Eagleville and pick up the grain order. Gavin said he'd be here in time to help unload and he's bringing home burgers from Uncle Jim's place. He and Aunt Regina called yesterday, and they want to give us, me and Gavin a baby shower."

Brigid winced, picking up her coffee cup. "Mom will have one of her raging fits about it."

"Tough nuggets." Kate shrugged. "Like Gavin says, either way she'll be a grandmother in four and a half months. It's her choice if she gets over it or not. And I need stuff for our baby. Aunt Regina already told me she intends to spoil the kid absolutely rotten. As soon as we pick a date, Aunt Marlene is going to contact all the Dawsons and invite them. Will you make a cake for it?"

"You know I will." Taking her coffee with her, Brigid headed for the shower. She didn't linger in the bathroom because the older farmhouse only had one. Living with a pregnant woman meant making concessions and truthfully, Brigid didn't mind. She loved children and always wanted a big family of her own.

However, she'd never found Mr. Right—well, that wasn't quite true. As a junior, she'd met a new transfer student in high school, Rob O'Malley and fallen head over cowgirl boots for him. They'd studied and hung out together. He was honest, sweet, loving and as goal oriented as she was, determined to earn academic scholarships for college. He seemed to understand her responsibilities at home, which included helping her divorced mother on the family ranch. Since she also had to look after her four younger sisters, she didn't have a lot of time to date.

Rob claimed his dad was in the Army and away on a mission, so he and his mother were staying with relatives in Liberty Valley. He couldn't see her over Christmas break because his father got a last-minute leave and was going to meet them in Hawaii. Brigid was thrilled for him, right up until she discovered he lied and was dating a half-dozen different girls in the area. When she confronted him, he pretended not to know who she was and cut her dead.

She told herself she was better off without him but had difficulty making herself believe it when he laid on the charm. One day, he'd be super sweet and bring her flowers. The next he'd ignore her and flaunt his latest sleaze in front of her. Later that spring, he'd tried giving her a long story about having a look-alike cousin. It was impossible to believe it because she never saw the two of them together, just one guy who either called himself Robert Zane O'Malley or when he was being an utter shit, his name changed to Zane Robert O'Malley.

When she walked out of the house a short time later, her gaze strayed down the street toward the remodeled two-story with dormers and a large wrap-around porch. She wondered again why and how Zane O'Malley had put so much effort into his family home when he faced trial on several animal cruelty charges. Her older sister, Audra and her brother-in-law Joe Watkins intended to testify against Zane because they'd seen the bloodbath after he slaughtered several domestic and wild creatures.

Brigid shook her head and strode toward her waiting SUV. It was hard to believe that a boy who insisted on taking gourmet cooking classes with her could turn into such a monster. *Forget the past and think about the future, Brigid Sloane Dawson. You have a job waiting that you love in Eagleville. There are cookies to make, birthday and wedding cakes to decorate.*

———

"Let's move it, slugabeds. Breakfast will be served shortly." Master Sergeant Rob O'Malley glanced in the bedroom at his slowly moving stepdaughters.

Nine-year-old Donna sat on the edge of her bed, hiding a yawn behind her hand while her twin sister, Helen, tried to awaken three-year-old blonde Angel still buried in the covers.

Rob frowned at the towheaded trio who'd obviously shared the bottom bunk again. "Bad dreams? I'm sorry. What can I do?"

"It's not your fault, Top." Their eleven-year-old brother, Peter stood behind him, holding the youngest of the siblings, fourteen-month-old Matthew. "That therapist you take us to says it will get better after a while. We just miss Mom and Dad."

"I know." Rob lifted Matt into his arms. "I do too."

That earned him a steady, brown-eyed look from the dark-haired boy who nodded and then moved into the bedroom. He took over, encouraging his sisters to get up, get dressed and Rob carried Matt into the kitchen. At least, the kid wasn't drooling on his T-shirt. Ensconced in his highchair, the little boy happily chewed on bits of cereal while Rob set the table and began popping frozen waffles into the toaster.

While the entire bunch was around the table, quietly eating syrup-soaked waffles, except for Angel and Matt who preferred strawberry jam on theirs, Rob drank coffee and packed lunches.

He'd drop the older three at the elementary school nearby. The two younger ones went to the day-care at the community college where he taught Reserve Officer Training Courses. He still thought of it as ROT-C, but never called it that.

Sometimes, when he looked at Peter, Rob saw his father. Dark-haired, dark-eyed, brawny Major Pedro Gonzales should be here raising his kids. They'd served together on three different tours, first in Iraq and later in Afghanistan. *Damn it, Gonzales. You ought to be cooking here, not me*, Rob thought, not for the first time. *Why did that IED take him? It ought to have been me. Nobody would miss me, but these kids need him especially since their momma died of cancer.*

He'd only intended to visit Jackie Gonzales when he returned Stateside, do anything she needed done like he'd promised his C.O. Except, she was down for the count, fighting the last stage of ovarian cancer. Her family wanted to split up the kids, sending the boys off to live with their dad's relatives while the girls would be living with various aunts and uncles. The five of them would be lucky if they saw each other on holidays.

So, Rob and Jackie struck a deal. They'd marry and he'd be the kids' stepdad. When she asked what he wanted out of the bargain, he suggested another boy once she beat the cancer. Bald, thin, and shaking like a leaf, she coughed and laughed weakly. He promised he'd keep their family together. When her time grew shorter, he contacted his parents and asked them to come back east and help them move to Washington State.

They had. He'd give them enough credit for doing it and keeping their mouths shut about his teenage years when they favored his cousin, Zane, over him despite his cousin vandalizing property, stealing cars, assaulting people, and always blaming Rob for his crimes. Their grandfather had put his affairs in order before moving to a senior living center. Since the relatives didn't want to live on the O'Malley farm, Zane had been allowed to stay here rent free.

It shocked everyone when they discovered the patriarch of the clan left the place to Rob and disinherited the rest of them. Gramps said if they were stupid enough to believe a psychotic like Zane instead of committing him to the looney bin, that was their look-out, not his. Last summer, when he learned the thirty-acre farm was his, Rob had the house totally gutted and rebuilt. Evicting his cousin was an added bonus!

Breakfast over, the kids helped clear the table, and load the dishwasher. They dispersed into the two bathrooms to wash up and brush their teeth before they walked out the door. Rob cleaned up Matt, changed his diaper and checked the bag he was taking with them. Clothes, diapers, an extra sippy cup, and a bottle. Yup, they were good to go.

In the eat-in kitchen, Peter held Matt long enough for Rob to shrug into his camouflage shirt and then they trooped out to the large Jeep Rubicon that had belonged to their mother. On the way to school, Peter drilled the twins on their spelling words and then all three of them practiced the multiplication tables.

"Top, are we still going to look at kittens today?" Helen asked. "You promised we could have them at our new house."

"Sure." Rob flicked a quick glance at the little girl in the rear-view mirror and saw her smile. "We'll go right after you kids finish therapy. Are two going to be enough? Or should we get three? One for you, one for Donna and one for Angel?"

"She's too little." Donna told him. "Momma says nobody gets a kitten until she can feed it and clean the litter box and hold it when it goes to the doctor."

Helen nodded agreement. "She'll share ours just like Mattie will share Peter's puppy when you find the right one, Top."

"Sounds like a winner." Rob pulled into the long, circular drive at the front of the elementary. The therapist had suggested the kids call him by his first name or Daddy Rob, but they weren't ready for that yet. For now, they called him the same thing their father had, "Top" because he was the senior non-com in their unit, just like he'd been in the *sandbox* with the major. "Have a good day and learn lots."

"We will."

Other children raced past them toward the playground, but not his. The three of them remained together, marching stolidly toward the brick buildings even though classes wouldn't start for fifteen minutes.

Rob stared after them before he followed the car in front of the Jeep toward the exit. "I'm doing my best, Jackie. Gawd, I hope it's good enough."

## 15

*Seattle, Washington*
*Thursday, November 29th, 2018*

SHE'D DELIBERATELY ARRANGED FOR HER FALL QUARTER CLASSES AT the University of Washington to end early on Thursdays. Rebekah Corbett headed for the freeway, grabbing a fast-food sandwich and bottled water on the way. Her mind wandered as she drove toward the waterfront and her apartment. She had few friends among the other veterinary students in her cohort, primarily because she needed to keep certain things in her life private. And granted, they all had heavy courseloads. They were always studying, researching topics for various projects, writing papers, making presentations, or assisting at the university veterinary clinic.

Her professors often praised her, saying she had a gift for helping the injured or sick animals during her practical labs at the clinic. They also appreciated the way she volunteered for extra hours, but she was careful not to admit to being an apprentice witch or a *High Healer* in training. Another difference between her and the other students was the fact she stayed off-campus, claiming it was too expensive to live in the dorms. She rarely socialized with the rest of the women her age.

As for dating the college boys, forget about it. There hadn't been much point before *Samhain* because she expected the elder witches in the coven to eventually arrange an appropriate mate for her when she finished vet school. Of course she was supposed to return to Corbettstown, a small logging town in Liberty Valley where she'd grown up, after she graduated from high school. The alpha of the shifter pack would have given her to one of the adult males to see if her children were able to turn into wolves. *If they couldn't, they'd be slain along with me. But I've never been what the rest of the Corbetts consider normal*, Rebekah thought. *Either way, I was destined to die before my twentieth birthday at the latest.*

Her estranged mother had fled once it became apparent, she only had girl children. Granted the first three were triplets. All were witches, but only one of them could shape-change. Diana left her older half-sister and Rebekah behind with their father, the town doctor. However, she hadn't counted on Astra Jamison's interference. Nobody had. From the time she was thirteen, Rebekah had waited on the pack's princess when she visited her father, the pack enforcer, Gunnolf Marvin who was also the police chief. She cleaned, cooked, washed Astra's clothes, and obeyed every order, even taking messages to the male shifters, the woman found attractive enough to share her bed.

The downside of that time was having to rush to Gunnolf's house after school and being a dutiful servant to the town diva. Astra didn't tolerate complaints. When the doctor protested about his youngest daughter's new role, it earned him a thrashing from the enforcer who made sure everyone adhered to the rules. Luckily, shifters healed rapidly so his broken arm only lasted a week until the next full moon. He never said another word about Rebekah having too many chores to socialize with her peers.

The upside was Astra's protection extended whether she was in Corbettstown or not. At the time, Rebekah hadn't realized what a blessing that was. She no longer had to fear the yearly testing or reaping of the children and what would happen when she failed to turn into a wolf. And Astra insisted she be allowed to attend high school in Eagleville with some of the other girls, including Corrine and Andrel Corbett, because Astra didn't want a 'stupid' maid. Neither Astra nor her father realized Rebekah was part of the shadow pack rebelling against the official one in Corbettstown. It hadn't mattered that she was a *healer*, not a shifter. She'd been claimed by the leader, Corrine, because her pack was open to all *magick* folk.

Granted, the enforcer contacted Rebekah regularly, demanding reports about his daughter when Astra was too busy in court to call, text or visit him, but that initially seemed a small price to pay. Gunnolf saw to it the pack paid for Rebekah to attend the U-Dub, originally as an undergraduate and now as a second-year veterinary student.

Rebekah's hands clenched on the steering wheel. She forced herself to relax, signal for the next exit and changed lanes. Everything had seemed fine until the weekend celebration last month when she met the man destined to be her life-mate. While she'd always known her *magickal* talents lay in the healing arts, she'd also accepted the fact they would increase as she grew older. At twenty-four in this incarnation, she didn't remember everything from her previous lives. Still, she was aware her *magick* was connected to her emotions.

And they were turbulent now because she dreamed of her past lives, learning how she'd lived and especially how she died, usually horribly as a blood sacrifice to Gunnolf Marvin, or the pack executioner, Latham Sellers or Frank Corbett, the alpha. She hadn't told Astra. *She'd block them and then I wouldn't recognize my enemies. I need to know who they are so I can defend myself.*

A few minutes later, Rebekah arrived at the renovated warehouse on the Seattle waterfront where she had a comfortable apartment. It wasn't as large as the one where her older half-sister lived who mentored Rebekah and taught her *magick* skills. Their powers were different. A dark sorceress who served *Hecate*, the *Goddess of*

*Death and the Crossroads*, Astra never hesitated to push the boundaries. She'd done it as a child, a teen and now as a high-priced lawyer trying to make partner in a well-established, Seattle firm.

Rebekah often felt far older than the criminal defense lawyer, especially when it came time to remind Astra that *magick* always demanded a witch or wizard pay the price. Large efforts used up their powers and they couldn't defend themselves afterwards from an attack—at least not until they had time to recharge their energies. Astra usually dismissed Rebekah's concerns, saying it was the *Healer* in her who wanted to take care of everyone.

She still worried about the older woman but at least she wasn't the only one, not anymore. Astra's mate, another *High Healer* had recently arrived from 1888 Liberty Valley and Rowdy Tall-Deer understood more about what they owed those who provided their powers. He'd look after his soul-bound mate when Rebekah couldn't.

She parked in the garage and headed for the elevator. She had time to take Astra's three huge ebony hellhounds to the secluded park owned by the coven for exercise. A mix between English bull-mastiff, Bernese Mountain Dog and Rottweiler with a dash of black wolf-blood, first Freya and now her two adult sons treated Rebekah with respect from the day she arrived, long before she healed the matriarch from two different attacks.

The trio met her at the penthouse door and waited patiently while Rebekah put on collars and attached extended leashes. It wasn't as if Astra's familiars truly needed them, but this was part of the dance they did to live in the city the senior witch preferred.

They headed down the hall to the elevator and the garage. Ivor and Bamse, the two younger dogs eagerly jumped into the back of her Ford Explorer while their mother took the passenger seat, ready to act as co-pilot. Gray clouds piled on the horizon and rain splattered on the windshield.

Sighing, Rebekah turned on the wipers and drove to the park. The weather was the easiest thing to change and thankfully in Seattle, most people didn't notice how often showers became intermittent. She tapped her fingers on the steering wheel when she pulled into the drive and waited for the caretaker to open the wrought-iron, spiked gates. She could do it herself with a mere thought, but it'd be considered rude by one of the stone creatures perched on the granite pillars that served as posts. And she had nothing to gain or prove by fighting with others in the coven.

The gates swung wide, and she drove through, waving her thanks to the gargoyles. The larger of the pair tilted her head in acknowledgement. Rebekah noticed they were the only visitors which would make the excursion more pleasant for the dogs. Out of the SUV, she removed the leashes, leaving the collars on the dogs so any new guest would realize they were so-called pets. She reminded Freya to take it easy since she was still recovering from her injuries the previous week which earned a disgusted growl.

Rebekah held the coiled leash in her hand and stared into the dog's eyes. "Last week, you were mortally wounded in that battle with those shifters."

A picture came from Ivor of his mother's injuries when he'd seen her carried into the house and up to the workroom. Blood covered Freya's neck and shoulder. One of her front legs was ripped open to the bone. Her hindquarters looked like raw meat, exposing tissues like obscene jelly, shredded from the wolves' teeth.

Bamse, the youngest dog whimpered at the memory and Rebekah rested her fingers on his massive head, offering comfort. "I *Healed* her, brought her back before she went to *Summerland* with the rest of our dead. She will be fine but no scrimmages."

Another few minutes while the threesome considered the request and then they raced off to run and romp on the grassy lawns. Rebekah noticed the two younger dogs saved their roughhousing for each other and ran shorter distances with their mother. She'd let them exercise for a while before she brought out their favorite ball launcher.

She returned to the SUV and collected her backpack as well as the toy, three balls and a fleece throw before locking the vehicle and crossing the rain-soaked grass to a wooden picnic table. The park was over a small node, so she tapped into the energy source enough to dry a small spot on the table before she sat down. She pulled out her laptop and began to read the articles she'd bookmarked for an upcoming paper.

Her phone buzzed and she looked at the incoming text from her sister, Trina, who wanted to know if Rebekah heard anything from the leader of the shadow pack in Corbettstown.

*'I'm worried. Corrine doesn't answer my emails or texts. I haven't heard from her since she helped me escape. Did the enforcer hurt her?'*

*'I'm sure he didn't. He took her as his mate so he wouldn't have to kill her.'*

*'She says nobody owns a shifter, but still calls him, her owner and master.'*

*'It happens all the time in Corbettstown. She's not the first rule-breaker who's had to do that, but he doesn't make her belly crawl to him in public. He doesn't break her bones. It's the other way around. If she's pissed, she hurts him.'*

Silence for a moment before another text came. *'When he wouldn't beat her with a dog whip in front of the pack, Frank ordered him to kill her at Mabon in September.'*

*'The enforcer won't do it. She's two months younger than me and he says she's not a grown-up yet, even if she's under a death sentence. It's why he uses a rolled-up newspaper on her behind when the other shifters see her being what he calls naughty.'*

*'I'm still worried about our real alpha.'*

*'It's okay.'* After working with the midwife in town, Corrine's foster mother, Rebekah knew their leader was safe with the police chief. Trina had been part of the shadow pack for less than two weeks. No wonder she didn't understand all the ramifications of the enforcer's public behavior. *'I'll touch base with her second and see what Andrel knows.'*

*'And let me know too.'*

*'Of course.'* Rebekah ended the chat with her older sister and sent off a message to the police detective asking about Corrine's

status. An answer came moments later. Their leader was in her wolf form, perfectly safe, sleeping on the couch in the chief's office. While Gunnolf held a meeting in the conference room with his senior staff, she'd already attacked three of the junior patrolmen who dared to enter his private sanctum.

*'Will he be angry about it?'*

*'Doubtful. He always tells us to stay out of there unless the door is open or he invites us inside. Corrine's in wolf form until Sunday because she wrecked his car again. I don't think he's figured out why she stole it and if he has, he's not talking about it.'* A laughing emoji accompanied the text.

Amused, Rebekah passed the word onto her sister and then started reading research articles again. Halfway through the next one, Freya joined her. She laboriously climbed up on the bench, then stretched out behind Rebekah to lie on the table. It only took a moment to dry the wood beneath the giant dog and the animal heaved a sigh of relief before she began to drowse. Rebekah shook out the blanket and laid it over top of the hellhound.

Ivor and Bamse sat watching and she nodded in answer to the unspoken question. "Go inspect the woods while she sleeps. When she's ready, we'll play ball."

They eyed her anxiously and she gestured toward the stone pillars surrounding the park, not only at the gateways. The assortment of elaborately carved, winged creatures sat on top of them as guardians. "We'll be safe. Go enjoy yourselves."

She made notes while she read the next two articles, occasionally glancing toward the cluster of evergreens bordering the grassy areas. The two younger dogs pelted in and out of the cedars and pines, running to her and then bolting back for another game of tag. She fed them well enough that they weren't hungry, so the local rabbits weren't in peril.

A faint warning whistle caught her attention and she looked at the main driveway. A red sports car sat in front of the gates, but they remained closed. Whoever visited wasn't part of the coven and didn't have permission to be here or the guards would have allowed entry. Rebekah narrowed her gaze, recognizing the tall figure.

Latham Sellers! One of Astra's former lovers. Six foot tall, sun-bronzed, and muscular in his three-piece, pinstriped suit, he must have come straight from the state capitol or a visit to Corbettstown. Sunlight reflected off his shaved skull. He mimicked the enforcer so much. The older man was going bald, but Latham just loved to be the proverbial copy-cat.

Dread swept through her, and Rebekah drew a ragged breath. She sent a quick mind message to the stone queen. *'Don't let him in. Don't let him. Don't let—'*

*'Hush, child. We remember everything we see. And we see it all!'*

Rebekah shuddered, hands shaking as she closed the laptop. Freya awakened, stood, and stretched, the blanket falling onto the table. She pressed close, a deep growl rumbling in her throat. A picture came of Latham setting a half-dozen wolves on her.

"I know." Rebekah rested her trembling arm on the black dog's brawny shoulders. "I saw you afterwards. But during the attack, I was helping Astra's mate heal that innocent."

Ivor and Bamse charged toward them and took up sentry positions between the table and the gate. All of them watched as Latham tried to open the gates with various sweeps of his hands and incantations. Nothing worked and eventually the stone guards grew tired of his *magickal* gyrations. They began to chuck bits of rock at him.

He warded those off easily enough, but when they started throwing shale at the expensive sports car, he stormed to the vehicle. A hail of rocks followed while he started the engine, backed, and turned, then peeled out. Oh, he was furious but at least he was gone. Hugging Freya, Rebekah stared after the departing would-be warlock.

Last spring, he'd been pursuing Astra, but she wasn't interested in anything serious. He'd come to the park one afternoon when Rebekah brought the dogs here. She'd listened to his protestations of undying love for her mentor and offered token sympathies. She hadn't expected him to grab her, kiss her and then tear off her shirt, laughing at her struggles.

Between the dogs and the stone guards who allied with her, he hadn't succeeded in raping her. *But he intended to, and he told me I wouldn't win the next time. I will.*

Bamse shifted on his haunches, rose, and padded close enough to rest his head on her knee. Rebekah petted him. "Don't worry. I remember what Meteor told me when she woke me from my nightmare last month."

When Ivor joined them and nosed her, Rebekah nodded. She revealed the tale in pictures of Meteor in her own dog-form coming into the bedroom where Rebekah tossed and turned in the queen-size bed, enmeshed in a terrifying dream. She'd worn the torn remnants of a blue *High Healer* robe, and three shape-shifters dragged her toward a fiery barbeque pit. Blood ran down the inside of her thighs, red and purple bruises covered her face, arms, and ribs. Bite marks lined her throat and breasts.

The three hellhounds growled, and Rebekah paused to comfort them before she continued the story of her death in a long-ago life. The men who intended to roast and eat her, had already raped and tortured her. That was obvious. Death would prove a release, but it didn't appear to be a merciful end.

Still in her dog form, Meteor nudged Rebekah's shoulder. *'Listen to me. Stop your pulses, heart, and mind. Choose when and where you die since there isn't an escape. Make your body anathema to these outlaws.'*

*'I'm the last to die. They killed my healers in front of me and purloined all our powers. I don't have much strength left.'*

*'You have enough. You haven't forgotten the first lesson a healer learns. To put a body together, you must know how to take one apart. Do it now! Discorporate!'*

Silence while the *healer* in the dream took a deep breath, used the last vestiges of her *magick* and dissolved into a heap on the ground, poisonous fumes rising from her corpse. A howl of rage erupted from the silver-haired mage by the fire, but it was too late.

Rebekah recognized him as the police chief from Corbettstown. She shuddered at the sight of the demon-mage prince, but now the hell-hounds would know he was one of their enemies and would be on alert, just as she was.

Rebekah slid off the table to her feet and put her laptop in the backpack. She collected the toys and fleece blanket. "Let's go home. We'll play fetch next time."

A warning came from the stone queen. *'And like last time that snake was here, you will tell our favorite witch so she will provide what he so richly deserves.'*

*'I will.'* Rebekah promised.

# 16

*Rocking J Ranch, Washington*
*Thursday, November 29th, 2018*

VENUS SIGNALED THE YOUNG BLACK APPALOOSA MARE SHE RODE for a slow jog. Dancer moved forward, picking up a steady shuffle step and circled the big corral. Clouds piled up on the horizon and a cold breeze blew. Venus tasted a hint of snow. Winter approached and she should be training in the indoor arena, but the Warmblood mix was destined to become a war-horse, so she had to learn to work in all sorts of weather.

She focused on training Dancer. They went from the trot to the walk, then up to a collected lope on the left lead. A turn toward the center of the arena, a downward transition to the jog again, followed by the walk, then up to a canter on the right lead. Clods of frozen mud flew behind them and the horse slipped, caught herself and leaped forward, landing solidly. Venus leaned forward, petted her ebony neck.

She slowed to the walk and worked through a serpentine, a

series of half circles on a straight line from one side of the ring to the other. At the far end, she tightened the reins, and sent the mare into a jog. Using her seat and legs, Venus urged Dancer into the 'passage', a measured, very collected, cadenced gait with higher steps than the regular trot. From that, they went onto the 'piaffe' or trot in place.

They weren't very good at it yet, but they had time. Nobody was ready to buy Dancer since she'd only been under saddle for two years. Venus glanced toward the barn when Hugh O'Connell walked out of the building toward her. She rode across the ring on a loose rein. Dropping her heels down below the stirrups and sitting deep, she asked the young horse to transition to a halt when they reached the fence. She sat still, enjoying the sight of him.

Hugh topped six feet. Broad shoulders, a wide chest, long legs, narrow-hipped, he was the epitome of a clichéd, sexy cowboy in faded jeans, a flannel work shirt under a denim jacket and boots. Blond hair curled beneath his Stetson. His slow smile always sent excitement rocketing through her, but she told herself she needed time and space. She wasn't falling into his arms even if they were strong enough to hold her.

At twenty-eight, she'd dated. All of her relationships ended at the proverbial front door. She thought she'd been willing to settle for less than love in this life, but that was before she met him. She took a deep breath and met his gaze. His eyes weren't dark brown, but a true black like obsidian and as unreadable. Whenever he stared at her, she shivered and tried desperately not to show how much he affected her. His mouth was wide and full, with little creases beside it as if he laughed more than he frowned.

"I thought you and Rowdy were building boundary fence today."

"We were until we ran out of wire yesterday. We've scrapped and patched with everything we could." Hugh rested muscular arms on the top rail, one boot on the bottom. "We have options, *Laspowima*. We could cut more alder poles and use them on the boundary, not just the cross-fences. I've built portable sawmills before and made boards, but the green ones won't hold up nearly as well as those seasoned for a year."

"I'm impressed. What else?"

"Rowdy found a few spools of barbed wire in the back of the toolshed. He's a *High Healer* and complained bitterly about what it could do to your blooded horses."

"He's right." Venus swung out of the saddle. "That's why I shoved it out of the way. I don't want the horses, or the cattle to be cut or damaged by it. I hate seeing scars on them. I'll talk to Estelle. If she'll agree to pay for more mesh, I'll stop by the feed-store after I pick up the boys from school and get a half-dozen rolls."

"Trina will accompany you." Hugh opened the gate and held it while she led the horse through it. "You don't go anywhere without a guard."

Venus stopped in front of him and met his dark gaze. "I'm the war-queen, Hughondear. I don't enter any battle unarmed."

"Leave your daggers sheathed for a moment, Princess."

She trembled when he framed her face with those wonderful, calloused hands and leaned down to kiss her. He knew she hid matching daggers under the full sleeves of her coat and had another pair in her low-heeled boots. Her favorite sword was in a scabbard on her back. When she went to town, she'd add a shoulder harness and her pink Glock loaded with the silver bullets he'd made for her in the event a rabid shifter confronted her.

His mouth claimed hers and she surrendered to the passionate pressure of his lips. Her fingers gripped his shoulders and her lips parted. He deepened the kiss, his tongue teasing hers. It could have lasted for hours or all time when he finally lifted his mouth from hers. She sighed and stepped closer, pressing against him. He held her and she tipped back her head. "I've told you for the past month that we don't have to stop with kisses."

"One day, we won't." He smiled, feathered his thumb over her lips. "For now, we wait until the war is behind us."

"We haven't fought the first battle yet. Not in this life. My sisters have—"

"Our time will come." He took Dancer's reins, turning the horse to walk beside them in the direction of the stable. "I'll see to your horse. You go ask the woman who raised you for the funds you want."

"She still infuriates me because she didn't protect my sisters."

"Ask her to explain her thoughts and regrets before you chastise her."

Venus scowled at him. "I know you're as angry as I am because they allowed Astra to be gang-raped by our father and his disciples and allowed those bastards to kill her in their demonic rites in three of her previous lives. They didn't even attempt to keep her away from him."

"True. But I also remember what Rowdy told us and you should as well. Before he and Astra travel to Corbettstown with Meteor and Jed to face the alpha, the executioner, and the enforcer on Sunday, you and your sisters need to *Heal* the divide between you and the leaders of your coven. We don't want it used against us. Witches who carry the burden of the past with them are always a hazard to their allies."

"And those who don't recall the past are condemned to repeat it." Venus slipped her hand into his. "I won't forget what I've learned. Not anymore. I didn't have to tell Astra to stop blocking my memories. She's been so busy with her own life she doesn't have time to mess with mine."

"Fair enough."

She kissed him quickly and then walked toward the large three-story, Victorian style house with its towers, wrap-around porches, a squared-off wing, and balconies. She bypassed the wing where she lived with the children she fostered for Meteor and her mate. Today, their two-and-a-half-year-old daughter, Fallyn was with Trina, the new enforcer of their budding pack.

Prior to discovering the leaders of their coven had substantially harmed her older sister, Venus often counted on them to look after the little girl and her two brothers. Not anymore. She didn't know what she'd have done if Meteor and Jed hadn't arranged for Trina to stay with her for martial arts and weapons training once she fled Corbettstown.

*I'd have thought of something. I wasn't trusting them with vulnerable younglings, not again.*

Venus walked around to Estelle's kitchen door and tapped on it, waiting for someone to answer. A sandy-haired, tall teenager on crutches, her half-brother opened the door. Venus nodded a greeting. "How are you doing, Orion?"

"Getting better." He stepped back and gestured for her to enter. "You don't need to be so polite. You're family."

"I still have some issues with that after dinner on Black Friday." Venus walked past him and waited while he closed the door. She glanced across the room to the table where her mother and aunt sat drinking tea.

It was true, Elder Witch Estelle Jamison had taken on the role of mother to the triplets. In actuality, one of the other women from a long-ago commune in Corbettstown, her mother's best friend, a sister in spirit if not in blood, Diana Yarbro had given birth to the triplets. When she fled the community, Estelle took the three girls with her and since that time, they'd referred to Diana as their aunt.

Petite and plump, she turned slightly in her chair. Gray-streaked red hair curled around her face, then fell halfway down her back. She blinked hard to keep tears from filling her dark blue eyes. "Venus, it's so good to see you. It feels like it's been longer than a week. Make yourself some tea or a cup of coffee and come join us."

"You're busy." Venus paused. "I'll stop back later."

"Nonsense." A tall, stately woman in one of her favorite flowing caftans, Diana pointed to an empty chair near them. "We're talking about *Yule* and how to celebrate the holiday with the coven. That can wait. What's on your mind?"

Rather than share her issues with them, Venus decided to wait. She went to the coffee maker on the counter, put in a pod and brewed a cup of strong java before she joined them. Orion pushed the plate of cookies her way and she took one. Apparently, either her mother or aunt had decided to visit Meteor at the bakery in town and Venus wondered how the overture went. She didn't ask.

Instead, she chose a frosted reindeer. "Hugh and Rowdy need more fence wire. I came to ask if it was all right for me to buy a few rolls at the feedstore."

Silence reigned while Estelle stared at her. "Venus, you're the one who manages the Rocking J. Normally, you handle purchases and I let you know when the budget is really tight. As far as I'm concerned, nothing's changed."

"Really?" Venus dropped her hands under the table and clenched her fists. "And as far as I'm concerned," she repeated, mocking her foster mother, "everything has. If I had somewhere to take the children and my horses, I would."

Estelle gasped, flushing. "I told you last week I was misled. I didn't know what happened to Astra—"

"You claimed she broke your rules and ran wild from the time she turned fourteen. She drank, smoked everything, not just tobacco, did drugs and of course, had sex with a variety of partners. You said you made sure she had birth control pills and condoms in her backpack so there wouldn't be unwanted complications." Venus took a deep breath. "All signs of trauma and you never asked what happened to her."

"As far as we knew, she'd disappeared after a football game the three of you attended when you were freshmen in high school." Diana took Estelle's hand in an attempt to comfort her sister-witch. "Hindsight is twenty-twenty, Katiranika. Your father must have abducted Astra for his own purposes and then released her afterwards, keeping her from remembering everything that happened for some time."

"And you didn't know he'd killed her in previous lives?" Venus raised a skeptical eyebrow. "When he didn't do it himself, he gave her to one of his minions for a blood sacrifice."

"I know it's easier for you to be angry with us for slights real and imagined than to confront Jarvesel." Diana leaned forward.

"Remember when I told you that memories of your previous lives would start to return after your thirtieth birthday?"

"That's a little more than a year away. Before Hughondear arrived, I didn't learn much from my dreams or fantasies."

"And I also said things would change when your soul-matched mate came. It's why we chose him for you."

Venus eyed the two older women. "That's what he says too. Why him?"

"He's a good wizard, not a warlock who opts for evil. He doesn't try to control your powers." Diana glanced swiftly at Estelle, then at Orion before turning her attention back to Venus. "I was twenty when I met your father, and I had the three of you the next year. I knew I was a witch. I wasn't the only one. A few other girls, Estelle and I were learning *magick* from our teacher, Opal who was mated to the alpha, the lead shifter in the commune."

"I didn't know Frank Corbett ever had a mate," Orion said. "Jed never mentioned it."

"It wasn't Frank." Estelle told him. "It was his older brother, Archibald. He and Opal had two other sons, but I don't recall them shifting yet. Under Archie's leadership, all were welcome in Corbettstown so the boys could have been healers or priests or wizards. Nobody knows. When Thojedescar was ten, his uncle killed his parents and siblings—"

"What?" Venus froze in her chair, staring at them. "He's never said—"

"He probably doesn't remember yet. Your sisters weren't the only ones who blocked his memories. Jarvesel and Frank did too." Estelle rose, came around the table and wrapped an arm around Venus' shoulders. "It was a horrible car accident. You and your sisters were little witches playing with your first wands, barely four years old."

"I overheard Frank and Jarvesel talking about their plans to sacrifice the three of you at *Yule* in one of their first blood rites." Diana shuddered. "And after they slaughtered you, they intended to use your bodies to feed their followers."

"We were his own children. How could he be so evil?"

"Because he traded off his soul to become a demon prince back on *Trilunon*," Diana said. "The closest he had to a conscience was Corrine, a shifter woman who lived with him when we met."

"Why didn't you recognize him?" Venus asked. "Why be with him again and again and again even to have us?"

"We have a theory about that, but you may think it's strange," Estelle said.

"What is it?"

"We live what could be considered a 'normal' lifespan to fit in with the people of this realm. We're born, live, die and are born again. But we don't think Jarvesel does. Somehow, he changes bodies when he's close to death. It'd explain why Diana didn't recognize him and couldn't fend him off."

"Or know how much evil he intended."

"Exactly." Diana glanced at Estelle and then continued. "Corrine was a lovely, kind woman. When we met, I thought she was Gunnolf's or Jarvesel's mother. He was really wonderful to her and as the saying goes, if you look at how a man treats his mom, you'll see how he'll treat you. She loved you girls so much and insisted he start college funds for each of you. She enjoyed watching you play with your wands and do little bits of starter-*magick*."

"What happened to her?" Orion asked. "Did she—?"

"Yes. She called our little coven to her when she was dying. She wanted us to see her off to *Summerland*." Diana ran a hand through her auburn hair. "We promised we would. We visited her regularly and one day—"

"I took her some beef soup." A blush formed on Estelle's face. "I discovered her and Jarvesel together—"

"He was her son, wasn't he?" Venus asked. "It'd be natural for him to visit her."

"No, they were together in bed." Estelle's cheeks grew brighter. "And I do mean together. From what I heard, I learned they'd been lovers for more than three hundred years. She was begging him to let her go, to let her die. He refused. He said he was keeping her forever, that she was his little pet."

"Now, that's just gross," Orion said.

"It gets worse." Diana drew a deep breath. "I went to her in private and told her we knew. She still wanted us to send her onto *Summerland*. She told me that whenever she died, he trapped her soul, put it in a new body and then kept her with him. He'd been doing it since he found her on *Trilunon*."

"She was in training to be a pack leader when Jarvesel saw her and wanted her. The *Ethlestials* tried to keep her safe. He romanced her and she ran away with him. Latham, his apprentice and executioner was sent to distract the priestesses guarding her." Estelle leaned over to touch Venus' hand. "When she died, Jarvesel refused to let us follow her wishes. He stole her soul and then he went crazy. He was determined to kill all the witches he could find. He blamed us because he hadn't found a new body for her."

"Is that why he planned to kill me when they ran my car off the road at *Samhain*?" Orion reached over to take Venus' hand. "Thankfully, your protection spells saved me, or I'd have died in flames, not gone off the highway."

"The Corbetts prefer their meat roasted which is what they call young witches and wizards as well as the mortals they turn into prey." Estelle struggled to keep her voice calm. "They really hate *healers*—"

"They're usually disemboweled, ripped to shreds, and eaten alive while they hear shapeshifters quarrel over their bones." Tears began to slide down Diana's cheeks. "I went to Estelle and the others in our group. I told them we were in danger, but they didn't believe me. She was the only one who did. She took you girls and fled that night. I was betrayed before I escaped."

"Oh no! *Lady and Lord*, protect you." Venus slipped out of Estelle's hold and went to her mother. "I'm so sorry."

Diana stood. She unfastened the collar of the caftan and top buttons, sliding it off to reveal the sleeveless tunic and knee-length leggings she wore. Tattoos of defensive and battle runes covered her arms and legs.

Venus saw the scars beneath them. "What happened?"

"Your demon father skinned me, then had his captive witches heal me so he could torture me again. One by one, he sacrificed them until the only witches left from our initial coven were me and Estelle. He thought he'd drained me of all my powers when he gave me to Gideon Corbett, the Corbettstown doctor."

"Rebekah's father?"

"And Trina's. Her mother, Mara Samuels, was as kind to me as she dared to be when nobody was watching. I promised to look after the girls. She was a few years older and when her memories began to return, she learned she was—"

Orion took Estelle's hand. "A witch?"

"Worse," Diana said. "An *Animal-Healer*. I kept her secret. Gideon discovered it and he—"

"Killed her?" All of her anger melted, and Venus hugged her mother. "I'm so sorry for your friend."

Diana shook her head. "That would have been bad enough. She loved him and he gave her to Frank and your father for one of their ceremonial dinners. She died, screaming Gideon's name. I failed when I tried to stop them, and I paid the price."

Venus gagged. "But she was the mother of his child. How could he?"

"Because the pack comes first to those shifters. If Astra hadn't intervened, Rebekah would have been eaten years ago and Trina would have been punished for protecting her little sister."

"Killed too?"

"No, just beaten and shared among the male shifters until she was pregnant." Estelle clung to Orion's hand. "Her children would have been taken away and raised by the women. If they couldn't shift, they'd have been eaten. Those who did *change* would be taught to hate their mother as a traitor."

"And eventually, she'd have been another of Frank's and Jarvesel's victims." Diana smoothed Venus' hair. "She's safe with you. Keep teaching her to fight as a woman, not just a wolf. Trust her to protect Fallyn, Quaid and Edwin."

"I will." Venus drew a ragged breath. "How did you escape, Mother?"

"Estelle came for me."

"She was barely alive, and we couldn't get Trina and Rebekah away from the shifter women."

"We have now." Venus collected the caftan and helped Diana into the garment. "May I share this tale with all my sisters, not just Astra and Meteor?"

"Yes." Diana fastened the buttons. "Please do. They need to know why I failed them as their mother. I can't bear to repeat the story again."

Pity stirred within Venus. She kissed her mother's cheek. "You were barely my age. I don't know if I could have survived what you did, much less saved my children."

"You would have died trying." Diana wrapped her arms around Venus. "I'm glad to be alive this time, to be with you and your sisters. Jarvesel killed me in so many lives. This time, Estelle managed to save both of us."

"Thank the *Lady and Lord* for that mercy," Venus said.

"There's more." Estelle glanced at Diana who nodded. "You have a student, a girl, a young shifter determined to learn warcraft. She ordered a sword and picked it up a couple weeks ago."

"Corri." Venus froze. "Corrine? Is she —?"

"Your father thought she was a suitable vessel for Corrine's soul and transferred it twenty-two years ago. You need to warn your sisters not to harm her." Diana folded her hands. "I recognized her marks on Trina, Junior and Cherry when we severed their ties to the Corbettstown pack."

"I'm not a shifter. What does that mean?"

"It means they're bound to her as well as Jed and your sister. Corrine won't harm them. She's the one who sent them here for their own safety and more will be coming as *Yule* approaches. Orion did a *Foreseeing* and discovered she's behind the birth control scheme."

"She's stopping the women in Corbettstown from having babies." Orion glanced around the table at them. "If Frank or Jarvesel learn that's why no younglings are being born, she'll be in big trouble. They'll probably give her to the pack executioner. Plus, she's friends with lots of people here and nobody's seen her in almost two weeks, not since Trina escaped. When I *Look*, all I *See* is a wolf sleeping in the police department."

# 17

---

SHORTLY BEFORE FOUR IN THE AFTERNOON, THE DINING ROOM closed. Daphne began cleaning, wiping down tables, walls, and booths before she sanitized them. Because she'd started working at the bakery that morning, Cherry Corbett immediately brought out a bucket of hot soapy water and the mop after she swept the floor. Meanwhile, Meteor continued waiting on walk-in customers who knew the routine. They could purchase cakes, doughnuts, scones, pies, sandwiches, and other pastries before the business closed in an hour and a half.

Bells rang as the front door opened and Venus entered, accompanied by the three children and Trina. "Remember, hands in pockets if you want cookies."

Meteor smiled as the youngsters immediately obeyed, even little Fallyn. "Wow, what a great surprise. I didn't expect you today."

"We're on our way to the feedstore." Trina nodded a greeting to her pack-sister, Cherry, who continued mopping the tile floor. "And we decided to stop for dessert on the way."

"We'll eat it after dinner." Edwin studied the array of frosted sugar cookies in the glass display case. "But Aunt—I mean, Momma said we could have a treat now."

"Good one." Meteor reached over the counter to ruffle his sandy hair, pleased he remembered to act as if Venus was his mother, just like his younger brother and sister did. They were safer with Venus than they would be with her. "Are you helping Fallyn choose one?"

"Me pick." The little girl lifted her dimpled chin, narrowing big blue eyes. "Not Wynn."

"Okay." Meteor walked behind the glass case, sliding open the door, preparing to collect the appropriate holiday cookies. "Which one do you want, sweetie?"

"Say, please." Venus rested a hand on Quaid's shoulder. "Manners, first. Or we'll leave."

"Dat cookie, Auntie Mettie. Pease." Fallyn looked at a unicorn-shaped one covered in thick pink frosting and sprinkles. Surprisingly, it stood up, stretched in horsy fashion, then pranced toward Meteor. "Mine."

Venus looked hastily around the empty restaurant while Meteor hid a smile and put the cookie on a saucer where it lay down and faded back into what most people would consider normality. The boys were more discreet. After Quaid chose an elaborately frosted *Wish Tree* and Edwin selected a snowman, Trina picked hers, a harnessed reindeer.

Meteor added three small cartons of milk and a cup of decaf coffee to the tray. Daphne signaled the group, gesturing to the front corner booth which was saved for last-minute guests and Trina accompanied the children. They sat down and promptly began enjoying their goodies.

"I haven't figured out how to explain to Fallyn about not doing *magick* in public." Venus waited as Meteor made her favorite mocha. "She won't be three until March, but she's going to be a powerful little witch like the rest of us. Our mother, Diana wants to give her a wand for *Yule*, and I said I'd talk to you about it."

"Her first wand." Meteor felt tears rising and blinked them away, passing the coffee cup to her sister. "They grow up so fast."

"I know." Venus sipped the sweet brew. "We need to talk about our family issues, Meteor. And after you and I have a sit-down, we'll need to discuss the same things with Astra."

"I don't know when or if that will work." Meteor grimaced. "We're going to Corbettstown on Sunday—"

"It has to be today, tomorrow or Saturday. 'Forewarned is fore-armed' as the saying goes and there are truths to be shared before you head into battle."

"More war *magick?*"

"I'm afraid so." Venus lowered her voice so only Meteor could hear. "I learned truths about our mother and aunt today. Perhaps you already knew Diana wasn't even our age when she was being tortured, skinned alive and having her *magick* stolen by our father. Then, he gave her to Rebekah's sire, the town doctor, essentially as a brood mare. Estelle managed to rescue her, but they couldn't get our half-sister and Trina away. All of this was news to me. By then, our aunt had already hidden us from Jarvesel."

"If she was so young, Diana had no idea how evil he was when she met him." Meteor glanced across the room at the happy children and the shapeshifting woman who guarded them. "I knew more when I saw Jed the first time."

"You and Astra blocked his memories for your protection, but our father already had. Frank Corbett killed Jed's parents and younger brothers when he was barely older than Edwin." Venus finished her coffee and put the mug on the counter. "It's something all of you need to know before you make that trip to Corbettstown. Jarvesel isn't the only killer who stalks prey and murders the inno-cent there."

The warning lingered in Meteor's mind after her sister left with Trina, Cherry, and the children. Thanks to Daphne and Cherry's efforts, the dining room gleamed when they went to help finish in the kitchen. By the time Meteor locked the front doors, shut the window blinds, put the last few chairs on the tables and joined them, most of the back-of-house closing procedures were completed.

Brigid and Lizzie focused on food safety, storing perishable items at the correct temperatures in the large walk-in coolers. This was crucial since it prevented spoilage and reduced the risk of food-borne illnesses. While Brigid finished putting away the carts that held several trays of items to be baked the following morning, Lizzie did a last-minute food inventory to identify anything that needed to be used the next day.

Meanwhile, Tolliver was in charge of cleaning and maintaining the kitchen appliances from the ovens to the steam tables to the large coffee pots and espresso machines. Daphne and Cherry thoroughly cleaned the surfaces including countertops, stovetops, cutting boards and loaded up the dishwasher. Like any other restaurant, it was essential for the bakery to uphold the highest standards of cleanliness and hygiene.

Since everything was under control, Meteor went to the small office and finished the grocery order. Supplies would be delivered the next day before they opened. When she returned to the commercial kitchen, Cherry and Brigid happily chatted on their way out the back door. Lizzie, Daphne, and Tolliver followed them. Meteor collected her purse and keys, then went after them, pausing to turn on the security system.

She'd contemplated going upstairs and fixing a meal but decided that could wait. So could changing from the jeans and blouse she'd worn to work. If she didn't go immediately, she'd put off sharing what she'd learned about Frank Corbett. Instead, she drove to Jed's place in the middle of town, a white two-story colonial house.

It wasn't the first time she'd visited his home. Shortly before *Samhain*, she'd changed into a large black cat close to the size of a half-grown cougar. When his cousin tried to run her over, Jed stopped him and then brought her here so he could look after her. At the time, he hadn't realized she was a shifter, or she was his soul-matched mate. He just wanted to save an injured animal.

The contradictions in his behavior always baffled her. How could he be a rowdy hellraiser one moment and an upright, decent person the next? Perhaps, it was as simple as his friends—the wizards from 1888 Liberty Valley—and her mother and aunt said. His spirit was blocked.

Taking a deep breath, Meteor walked up the concrete path to the front porch. Before she rang the bell, the door opened, and Jed loomed in the doorway. She lifted her chin and met his amused dark gaze. *Lady and Lord, bless it. He was such a hunk.* Obviously, he'd only arrived home a short time ago.

He wore heavy work jeans, cut-off about halfway between the knee and ankle. Red suspenders over a zip-up striped hickory shirt and thick gray socks. She spotted his spiked boots in the hallway, just inside the door. He eyed her, curiosity filling his ruggedly handsome features. "Well, this is a surprise."

"Are you inviting me inside or keeping me outdoors?"

His eyes widened for an instant. Then he reached into his shirt pocket, pulled out a wide antique rose and yellow gold bangle bracelet. The three-dimension filigree design featured old-style suns and tiny animals, complete with ruby, sapphire, and diamond eyes. It matched the necklace she'd given their daughter. "If you want to enter my house, wear this first."

"Where did you get that?" Meteor demanded. "I haven't seen it in more than three hundred years."

"Your mother has been saving it for you." Jed folded massive, muscled arms and waited. "We both know someone has been taking our shapes and killing us in our past lives. And if you're that killer, you won't be able to safely touch any part of the *talipenlace* set I made you."

"True." On their long-ago soul-matching night, he'd put his enchanted set of jewelry on her, the elaborate necklace with its golden sun around her neck, the matching bracelets on thin wrists, the earrings. Like his compatriots, he'd thought she was agreeing to honor the traditions of his patriarchal homeland and didn't realize she subverted the spells he'd interwoven into the pieces, taking his *magickal* powers for herself.

Instead of accepting the bracelet, she held out her wrist. "You do it."

He inclined his head, then followed her directions and slid it into place on her arm. "Why are you willing to wear this when you give away the necklace I created?"

"I need to talk to you." She paused while he clicked the clasp. "If this is the price of admission for me to join you tonight, so be it. I'll wear one of the bracelets." She ran a finger over a beautifully carved wolf and could have sworn she felt it wag its tail. "Besides, this was my favorite in the set. I always admired your craftsmanship."

"You've never told me that before."

"You're so arrogant, Thojedescar." She shrugged. "Maybe, I didn't want to pander to your ego by saying how much I appreciated your *magickal* abilities."

"Fair enough." He chuckled, leaned down to kiss her, barely brushing her lips with his. "Come inside, Matiranika, and join us for dinner. Gard's grilling steaks on the back deck. Is he allowed to hear what you want to say? Or shall we stay in the living-room?"

"He should hear it too."

She followed him through the open-concept living room with its giant couch, two large matching recliners and the humongous flatscreen TV over the river-rock fireplace. Lamps sat on the end tables and a long coffee table was perfect for refreshments. She'd bet he enjoyed watching sports with his friends from the pack on weekends. She didn't ask.

When she glanced around the room, she spotted the string of quartz amulets hanging from the lines over the doorways. Another set of rocks, star-shaped clear stones outlined the windows. So, Rowdy Tall-Deer had been here and set up wards to protect Jed from the would-be killer, similar to what he'd done at the bakery.

When she and Jed arrived in the kitchen, Meteor saw Cherry Corbett checking potatoes in the oven while her husband arranged the trimmings, sour cream, butter, chopped green onions, and bacon bits on the center island. "I didn't realize you were coming here, Cherry, or I'd have given you a ride."

The petite, curvaceous brunette smiled. "I didn't know until I got home, and Junior said we were joining Jed for dinner. Our new pack needs to plan the December hunt on the night of the full moon before *Yule*."

"Good point." Meteor took the glass of red wine Junior offered. "We have other business to discuss too."

"Like what?" The shorter man in logging attire bore a strong resemblance to Jed, except Junior had dark brown, almost black hair and gray eyes. Both had muscled bodies, but Junior barely topped six feet. "Is something wrong?"

Meteor hesitated, sipped her wine, and rubbed the wolf on the bracelet again, seeking courage. "When my sister came to visit me at the bakery today, she had a story to share about your father and the way he became the alpha of the Corbettstown pack."

"We all know he took it over when Jed's father died." Junior said. "Shifters depend on strong leadership. Packs have been known to fail without it."

"Yes." Meteor scanned the younger man again, trying to read the truth in his gaze. He didn't seem to see anything wrong in Frank Corbett's actions. Did he even know about all of them? She stepped closer to Jed. "Venus had a long conversation with Diana and Estelle today. They told her some long-hidden truths."

"Ones you feel I need to hear?"

Meteor nodded, enjoying the comfort of the arm he slipped around her waist. "Did you know your parents and younger brothers died in a car accident when you were barely ten years old?"

"I was supposed to be with them, but I'd stayed overnight at a friend's. Uncle Frank took me in afterwards." Jed eyed her. "What aren't you saying?"

"My mother and aunt claim your uncle arranged it. He had my father block any suspicions you might have."

Jed stiffened, his grip tightening on her for a moment. "He couldn't. He wouldn't slay his own brother."

Cherry and Junior shared a meaningful glance before the other man spoke. "I believe he'd do anything to be alpha. My memories of past lives are stronger after my ties were broken to his pack."

"So, are mine." Cherry took a deep breath, wiping her hands on a dish towel. "He sent Junior on a suicide mission in our last incarnation, and it wasn't the first time. A man who kills his own son wouldn't hesitate to murder his alpha."

Junior rubbed his jaw thoughtfully. "It makes me wonder if he murdered our *Stalenary* back on *Trilunon* before we left."

"What or should I say who is that?" Meteor tilted her head to one side, curious. "I've never heard that word before."

"It's a hereditary leader for all the wolf shifter packs in a region. Whoever is chosen agrees to serve for at least a thousand years." Jed kissed her forehead. "My family was honored when the *Ethlestials* selected one of my distant cousins. She disappeared during the middle of the plague waves, and we never heard what happened to her."

"My father refuses to establish diplomatic relationships with other shifter societies, so I don't know if their clan rulers survived to come to this realm with us," Junior said. "We haven't seen the bears or cats or birds in years."

"And Frank only visits other leaders who feed humans to their shifters, so we haven't socialized with other wolf packs." Cherry picked up her glass of wine. "When Gunnolf met Frank in California twenty-two years ago, the alpha there gave an orphaned wolfling to the enforcer. Frank has been pissed for years about how Gunnolf treated her."

Nausea bubbled up inside Meteor. "He killed a baby?"

"Oh no." Junior grinned appreciatively. "He found a she-wolf to foster and raise Corrine. I'm surprised you don't recall her. She loves your bakery and brings home cookies whenever she visits Eagleville. Gunnolf arranged for her to go to high school here."

"What?" Meteor gaped at the three shifters, remembering the

dainty blonde who was one of her best customers. "Corrine doesn't smell like a wolf. She wears classic perfume, one with violet, rose, jasmine and lily. I've never seen her without cosmetics. She gets manis and pedis more often than Lizzie does. Venus complains because Corrine's attendance is so erratic in class. Sometimes she shows up in a dress and stilettos. She is so, so—"

"Girly?" Cherry grimaced. "That's what the enforcer wants. She follows his dictates, or else. Women don't have much power in Corbettstown. If he's pleased with her, she helps at the clinic or daycare or teaches reading at the elementary. If he's not happy with her, she stays at the cop shop or his home. And if she really pisses him off, he keeps her in her wolf form for weeks."

"Say what?" Meteor's hands clenched into fists. "Is he trying to be a total asshat?"

"Not really." Junior leaned against the counter. "He's fifty-something and set in his ways. But he protects her from everyone in town. She's been under a death sentence for the past year.

"But she's so young," Meteor protested.

"Twenty-four this *Yule*." Junior checked the potatoes again. "We went to the birthday party the enforcer had for her last December. Gunnolf gave her a mate-gift, a vintage necklace and my father promptly sent him out of town to renew an alliance with a pack in Idaho."

"Well, that actually made sense," Jed said. "She's too young to be anyone's mate."

"Oh, Frank wasn't trying to protect her from being mated so early." Cherry met Meteor's gaze. "Rumor around town was he took her for himself. When he assaulted her, she almost killed him. It's why he issued a bounty on her. It amazed everyone that she survived in jail until Gunnolf returned a few days later. He claimed her as his mate and took her home with him. Shifters are more afraid of the enforcer than they are of the alpha, so nobody's executed her."

"She shouldn't be with either of them." Jed's eyes darkened with annoyance. "There's no way she can please such an old wolf like my uncle or a sorcerer like Chief Marvin."

"Frank claimed he'd rescind the order if she lived with him again and ordered the enforcer to return her a few months later. It didn't last long. She kept running back to Gunnolf. Since he claims to 'like' me, I suggested Frank stop trying to interfere with a mated pair because it never works." Cherry took a bowl out of the cupboard and held it while Junior forked the potatoes out of the oven and into the container. "So, then he chose Trina, Gideon Corbett's daughter at *Beltane*. She's such a perfect female shifter. None of us could believe it when Frank gave her to the enforcer at *Samhain*."

"He and my father execute rebellious shifters. It's lucky they didn't kill Trina before she escaped. It's a wonder Corrine has survived this long." Meteor frowned when she saw the look that Cherry and Junior exchanged. "What?"

"After Corrine had a major meltdown at the *Mabon* harvest festivities in September, my father ordered Gunnolf to slay her—"

"He didn't do it." Cherry added hastily. "He left town with her and when he came back, he did something so Frank couldn't see or hear her. Nobody can tell him she's still alive or the enforcer disobeyed a command. I went to her when Frank kept trying to jump me—"

"And she suggested I come to you, Jed," Junior said, "so I did."

"We need to get her out of Corbettstown." Meteor saw the agreement on Jed's face before he nodded. "Let's bring her home with us on Sunday."

"She's determined to save the children." Cherry carried the bowl of potatoes over to the island. "She won't leave until after the sorting for *Yule*. Those who can't change will be killed and eaten."

"So, we protect them too." Jed glanced out the French doors to the back deck. "Well, let's include Gard in the rest of the discussion."

Three hours later when dinner was over and the kitchen cleaned, Cherry and Junior left. Gard went to his room and Meteor tracked down Jed in the living room. She wanted to speak to him before she headed home. She'd expected to find him doing a guy thing and watching TV. He wasn't. He sat on the couch staring off into the distance.

She crossed the room and pulled up a seat on the coffee table. "Talk to me. How can I help?"

"I haven't thought about it in a long time." He heaved a deep breath, shook his head. "I don't have any pictures of my family and I barely remember what they looked like."

Pity stirred within her. She reached into the back pocket of her jeans, pulled out her phone and connected to the Internet. "Let's see what we can find. There must be something. The newspapers would have covered their wedding—"

"Seriously?"

"And probably a few more events like your birth and that of your brothers." Meteor didn't add there would have been coverage of the fatal car accident. She didn't want to see that, and neither would he. "When we find some, I'll email the articles to the bakery and print them off for you."

He leaned forward, close enough to kiss her. "Will you send me photos of our pups?"

"Sure." She rested a hand on his cheek, feeling beard stubble against her palm. "I'm sorry I didn't do it before."

"We haven't been together before. Not really." His lips brushed hers again. "My uncle and your father have done their best to keep us apart for far too long."

"And we've helped them too much." It was her turn to kiss him. "Let's do better in this life, Thojedescar."

———

Researching on her phone began with her sitting on the coffee table, but in a short time they were side by side on the couch, their gazes locked on the small screen. She was right. They found several photos of Archie Corbett, a young, dark-haired man, a rising star in the legal field and his wife, Opal, another lawyer who worked with him in their firm.

Dimly, Jed remembered them cheering him on at a baseball game, his father jumping up and down when he hit a home run while his mother helped his youngest brother, an infant on her lap wave at him. More memories would come, and he'd welcome them. Jed frowned. Why didn't he have anything that belonged to his parents?

They'd died in a car wreck, but what happened to their possessions? Several of the articles mentioned cases his parents won. He recalled his mom, a warm, loving woman reading him and his brothers' stories at night when she tucked them into bed. She was the one who taught him to shift and then took him on his first hunting trips.

Jed and his father often went hiking. On one of those adventures, it amazed his dad when Jed changed into a hawk. Normally, shifters were limited to one shape. Archie had warned Jed to keep the new ability a secret, that the older wolves in the pack would find it freakish. And they would kill him for being different.

"Are Edwin and Quaid like us?" Jed framed Meteor's face with his hands, staring into the bright blue eyes. "Do they have freedom of shape? Can they change into more than one creature?"

"An interesting question." She licked her lips. "I know Fallyn has talked to me about changing into birds and fish, but the boys haven't. I'll ask them next time I'm at the ranch."

"And we'll both teach them." Jed's mouth teased hers in a whisper soft kiss. "I'm glad you came tonight. Are you?"

# 18

*Eagleville, Washington*
*Thursday, November 29th, 2018*

On her way out of Eagleville, Brigid stopped at the large wood and steel pole barn on the right side of the main street. A sign on the front of the building read, Murphy's Feed, Seed, and Tack. She pulled into the slot closest to the warehouse to make it easier for the grain to be loaded. Collecting her purse, she headed inside.

The store had everything from display racks of outdoor clothes, gloves, riding boots, and barn boots to the left. Shelves of gifts and souvenirs, including a few used paperback novels on a spinner were off to the right. Three young girls surveyed the left wall and several crates holding a variety of kittens who ate, slept or played. Pet gear, horse tack, medicine, and farm equipment filled the rear of the store. Hay and grain were through the back door in the adjacent warehouse.

Brigid strolled toward the counter in the middle of the large room and the cashier apparently waiting on a dark-haired boy with a diaper bag hanging from one shoulder and a toddler clinging to his hand. As she neared, she heard the twenty-something, Jonel Murphy, repeat there wasn't a changing table in the men's room, so he'd need to have his mother take the baby to the other restroom.

The boy sounded slightly irritated and overwhelmed. "My mom isn't here." He looked down at his younger brother, then back at the girl standing behind the counter. "Can you spell?"

"What does that mean?" The blonde cashier glowered at him, popping her gum. "I'm not stupid."

"Okay, my mom is D.E.A.D. My stepdad is getting stuff for my sisters' new kittens. I need to change Mattie's diaper. Where do you suggest I do it? Right here on the counter in front of everyone?"

Sympathy swept through Brigid, and she advanced on the small group. "Jonel, give me the key to the ladies' room and I'll handle this for you since I'm sure you don't want to do it. And if I call your dad or brother from the warehouse, we both know they'll tell you to step up." While she waited, Brigid introduced herself. "I'm Brigid Dawson. What's your name?"

"Peter Gonzales." Relief swept into the boy's features, landing in the somber brown eyes. "Are you really going to help me?"

"Of course. You and Matt." Brigid accepted the red special, plastic flapjack turner holding the key and led the way around the corner in the direction of the offices and the bathrooms. "Actually, since Ronan Murphy, the owner of the store, keeps the doors locked to the restrooms, we'll both handle this project. I'm pretty sure your brother will scream like a banshee if I'm invading his personal space. My little sisters always did."

"How many sisters do you have?" Peter followed her. "I have three."

"Awesome. I have five. They're all grown up now, of course." Brigid continued to make conversation as they wound through the racks of discounted T-shirts and sweatshirts. She'd have to take a few minutes to look and see if they had any snarky ones, suitable for her sister, Clancy, who loved sarcasm and wielded it as a weapon at family gatherings.

———

He'd gathered cat supplies including a bag of clay litter, a cat box, dry and wet food, treats and toys. Robert carried the assorted items to the cashier. He spotted his three girls still considering the display of kittens in the various cages. They'd been joined by three other children, two boys and a little strawberry-blonde who had to be their sister. A woman in jeans and a denim jacket, long pale hair in a hip-length braid stood close by, monitoring the new trio.

Robert left the merchandise by the L-shaped desk with the cashier and went toward them. As he neared, he heard the little girl insist she wanted the long-haired, black, and white tuxedo kitten staring at her. "Him mine."

"We have lots of cats at home, Fallyn." The oldest boy shook his head. "We don't need more."

"Him too." Fallyn plopped tiny fists on her hips and lifted her chin. "He come now. Him say."

Robert chuckled and glanced at the woman in her early thirties, about his age. "I didn't hear him say anything. Did you?"

"No, but it's not my gift. It's hers." She turned her attention back to the boys. "Edwin, you, and Quaid go find your mother. Tell her the situation. It looks like we're adding a new kitten to the cat colony on the ranch."

"Okay, Trina. But Mama will tell you we really don't need another one."

"And we'll let her explain that to Fallyn." Trina gestured toward the distant door to the warehouse. "She's getting fence wire."

"We know." This time it was the smaller, sandy-haired boy who spoke. Bumping his older brother with an elbow, the pair walked away. Barely out of earshot, they started to argue whether or not their sister would be able to take home the kitten. Edwin was a staunch 'no' while Quaid felt Fallyn would win this battle.

Still amused, Robert stepped closer to his stepdaughters. First things first. "Where are Peter and Matthew?"

"Peter took him to the bathroom to change his diaper. He told us to stay here." Donna gestured toward the cage holding two long-haired kittens, one gray and the other a tabby. "We want these, Top."

"Them family." Fallyn announced. "They go 'gether."

Robert took a step close enough to read the sign on the cage. Sure enough, she was right. The pair were brother and sister. He wondered how she knew they were siblings and decided Trina must have told her. Either that or his girls had. "What do you think, Helen? Did you help choose the ones you want?"

She nodded, her dark gaze pinned on him. "Are we really getting them, Top?"

"Yes, we are." He picked up a cardboard carrier. "Let's do it."

"That won't work for long," Trina said. "They'll be out of it before you're a mile down the road. You want a plastic container."

Robert grimaced. "Why do I think this is going to be an expensive endeavor?"

"Because you're smart." Trina smiled at him. "They'll be happy sharing the same crate and I'll stay here with the girls while you find one. Put a pad inside so they can sleep. You're lucky Ronan Murphy is an honorable man. They've already had their shots."

"Thank you." Robert started toward the pet supply area, then froze when he saw his stepsons coming toward him. They weren't alone. A tall, curvaceous redhead accompanied them. A light blue blouse clung to full breasts and a slender waist. Blue slacks hugged long legs. She wore running shoes, not the laced-up riding boots he remembered. But her face was the same. High cheekbones, dark red brows, brilliant emerald-green eyes that saw all the way to his soul.

Trina nodded a greeting. "Hey, Brigid. Those cookies were delicious. If your peach cobbler is anything like them, we'll be in hog heaven tonight after dinner."

The comment earned a smile, but it barely reached Brigid's green eyes. "What are you two doing?"

"Waiting for Venus to explain the facts of life to her daughter." Trina flicked a quick downward glance at Fallyn. "Somebody wants that kitten or else."

"Makes sense to me." Brigid drew out her phone. "Fallyn, shall we send a picture to your Auntie Meteor?"

It'd taken a moment, but Robert realized she fully intended to cut him dead. Decision time. Was he going to let her get away with it? No, he thought. "It's been a long time, Brigid."

She swept a scathing glance over him. "Not long enough."

———

While the Murphy men loaded six rolls of fence wire in her truck, Venus allowed her foster sons to escort her into the feedstore to resolve the conundrum with their sister. Fallyn's rages could be intimidating so Venus didn't blame Trina for not wanting to deal with a tantrum in public. A few days ago, Astra shared the news that the little girl had the *magick* talent to become an *animal-healer*. It was little wonder she'd decided a kitten needed to come home with them.

Venus frowned as she neared the front corner of the store. Other people were with Fallyn and Trina, which wasn't much of a surprise since little creatures needing homes were always an attraction. However, recognizing Brigid Dawson, Meteor's apprentice, another family including a stalwart, dark-haired man in a camouflage Army uniform and a sheriff's deputy was unexpected.

"What's the story, Trina?" Venus glanced at the silvery blonde woman. "Bring me up to speed."

"We told you, Mama." Quaid pointed to his scowling younger sister. "Fallyn wants that kitten."

"I know." Venus looked at the other children. Two of the girls were obviously twins, a little taller and older than seven-year-old Edwin. Their smaller sister clung to the soldier's leg, tears swimming in her big brown eyes. The man held a toddler and his oldest, another boy stood in front of him as if he wanted to protect his father.

Trina drew a deep breath. "Well, Deputy Dudley Do-Wrong here says Master Sergeant O'Malley jumped bail and needs to go to the sheriff's office with him. I suggested he call a *real* cop who had prior military service, and he got snotty with me."

Venus swept her gaze over the burly young man in the green uniform who glared at the nanny who mocked him, adding "Do-Wrong" to his name. Trina had issues with law enforcement after the alpha of her former pack gave her to his enforcer, the police chief in Corbettstown as a reward. It'd taken her two weeks to escape.

She hadn't shared many details of the sexual assaults during her captivity, but then again, she'd only been at the ranch for a few days. And she'd never mentioned knowing Corrine Corbett, a younger woman from the shifter town who took self-defense classes with Venus.

"Did you show him your military identification, Sergeant?" Venus opted for a polite smile and courteous tone. "That should certainly clear up any misunderstandings."

"I did. He doesn't believe I'm Robert O'Malley. He thinks I'm my cousin who's been breaking laws forever."

"Because you're lying. ID cards are faked all the time, and Zane O'Malley is coming with me. Do I need to call for back-up?"

"It's not necessary." Venus studied the man in front of her. Short dark hair in the proverbial high and tight style favored by career soldiers and his camo pants, shirt and combat boots appeared genuine. So did the black insignia on his collar tabs. "Do you have a lawyer, Master Sergeant O'Malley?"

"Why does Top need one?" the oldest boy demanded. "He hasn't done anything bad. We'd know."

"Kids always want to defend their parents." Dudley adjusted his gunbelt, glowering at the boy. "O'Malley is coming with me whether you like it or not. He's scum."

"Let it go." Brigid shook her head at the boy when he started to speak. She finished texting someone on her phone and returned it to her purse. "I've contacted my cousin, Donald Dawson. He's helping with the murder investigation up in Corbettstown, but he'll meet you at the sheriff's satellite office here, Robert." She reached for the toddler, and he immediately went from his father into her arms.

"Don did his time in the Marines, but like Venus always says, one professional soldier recognizes another."

"My turn to use my phone." Venus smiled, although she didn't mean it. "Who is your lawyer, Sergeant?"

"I don't have one yet. I just transferred here from Georgia."

"Then, I'm calling my sister. It will take a while for Astra to get to Eagleville from Seattle." Venus drew out her smart phone. "Don't say anything to anyone at the cop shop until she arrives."

"My kids?"

"Are coming home with me." Brigid held out her hand. "I'll need to borrow your rig because I don't have safety seats in mine."

Robert O'Malley hesitated, then slowly handed over a ring of keys. "Are you still living at the Lazy B? What will your family say about unexpected guests? I'll come get them as soon as I can."

"I manage the Silver Lake Pony Ranch across the street from the O'Malley place." Brigid turned her attention onto the blonde twins. "You and little sis, go get a crate for your new kittens. We'll need to take them with us before Ronan sells them to somebody else."

When the girls headed off to the pet section, Brigid eyed their older brother. "Hit the clothes section and find pjs for your family, Peter, because I'm taking you kiddoes to my house. You're in luck. I have extra toothbrushes already."

"Thanks, Brigid." Relief spread across Robert's rugged features while he watched Peter walk away. "You're a saint. I owe you." He paused. "Their mom passed last summer. Cancer. They don't sleep well, and Angel has fits if she doesn't like what's on the menu."

"We'll be fine." Brigid gestured toward the front door. "Go with Dudley." The deputy reached for his handcuffs, and she shook her head. "Don't. Robert is going with you to sort out this mess. Don't embarrass him any further in front of his kids."

Venus turned slightly away to talk to her sister. When she swung back around, she discovered the men had left the building. Outside, the deputy had Robert O'Malley in restraints before urging him into the back of the squad car. She curtailed the urge to swear when she saw Fallyn gazing up at her, a long-haired black and white tuxedo kitten purring in her arms.

"All right, sweetie. Show me what you have." Venus smiled at Trina. "Did you take him out for her?"

"No. I don't know how she got him." Trina gestured to the empty cage in the top row, still closed and locked, well out of Fallyn's reach.

"Him no like it there." The child tilted her head, projecting total innocence. "Him mine. We go home now."

Venus tucked away her phone and studied the two sandy-haired boys, Quaid, and then Edwin. "Do you know how she got him?"

Quaid shrugged, unimpressed by his sister's antics. "Same way she always gets what she wants. She '*poofed*' him."

"What does that mean?" Brigid asked, cuddling the sleepy little boy yawning in her arms. "I don't get it."

"That's okay. You're a new witch." It was Edwin's turn to explain. "We call it, '*poofing*' when you make something reappear that was lost. You know when you misplace your keys or a book or your homework. You '*poof*' it and it comes back."

"I do that with recipes sometimes when I can't find them in my cookbooks or keepsake box," Brigid admitted. "What does it have to do with the kitten?"

"Well, everybody was busy with Sarge Top's stuff and Fallyn wanted her kitten. So, she asked him if she could '*poof*' him." Quaid took a step closer to his sister in an attempt to protect her. "And he must have agreed because next thing, you know, he was with her."

"We go now. Him hungry." Fallyn considered that a moment longer. "Me too."

Venus heaved a sigh. "I so have to talk to Meteor about how to deal with you three and your emerging talents. Meanwhile, Edwin, we'll need a harness and leash for the kitten. I'm not taking him outside this store without one. And your sister will pitch a fit if we put him in a carrier."

"Him stay wif me." Fallyn snuggled the kitten closer. "No cage."

"You also have to come up with an explanation of how he got

out of that locked crate." Brigid flicked a glance at the registers and the waiting cashier. "Jonel has to open those with her special key, or people would be stealing pets rather than paying for them."

"Good point. I'll take care of that," Trina said. "Go play distract with her and kick her butt for calling the cops on Robert O'Malley. Even that twit should have been able to tell the difference between a warrior and a wanna-be."

# 19

*Eagleville, Washington*
*Thursday, November 29th, 2018*

ROBERT SAT IN THE SMALL INTERROGATION ROOM AT THE POLICE station and waited. He glanced at his watch. Almost twenty-one hundred hours, nine p.m. civilian. It wasn't the first time he'd been searched, fingerprinted, or had his photo taken at a precinct. Growing up, he'd constantly been blamed for whatever his cousin Zane did. Back then, it was lying, stealing from the grocery store, bullying younger neighbor kids, arguing with authority figures from relatives to teachers to the minister, breaking windows—the list went on and on.

When they were teens, Zane escalated to burglaries, stolen cars, vandalism, assaults—and Robert was the scapegoat in most instances. *Bad enough when strangers accused me of what he did, but when my own parents did, it was hell.* Losing his first girlfriend to Zane's machinations was a heartbreak. Being sent to military school shortly afterwards, when he was barely seventeen, hadn't been the punishment anyone expected. Even now, his dad tried to claim it'd straightened out Robert, but he'd been smart enough not to share how he was treated.

While the instructors were strict, they weren't capricious or arbitrary, so it was much better than life with an uber-controlling father and a passive-aggressive mother. Robert was judged fairly for his actions and rewarded or punished accordingly. Little wonder, he'd opted for the Army as a career. He'd risen through the ranks during the last seventeen years, survived five combat tours in Iraq and Afghanistan. He'd found a new home wherever he was stationed in the US and abroad.

He hadn't expected to inherit the O'Malley farm but since he'd had it renovated, eventually it'd be perfect for him and the kids. He glanced at the door when it opened. A big, brawny blond followed two deputies inside. The first was Officer Dudley, the arrogant know-it-all who'd brought him here. The second was slightly older. Short auburn hair, bright blue eyes, he bore a resemblance to Brigid, but was taller, not quite six feet. He kept more weight on his right leg, compensating for some old injury to his left. Most civilians wouldn't realize he'd been the walking wounded in the past.

Robert nodded a greeting. "I.E.D.?"

"Yes. Donald Dawson." Crossing to the far side of the table, he held out his hand, ready to shake Robert's. "Welcome home, Master Sergeant or is it Top like your kids call you?"

"I'm not a First Shirt right now." Robert held up his wrists, showing the stainless-steel handcuffs. "I have a new assignment. I'm the ROTC instructor at the college in Everett."

The older man walked around the table. He didn't wear a uniform like the other officers, but a tan jacket over a white shirt and a striped tie. Light brown pants touched shiny black shoes. He obviously outranked the two deputies and carried a pistol in his shoulder holster. "Detective John Watkins. Let me unfasten those restraints. Dawson tells me that he's seen Zane O'Malley in Corbettstown before, but he's been least in sight for the last couple of days."

"I'm not surprised. He tends to avoid law enforcement whenever possible." Robert stood, leaving the handcuffs on the table, glancing at the former Marine. "Brigid said you're helping with an investigation up there."

"We're trying to find a trace of two missing people and the man we suspect killed them." Donald handed Robert his wallet, then nudged the other officer. "You owe Master Sergeant O'Malley an apology. Detective Watkins is here to make sure you do it before—"

"His lawyer arrives." John Watkins cast a censorious look toward Officer Dudley. "Astra Jamison always enjoys filing charges against the department and she's packing a grudge because she suspects her clients were murdered and we didn't do enough to protect them."

"Only because you didn't. And Nina Armstrong and Kyle Morgan paid the price for your ineptitude." A red-haired woman in a dark blue power suit that matched her eyes walked through the open door behind the officers. The room was already full even before the Native American man who accompanied her stepped inside. Long black hair speckled with gray tied in a ponytail with a leather thong, he wore a suede shirt, brown pants, and low-heeled boots. Wiry, lean, and muscular with the lethal grace of a trained warrior, he lingered in the doorway.

"I'm Astra Jamison." Carrying her briefcase, she smiled politely at Donald Dawson and nodded at the other two officers, before beckoning at Robert. "If you're finished harassing my client, we're leaving."

Suppressing a smile, Robert obeyed the summons. Her companion glanced at Donald. "Use heat to reduce the pain."

"I've been told to use ice at the end of the day."

"Heat provides relief for chronic muscle and joint pain." The stranger looked at Donald's leg. "You've had that injury a while."

"Three years." Donald nodded. "Thanks. I'll try it. I didn't get your name."

"He isn't offering it." Astra led the way from the room, stiletto heels striking the tile floor. Outside in the parking lot, she shot a glare at her companion. "I didn't need your interference."

He seemed unimpressed by her annoyance and placed a hand on

her shoulder. "I told you before. You may not want my protection, but the mother of my child does. You'll never confront danger alone again."

"There wasn't any threat here." She stalked to a late-model Lexus and used the key fob to unlock the doors. "I'm not afraid of them."

He gestured toward a white patrol car with a wolf's head on the door. "They are in league with your father who already plans to kill you. We've discussed this before. You and your sisters go nowhere alone."

Robert stiffened, eyeing the pair. "How can you say that? Venus was alone at the feedstore."

"No, she wasn't. She had her bodyguard." Astra pointed to the car, revealing a gold bracelet on her wrist. "Front seat, Robert. We need to talk. Rowdy will take the back. As for my sister, she sent home her children and went to protect yours. Let's go."

Before he followed directions, Robert turned to the other man, holding out his hand. "Thank you for coming, Mr..."

"Rowdy Tall-Deer." The man smiled, faint amusement gleaming in the dark gaze. "You're welcome, Robert O'Malley. Let's head to Brigid's place now before it gets any later."

———

She'd tucked the girls into the queen-size bed in her room, the new kittens cuddled up with them. The boys slept in the guestroom on the other side of the living-room. When Brigid returned to the kitchen, she found her sister sitting at the table. A basket of clothes, fresh from the dryer was on one of the other chairs. Venus loaded the dishwasher while Gavin Killian, Kate's fiancé swept the floor. "Thanks, everyone."

"It's the least I can do when you're babysitting the neighborhood psycho's kids." Kate shook out a pair of jeans. "Now, that they're zonked, bring us up to speed. How on earth did Zane O'Malley find a woman stupid enough to have his children? Especially those five cuties?"

Venus closed the dishwasher and swung around. "They're not Zane's. They're his cousin, Robert's. Career military. Just got an assignment at the college in Everett. And his wife made him promise to bring the kids here before she died. She was afraid her family would separate them."

"I didn't hear any of that from him or them." Brigid gaped at the other woman. "How do you know?"

"My sister needs to teach you more than kitchen craft." Venus wrung out a dishcloth and began wiping down the counters. "Hugh and I have both told you. One true warrior always recognizes another. I read Robert's truths at the feedstore."

This time, Kate and Gavin stared at her. Finally, Gavin said, "I didn't know you were in the military."

"My family calls me the war-queen for a reason." Venus hung the damp cloth on the faucet of the farmhouse sink. "We have company."

"I locked the gates when we arrived." Brigid followed the younger woman to the back door. "Whoever it is, can't come through them."

"It's Astra's car." Venus opened the door and started across the porch, pausing to draw the sword out of its sheath on her back. "Bring the keys."

"We have really weird cousins." Kate kept folding clothes. "I have to talk to Audra and see what she knows about them because I'm pretty sure she hasn't told us everything."

Brigid didn't respond to the comment. She remembered what their older sister had said when she heard about the new job at Captivating Catering. 'Keep an open mind and see what you learn. The world's a bigger place than most people think.' Obviously, Audra knew more about the mystical nature of the Jamisons than she admitted to her sisters or their other relatives.

It didn't take long to open the set of gates and allow Astra to pull inside. Brigid went to join the others when Astra parked her car next to Rob's Jeep Rubicon and Brigid's older Chevy pickup.

Venus put away the sword and greeted her sister with a kiss on the cheek. "Blessed be. I'm glad you came. Thank you."

"For what?" Astra lifted her chin, gold earrings glinting in the moonlight. "What else did you expect? I always come when you or Meteor call."

"True." Venus flashed a dazzling smile at Robert. "I just didn't know if she'd have time to take your case since she's dealing with a murder trial right now."

"It was a good time for her to leave it behind." Rowdy closed the car door. "I want her to protect only the innocents, not those who hunt them. It diminishes her soul when she sends the wicked to die at the hands of your father or his minions."

"And as you've said before, it's my choice," Astra retorted. "I know you don't like it, but it's how I choose to protect your innocents."

"Let's go inside." Brigid intervened before the argument escalated. "We have leftover pasta, garlic toast and salad unless you stopped to eat on the way here."

"Trust a kitchen witch to offer food to distract us." Astra smiled at her. "I'm sorry, Brigid. Rowindache and I will undoubtedly be arguing about the difference between legality and justice for the next three hundred years, but we won't do it here."

"Not when it makes you uncomfortable." Rowdy slipped his arm around Astra's waist. "And if you feed my son, you may not be so quarrelsome."

"If my daughter is anything like her cousin, Fallyn, she will teach you about tempestuous women."

"Seriously?" Venus stepped up next to her sister. "You're expecting a baby, and you think I'll let you go to Corbettstown with Meteor on Sunday to face our father?"

"I'm going." Astra held up her hand to quell any protests. "For now, I want to eat and talk to my new client. You and I will discuss our issues later, my darling Kat—"

"Believe me, we will," Venus interrupted.

Inside, Brigid discovered her sister had finished the laundry. The kids would have clean clothes for the next day. She urged her guests to sit down while she filled three bowls with salad. Venus proceeded to warm up the leftover lasagna and chicken fettucine so the new arrivals could choose whichever they preferred. Gavin filled glasses with wine for Rowdy and Robert while Kate made a cup of raspberry tea for Astra.

"I appreciate the meal, Brigid." Robert passed around napkins before he sat down. "Where are the kids? You had my keys. You could have taken them home and they'd be able to sleep in their own beds."

"No." She put bottles of dressing on the table. "Eat something. They barely stayed awake through dinner. We opted for quick showers and shampoos. While the boys were waiting their turns, they fell asleep in front of the TV."

"They never do that. It takes forever to get them into bed and even then, they always want more drinks of water, more stories." Robert added ranch dressing to his salad. "I can't believe they're not out here talking to us when it takes so long to get them to sleep at home. Constant nightmares, bad dreams, and all of them wake up screaming even if they do sleep. Their therapist says it's part of the grieving process because their mom died a few months ago."

"Bad juju." Brigid poured herself a glass of red wine and sat down at one end of the table. "Not one of them was upset when we came here instead of going down the block to the O'Malley place. They'd be awake if they were stressing about their mom and dad."

Dressed casually in jeans and a sweatshirt, Gavin didn't look anything like the proverbial university professor. "The older three loved helping take care of the ponies, horses and other livestock. They're hard workers."

"And I'll bet they didn't even ask to go to the O'Malley place, did they?" Kate handed a cup of tea to Astra, then sat across from her. "They didn't ask me either. Bad juju."

"Okay." Robert eyed the women. "I don't get it. What do you mean by bad juju?"

"Open your mind, Robert." Brigid folded her arms and kept a narrowed gaze on him. "It's bad luck or negative energy of a colossal, unworldly magnitude. The O'Malley place reeks of it." She heaved a sigh. "It needs a total cleansing."

"I pay a cleaning service to come every week. I don't expect the kids to do more than put their clothes in the laundry, help load the dishwasher and take out the trash. And I don't have a lot of time to G.I. the place."

"Cleansing," Brigid repeated. "It's a warding to keep out evil, a protective ritual to destroy bad juju."

She saw the confusion on his rugged features before it was replaced by skepticism. He didn't understand that the kids felt the same thing she did. The malodorous atmosphere still lingered even if Zane O'Malley no longer lived on the family property. "Did you know your cousin tortured and killed animals for years there?"

"What?" Robert lowered his fork. "My family said he was falsely accused, that people manufactured evidence against him."

"Wrong." Kate glowered at him over her mug. "My sister, Audra is married to Joe Watkins, a veterinarian. They discovered the carnage. Joe stabilized an injured fawn and sent it off with its twin to a wildlife sanctuary after their mother was killed. There were five dead dogs, four more dying, and six more shot. Cats, raccoons, rabbits, some lethally wounded, all shot in a mad frenzy. If your family hadn't paid Zane's bail, he'd still be behind bars, not romping around the county."

"Bad juju," Brigid repeated, her gaze locked on Robert. "The house may be renovated, but the spirit of death and destruction still lingers. We haven't even brought up him poisoning wild and domestic animals with antifreeze. No wonder your kids hate it there."

"So, what are you saying I need to do?" Robert demanded.

"Have the place healed and cleansed." Rowdy cut into his lasagna. "We'll do it as soon as we can. We're busy for the next two days. Brigid, will you keep the younglings here and protect them until we do what's needful?"

"I can and will." She met Robert's dark brown gaze. "And because I love children, I won't even charge the going rate for babysitting them. However, you will pay for riding lessons and groceries. If you don't piss me off too much, I'll take Peter with me to visit my brother-in-law Sean to see his latest batch of puppies. And if you do, I'll arrange for Sean to sell one to Peter."

## 20

PROMISING TO CALL SOON, HIS NEW ATTORNEY LEFT, ACCOMPANIED by her partner and her sister an hour and a half later. The farmhouse Brigid and Kate shared was much smaller than his house, but somehow it felt more comfortable. Robert glanced around the fairly large kitchen. It was probably the biggest room. The counters, sink, dishwasher, and electric range were on the far wall. The doors to the bath and a small bedroom shared by Kate and Gavin were on the right-hand wall and in the corner was a desk and filing cabinet.

Adjacent to that was the outside door to the back deck. In the left-hand corner of the kitchen were the table and six chairs. The washer, dryer, and refrigerator were on the left wall. No center island with its stools like the huge one in his renovated chef's kitchen. Brigid finished rinsing the last of the plates and loaded them in the dishwasher. "Are you staying with the kids or going?"

"Thought my place had bad juju." Robert wiped off the table before he crossed the room to rinse out the dishcloth. "Sorry, I shouldn't tease you. I didn't expect you to look after my kids or arrange for your cousin to meet me at the precinct. If it's okay with you, I'd like to stay."

She turned to look at him. "When I was changing Matt's diaper,

Peter told me you served with his dad in Afghanistan, that it wasn't your first time in combat."

"Five tours in America's longest war." Robert gestured to the half-full wine bottle on the counter. "If we're going to talk about that, I could use another drink. How about you?"

She nodded, opened the cupboard, and removed two glasses. She waited until he filled them, picked up the bottle and led the way into the living room. She put her goblet on the coffee table and signaled him to follow her to a bedroom door. When he did, he saw the three girls snuggled in a king-size bed, sound asleep. After she closed the door, Brigid led the way to a matching one on the other side of the room. This time, he spotted the boys in a large bed pulled out from a sleeper sofa.

Robert gently shut the door. "I don't believe it. I haven't seen the five of them sleeping like that since we got here. I know what you're going to say, but it's difficult for me to believe the O'Malley house has such a toxic atmosphere. My grandparents lived there forever."

"It was probably fine before Zane moved into it." Brigid picked up her glass and found a seat in a recliner. She gestured to the matching one. "Let's talk. When did you go in the Army? Peter said you'd served longer than his dad, almost twenty years."

"I enlisted as soon as I graduated from the military boarding school." He swirled the red wine in his glass and watched light from the pole lamp play on her face. "Didn't you wonder why I disappeared shortly after spring break during my junior year?"

"I don't know what to believe anymore." She heaved a sigh. "I thought I'd met a really great guy and then it was like you changed into a totally different one, a real shit."

"That was Zane." Robert raised the glass to his lips. "Not me. For fun, his fun, he'd pull all sorts of dirty tricks and then claim I did them. I thought everybody believed him. It surprised the hell out of me when I learned my grandfather saw through him."

"Say what?" She shook her head. "I don't get it."

"Before Grandpa went into assisted living, he signed over all his property to me, including the family farm. He was dying of cancer, so he kept enough to pay the costs for the retirement center and his funeral. He didn't share what he'd done after they moved Zane into the house." Robert drank some red wine. "Grandpa passed when I was overseas. I missed the service and the family raised hell when the lawyer read his will. Since I was up to my ass in alligators in a warzone, I ignored them."

She frowned, her attention on the drink she held. "Didn't you ever return after high school? This seems really weird."

"I came back to visit the summer before I went to basic training for a couple weeks. You were working at Billy-Bob's, your uncle's place. I brought you flowers, long-stemmed red roses. You agreed to go out with me later that night." He shrugged. "You changed your mind."

"No, I didn't." She took a swallow of wine. "I met you in the parking lot. I hurried when I finished cleaning the kitchen—" She paused. "At least, I thought it was you until you drove up to an old, abandoned logging road in the middle of nowhere and tried to jump me. I managed to get out of the truck and ran into the woods."

"No!" He jumped to his feet, the dregs of wine splashing onto the carpet. "He didn't. I'll kill that son of—"

"Stop." She held up her hand. "Just stop, Robert. I got away. I hiked down the mountain. I didn't have a cell phone so when I found a payphone, I called Gavin's older brother, Ethan, and he came to get me. Later, Sean tracked Zane down in a logger bar in Eagleville. Sean kicked the crap out of—well, I thought it was you —but it must have been Zane. He had a broken nose, black eyes, and busted ribs."

"Jesus, Mary, and Joseph! Wow, I'm impressed." Robert put his glass on the coffee table long enough to wipe the carpet with the spit cloth he kept in his pants pocket for Matthew's drooling. "How old was Sean? Why didn't he end up in jail for assaulting Zane, the O'Malley family fave?"

"The war between them started when Sean was fifteen and carried on until that last battle. His father, Wallace is a career politician." Brigid held out her glass for a refill. "And even if he didn't approve of his youngest son's actions, there wasn't any way he'd allow people he considered 'low-class' to file charges against him or let Sean end up in the Gray-Bar Hotel. The O'Malleys may own one of the largest feed mills in the county, but they've never been any competition for the Dawsons or Killians."

"Okay, so that explains a lot." Robert topped their glasses then returned to the recliner. "No wonder you refused to speak to me when I visited. Not that I did very often. I was stationed all over the country and in Europe for nearly twenty years. I'm sure Zane ran amuck."

"And apparently, he continued stealing your identity whenever possible." Brigid narrowed her green eyes. "Have you talked to Astra Jamison about that?"

"I didn't know everything he was doing, so I'll bring her up to speed. I can't let him ruin my reputation or it'll affect my custody of Jackie and Pedro's kids and they come first. I've got to keep my promise to their parents."

While they finished the bottle of wine, Robert told her about his former commanding officer asking him to look after his wife and family. Brigid completely understood why he married Jackie to save the five kids from being split up among various relatives or even being put in foster care. Afterwards, she slept on the couch while he sacked out in the recliner. He'd bunked in worse places and at least nobody would be shooting at him here.

———

Friday morning, Brigid put on the coffee before she headed to the barn to look after the livestock. Halfway through feeding hay to the ponies and horses, Gavin joined her. She flicked a sideways glance at her someday brother-in-law. Gavin bore a strong resemblance to his brothers in the fierce angles of his handsome face and square jaw. Silver threaded his dark brown hair and the lines around his mouth and gray eyes. He only dressed in what his sister-in-law,

Elinor, called nineteen-piece suits on formal occasions at the university. The rest of the time he opted for more casual attire, jeans, flannel shirts and boots.

"What's on your mind?" Brigid dropped a flake of hay in the next manger. "You're contemplating something and I'm pretty sure it's not my evil baby sisters who never have apologized for their antics almost a year ago. They still don't see anything wrong with telling Kate lies about you until she broke your engagement."

"Not holding my breath on that one." Gavin pushed the wheelbarrow after her. "They should have paid attention in the few classes they attended when I lectured about actions having consequences."

"Good luck with that. They never believed it applied to them when Mom or Audra tried saying it to our entitled, spoiled brats." Brigid continued feeding the alfalfa-grass hay. "What do you think about the O'Malleys? It really surprised me to learn Robert was telling the truth so many years ago. He insisted he had a doppelganger, but I never believed him."

"Not quite." Gavin smiled at her. "That's a spirit who looks exactly like a living person or is someone who looks exactly like someone else but isn't related to that person. Robert and Zane are first cousins."

"Good point." Finished with the hay, she gestured toward the second wheelbarrow, the one containing the grain. She walked toward it while he parked the first one in the corner of the barn. "I called in my cousin, Donald because I figured if Zane was pulling a fast one and pretending he was a soldier yesterday at the feedstore, Don would kick his butt to the moon and back."

"I thought he lost part of his leg in combat."

"Yeah, but he's a Marine. He could do it with his prothesis or other leg. Of course, I was like Kate. I didn't know how on earth Zane got five kiddoes."

"I could see him pulling a fast one on their mother for the insurance, but I didn't see him leaving them alive—" Gavin paused. "Anyone who abuses animals would abuse children."

"Preaching to the proverbial choir." Brigid measured grain into the first row of buckets. "And I wasn't sure how Robert had military ID either. After they met, Donald texted me that according to his contacts, Robert is the real deal."

"Not hard to fake or buy phony ID. I'm not discounting your cousin's opinion, but I want more facts before I buy what could be a B.S. story." Gavin began to carry the individual buckets to the various ponies and horses. "Glad you labeled these or I'd be asking directions."

"Me too. I had to change things up when I took over the place after Audra married Joe and moved to Pullman." Brigid scooped more feed into the second row of buckets. "She has a brain like a steel trap. She never forgets anything, so I'm amazed she didn't know there were two O'Malley boys."

"I still want to see them together." Gavin considered that idea for a moment, then began ferrying the next set of buckets to the appropriate stalls. "You're going to play hell getting Sean to sell you a puppy for Robert's oldest boy."

"I know but I wanted to see what Robert had to say about it after the way he and Sean fought for years. Except it wasn't him. It was supposedly his cousin, Zane." Brigid poured the rest of the grain into the remaining bucket. "Robert freaked when I told him what happened on our supposed first and last *real* date seventeen years ago. It seemed genuine."

"But you don't quite believe it yet."

"No. Does that make me stupid?"

"Not to me."

She waited while Gavin took the wheelbarrow to the feedroom. "Venus seems to think Robert is an Army vet, but I still want to hear it from Astra. I'll text her but she won't get back to me until after court today."

"She's a good lawyer. She'll be able to confirm what Donald told you."

"I'm counting on it."

On their way to the house, Brigid took care of the chickens. Gavin collected the eggs. In the kitchen, they found Robert drinking coffee while he looked in the refrigerator and then in the cupboards.

Brigid eyed him. "What are you doing?"

"Trying to find something to feed the kids for breakfast. I can't find any cereal or frozen waffles or—"

"You won't in Brigid's kitchen." Gavin laughed on his way to the sink to wash the eggs. "I may not believe in her and Kate's bad juju, but I know better than to look for fast food in her house."

"If you tease me, you'll be buying one of their muffins at the espresso stand on your way to the university." Brigid crossed to the counter and poured two mugs of coffee. "Do your kids like French toast?"

"Sure. They aren't fussy."

"Good. Set the table while I cook." Brigid removed a bowl from the cupboard. "Gavin, store those eggs in the fridge and get me the ones that are already there plus a pitcher of milk. I'll need the ham too. Cut off a few pieces for me."

"Why isn't it in a carton?" Robert carried a stack of plates to the table. "Where's it from?"

"Elinor Killian, Sean's wife is the owner of the farm. She brings it when she visits. She took the cow with her when she moved to his place in Snohomish." Two loaves of sourdough bread wrapped in dishtowels sat on the counter and Brigid unwrapped them, glad she'd taken time to slice them when she was at the bakery. She left the cranberry-orange loaf for Kate since it was her favorite.

Two hours later, Brigid joined Kate at the kitchen table while her younger sister drank peppermint tea and crunched a piece of dry toast. Robert had left for work, taking the children with him to drop them off at school and day care. Gavin went to the university after helping clean up after breakfast.

Brigid leaned back in her chair, sipping coffee. She had a late start at the bakery today because people would be picking up decorated cakes this afternoon for weekend celebrations. "Okay, I'm sure you have something more to say about Robert. Spit it out."

"Actually, the man is growing on me." Kate's smile warmed her blue eyes. "I've never seen a guy pack lunches so quickly. I couldn't believe it when he had the kids organizing backpacks or Peter packing a diaper bag for Matt. It was impressive. I think Gavin and I better take notes."

"Are you serious?"

"Sure. I don't remember our dad helping out Mom or Audra. It was always the two of them running the house and the ranch. He never paid a penny of child support after the divorce."

"The Dawsons did their version of a family intervention when they arranged for us to live on the Lazy B." Brigid finished her coffee and reached for the carafe in the middle of the table to refill the mug. "I don't know where we'd have ended up if they hadn't. Probably on the street, somewhere."

"Yeah, well the twins are still complaining about Audra telling them the facts of life last summer. She even shared that Dad sells his blood to get a poker stake."

"Sounds about right." Brigid heaved a sigh. "Don texted me last night and said he'd seen Zane O'Malley up in Corbettstown this past week, but now the guy has disappeared. Don is going to ask around and remind some of the city cops there are outstanding county warrants for Zane."

"Everybody knows it's a low-class place. Too many drunks and skanks. Did you ask Don to be careful? He's sacrificed enough, Brigid."

"I know. I reminded him what Beth used to say about finding someone to 'watch his six' and he promised he would."

———

As she went through her morning routine on Friday, Meteor remembered the evening at Jed's home. Surprisingly, she'd enjoyed the meal and the company more than she expected. Her gaze landed on the wide, vintage bracelet she still wore. She'd attempted to remove it when she arrived home but couldn't locate the clasp. It wasn't as if she'd been able to ask Jed who'd shown up on her balcony in his hawk form. Once he knew she was safe in her apartment, he'd flown away.

She stroked one of the wildcats embossed in the gold. She almost swore she felt it stretch, close its sapphire blue eyes and purr. That never happened when she wore the bracelet before, not even during the mating ceremony when she was matched to Thojedescar three hundred years ago. What was different now?

She frowned thoughtfully, remembering when her foster mother, Estelle Jamison, one of the head witches of the coven, gave the *talipenlace* collections to each of the triplets on their twenty-first birthdays in this life, seven years ago. In rare attempts to placate Estelle and avoid her rage, Meteor occasionally wore the necklace, but not the bracelets or earrings, making up the set. *I'd almost forgotten about them. I hadn't seen them in so long. Why did she and Diana give them to Jed?*

Meteor placed the tray of freshly baked and frosted maple bars in the display case. She'd think about it later. If she hadn't come up with an answer by the time the bakery closed, she could always ask Astra. Her older sister was only in court four days a week and would be at the Rocking J with Rowdy this morning so they could prepare for the trip to Corbettstown on Sunday.

When she returned to the kitchen, she found Brigid putting the finishing touches on a merry-go-round horse shaped birthday cake. The other woman made it look easy as she swirled frosting around the traditional center pole. "I have a question, Meteor. You and your family keep calling me a new witch or a fledgling or even a witchling."

"True, because you have a great deal to learn."

"All right. Yesterday, when we met Robert O'Malley at the feedstore, Venus said she read the truth about him, and he was a career soldier—"

"She'd recognize the qualities of another fighter. She's the war-queen."

"How do I tell the difference between him and his cousin? He and Zane look so much alike. Their mothers were identical twins."

Brigid switched to a different bag of frosting, a blue one this time. "The guys mixed me up when I was younger, and I don't want to go through that again."

"The easiest way to begin is by reading their auras." Meteor leaned against the counter. "Have you ever done that?"

"No. Tell me more about it."

"Okay, an aura is a field of colored energy around someone. Humans, animals, plants – we all have auras. Each one is about three feet and surrounds a body. Seeing those is a good way to protect yourself. You'll be able to perceive the differences between good and bad life forces."

"And that will tell me the difference between the O'Malley men?"

"Definitely, Brighty." Meteor carefully patted her apprentice witch's shoulder lightly so she wouldn't disrupt her work. "It will also help you with everyone else you meet. We'll start the lessons during your lunch break."

## PART III

---

# "NOBODY OWNS A SHAPE-SHIFTER!"

—Corrine Corbett, Primal–Alpha
and She-Wolf Shapeshifter

# 21

_Corbettstown, Washington_
_Friday, November 30<sup>th</sup>, 2018_

READY FOR HIS OVERNIGHT SHIFT TO END, TREYTON CORBETT drove through the rain toward city hall in the early morning. He grimaced when he pulled his patrol car into a reserved spot. There were still several county, state and federal law enforcement vehicles taking up most of the parking spaces around town.

That meant A.J. Corbett, his supervisor, would be testy and ready to rip into him for any infraction, no matter how minor. Nothing like dealing with a shifter angry about spelling errors on a witness report. Treyton took a deep breath. He'd report in, then head home to sleep for a few hours before he had to return to work.

Friday nights tended to be wild and crazy in the local bars. Some of the other male shifters couldn't handle their booze and seized on any opportunity to start a fight. Females would egg them on, determined to learn who were the most dominant and take away the winners for sex. Often, that happened in alleys or parking lots.

Most of the she-wolves didn't look at him as a possible mate because he was a 'beta' wolf, someone not as successful or powerful as the other males. Generally, an alpha or leader would put a stop to the brawls and public sexual encounters, but Frank Corbett encouraged the strife. He said the violence and sex meant there'd eventually be more youngsters. No pack could survive without children. So far, his theory wasn't working. The birth rate continued to drop. No new babies had been born in the past five years.

When Treyton entered the office, he spotted his mother, Hester Corbett sitting at the reception desk, ready to greet visitors. The slender woman with curling brown hair wore her usual uniform, a well-fitting beige blouse, matching slacks, and polished, lace-up boots, equipped with a pistol belt, radio, and other police paraphernalia. She smiled at him. "How was your night, Trey?"

"The usual." Treyton paused. "A few speeders. Younglings out past curfew drinking at one of the gravel pits—"

"Not your brothers or sister?" Concern filled Hester's voice. "I had to interview some female shifters about Cherry Corbett, so I left them home alone for a little while."

"Not them, just a few of their wilder friends. What about her?"

"She and her husband disappeared. Chief Marvin wants to see you." Worry slipped into her brown eyes. "Be careful. Treat the pack enforcer with respect. I can't lose you like I did your father." Her voice trailed away and then she changed the subject. "He has Corrine in his office. Tomorrow is the last day of her punishment for wrecking his car, but he's still angry about it. He's already had her screaming twice this morning."

"It's all right, Mom. Yes, we dated last year before he claimed her, but we're just friends."

"She belongs to him now." Hester twisted her hands together. "He's not a shifter, but the older members of the pack know he's a sorcerer, not just the enforcer. He can and does call on pack *magick*. Since Frank doesn't have a second in command, the role falls to Chief Marvin. Be polite. I've seen the way he looks at you. He thinks she still cares about you and—"

"Stop. Mom, just stop." Treyton held up his hand. "He knows

I'm not any competition for him, especially after she kicked the crap out of me a few weeks ago when he sent that patrol to bring her home. She trashed his place again when he brought Trina to live there and—"

"If he decides you still want her, he'll kill you." Hester trembled, rare tears shining in her brown eyes. "This town is so rough. Nobody will criticize him for it. I can't lose you too."

"You're not losing me." Nobody else was around the reception area. It was safe to hug her. "I'll go see what the chief wants. It will be fine. Now, don't worry. I always remember my place in the pack."

On the way to the private offices, Treyton stopped by the restroom to be sure his dark brown uniform was as neat as could be expected after his shift. He needed a shave but that wasn't possible right now. He combed his hair and then strode down the hall.

He'd only been on the force a little over a year after completing his degree in criminology. He'd never received any special assignments, unlike some of the other deputies. Not for the first time, he wished the alpha would have let him leave Corbettstown for a position with a larger law enforcement agency in a different community, but every request was denied.

He knocked on the door and waited for the police chief to summon him. No answer at first, but then someone called for him to enter. He was barely inside when a silver-gray body launched off the couch in the middle of the room. Her hundred-pound body slammed into his chest, and he fell backwards onto the floor.

Dizzy, he stared into the slits of her golden-brown eyes. "Damn it, Corrine. Get off me. This isn't funny. The chief will kill me."

'*Beta Boy!*' She opened her mouth, teeth gleaming as she grinned at him. She licked his cheek, his mouth. '*You taste like sugar.*'

"I had a maple bar with my coffee." He flushed, remembering when they used to meet at the town doughnut shop during his breaks and she'd tease him about being a stereotypical cop.

'*Ooh, I miss those so much. Bring me another one sometime.*'

She paused, tilting her head left and right. *'Well, when I come to Eagleville. The bakery has the best. The kitchen witches are sooo nice and very good cooks. You go there.'*

"I'm hardly ever allowed to leave Corbettstown, but I will next time I'm on the road." He winced and tried to push her off him. "*Lord and Lady*, you weigh a ton. Get off me."

*'No! Listen. We don't have much time. Does your sister shift yet?'*

He froze, barely managing to shake his head. "Why?"

*'They're testing her on Sunday, and she dies then so they can eat her at Yule.'* Corrine lifted her head, glancing at the door. *'He's coming. Cry.'*

"What?" He lifted his hands, determined to push her away.

She bit him, breaking the skin. He yelped in surprise. He'd had more painful nips from his mother when he was a pup, but this one seeped blood.

She licked it away. *'Good! Beta Boy! My wolf. Say it, quick!'*

"Your wolf," he murmured, remembering the way they kissed when she was his girl, before the alpha and the enforcer took her away. They rarely found places where they could truly be alone and together, so they didn't have sex very often. He still had great memories of her touch and the way she smiled when she pulled off his shirt. "Your wolf, always."

*'Good! Take your sister away. Go to Jed Corbett. Now, cry!'*

He followed the order, slowly realizing she'd severed the tie to the pack here and claimed him as hers with the blood from that little scratch. Tears filled his eyes and slipped down his cheeks. "Please don't hurt me."

She nosed his throat and growled. It sounded like she meant to kill him.

"Bad girl! Let him go. Now!" The enforcer strode in the door and came toward them.

From his position lying on the floor, Treyton glimpsed his brightly polished boots and part of the brown slacks. "Please, sir. My mom said you wanted me. I—"

"I do." Chief Marvin scowled at Corrine. "I said, let him go."

*'No. My Beta Boy in my space. I'll train him.'*

"I'm training you." The police chief reached for her collar. She turned her head, baring her teeth. "Don't do it. No biting. Bad puppy!"

*'I'm not a puppy.'* She snarled at him. *'I'm a wolf and he's my beta boy, not yours.'*

"My wolf. My very bad wolf who is going in the kennel as soon as we get home after a real spanking." The muscular older man grabbed her collar and pulled her toward him. "Get up, son. Are you all right?"

Corrine lunged toward Treyton, and he scrambled backwards until he could stand. He flushed when he heard her mocking laughter. "I'm sorry. I thought you told me to come inside, Chief and—"

*'I did, Beta Boy. I said, come and you did.'* Corrine tossed a wolfish grin his way. *'I'm alpha.'*

Chief Marvin dragged her toward his large oak desk and picked up a coiled leash. He snapped one end on the antique silver and gold chain collar around her neck. "You're alpha? What am I?"

*'He's beta. I'm alpha.'* If she was in her human form, she'd have shrugged. *'You, Grandpa? You're not shifter. Not wolf. You're nothing!'*

Treyton's eyes widened and he backed another step toward the door. He'd never have insulted the enforcer like that. "I'm sorry. I'll go. I can come back later."

"Not yet. I have an assignment for you." Gunnolf pointed to the large, thick dog pad behind his desk, his attention on the silvery gray wolf. "Lie down. On your bed."

Corrine stood stiff-legged, lips curled and growled at him. *'No. I'm alpha. And I've been punished enough for your stupid car! Get over it, Grandpa!'*

Treyton saw a short whip on the corner of the desk, along with a bag of dog treats. Reward and punishment—a hell of a way to treat another human being, even if Corrine was acting like a real bitch right now. Pity for his former girlfriend swept through him and he struggled not to let it show. During the past two weeks, he'd seen other deputies, more favored ones, standing and laughing in the hallway when she began shrieking and calling the police chief her master, her owner. Some even enjoyed watching her be disciplined, saying she needed either a good beating or a good fucking.

Not Treyton. The words sickened him. Yes, they answered to the alpha as a leader of their pack, but he'd been taught nobody truly owned a shifter. He always slipped out of the building until Corrine's screams subsided. If he couldn't help her, he didn't have to witness the torture.

He didn't look at Corrine again but focused on the bookcases that held nearly a hundred wolf-shaped decanters. The enforcer received them as gifts from traveling shifters. Maybe he could distract the man from the stubborn female shifter looking for a fight. Being a 'beta' wolf wasn't all bad.

Treyton knew he was good at resolving issues, not only between the humans who lived here, but also the shifters. "You wanted to see me, sir?"

Gunnolf looked him up and down before he picked up a file folder. "I have some outstanding warrants here from the county. When you're making your rounds, you'll probably find these fellows. If you do, bring them to my house. Lock them in the tool-shed, one to a cell."

Corrine turned her head, narrowing golden-brown eyes and barked at Treyton.

He retreated a step. "I—"

Gunnolf glanced at him, then at the wolf. He bent, rapped her nose. "He heard me. Now, stop being so naughty. They won't be near your doghouse."

Another growl and she took a step, ready to leap at Treyton again.

"Stay away from her kennel too," Gunnolf said. "She gets a bit territorial when she's home alone or at night or when she doesn't like someone's smell, or if there's out of control humans, or—"

"I'll be careful. And I'll keep the prisoners away." Treyton eyed her warily, straightening to his full six feet. "Will she go after other shifters? What do I tell the alpha?"

"Don't worry about him." A faint smile edged Gunnolf's mouth. "He already knows I'm handling outsiders like I always do, and he's aware my mate is a lone wolf. Any shifters stupid enough to raise hell before *Yule* will be locked in the special cages here. They contain silver in the bars so the shifters can't escape my justice. I'll deal with them tomorrow morning." He reached over to ruffle Corrine's fur. "They won't like it any more than she does when I leave her behind, but that's the point."

"Yes, sir." Treyton took the folder. He backed up a step, saluted again, executed an about-face, and marched to the door. Before he closed it behind him, he heard the chief lecturing Corrine for attacking him and being so disrespectful.

Treyton looked quickly over his shoulder in time to see a rolled-up newspaper in the chief's hand. He didn't use it. He didn't have to —she immediately crouched at his feet, her belly on the floor, tail down between her back legs, ears flattened, not making eye contact, so obviously he'd beaten her before. All the signs of submission upset Treyton, but apparently, they pleased the enforcer who put the paper next to a dog whip, a plaited cowhide strap.

The chief snapped his fingers three times. She shuddered before she writhed at his feet. What kind of torture or *magick* was that? It didn't come from the pack because Treyton didn't feel it. She moaned softly when Gunnolf stroked her fur.

She whined and panted, looking up at him. *'No more, Master. I'll be good.'*

"Are you sure? No more sassy mouth? Are you done?"

*'Yes, Master.'*

"All right. Let's go." When he signaled her, she rose to stand in front of him, still shaking. She pressed against his leg. He chuckled and stood, holding the leash on her jeweled collar. "It's time to do a walk-through in town and check on things. Then, we'll go for a car ride."

*'Come back here?'* She licked his hand. *'Please, Master. It's*

*freezing on the mountain. Don't want to Change and have you fuck me in the snow. Hate it.'*

"You should have thought of that before you jumped the boy and got snotty with me. You know what happens when you call me, 'Grandpa'. If you're very, very good, I'll buy you a special 'doggie' burger for lunch at the café near the mountain. You can watch me eat one of their big T-Bone steaks. And then we'll go to the dog park in Eagleville so you can play fetch with the college kids. If they like you, really like you, maybe you won't get a spanking when we go home."

*'Make you run in the snow, old man and catch me first. Hate those burgers. Hate them kids. Hate chasing their stupid toys. Hate you. Hate you. Hate you! Going to kill you someday soon.'*

"Yes, but it won't be today. And you'll be staying in the down-stairs kennel for bad girls tonight after that spanking if you keep being naughty. Now, heel."

Treyton winced. He'd go home so he wouldn't have to see her parade through town like a well-trained dog while the chief visited local businesses. When things were quiet, there would be a way to get to Eagleville and Jed Corbett. Meantime, his brothers and sister could start packing. Treyton paused for a moment in the hallway to carefully open the file. The top page described Zane O'Malley, a man who'd faced several animal cruelty charges and skipped town when he made bail.

Treyton shuddered, remembering the case from last summer. He'd overheard the alpha, Frank Corbett and Gunnolf Marvin, the pack enforcer discussing it. They detailed what they'd like to do to someone who wasted meat after a hunt, killed a nursing doe, and poisoned small animals with antifreeze so they couldn't be eaten.

It started with turning him loose in the woods and letting an assortment of the more vicious deputies track him down. When Zane O'Malley was captured, they'd disembowel him, rip him to shreds, and eat him alive while he heard the shifters quarrel over his bones. Treyton took a deep breath and headed out the side door, avoiding his mother. He'd swing by the fried chicken place later and bring her a big lunch. Then, he could share what he learned from Corrine.

His mother warned him more than once to be careful, to follow orders so he wouldn't be disciplined or killed. She couldn't bear the thought of losing him like she had his father, a widower who fled with his children who couldn't shift before he and Hester went through the mating ceremony.

Pregnant at the time, Hester had been given to a different male, an older one who was kind enough to Treyton. He'd grown up seeing the blood sacrifices of those who flaunted the alpha's demands, like the children who couldn't change into wolves. They were killed and eaten by the pack.

*Not me, he thought, and not my little half-brothers and baby sis. Thanks to Corrine, I've been warned.* Now, he could save his family while she kept the enforcer busy! *I owe her big time and somehow, I'll repay her. If she needs help killing him, I'm on it! Right after we save my family!*

## 22

 ·

---

*Rocking J Ranch, Washington*
*Friday, November 30th, 2018*

THE PREVIOUS NIGHT, HUGH REMINDED HIMSELF REPEATEDLY THAT worrying was negative prayer and a waste of time while he waited for his chosen mate to return from visiting her sister's witchling. At the sound of boots on the plank floor, he stopped brushing his stallion and glanced toward the barn door. He watched Venus enter the building, pausing to lock the gate behind her.

She'd dressed for work. Riding pants clung to curving hips and long legs before they were tucked into knee-high, low-heeled boots. A fleece-lined jacket covered most of a plaid flannel shirt. She'd braided her waist-length red hair and wore a blue knit hat that matched her eyes. She walked toward him and handed him a cup of strong, black coffee in what she called a travel mug.

She turned away to feed carrots to the horses. Fourteen of them were hers. The other two belonged to him and Rowdy. Hugh eyed her and decided to accept the coffee as a peace offering when she returned to the aisle outside his horse's stall. "I'm still angry when you take risks, *Laspowima*."

"And you'll just have to get over it by yourself." She lingered, scratching the buckskin's cheek after she gave him the last treat. "I've told you too many times, Hughondear. I'm the war-queen. I decide what battles I'll fight."

"I want you to survive this war and the others to come."

"I will. With you by my side. You're my ally, my *chapalmatand*, not my owner. Praise the Goddess for that. Orion did another *Seeing* and told me one of my students who is a shifter has to call my father that. He uses her like a sex slave he bought from the marketplace on *Trilunon*. I was going to outlaw those as soon as I had my throne." Venus shook her head. "Next time, Corrine comes to class, I'm gifting her with a 'Bowie' knife from my collection. It's steel, not silver like the antique dagger I gave her to use on rogue shifters. She'll be able to wield it."

"On your father?" Hugh leaned close enough to kiss her. "If we get there first, we'll kill him and rescue her."

"You do know how to brighten my day." Venus smiled at him and continued drinking her coffee.

Hugh drank his while he considered her point. Under normal circumstances, she was right. She could and would protect herself. However, a week ago, her older sister, Astra and her familiar, a black hellhound had nearly died in a battle. It'd taken the talents of Rowdy, a *High Healer-Mage* and Astra's apprentice to save them.

Hugh put the empty cup on the wall near his waiting saddle. He caught her chin between two fingers and leaned down to kiss her. "Don't do it again, Katiranika. You're mine and I've waited too long to have you in my life."

"If that's supposed to be love talk, you're failing the charm test."

"I don't use charm. It's a shifter tool, not a warrior's."

She smiled, opened the half-door, and entered the stall. She rested her gloved hands on his chest. "I'm sorry I frightened you. That wasn't my intention. I'm not accustomed to anyone taking care of me."

"Your sisters—"

"When they tried, they blocked my memories so I wouldn't realize what was happening around me and I'd have no recollection of you or our past on *Trilunon*." She heaved a sigh, sliding her arms around his neck and pressing against him. "They didn't know, couldn't realize how much they limited my powers."

He stroked her bright red hair. He disagreed with the assessment but wouldn't say so. He had his own issues with the other two witches, especially Astra who was bound to Rowdy. She was sent to her demon-father to serve him and his minions as a virgin sacrifice in each and every one of her lives when she reached puberty, as a punishment for writing the *banexort* spell she'd given Venus when they arrived in this realm three hundred years before.

Granted, Venus was the one who cast it and that spell threw him and Rowdy, along with his army, into the Middle Ages. But she hadn't realized the extent of her older sister's machinations. Even so, Astra didn't deserve to be raped before she was horribly murdered in a blood sacrifice rite in life after life. Because she feared their father would use Venus and Meteor the way he used her, Astra kept him away from them and blocked Venus's memories of him.

Hugh often reminded himself to protect all three witches known as the *Trecesalty*. He understood why Astra tried so hard to defend her younger sisters in this life with any weapon at hand. Being reborn five times to the same parents who couldn't be trusted to look after her and abused her in every way possible would take its toll on any witch, turning her bitter and angry.

He wondered how well he'd have done in the same situation. Would he be like Rowdy, determined to heal the past and survive into the future or like his mate willing to sacrifice herself one more time to save those she loved?

Mustard nudged them in an apparent search for another carrot and Hugh turned slightly to pet the horse's neck. "Saddle up and we'll ride out. I'll show you what we've done on the boundary fence."

"I'd like that." Venus took a deep breath. "Next time, I go into town, I'll get you and Rowdy cell phones. Orion can teach you how to use them because he has more patience with technology than I do and then I'll call you if something comes up."

Hugh framed her lovely face in his hands, staring into the violet-blue eyes. "Either that or when you're more in touch with your talents, I can teach you to speak to me, mind to mind."

"I never heard of such a thing. Seriously? We can do that?"

"Of course." He kissed her. "How do you think generals communicate with their troops on the battlefield? Even if you haven't done it in this realm, you'd have done it before on *Trilunon* when you went to war."

"Show me." She shivered eagerly in his hold. "Do it now."

He chuckled. "Tonight. I'll come for supper and afterwards—"

"I want to know right now. Teach me. This minute, not when you get around to it!"

This time he laughed and rocked her against him. "Now, I know where little Fallyn gets her temper. Princess, it takes time, practice, and a safe space to learn a new *magick* skill. This barn offers none of that. Let's ride. We'll do it later."

She pulled free, scowling at him over her shoulder before she stomped out of the stall. "Well, when I'm able to communicate with you telepathically, it's going to be much easier to tell you what I think of your macho crap."

Amused, he watched her storm toward the tackroom. There was more than one way to link with another, he thought, smoothing Mustard's black mane. Hugh had recalled most of them five years ago when he regained his memories and powers after his thirtieth birthday, but he never forced a connection with any creature. He always allowed his two-legged and four-legged companions to make their own choices.

In his last life, he'd been left afoot when his previous mount died in an ambush. He'd reached out to the herd of wild horses and asked for a partner. Mustard answered that call and the two of them had been attached ever since. The young stallion hadn't hesitated when they came through the *Time Portal* that brought them from 1888 Liberty Valley to their new home more than a hundred years later.

The buckskin nosed Hugh's shoulder. *She will be with you tonight and tomorrow have her bring me more carrots. Apples too. There are never enough of those. She must reward me for sharing you.*

*I'll let her know.*

---

When she woke Friday morning, Rebekah discovered she was alone in the guestroom. She glanced at the radio-clock on the nightstand beside the double bed, noticing it was after ten. No wonder her older half-sister, Trina, had already left the room. She undoubtedly was downstairs helping Venus with a myriad of responsibilities. Yawning, Rebekah slowly pushed the blankets aside and sat up. She'd brought the three dogs with her the previous night, and they'd met Astra and Rowdy here at the Rocking J.

After she showered and dressed, Rebekah headed downstairs. She found Astra sitting at the kitchen table drinking tea and skimming through a stack of legal papers. Instead of one of the suits she wore to court, the older witch dressed casually in a blue tunic and black leggings, ballet slipper shoes on her feet. Freya, the matriarch of the hellhounds lay beneath the table, half snoozing while a tuxedo kitten attacked her slowly wagging, plumed black tail.

Rebekah glanced at the little girl clad in a pink t-shirt and blue overalls, tiny sneakers on her feet. A gold sun-shaped necklace, a gift from Meteor, hung on a chain around the toddler's neck. She happily sat with the animals in their cave. "When did the new kitty arrive, Fallyn?"

"Him mine." She petted the big black dog. "Her mine too."

"When it comes to her critter friends, she's definitely her mother's daughter." Astra looked up from her paperwork. "Trina and Rowdy are down training in the 'salon', the basement war-room. Venus and Hugh went riding. The young dogs went with them. I said we'd finish making lunch. There's 'Cowboy Soup' in the slow cooker. I've never seen anything like it before. I thought Rowdy was making chili, but he wasn't. It has meat, beans, onions, tomatoes, corn, potatoes, vegetables, and spices. Whenever I take the lid off to stir it, I want to eat it now, not wait for the cornbread he wanted to go with it."

"I'll make it in a few minutes." Rebekah dropped a pod in the brewer and stood near the counter, waiting for coffee to fill her mug. She eyed Fallyn again. "What's your kitty's name?"

"Him no say yet." Fallyn crawled out from under the table and sauntered toward Rebekah. "I want cookie."

"Wash your hands first or the cookie will taste like kitten and dog." Astra turned a page, not lifting her gaze from the work in front of her.

"No!" Fallyn stomped to Rebekah. "Cookie now! Gimme!"

"Clean hands or no cookie," her aunt ordered, attention unwavering from her work.

Rebekah grinned appreciatively before she used her *magick* to lift the child, floating her in the air to the sink. The unexpected thrill ride earned a squeal of delight when the faucets turned on by themselves. A short time later, Fallyn was ensconced below the table again, a giant chocolate chip cookie in one hand for her and treats for the dog and nameless kitten in the other.

"You spoil that child," Astra pointed out with a smile. "I hope you do the same when I have a daughter."

"I will." Rebekah popped a bagel in the toaster while she sipped coffee. "Do you need more tea?"

"Yes, please. Since Fallyn is making that cookie look so good, would you find one for me too?"

"Sure." Once she joined Astra at the table, Rebekah silently debated whether or not to share the adventure at the dog park the previous day or to wait until they were alone. The long steady stare from the dark cobalt blue eyes provided the answer. Her mentor already knew something had happened. "After school, I took out the dogs yesterday—"

"What happened? I had a message from the Stone Queen you were in trouble."

"She and her guards kept us safe." Rebekah heaved a sigh. "Latham showed up and tried to break inside the park, but he couldn't get through the wards you set on the gates. He had a fit when he couldn't open them."

"I updated the security after he attacked you last summer." Astra swirled the tea in her cup. "In the past five years since you came to live with me, I told him more than once to show respect and remember you were off-limits. You serve me, not him or my demon-father or the pack."

"Did Meteor tell you what they did to me in my past lives?"

"She didn't need to." Astra stretched out her hand to take Rebekah's. "I learned how they tortured and killed me when I was fourteen and served as my demon-father's altar the first time. As one of *Hecate's* priestesses, I saw your fate mirrored mine in too many lives. It's why I insisted on having you as my servant when I had to visit my father in Corbettstown. He may have waited, but he still has inappropriate plans for you and he's not the kind of man who takes 'no' for an answer."

Rebekah squeezed her older half-sister's hand. They had the same mother and different fathers while with Trina, it was the other way around. "I've been having nightmares about him raping and killing me since *Samhain*. Meteor has encouraged me to remember that as a *healer*, I know how to take bodies apart, not just put them back together."

"Fair enough. When Rowdy and I go to Corbettstown with her and Jed Corbett, I want you to start classes with Venus. Train with Trina and learn to use a blade. Then, if Latham manages to get you alone, you'll be able to defend yourself in more than one way."

"I miss my friends." Rebekah didn't say they were members of the shadow pack and she wanted to see Corrine the leader. "I'll come along and make sure they're safe."

"No." Astra shook her head. "Venus needs a *healer* here in case of an attack. Promise you'll stay with them and help Trina keep our sister and the younglings safe."

"I hadn't thought of that." Rebekah eased back in her chair. "You have a deal. I'll wait at the ranch this weekend and do my part to save lives."

———

Rowdy lowered his sword and allowed Trina Corbett, a tall, slender shifter, a chance to recover her balance. She'd dressed for a fight, opting for close-fitting black pants, a long-sleeved tight black shirt, and low-heeled boots. Similar to the style Venus preferred, Trina braided her long, ash-blonde hair, coiling it into a bun on the back of her head. She narrowed her sky-blue eyes, taking a few minutes to catch her breath.

He smiled at her. "You're doing well. Thanks for agreeing to practice with me."

"Don't patronize me." She stood out of reach and scowled at him. "I suck at this. I can't believe Venus told me to come down here with you."

"I told you. I have to sharpen my skills. I have an upcoming duel with Latham Sellers, and I intend to kill him for what he's done to my mate."

Trina shuddered. "If you go after him, Gunnolf Marvin will attack you for slaying his favorite executioner. He may thrash Latham occasionally, but Gunnolf doesn't allow anyone else the privilege."

"He may try to stop me, but he'll fail in this life." Rowdy glanced around the large cellar. They used the center of the room, staying on the wooden floor. Venus had rubber mats under some of the equipment and what she called a stationary bike. Large mirrors lined one wall and he used those so Trina could see how she looked when she used the broadsword Venus gave her.

"Gunnolf punishes any shifter who annoys him, not only the

ones the alpha wants disciplined like me. His deputies are the most dangerous. They won't hesitate to kill you. Even Corrine, Gunnolf's mate and favorite she-wolf can't stop all of them, but she'll die trying and the enforcer will go berserk again."

"I won't hide behind a woman." Rowdy lifted his sword. "Rest time is over. Attack me."

By the time they finished an hour later, she was able to block his strikes, then bring the fight to him. She focused on the battle and stopped telegraphing her intentions with her gaze. She was still a novice with a blade, but she had potential.

He sheathed his sword in the scabbard on his back and gestured toward the stairs at the end of the room. "You're a shifter and Thojedescar says he wants you to enforce the rules of his new pack. Think of the sword as another set of claws. When your skills improve, it will become a good tool, bigger than a knife but it will serve the same purpose."

"I hadn't thought of that." She put the blade in its place on the wall and led the way upstairs. "I need more practice. You gave me time and space, but a real adversary won't."

"Do you ask for it when you fight another shifter?"

"Good point. No, I don't."

Rowdy left the subject there. Part of being a *High Healer* was knowing when to advise a potential patient and when to bide his time. After he showered and changed to his usual attire of a suede shirt, brown pants, and low-heeled boots, he tied back his hair with a leather thong. In the kitchen, he found Astra setting the table while Rebekah put the finishing touches on the meal.

He ushered Freya outside where she promptly found a comfortable dog bed on the porch and curled up for a nap, one without a mischievous toddler and her new kitten. Back inside, he lifted Fallyn into her highchair. The tuxedo kitten stalked across the room to the center island, jumped onto a stool and began to wash its snow-white paws.

"How did the lesson go?" Astra flicked a quick glance at him, then proceeded to use a damp cloth to wipe cookie remains off

Fallyn's face and hands. "Did Trina provide you enough of a challenge?"

"She's talented and very aggressive." Rowdy ladled soup into bowls. "New swordsmen can be more dangerous than experienced ones because they don't know what works and what doesn't."

"That definitely helps you prepare. I'm glad she can fill in for me right now. Later, I'll be happy to have a bout or two with you."

"Much later, my own." He glanced at her, his gaze as warm as a kiss. "No swordplay while you carry my son."

Astra sniffed. "As if my daughter would complain when I teach her father a needed lesson in manners."

Rowdy heard footsteps on the porch moments before the door opened. Venus entered, followed by Holt. Before too much longer, all of them were seated at the table enjoying the meal. Topics of conversation ranged from the new fences to other improvements on the ranch to more training sessions in the basement salon.

After lunch, Trina carried Fallyn off for a nap and the kitten went too. Saying she had some legal responses to write and email to her paralegal, Astra headed upstairs. When Rebekah and Venus offered to clean up, Rowdy followed. It didn't surprise him to find his mate sitting on the edge of the double bed removing her shoes.

He glanced at her briefcase near the nightstand. "I thought you were going to work."

"Wake me in an hour." She yawned. "I'll do it then."

He chuckled, then sat beside her to take off his boots. "I could use a nap too."

She nestled close. He drew the crocheted blanket at the foot of the bed over them. In moments, she'd closed her eyes, her breathing slowed, and she drifted to sleep. His arms tightened around her. *Sex Magick* with her was surprisingly blissful even before she admitted she loved him, especially when she allowed him to hold her like this.

———

When he drove by the bakery on the way home, it was closed, and he didn't see Meteor's red Ford Explorer in the parking lot. Jed drove toward his house. "She must have gone out to the Rocking J to see the kids. Let's clean up and join them."

"Good idea." Gard stretched out long legs in the passenger seat. "Do you think we'll catch hell from your uncle when he hears you gave the crew tomorrow off? Wasn't he still upset because we're behind on our quotas?"

"He'll have to get over it." Jed pulled into the driveway, frowning when a Corbettstown patrol car parked behind his pickup. "I have to prepare to face him and the enforcer on Sunday. Now, I need to know why he sent one of his messengers."

"I've got your back." Gard adjusted his jacket, hiding the shoulder holster and pistol he'd loaded with silver bullets from view. "Keep it on the down-low, Jed. I don't want to shoot a cop."

"No worries." Jed opened his truck door and stepped out of the rig. He started toward the white sedan with the distinctive emblem for the Corbettstown Police Department, a five-pointed star with a wolf's head in the middle and lettering around the side proclaiming they protected and served. Not for the first time, he wondered who.

He nodded a greeting to the young, dark-haired man in the dark brown uniform, a beta shifter. "What's going on, Trey?"

"Three messages. Least of all, your uncle wants you there for dinner tonight." Treyton Corbett planted his feet, obviously ready for a smack-down. As a beta wolf, it wasn't in his nature to challenge an alpha. "Second, the police chief texted me and said to take you to your uncle. And most important, Corrine sent me. She'll keep the enforcer busy while you help me save my family."

# 23

"WHO IS CORRINE?" GARD CAME A LITTLE CLOSER. "I DON'T remember meeting a woman with that name at the Halloween Party at Frank's or during those interminable Sunday dinners."

"You wouldn't have. He ordered the enforcer to kill her at *Mabon*, the harvest festival in September. It's the first time the chief disobeyed an order, but Corrine is special." Treyton frowned thoughtfully. "I don't think you were there until after dinner, Jed. When they arrived that afternoon, Corrine came as Chief Marvin's pet wolf, wearing a collar and leash. He claimed she was being punished because she was still under a death sentence even though he hadn't done that to other lawbreakers."

"He did what?" Jed took an angry step forward, then forced himself to remember he was an alpha. He controlled his emotions now, not the other way around. "We're shifters, not toys. How dare Frank allow such an insult? I'll kill him and his damned lackey too."

"You can't. I know my mother begged the alpha for mercy, but he was furious after Corrine shit on his shoes and all over his house."

"Wait a minute." Jed ran a hand through his hair. "I'm confused. You just said she sent you here."

"She did. Okay, let me back up. When they got to the party, the enforcer sent Corrine to play in the backyard with the pups, the children while he drank beer and hung out with the guys on the deck. He said he needed to watch her and make sure she behaved appropriately. She didn't." Trey grinned appreciatively. "I mean all three of them were sitting there, the enforcer, the executioner and the alpha and she marked the kids as hers right in front of them."

"I don't get it." Gard shook his head, eyeing Jed. "What does that mean?"

"An alpha wolf claims members when they create a pack," Jed explained. "It means the kids won't come when Frank calls them or do what he says—"

"Or eat the meat he serves at his house. Corrine says, no more hunting humans or killing them regardless of the shapes that Latham makes them wear and her shifters will not eat them. Pretty damn funny when twenty kiddoes started throwing tantrums about the menu after she and the enforcer left that day."

"How many wolves does she have in her pack?"

"I'm not sure, Jed. When I got home, I told my brothers and sister we were leaving. They already knew. My little brother told me that Corrine marks the children she teaches to read when she's tutoring at the elementary school. My sibs were packing and some of Corrine's girlfriends were sanitizing the house. I went back to the office to have lunch with my mom—"

"How does she feel about you taking away your sibs?"

"She says for you to call her, Jed. Corrine arranged for Mom's cell phone to lose any numbers from Eagleville."

"I don't get it." Gard folded his arms. "What's the big deal? Why do you have to come right now? There's no statute on murder. Why can't it wait until after Frank is arrested? And who is Latham? I thought Gunnolf Marvin was in cahoots with Frank."

"My mom says there was a different Corrine before. When she died twenty-five years ago, Gunnolf lost it. Wolves mate for life and he's not one, but he left Corbettstown after her funeral. On his way out of town, he told my mom he was going to find a new Corrine and he wouldn't be back until he did."

"But he's been the enforcer more than thirty years." Jed rubbed his jaw. "How could he just leave? Who'd back up the alpha?"

"Latham did. He's a sorcerer, the pack executioner, and he enjoys killing. The enforcer doesn't so he lets Latham do it. He'd been working with Frank a long time. The two of them told your dad they could handle Gunnolf's job while he grieved. And Mom said everyone understood how devastated Gunnolf was. Well, the shifters did." Treyton shrugged. "Who knows about witches? They all stormed off on their broomsticks. And their allies, the fairies, elves, satyrs, *healers* went with them, including my bio-dad, my mom's original mate."

"A little bit more to it than that. My mate's a witch and you haven't heard her side of the story. Okay, answer Gard's question. Why today? Why now when I come to my uncle's house most Sundays."

"They're testing my little sister on Sunday. She doesn't change, Jed." Treyton took a ragged breath. "Corrine says they'll kill her then so they can eat her at the *Yule* parties. My mother will go crazy. She lost her first mate, and the alpha gave her to my stepdad. He went to *Summerland* three years ago."

"Is your mom still at work?" Gard asked, standing behind Jed.

"No, she has the day shift. She should be home by now. She's off this weekend. She's due back in the office on Monday morning."

"All right." Jed held out his hand. "Give me your cell phone."

Treyton hesitated, then slowly obeyed. He was a younger wolf and knew his place in the pack. He didn't dare disobey an older, more dominant male. When he had the phone, Jed scrolled through the contact list and found Hester Corbett's number.

When she answered, Jed asked if she was ready to leave. She said she was, that Corrine had arranged for transportation. Her friends were mythical creatures who couldn't be tracked by the shifters and the deputies wouldn't see them.

"Frank's angry because different parts of Eagleville are warded against him. I heard him complaining to Chief Marvin about it and the enforcer said he had enough trouble controlling the shifters. He wasn't going after the biggest coven in Washington State without help and his deputies weren't ready to fight witches."

"Well, that gives us some breathing room." Jed met Treyton's gaze. "I'm having Trey drop off his rig at the cop shop here and will keep him with me. We'll meet you and your other children in Eagleville."

"What happens if they can't change into wolves?"

"Nothing. I will not kill children." Jed contemplated sharing his own daughter was destined to be an *Animal Healer* and decided to keep the news to himself. He wouldn't jeopardize her safety and for now, he didn't know how trustworthy any of the Corbett wolves would be.

Silence while Hester contemplated the idea and then she said, "All right. We're coming. You'll really keep Trey safe?"

"I really will." Jed ended the conversation and returned the cell phone to its owner. "When your mother and sibs arrive safely, I'll call my uncle and tell him I'm busy tonight. Do I need to call the enforcer and give him the same message?"

"I wouldn't. Corrine's in trouble for stealing and wrecking his car. She said she's going to run him in the snow on the mountain when he threatened to make her eat dog food and chase 'Frisbees' at the dog park with humans. The enforcer will be fending off her attacks most of the evening."

"That should definitely keep him occupied until I kill him for insulting her."

"Give it up, Jed." Surprisingly, Treyton laughed. "She already warned him that she's going to kill him herself."

"Fair enough." Gard grinned. "A woman's gotta do what a woman's gotta do."

Treyton glanced at his vehicle, mingled hope and concern filling his youthful, handsome features. "What about the patrol car?"

"I'm calling my mate. She is related to the new *Bard* who will speak to her husband's cousin. By the time we finish, you will have the choice to remain with the Corbettstown police department or join the officers here."

"Your uncle will never allow it. I wanted to apply to different law enforcement agencies, but he refused to let me. Corrine said I should keep sending out my resumes and maybe he'd change his mind."

"I. have different rules in my pack." Jed kept his tones even. "As long as you follow them, I won't stop you from choosing your house, your job, or your potential mate. If you disobey me, I will punish you, but I won't kill you unless you've harmed an innocent. And your siblings won't be held accountable for any sins you commit, only their own."

———

*Rocking J Ranch,*
*Friday, November 30th, 2018*

Meteor's original plan to talk to Astra about the faulty clasp on the bracelet faded when Jed called about a shifter family seeking refuge. He brought the woman and her five children to the Rocking J and the Jamisons leaped into action. While Estelle, Rebekah and Trina cleaned and warded an old cabin, Orion took Gard and Holt to the attic to find appropriate furniture. The other men moved furniture, beds, tables, chairs, and dressers from the large house to the smaller dwelling.

Once it was agreed that they'd remain connected to their beloved Corrine, Astra helped Diana and Rowdy sever the family's bonds to the Corbettstown pack. They were attached to Meteor and Jed. When they finished the ceremony, everyone was ready to eat the meal Venus prepared. Pizza and salad accompanied the leftover soup and cornbread from lunch. Afterwards, the children joined Edwin and Quaid in the family room to watch a cartoon movie. Rowdy and Diana went with their older brother to help finish organizing their new home.

Fallyn didn't leave the kitchen with the other youngsters. Instead, she clambered up on Meteor's lap, reaching for the vintage gold necklace she'd worn for the rite. "Want back my prettie, Auntie. Gimme!"

"Not anymore, sweetheart." Jed drew a smaller version of the spoked sun with tiny animals from his shirt pocket. "Look what I made for you."

"Mine?" Fallyn's big blue eyes widened, and she lunged for it. "Gimme."

Meteor caught the little girl, holding her tight so she didn't tumble to the floor. "Careful. Don't fall. What do you say to him?"

"My fadda, the wolf. He make my prettie." Fallyn held out her hands again. "Gimme. Pease."

"Okay." Jed chuckled. He advanced on them, dropped to one knee, and slid the chain around the child's neck. "Now, you have your own and so does—" He paused, looking at Meteor. "So does your Aunt Meteor."

She appreciated the fact that he didn't share the fact she was the mother of their children in front of Hester Corbett. The older woman stood at the sink rinsing the dishes while Venus loaded the dishwasher.

Meteor rose to her feet. "Time for this little one to go to bed, Venus. I'll take her tonight."

"And I'll help." Astra gave Jed a solid onceover. "It looks like you're going to have a decent sized pack before we go to Corbettstown on Sunday. I remember Corrine as being a little doll that my demon-father preferred to my sisters and me."

"I'm sure none of you ever tried ripping out his throat in the middle of town in front of half the pack and a busload of tourists or shit all over Frank Corbett's house at a festival or lives under a death sentence for attacking him." Hester passed a large bowl to Venus. "I've warned Corrine several times to watch her temper. She's a primal-alpha, a dominatrix who can lead a bunch of shifters, but it doesn't mean the enforcer will be able to continue protecting her from a mob of misogynists like our old alpha, Latham, the pack executioner, and some of the deputies."

"Will my father even try?" Astra demanded, narrowing her

sunset dark eyes. "I remember him going more for expediency than morality. Of course, he is a demon."

"We'll talk about it later." Jed took his coffee cup to the counter. "I need to lay out the rules for my pack and I've already promised there won't be any sacrifices."

Meteor nodded when she saw the unspoken question rise in her older sister's face. That was something she and Jed agreed on, even if they weren't ready to resolve all of their differences. She would lead the pack with him until he found another alpha female to take her place. She left the room, climbing the stairs to Fallyn's bedroom. "Bathtime, first."

The black kitten rose from the landing and followed them. Astra eyed him. "So, where did he come from?"

"Fallyn found him at the feedstore yesterday." Meteor dropped a kiss on her daughter's forehead. "Do you know his name yet?"

"He say, Wibberfuss."

"Hmm, that's an unusual one." Meteor led the way into the room, catching a glimpse of Astra's amusement. "What?"

"It's actually, Wilberforce." Astra leaned down to pet the long-haired tuxedo kitten. "However, Fallyn has her own interpretations. You get the jammies and I'll go start the water running in the tub."

"Works for me."

While the little girl happily splashed and played with her toys a few minutes later, Meteor sat on the edge of the tub and watched. She held out her right arm toward her sister who sat on the toilet. "The other night, I was at Jed's for supper, and he gave me this bracelet. It's part of the *talipenlace* set. He said he was concerned someone might have stolen my shape."

"Fair enough." Astra nodded, narrowing her cobalt blue eyes. "We know somebody's done it before and K.I.L.L.E.D. the pair of you. What's the issue?"

"I tried to take it off and put it away when I got home, but I can't find the clasp."

"I told Venus to warn you about these thrice-damned things after *Samhain*." Astra pulled on the chain around her neck, revealing the center disk of her necklace, a five-pointed star inside a circle. "I haven't been able to take off any of the jewelry, not since I participated in a *S.E.X Magick* rite with Rowindache at *Samhain*."

Meteor gasped, staring at the other witch. "You didn't?"

"I was distracted by what we were doing." Red crept into Astra's cheeks. "I thought it was just S.E.X. Great, but it shouldn't have meant anything except he asked me if the set was mine or our father's. It was a trick and I fell for it. I insisted the *talipenlace* belonged to me as well as Rowindache's powers. Did you agree to wear the bracelet willingly?"

Meteor slowly nodded. "And I swear the creatures on it respond to my touch. They never did before."

"Because it's truly yours now." Astra drew a deep breath. "After *Samhain*, I told Venus to warn you about the *talipenlace* set."

"She did, but I thought the rules only applied to the necklace."

"Well, apparently, they don't. No matter what, you have to refuse to wear the rest of the set willingly. You must deny it's yours. Don't repeat the soul-matching vows, or we're all lost."

"All right." Meteor pointed to the necklace she wore. "What about this? Why can I remove it?"

"Have you ever claimed it as your property?"

"No. I use it as a focus when we're severing the bonds to the Corbettstown pack, but I can give it to any of my children." Meteor glanced at her daughter, yawning in the tub. "Time for someone to be washed, dried, then tucked into bed. We'll talk more about this later."

"Sounds like a plan."

A short time later, Meteor lowered the child into her new bed, tucking a handmade patchwork quilt over the small body.

"Want my blankie and my pony and—

The stuffed horse came next, along with its companion, a shaggy wolf. Wilberforce jumped up and found a spot between the toys, cuddling next to the little girl.

Fallyn yawned. "Story now. 'Bout Eggie-bert."

Meteor took the favorite picture book Astra handed her and

opened it. Halfway through the tale about a young dragon with rainbow scales, brilliant pink wings and popsicles down her back, Fallyn fell asleep.

Putting the book on the nightstand, Meteor kissed her daughter's cheek. "Sleep tight, sweetie."

Astra turned on the unicorn-shaped nightlight and the two of them headed into the hallway. "Let's go have a meeting of the minds in my room."

"Works for me," Meteor said.

———

On the way back from the dog park to Corbettstown, A.J. was on the radio pitching a fit. Nobody could find Treyton who disappeared during the early part of his shift. Someone parked his patrol car, in pristine condition, in front of the police department. After looking at it, Gunnolf drove to Hester's old two-story house on the outskirts of town.

Her crew did a good job, Corrine thought. Despite the rain, the landscaping was perfect. The rolling lawns had been mowed. The fallen leaves from the maples were raked into piles. The windows gleamed, glass shining in the twilight. She couldn't tell from here, but she expected the inside would reek of bleach and household cleaners.

He snapped on the lead. "Come along, my wolf. You can sniff around and see what you learn."

*'Not a K-9. Hire one.'* Corrine growled when he pulled on the leash. *'Don't do that!'*

"Then, heel."

Deliberately, she sauntered closer to him. It was snowing on the mountain. He hadn't enjoyed running through the woods after her, but she figured if she was going to freeze while he fucked her, he should share the misery. By the time he caught her, and they returned to the car, the snow soaked through his coat and boots.

He said he'd wait to have her, and she remained in her wolf

form. She dried off under the table at the café during lunch, smirking when he sneezed a few times while he ate a huge steak, fries and drank numerous cups of hot tea. He had to use his personal *magick* to keep from catching a cold. Payback was hers.

It rained most of the afternoon when they reached lower elevations. She kept sliding through mud puddles at the dog park while he stood and snickered. Everyone thought he was a wonderful law enforcement officer, trying to build community when she was the one doing the work. She was totally wet and muddy from chasing stupid toys from humans who could barely throw them a decent distance. She was a wolf, damn it. She added a touch of shifter *magick* and proceeded to shake herself dry.

Mud and water covered Gunnolf from head to toe. She gave him a wolf grin. *'Being a good hostess and sharing, Master. You like it?'*

"Very amusing." A towel appeared in his hand. He dried his shaved head and then his face. "You're still not clean enough to sleep in my bed. Looks like a 'doggie' bath is on the agenda when we get home."

# 24

*Rocking J Ranch,*
*Friday, November 30th, 2018*

ROWDY SAT IN ONE OF THE ROCKERS ON THE BUNKHOUSE'S COVERED porch, watching the moon play hide and seek in the clouds. A cold winter wind blew across his face, and he tasted snow in the breeze. They might have a few flakes before morning, but he doubted it'd be enough to close the roads or keep them from visiting Corbettstown on Sunday. Hugh stood sentry near the other houses in the event any of the shifters came calling and Rowdy had sent the two younger hellhounds to help him.

Their mother lay close by Rowdy, still recovering from the attack last week. He leaned back in the chair, closing his eyes for a moment. He'd sent word to the *dracklegons,* that were half human and half dragon, about the proposed challenges, his to Latham Sellers and Jed's to his uncle. At the very least, the giant, winged lizards intimidated the inhabitants of *Trilunun.*

At the most, the *Mage-Priests* enforced the long-established laws, burning those who broke the sacrosanct ones in the *Fires of*

*Eternity* and eating them. There hadn't been an answer from the lawgivers yet. One would come. Rowdy didn't doubt it and hoped it'd arrive before he confronted Latham Sellers, once known as Lavarutesel, the apprentice mage to Astra's demon father.

A memory stirred, not from one of Rowdy's past lives but of the original soul-matched night with Satiranika, who'd been given to him in a ceremonial rite. After he treated a patient, he'd returned to their chamber to discover she'd left to go to her one-time lover. Rowdy went after her, heading into the forbidden halls of the *Ethlestial* priests. He expected to fight for her. It might only be words, but it could also be a battle with more than one opponent.

Facing their swords might mean his death. It was a good day to die, but he prayed to the *Goddess* that it'd be a better time to live. If at all possible, he'd see to it that his new *Chosen* regretted this insult. She was his mate, given to him by her aunt, the regent of her land. By the *Lady and Lord*, Satiranika wouldn't forget that again.

Finally, at the end of one wide aisle, he recognized Lavarutesel, accompanied by two other male *dracklegons*. Rowdy had advanced on the trio, attempting to measure which was the most dangerous.

"You trespass, wizard." It wasn't Lavarutesel who spoke, but the fierce, young soldier wearing armor beside him. "Explain yourself and prepare to die."

"I come for my *Chosen*." Rowdy had raised his own sword to guard himself, but not to attack, at least not yet. He looked past the young *drack* in warrior-red to the older one behind Lavarutesel. "He called her from our chamber on our soul-matching night."

Horror filled the warrior's slitted green eyes. Sheathing his sword, he took a step forward. He dropped to one knee, baring his neck for a killing stroke. "I knew nothing of this disgrace. Slay me now for my misspeaking."

"No. There's been too much dying in all our countries." Rowdy admired the youngster's honesty. "Live and learn, *drack*. All is not as it seems."

"A good lesson for anyone to know," The silvery-scaled priest turned a furious gaze on Lavarutesel and hissed. "Nephew, does this

*Warpathian* speak truth? Did you steal his *Chosen* mate? The one he traded his soul to have?"

"She came on her own, saying she preferred my nest to his bed." Words tumbled from Lavarutesel's mouth. "I tried to talk her into returning to him."

"Words lie. Actions do not." The ancient lashed his tail against the floor, before pointing with a clawed hand to the covered dishes on a tray outside a door. "You fed her when you should have killed her and sent her on a *Journey to Rebirth*. Now, she must be meat forever, as must you."

The judgment evoked a sudden outpouring of excuses from Lavartesel as he attempted to defend himself. All blame was cast on Satiranika who had misled him, a heinous offense to most *Ethlestials* who respected the laws their councils created and insisted everyone else do the same.

Rowdy waited until there was silence, then repeated his initial claim. "I've come for my *Chosen*."

"Having her as a mate disgraces a *High Healer*, a man of honor." The eldest *Mage-Priest* decreed, fury filling his face. "We will kill her for you."

"No. Serving as my *vaslattel*, a secondary mate, subordinate to the other wives and any female servants in the household will be punishment enough for one of royal blood, especially when her children reflect this lower status."

The old *dracklegon* considered the point and then glanced at Lavarutesel. "And this priest who disgraces his *relkinam*? What do we tell his family?"

"Let him live and suffer too. Send him as an envoy to speak for us to the mortals. That duty will preclude him having a mate or younglings for at least a thousand years. Neither he nor my mate have earned a glorious death in the *Fires*."

His words earned a smile from the ancient priest. "You are the one who has been wronged. Let it be as you say."

"I will not return to him." Satiranika's voice came from behind the three *dracklegons*. "He is of low birth, a peasant who never knew his mother."

"Aah, then his punishment fits you better than I thought." Faint amusement touched the elderly priest's eyes. "Welcome to our *relkinam*. Her dishonorable sire was my grandson. I am Kudesarvel."

The offering of one's name was true acceptance to the *dracklegon* clans. "I am Rowindache. My *Chosen* speaks truth. I do not know much about my parents. My mother was a pilot who died when her sky-ship crashed. My father was an entertainer who took the *Journey to Rebirth* when the hotel where he worked caught fire. He saved as many guests as he could, but his injuries—"

"Their son honors the ones who went before by showing mercy to those who've wronged him," Kudesarvel announced. "Take your *Chosen* and leave our halls. Enjoy your soul-matching time together if such is possible with a recalcitrant *vaslattel*."

The trio stepped aside, and he glanced at the woman in leggings and a star-splashed tunic. "You have found a better match than you think, *Majeenler*. Be happy with your new mate."

"Never." She ignored the respectful use of her title and lunged past him. Something glimmered in her hand, a sword. "He will be meat for your roasting first."

"You left your blade where she could take it?" the young warrior demanded. "Cousin, what were you thinking?"

"I gave up my sword when I joined the *Poltaltet* Guild. We talk about our disputes. We do not battle, Iarvosarvel."

"No, you always send my guild to die for you." Iarvosarvel whirled, caught Satiranika's wrist and wrenched the hilt of the blade from her grasp with little effort. He propelled her toward Rowdy. "Let it be as the *Highest of the High Mage-Priests*, my grandsire declared. No blood this night, not in our quarters."

"A fair bargain." Rowdy sheathed his own sword. He avoided the blow when she struck him and snagged her wrist. He ignored it when she kicked him, grateful for the protection of his boots. He pulled her close enough to sling her over his shoulder, the proper way to carry a captive when he might have to fight.

Rowdy accepted the blade Iarvosarvel offered, noticing the runes spelled out his mate's name. "Send whatever else she brought to my chambers."

"I'll see to it." Iarvosarvel nodded agreement. "When you have your *vaslattel* secured, perhaps you would care to join me and my guild-mates for our sword practices. It will take a long time for the *Mage-Priests* to open the *Time-Portal* to our new home."

"He's nothing but an old *healer*," Satiranika pointed out. "You could kill him a hundred times and I will rejoice when you do."

"She has much to learn." Rowdy met the other warrior's gaze. "I will enjoy the opportunity to cross swords with you. I'll send word when my affairs are in order."

"After your war-games, then you may join me for a glass of wine. We will discuss honor and *Ethlestial* lore," Kudesarvel said. "I have sought a new student for many years, one fit to hear and pass on my truths."

"Indeed, you give me too much credit." Rowdy bowed slightly. "My pride sent me after my newly chosen mate."

"To be truly proud, you must have honor. You have a great deal to learn as well, Rowindache. Come to me when you are ready."

"That will be eons after forever." Satiranika tried to twist free. "He's less than the sludge at the bottom of sewers, real *garungap*."

"And you are mine. What does that make you?" He tightened his grip on her legs and bowed again before he turned away. He strode back toward their chamber in the opposite direction of the castle. He'd save his energy to take and tame his new *vaslattel*. For now, it'd shame her enough to be carried away like a parcel or sex-slave from the marketplace.

---

After the discussion with Meteor, Astra found Venus and reminded her about the price the *talipenlace* set would extort. The enchanted set of jewels were created by a wizard and then he sealed them with his heart, mind, blood, and soul in an eternal spell-casting before

giving them to his mated witch. Once she participated in a ceremonial rite, she'd wear the ornaments, the *talipenlace* sets for the rest
of her life. She and the wizard would be bonded forever, through
*Time, Death, and Rebirth.*

While Venus admitted the necklace or *amunecdant* was hers, and
Meteor wore one of the bracelets, neither of them had repeated the
soul-matching vows. It meant they had their own powers and
weren't committed to the wizards who wanted to claim them. They
were still the *Trecesalty,* the three-royal witch-queens born at the
same time, a sign of immense favor by the *Goddess* and her consort,
the *Horned God.*

Venus had said she intended to sleep a few hours before she
relieved Hugh to stand watch. Meteor had gone to bed as well.
When Astra went to her room, she discovered it was empty. She
swung a jacket around her shoulders and headed downstairs, leaving
through the side door. She headed for the path to the bunkhouse.

She found Rowdy sitting in one of the rocking chairs, Freya
sleeping nearby. "What are you doing?"

"Remembering our first night together." He held out his hand.
"Your grandfather, the *High Mage-Priest* offered to teach me what
he'd learned in his long life."

"I don't remember much about him yet, other than he led the rest
of the *Ethlestial Mage-Priests* in their ceremonies and wanted to kill
me." Sighing, she let Rowdy draw her down on his lap and pillowed
her head on his shoulder. "Did you ever go to him?"

"A few times." Rowdy tipped up her chin. "Have you been
making trouble for my saddle partner, Hughondear and my good
friend, Thojedescar, *Vaslattel?*"

Rowdy's use of that term created a *geas* that according to their
ancient laws, impelled her to tell him the truth. She narrowed her
eyes and glared at him, meeting the dark gaze. "I protect my sisters,
always. I won't let them be bound like I am or see them lose their
*magick.*"

"Have I taken yours?" He feathered his thumb across her lips.
"Or are we stronger together than we were apart?"

She hesitated, unsure of the answer. Although she loved him more than she'd ever thought possible, she was afraid of what the future held. She served *Hecate, the Goddess of Death and the Cross-roads*, but she couldn't see their destiny or even if they had one together. "I don't know, Rowindache."

"An honest reply." He shifted, rising to his feet, somehow managing to continue to hold her in his arms. He carried her toward the door. "So, let's go to bed and you can repeat your vows again during our *Sex-Magick* mating."

"I've already said them twice while you had me." She laced her arms around his neck. "It's not my fault if you didn't listen."

"And you'll say them again tonight." He closed the door behind them. "Payback, *Vaslattel* for disobeying my wishes. I've told you more than once to allow your sisters and their mates to decide their paths and leave the four of them alone."

She gasped when he turned, held her against the door and his mouth claimed hers. She kissed him back, somehow knowing that he intended to take her the same way he had the first time at *Samhain*. When he lifted his head, she moistened suddenly dry lips. "I do what I want, Rowindache."

"And now you'll do what I want, my own." He smiled. "More than once. Tell me the truth. Have you ever used *magick* to remove your clothes?"

"Of course not. All *magick* comes with a price, *Capostrol* and I wasn't paying it for something so frivolous."

He chuckled. "Well, there's a first time for everything. And I'm not waiting to have my witch. I'll have you up against the door before I take you to bed. I'll make sure you like it."

"I always do. The spell you cast the first night in *Trilunon* when you made me your *vaslattel* sees to that."

———

Meteor joined Trina and Rebekah in the kitchen to make breakfast on Saturday morning. It came as little surprise that after feeding the livestock, Venus and Hugh were still patrolling the ranch. Jed and Gard had left to meet their logging crew at the new site so nobody would realize they weren't putting Corbett Logging first. Rebekah said Astra was at the bunkhouse discussing potions with Rowdy.

Meteor wasn't sure if she believed that story or not but didn't pursue the topic. She stirred up a batch of pancake batter and began cooking. Saturday morning cartoons wouldn't occupy the three children for long.

Trina stood at the center island, slicing fresh fruit for a salad. In the middle of setting up the coffee pot, Rebekah pulled out her cell phone when it rang. She didn't swipe the screen and the ringtone buzzed a second, then a third time.

"Who is it?" Meteor flipped the hotcakes on the griddle and turned from the stove when the phone sounded again. "Why don't you answer?"

"It's your father." Rebekah shuddered. "And if I don't talk to him, he'll make me pay for it. He'll send Latham after me or another of his obedient deputies—

"Not now, not here at the Rocking J." Meteor interrupted. "I'm the kitchen witch and I consider this hallowed ground." She didn't have her wand so the flapjack turner would suffice. She pointed it at the smart phone in Rebekah's shaking hands. *Lady and Lord, bless and keep me and mine safe in our sacred space. White-light us, protect us and those we love in this place. Nothing evil may enter here. And we live in this house without fear....*"

Rebekah stared at the blank screen. "What did you do?"

"Used *magick* to block him." Meteor swung back to scoop the pancakes onto a serving platter and slid it into the oven to stay warm. "From now on, his calls will be dropped. He'll probably assume there's a problem with the cell towers and never realize they're going wherever the *Goddess* chooses."

"I'm impressed." Trina carried the bowl to the table. "Could you do that to my new phone too? There are certain people in Corbettstown, I don't want to hear from."

"No worries. We'll fix it after we eat." Meteor ladled more

batter onto the griddle. "Did Treyton do evil deeds for my demon-father or the alpha?"

"He only came to the enforcer's house once when I was there." Trina placed napkins at each setting. "Last summer he visited the alpha a few times and asked Frank about moving to a different police department, but the alpha refused to let him."

Rebekah began to fill glasses with milk. "Did the enforcer beat him for wanting a transfer?"

"No, he was very careful and polite. He seemed to accept Frank's decrees about keeping young wolves close to the pack until they were mature enough to be on their own."

"Very smart." Meteor glanced toward the back door when it opened, and Astra entered. "He wasn't one of those who attacked us last week in Monte Cristo. I'd have recognized his smell."

"I think he'll be a good addition here." Trina nodded a respectful greeting to the older witch. "He and his mother are happy to have their younglings safe from the "sorting" tomorrow. The alpha will be looking for what he calls 'sweet meats' to serve as dessert at *Yule*. Corrine is trying to stop him, but there are risks."

"How do we know they won't be tracked from Hester's house?" Meteor put the last of the batter on the skillet. "Cherry scoured her home. You may have hidden your tracks, Trina, but how could Hester with such short notice?"

Rebekah and Astra shared a meaningful look. Then, Astra said, "There is a subversive female element in the town and now I know the leader. Once Hester left with her children, Corrine's women will have sanitized everything. Nothing will remain that could lead anyone to Hester or her family."

"Corrine arranged for her followers to cleanse Cherry's home after she left. The women will scrub every room, including the carpets at Hester's," Trina said. "Sheets, blankets, curtains, and small furnishings will be removed. The bathrooms and all the appliances will reek of strong household cleaners, ones that burn a shifter's nose and throat. Bleach will have been poured down the drains too. I did that in my rooms at the enforcer's and Corrine promised to take care of the rest of the house after I fled."

"Once she was taken by the alpha who refused to let her change packs, Trina, Cherry and I made sure that none of the higher-ups or the older females know most of the younger women are practicing birth control and plotting their own escapes from the pack," Rebekah explained. "As they filter out of town, the ones still waiting hide their trail."

"Rebekah and I warded the rebels. It's why our demon father hasn't learned their plans." Astra froze at the sound of boots on the back porch. "This is female business, so we don't share it with wizards or male shifters, Meteor."

When her sister used that matter-of-fact tone, Meteor knew better than to argue. If she did, Astra wouldn't hesitate to block memories or future actions. She'd been a judge in a long-ago time in a distant realm, one who used the law for her own ends. *And I don't want to start and lose an argument with her.*

"All right." Meteor turned off the burner and moved the griddle to the cool side of the stove. "You're the eldest of the *Trecesalty*, Astra. You know best when it comes to dealing with our demon-father. Now, let's fetch the children and help them wash up for breakfast."

# 25

---

"WAKE UP, MY PUPPY. TIME FOR BREAKFAST."

"Tired." She slid deeper into the blankets, burying her face in the pillows. "Not hungry."

Yesterday exhausted her. She'd spent too much time switching between forms so she could read the files on his desk while he was in and out of the office. It cut deep to learn he wouldn't stop Treyton's eight-year-old sister from going early to her testing. Like most in the Corbettstown pack, she was too young to shift. There was no way the little girl could turn into a wolf and when she failed, she'd be killed and eaten by the pack at their *Yule* festival.

Corrine rarely cried. It didn't do any good. She'd hastily changed back into her wolf when she heard Gunnolf's boots in the hallway and pretended to be sleeping on the dog bed behind his desk. Silently, she sobbed and contemplated how she'd facilitate getting an entire family out of town, something she'd never done before. Once she made those arrangements, she had to find a way to notify Treyton and not allow Gunnolf to interfere with her plans.

That meant claiming her old boyfriend as part of her tiny, emerging pack and staging an argument with the enforcer so he wouldn't think she was cheating on him. He'd been with the pack too long, more than three hundred years. Even if he didn't realize it, he thought like a shifter. He'd have killed Treyton. Then, Gunnolf would have taken her until she conceived and started whelping his younglings. He didn't have any idea that she was part of the group of young women who practiced safe sex. There wouldn't be any new wolflings in Corbettstown until the sorting and killing stopped.

Once she'd had Gunnolf's attention, she kept him distracted the rest of the morning, all afternoon and throughout the evening. Of course, the man thought it was his idea. She certainly wasn't telling him otherwise.

He patted her butt. "Stop sulking. We're leaving for work in an hour and a half."

"Go by yourself."

"Not happening, my pet. Your 'beta boy' is running loose somewhere. He's cut his tie to the pack, and I haven't found him yet. When I do—"

"Don't hurt him. He's sweet." She rolled over, facing him and propped up on an elbow. "Please. He—"

"That's up to him." Gunnolf trailed a finger down her cheek. "He confesses, gives up the names of his confederates. Brings back his family so the alpha has his sister for *Yule*. Your old fuck-buddy dies easy. He doesn't talk? Then, he still dies. It's just a little worse." Gunnolf paused. "Actually, it's a lot worse. Latham shows no mercy when I let him execute a shifter."

She gasped, staring into his darkening gaze. "No. I won't let you. Either of you."

"You're mine, Corrinadora." He already wore his light brown, uniform shirt and the slacks she'd ironed last week. His jaw tightened, turning his rugged features into an expressionless mask.

"You've been mine since I met you the first time. Now, get up. Take your shower. Come have breakfast."

He left the bedroom before she answered. She buried her head in the pillows and burst into tears. *What did I do? I had to save them. I had to. And now Trey's going to be tortured, murdered. Gunnolf didn't say it, but he'll have him ripped to pieces and let him hear the pack quarrel over his bones before he dies. What did I do?*

Dimly she heard a woman's voice in her mind. One she knew from childhood. One she'd known before that. "Your job, Corrinadora. You're doing your job. And your enforcer is way out of line. You need to rein him in before he gets worse."

"What?" Corrine murmured. "I don't understand. What's my job? I'm an alpha. I have to protect my pack, save them from Frank —" Her voice faded for a moment. "Make things better."

"And you will. We will. First, you have to remember who and what you are. Let's start with something easy. Our last few lives."

"No, let's start with the name both of you are calling me. Explain that. Then, tell me who you are."

"Sounds good."

By the time she showered, dressed in jeans and a T-shirt and headed into the kitchen, she knew all about the realm they'd traveled from to come here and why. It didn't surprise her to learn Gunnolf was a *priest-mage* who'd destroyed the place in a jealous rage when he discovered he'd been sent to service a witch queen and give her children. He'd never be king, although his three infant daughters would rule their world someday.

"They're in Eagleville."

"That's right. And he's still furious about being passed over. So, he traded his immortal soul and became a warlock first. Since he felt he was used for stud service, he demanded the talents of an incubus, a minor demon who derives his power from sex. He needs a lot of it, but he can store the energy he receives."

"I know about the storage jars. What about you?"

"That's another story. Eat first and I'll tell you later."

Corrine followed directions. At least, now she understood why her scrambled eggs, rashers of bacon, slab of ham, and toast were still hot. He hadn't dished up when he heard her footsteps, the way he always claimed. He'd used a tiny bit of *magick* instead to keep the food warm. She eyed him under her lashes. "Did Treyton arrest any of the people you wanted him to find?"

"All of them. He completed the assignment I gave him before he took his family away. Stay out of the toolshed. Latham will be here to get them later today." Gunnolf cut into his ham. "Finish your meal. We need to go."

"They're criminals. You said they're wanted in other parts of the county." At his stern look, she picked up her fork. "You have to send them to those departments. It's the right thing to do."

He laughed, leaned across to kiss her. "Oh, my sweet, hot little pet. Don't you know by now I do what I want, and it usually isn't what people consider right?"

"You did right by me when I was a wolfling. You've saved me more than once from being killed by a crazy alpha like Frank."

"Another reason not to eat humans."

"But you're going to let the pack eat the ones in the toolshed."

"Don't worry. If they manage to stay out of reach for a full day and night once Latham changes them into prey, they earn their freedom."

She scooped up more eggs. "Have any of them ever done that?"

"Not since last spring. They spend too much time sitting around playing on their electronic devices. They're fat, out of shape and can't outrun the hunting party. Most of the meat is brought to Frank and he roasts it for the festivals. Latham always chooses either the worst criminal or the smartest one to be the reward for a good hunt. He is disemboweled, ripped to shreds, and eaten alive while he hears the shifters quarrel over his bones."

Gunnolf's matter-of-fact tone shocked her although she'd heard as much from the woman who'd shared their past. Once they finished eating, she cleaned the kitchen while he took food and water out to the prisoners. She hurried through her chores, then hustled into the main bedroom to take her burner phone out of the tampon box in the bathroom.

She debated texting Treyton, since Andrel had sent word, she was on a special assignment for the police chief this weekend. Then, Corrine decided against it. If her phone was tapped, they'd use it to find Trey and his family. She didn't want to jeopardize Andrel's position in the department because others might realize her bestie was part of the shadow pack.

Instead, she contacted the sheriff's office in Eagleville. For safety's sake, she made it look like it came from the cop shop in Corbettstown. She said the police chief was holding wanted felons on his property because he didn't have anyone trustworthy to take them out of town until Monday and needed assistance. Once she added details about where to find them, she hastily ended the call.

Still in the ensuite, she did her hair and makeup before she went into the main bedroom to dress. She was buttoning her scoop-necked beige blouse when Gunnolf came into the room, carrying the leash. A very short, flowered skirt and brown thigh-high stockings lay on the bed. Her chocolate-brown stilettos sat nearby. "I'm almost ready."

"Didn't you forget something?" He paused on the way to the closet to get his jacket.

"You're the one who freaks out if I wear panties." She reached for her skirt. "Not me."

"Always testing, my puppy. You're always testing." He snapped his fingers.

An orgasm raced through her, followed by a second, then a third. She collapsed onto the bed still shaking, wanting more. "Have me now."

He chuckled and shook his head. "You're going to have to wait."

When he came close enough, she snagged his tie and pulled him close enough to kiss. "Not my thing." She laced her arms around his neck and pressed against him, excitement building. "Let's stay home today."

"You're such a temptation." His mouth teased hers for a

moment. "Sorry, my pet but after running away yesterday, we have to be responsible now."

She gasped when he cupped the golden curls between her legs. "Please."

"I wish I could, but I don't like being late for work."

She rose to meet his hand when he slid two fingers into her and matched the strokes, spasming again and again. He unbuttoned her blouse with his free hand, bent his head to kiss her neck, then moved onto her breasts. After two more climaxes, he left her on the bed. He put away her clothes, the equivalent of a uniform for the cop shop and her shoes.

He glanced over his shoulder at her. "*Change.*"

"What?" She stared at him, baffled. "You took my things. I don't understand."

"Yes, you do. *Change.* You don't come to work as a human until tomorrow. *Change.*"

Moments later, she was a wolf. Lips curled, teeth bared, she stalked toward him. He clipped the leash onto her collar. When he ruffled her fur, she snarled and snapped at him. "Soon, my pet. As soon as everything's organized at the office, I'll fuck your brains out."

*That's his stock in trade,* a woman's voice murmured inside Corrine's head. *He always thinks sex will solve anything and everything. You'll teach him better.*

---

*Liberty Valley, Washington*
*December 1888*

It'd taken Marshal Rad Morgan and his posse almost a week of long days in their saddles to reach Corbett's Town. The biggest problem had been making enough silver bullets since it required extra high heat to melt the metal. Somehow, the two women, Astrid and Kallisto Hunter who called themselves witches were able to help with the task. It meant they could pursue the rogue shapeshifters who'd come after his adopted daughters much sooner.

Cedar shake buildings lined the muddy street. Oddly enough, Rad didn't see many people and there wasn't any music coming from the saloons. To the right were several houses but before they reached them, he spotted the town marshal's office. Rad rode closer. He dismounted, wrapped the reins around the hitchrail.

He glanced at those who accompanied him, his younger brother, Kyle, sister-in-law, Nina, the witches, Trace Burdette, her husband Zeb Prescott and their segundo, Lars Swenson who'd made the silver ammunition. All of them were crack shots and even better, they didn't doubt their enemies could turn from human to wolf and back again.

"Wait here while I check in with the law," Rad said, unfastening the loop that tied down his pistol while he rode. He removed the warrants from his saddlebags. "Then, we'll find the men we're after."

"He's one of them." Kallisto Hunter pointed out.

"Don't know that for sure. We'll give him a chance to do the right thing." Rad stepped up on the boardwalk. When he walked inside, he noticed the office was similar to his own, a central room, three cells and a curtained off alcove. Surprisingly, he glimpsed a large cradle near the bed.

Grayson Mallory, a wiry, lean man with a shock of white hair sat behind the desk, whisky bottles on a shelf nearby. A silver wolf lay behind him on a folded blanket. She lifted her head and looked at Rad but didn't bark or make a sound. She kept her golden-brown eyes on him.

"Haven't seen you in damned near a year, Morgan." Grayson's polite smile didn't touch dark eyes. "What's the occasion?"

"Some miscreants from here tried abducting my daughters. I want to arrest them, take them back to stand trial."

"Sounds reasonable. Got any names? Witnesses?"

"Both. And the judge signed off on the warrants." Rad walked across the room and handed the paperwork to the other lawman.

Grayson's gaze narrowed as he read the orders. "Me? The mayor? Are you loco?"

"No. Figure you were when you sent killers after my children." Rad glanced at the wolf. "I'll be back for you when I have the others. Find someone to look after your pet."

Turning, he headed for the door. He sensed, rather than heard Grayson move and spun around to see the older man pull a gun, aiming the pistol at him. He pulled the trigger.

Rad went for his own '45 Colt, afraid he was too late, and he'd never see his wife again or meet the baby due in the spring. *Bethany, I'm sorry.*

The wolf leaped, a chain rattling. Her teeth sank into Grayson's arm and a hundred pounds of angry animal pulled him out of his chair. The bullet hit the plank ceiling, but Rad's silver rounds landed in Grayson's chest.

Rad advanced on the dying man, booted the pistol out of reach. "Didn't have to be this way."

Grayson managed to turn his head, blood covering his chest. He eyed the wolf. "Bad girl."

"Not to me." Rad looked at her too. He knew it sounded foolish. "Thank you."

She sat down on her haunches, tilted her head to one side, gave him what was almost a dog's grin. Her voice sounded in his head, low and sweet. *'Mean that?'*

"What?" Rad continued to hold his own weapon, although he didn't intend to shoot her. He just wanted to be safe if Grayson Mallory rallied. "Yes, of course, I do. You saved my life."

*'Turn me loose. Save my pups.'*

"No!" The town marshal choked on his blood. "They're dead. They're meat now."

*'Mine. Not meat. Never!'*

It sounded right to Rad. Let her have the wolf pup lives in exchange for his. He moved toward her and unfastened the large silver lock on the chain attached to a jeweled collar.

She licked his hand. *'Thank you.'*

"Be sorry, Morgan." Grayson tried to lift his head. "She's grief-stricken."

A moment later, she'd flown through the door before Rad could warn her about his posse. He hurried after her. When he reached the door, he saw the group cantering behind her as she raced up the street. Grateful, they hadn't shot her, he untied his horse and joined them. The wolf didn't head for a barn or leave town. Instead, she ran into a small, wooden building with a cupola holding a large bell.

"It's a school." Rad stared at his younger brother. "Why would they have her puppies there?"

Kallisto Hunter vaulted from the saddle, rifle in hand. "Did she say, pups? That's what shifters call their children. They can't transform before they're fourteen or fifteen years old. The feast takes place in the school because they don't have a church." And she ran into the fray, her sister right behind her. Trace and Zeb were quick to join the battle.

Fighting and shots rang out. Screams, yelling and cursing erupted from inside the building.

Rad appreciated the warning. It meant he wasn't amazed when a group of children boiled outdoors as if they were going to recess. He heard two little girls crying and a boy yelling for Miss Korinna.

He swung off his own horse. He looked at his younger brother, sister-in-law and Lars Swenson. "The three of you find a wagon and team to get these kids out of town."

"We will. Be careful."

Inside, he saw men and women lying, dying on the floor. Trace and Zeb walked through, administering the *coup de grâce,* the final death blows to the shifters. His sister-in-law entered, asking if anyone wanted to go to *Summerland*, their version of Heaven. Then, Rad spotted the wolf. She was by two cradles near the front of the room, keening over the babies. *'My pups. My pups.'*

"Are they—" Rad couldn't ask the question. Dead? Mauled? Partially eaten?

"Not gone. They were sleeping until it was time for them to be dessert." Astrid looked at the wolf. "If you revert to your human form, you can carry them out of here."

*'Can't change.'* She yelped as she tried again. *'Grayson did something so the collar won't let me.'*

Kallisto approached, carrying a blanket. "She'll need this because she doesn't have clothes."

*'At Grayson's. Chained me. Gave them my pups to eat. Sweet meat.'*

"Hold still. This may hurt." Astrid gazed at the collar and began to chant a strange poem about being free. Kallisto joined her. The wolf whimpered, whined as the collar turned from silver to red to blue to purple. Then a chain link broke, and the collar fell onto the floor.

The wolf shimmered in what looked like a cloud of more colors. Suddenly, she was gone and a beautiful, young girl with waves of golden hair appeared. Ignoring her nudity, she snatched up one crying baby and then the other, rocking them against her bare breasts. "You're safe. Mama's here. You're safe."

Kallisto wrapped the blanket around the three of them. "What's your name? I'm Kallisto Hunter and that's my sister."

"No. Names have power. Don't give them away."

"You're right." Astrid ran a finger across a baby's downy brown hair. "It's why we never share our true, 'witch' names. Only our mortal ones."

"Where's their father?" Kallisto asked. "Do you want us to find him?"

"Dead." The former wolf looked at Rad, gratitude shining on her lovely features. "You killed him. Thank you."

"I only shot one person." Fury rose in Rad's heart. "Grayson. He's their—"

"Not anymore." The girl beamed happily. "He's dead. We'll go now." She looked at Kallisto. "Burn this place, War Witch. All of it. All of them."

"I will."

When Rad's people left the school, Kallisto turned. She pulled a sword out of a scabbard and pointed it at the building. Fire shot out and the building exploded in flames. The waiting children cheered and ran to the girl.

Two of the older ones took the babies and she pointed to the waiting wagon, keeping the worn blanket around her. "Go there. I need our things. Wait for me."

"What if he's alive?" one of the boys asked.

"Can't be. He was shot with silver."

"Wait." Rad drew his six-gun. "I'll go with you."

Amazingly, Grayson was barely alive when they entered. Someone had ransacked the place, only taking the whisky bottles, money from the desk and a few clothes. The girl walked into the alcove. She came out a short time later in a gray dress, her golden hair pinned up, a shawl around her shoulders.

"Help me," Grayson muttered. "He killed—"

"I know I did. You never should have started the ball, if you didn't plan to die," Rad said.

The girl lifted her skirt enough to remove a knife from its sheath on her leg. Pity filled her face and voice as she went to the dying man. "I'm sorry."

"So am I. First day in this town and it's my last."

That made no sense. Grayson Mallory had been the town marshal for the past twenty years. Still people often got rattled when they were dying. The girl didn't move. She pulled over the quilt where she'd lay as a wolf. She sat down next to him.

Rad wondered what she meant to do. Finish him with the knife? But she was different. Special. She held Grayson's hand and prayed with him. She said the rosary with him when he asked. She comforted him when he realized he'd lost his prayer beads and cried. She promised his God would forgive him for his sins. She must be some sort of saint. Who else could forgive someone who meant to kill her children? Their children? He couldn't.

Kallisto entered the building and joined the girl. After a moment, she spoke to Grayson in an unknown language. He stared at her, uncomprehending. The warrior woman heaved a sigh. "He's gone, isn't he?"

"Not quite," Rad said, "but soon."

"Oh, not this poor soul." Kallisto glanced at the shapeshifter woman. "The children are ready to leave. We've finished our hunt and I've burned the town. I'll stay here until this one goes, before I set the office ablaze. Your babies are hungry. They need you."

"We must take care. *He* will be after us." The girl put away her knife. "After me. When you find someone who will nurse my babies, I'll lure him away and kill him. And until I kill him, I'll try to keep him from you, your sisters and your *relkinam* no matter how long it takes. Guard, love and raise my pups for me."

Kallisto nodded. "We will. My family will until you return, no matter how long it takes."

# 26

*Eagleville, Washington*
*Saturday, December 1ˢᵗ, 2018*

JED SCOWLED AT THE CAR IN THE DRIVEWAY AT HIS HOUSE AND carefully parked on the street, so he didn't block the other vehicle. He hadn't expected company this afternoon, much less the shapely woman waiting on the porch. The other crews at Corbett Logging didn't work weekends, but his were still behind on their quotas. So, Jed insisted his loggers ship the logs they'd cut this week to the local mills. Nobody complained, at least not when he could hear them.

"Who's that?" Gard eyed the visitor in a tight sweater, fashionably torn jeans, and high-heeled designer boots warily. Red hair billowed halfway down her back. "Is it one of the Jamison relatives?"

"I think we're supposed to believe she is my mate." Jed reached into his shirt pocket for his cell phone. "Let's see where Meteor and her sisters are today."

"All three of them were at the Rocking J earlier and didn't have plans to leave." Gard watched the woman stroll toward them, exaggerating the sway of her hips. "I don't think she's going to give you much more time."

"I won't need it." Jed waited a moment for Meteor to answer, but apparently, she didn't, and he ended up talking to her sister. "She's doing what?" He chuckled. "Can you send me a picture to show Gard? We'll be along soon, and I don't want to miss it."

"What's going on?"

"Meteor is playing with the kids and teaching Fallyn to shift." Jed passed his phone to the bodyguard. "Isn't my little princess adorable?"

Gard stared at the video of three wolf pups. The smallest was attacking one of the others, assaulting his wagging tail. "Are you serious? These are your kids?"

"If you wait, you'll see Meteor with them in her wolf form. She's stunning in whatever shape she chooses."

"Well, if she's at the ranch, she's definitely not here."

"That's right, Gard." Jed took the phone, switched it off and put it back in his shirt pocket. "Let's go talk to our guest."

"Works for me." Gard removed his weapon from its holster. "Glad I got those silver bullets from Hugh. Do you mind if I shoot her?"

"Only if or when she tries to kill me." Jed opened his door. "Make it a wound so we can still interrogate her."

Gard nodded and slid out of his seat. They headed across the frost covered grass and met the woman partway. Jed stopped before he was within her reach. "Are you lost? Looking for someone? Needing directions?"

She smiled sweetly but it didn't touch her blue eyes. "I wanted to apologize—" She paused, tilting her head to one side. "I'd really like to talk in private, Jed."

"Not gonna happen." Gard eased forward, so he'd have a clear shot at her. "Why do you need to apologize, Ms.—"

"Jamison. Meteor Jamison." She took a step closer to Jed, her tone becoming low and sexy. "I heard from the county attorney today and thought we should talk about the charges from October—"

"You have a credibility problem." Gard kept his attention on her. "No prosecutor works on weekends."

"What he said." Jed folded his arms. "You may have tried to look like her, but you don't smell like that witch, Andrel Corbett. Didn't you think I'd recognize the shifter my uncle sent to constantly paw and rub against me at every festival even when she wasn't in heat?"

"Well, that's rude. Why are you pretending I'm someone else when I'm Meteor?"

"Not talking about that." Jed wrinkled his nose. "You stink like the dying plants and the disgusting meat hanging in the garage at my uncle's house. Shoot her now, Gard."

She retreated one step, then a second when Gard lifted the pistol. "You can't do this, Jed."

"I'm not doing a thing. Go back to Corbettstown, Andrel. Tell my uncle, his executioner, and the enforcer I'll be there tomorrow."

She turned and sprinted to her car, not giving Gard the opportunity to fire the weapon. He waited until she started the engine and backed into the street before he holstered the Sig Sauer. Tires squealing, she hit the gas and sped away. "Would you have realized she wasn't Meteor if Rowdy and Holt weren't here?"

"I don't think so." Jed frowned after the car. "Now, I wonder if she wasn't sent to kill me before. Did she succeed in the past?"

"Good question. Is there a way to learn the answer when we go to the ranch?"

"I don't know, but I'm definitely asking Rowdy to increase his protection spells."

———

Corbettstown, Washington
Saturday, December 1st, 2018

Gunnolf Marvin frowned at the sleeping wolf. She'd curled up on the dog bed behind his desk as soon as they arrived at the office. She didn't move, almost as if she were in stasis, a *magickal* coma. He'd never put her in one of those, so why did she need one today? Granted, she'd run through the woods for more than two hours yesterday, ignoring his whistle. He'd finally managed to catch her after she romped past some cross-country skiers. Of course, she barely touched the rare 'doggie' burger he ordered for her at lunch. He thought it was pure temper because she'd have preferred a steak like he'd had. She'd eaten two grilled T-bones at dinner as well as a huge baked potato with all the trimmings.

What was wrong with her? He'd called Rebekah Corbett, a *healer* in training several times but his calls kept getting dropped. Cell service was so erratic here. Occasionally, Corrine whined, moaned and growled in her sleep, but she didn't awaken. He should do a walk-through of the town hall and make sure everything ran smoothly at the department. The thought didn't stir him to action. Her adopted mother, Lorena, was filling in at the reception desk and so far, she hadn't needed him. He'd stay with Corrine until she finished dream-walking.

The door flew open, banging against the wall and Latham Sellers slammed into the room. Gunnolf reminded himself of the old platitude about imitation being the sincerest form of flattery, although he'd never liked the sycophant element of the younger *mage-priest*. Not in the old days on *Trilunon* and not three hundred plus years later.

"Quiet. She's resting."

"I don't care about your damned pet. I never did." His head newly shaved, six foot tall, sun-bronzed, muscular in his three-piece, pinstriped suit, Latham charged across the office. "How could you? Why did you give away our meat?"

"What are you talking about? I left the key above the front door of the tool shed because you were late. Like always." Gunnolf glanced at his watch. "The pack will be getting ready for the hunt. You should have had the prey in the forest hours ago."

"I would, except you—" His enraged bellow roused Corrine from her slumber. "You gave them to the humans!"

She vaulted to her feet, her gaze locked on Latham. *'You! Killer!'*

"What?" Gunnolf rested his hand on her back. "He's the executioner. You know that. You've always known."

She shook off his touch. She stormed toward Latham. She leaped and struck him mid-chest. He staggered, fell backwards onto the floor.

*'Killer. My pups! You took my babies for meat!'*

Her teeth tore into his arm and blood flew. He raised his hand to bespell her. She ripped his fingers to the bones. She spat skin and tissue on the floor. She went for his face. The unearthly howls continued. *'My babies! My babies! My babies!'*

Gunnolf grasped her collar. He dragged her a step away before she slashed Latham's throat. How did she know that? Remember it? He'd been away, tracking two runaway female shifters. He returned to Corbettstown only to find her half-crazed over the deaths of their three-month-old, twin sons. She refused to let them be roasted and eaten despite the fact it was what the pack did with their dead. He'd had to force her into a wolf shape, chain her before he could give Latham the little bodies.

*Maybe, if they'd been buried, she'd have allowed me to comfort her. She could have visited their graves. Instead, she helped the Liberty Valley marshal kill me. Then, she ran into that witch-set fire and burned alive.*

"Corrine, stop! It wasn't your fault. They died in their sleep—"

*'Liar!'* She yowled. *'Liar, liar, liar!'*

She twisted, writhed and he barely managed to hold her. Her teeth grazed his arm. She broke free and lunged for him again. She leaped. Her claws ripped his shirt. *'My pups! You gave them for meat.'* Her screams seared his ears, his brain. *'My babies! Mine!'*

Dimly, he glimpsed county officers piling in the door. One pointed a gun at her. All they saw was a wolf gone mad, trying to kill her owner and master.

"No!" Gunnolf grabbed her when she jumped at his throat. He managed to draw all of her *magick*. She collapsed onto the floor in a heap, still crying over the pups.

Lorena shoved her way past the visiting officers. Medics raced to Latham, but that wasn't Lorena's goal. She dropped to her knees beside Corrine. "What did you do to her? What evil thing did you do?"

*'Mama, they... They took my pups, Mama. For meat.'* Corrine crawled into Lorena's arms, moaning. *'My pups, my babies—'*

Gunnolf reached for Corrine. Fury sparked in Lorena's yellow-brown eyes, and he saw her wolf. Thankfully, she didn't shift to it in front of the police from visiting departments. "She's mine, Lorena."

"No! Get out!" Lorena rocked Corrine against her. "It's okay, sweetheart. It will be okay." She glanced over her shoulder at Latham still suffering through medical treatment from the humans. "Take your bastard son with you."

"He's not my son. They died years ago." Gunnolf gave up the battle. He stripped off the remains of his shirt, stomped to his desk and threw it in the trash. He went to the locker in the bathroom, and found a clean, ironed one. Taking a deep breath, he healed his wounds before he shrugged into the shirt. He buttoned it, tucked it into his pants.

He returned to his office. A big, brawny blond man stood near Lorena. He didn't wear a uniform like the other officers, but a tan jacket over a white shirt, a striped tie and brown slacks. His nametag read, Detective John Watkins. He'd removed the pistol from his shoulder holster. He pointed it toward the floor, but obviously intended to shoot Corrine if she showed signs of aggression again.

She didn't. She kept keening for their sons.

Lorena glared at Gunnolf. "She needs a *Healer*."

"One of the medics could look at her but she's not bleeding. They are." Watkins paused. "My cousin's a veterinarian. He's a professor at W.S.U. in Pullman. He treated a wolf-dog last month when he visited over Thanksgiving. He could recommend someone."

"Not a vet, you damned fool. A *Healer*, preferably a *High Healer*." Lorena held Corrine tighter. "You should have realized a long time ago that we needed them instead of getting rid of them, Enforcer!"

"Astra has one." Latham took a new bandage from one of the medics and wiped the blood off his face. "Call her."

"She won't answer." Gunnolf saw the rising anger on Lorena's face. The humans froze when he stopped time for the moment so they could speak freely. "I probably shouldn't have threatened her new man when we met last week."

"You think? You're a lousy father." Lorena reached for her cell phone. "I'll call her. Get out!"

Gunnolf hesitated, then walked over to the shelves that held his *magick* containers. He selected two, took them to Latham. "Use these. Heal yourself before they see it. Quickly!" Then, he gazed at Lorena again. "Tell Astra I'll pay whatever the *healer* desires."

"Latham. Give him, Latham." Lorena scrolled through her contact list. "He attacked Astra last week when you were out of town. Again! The *healer* wants him. Call it a *Yule* gift. Make amends."

"It's not my fault," Latham hastily squawked. "The alpha sent a patrol to clean up a mess Gary Smith made, and I was ordered to go along."

"You could have refused. We'll discuss it later." Gunnolf retraced his steps so everything would appear normal. His spell faded and the humans returned to their activities. The first responders patched up Latham. Detective Watkins stood guard.

Lorena waited while the call went through. "This is Lorena Corbett. I'm looking for Astra Jamison."

"Rowdy Tall-Deer. My woman naps. What do you need?"

"I'm in Corbettstown. I need *you*."

Rowdy's voice filled with regret. "I'd come if I could, but after what your people have done to me time and again, I will not tend your ill or injured, Lorena."

"It's my child." Lorena smoothed Corrine's silver fur. "My wolfling. She's trapped in a dream. Help her. Please. I will owe you."

"A moment, Lorena." This time it was a woman. "Let me switch on the video for Rowdy. Show him. And tell my demon-father to rot in hell! This is for Corrine, not for him. Never for him."

"I hear you, Daughter. Save Corrine for me and I will let bygones be bygones."

"Very good of you after everything you've done to me and mine," Astra mocked. "I won't forget or forgive."

The sound of her voice caused Corrine to open her eyes. She yipped and Lorena lowered the phone to reveal the other woman's face.

Astra looked at Corrine. "So, what's the issue? Why haven't you killed him? That was the promise you made my sister. You would lure him away from us and kill him. He's a demon who deserves to die and rot in hell."

Corrine growled softly. Detective Watkins took a step closer, raising his weapon. Lorena angled the phone slightly to reveal the threat he posed.

"I see. Well, you're just going to have to wait a bit longer for your revenge, Corrine. Until then, we keep our side of the bargain. Your two sons flourish with us as always."

"The pups were dead when I gave them to Latham." Gunnolf protested. "I saw them, held them, grieved for them. They were gone."

This time, Rowdy spoke. "Ask your novice about that. He knows poisons all too well. It'd be easy enough for him to drug infants until they appeared dead and then take them away to eat later. Let me see Corrine."

Detective Watkins slowly holstered his pistol. "Let's go somewhere to talk, Chief Marvin. I don't understand everything that's happening, but the situation appears under control." He walked toward Latham. "Did you really kill her wolf pups? And plan to eat them? No wonder she attacked you. You're nuts."

"She's insane and shouldn't be allowed to breed." He glanced toward Gunnolf. "I was doing you a favor when I got rid of them. You ought to be grateful."

"As you will be when I let you live." Gunnolf looked over his shoulder at Lorena who still held the phone for the consultation with the *High Healer*. Rowdy appeared to involve Corrine in the conversation which calmed the young she-wolf even more.

"And now, I will have to accept my daughter's new partner. A witch and a damned *healer*. Still, I'm glad she had sense enough to reject you." Gunnolf watched the medical team pack up their equipment.

Their scowls and low-voiced curses showed what they thought of a man who destroyed what they considered small animals. How would they feel if they knew the babies still looked human? There wasn't any proof they'd be like their mother and immediately able to shift into wolves.

"Prepare, Latham. I will give whatever he wants even if it's you." Gunnolf strode from the office, aware the Eagleville detective followed. In the breakroom, he gestured toward the coffee pot and the cups arranged on a wall rack. "Help yourself."

"Thanks. Why on earth would that idiot approach a wolf after killing her pups?"

"You said it. He's an idiot." Gunnolf stared at the electric teakettle. "Why are you here?"

"Appreciated your call and wanted to let you know we finished collecting those prisoners at your home. We sent them off to the jail at the county seat. Not really a crime scene, so I meant to come and thank you. We've been looking a while for some of those bail-jumpers." John Watkins sipped the strong brew. "Every cop shop is the same. It always tastes like mud."

"And that's why I drink tea." Gunnolf turned, leaning against the counter. He hadn't called, but suspected he knew who did. Nobody would believe it was the grieving wolf in his office. He'd have to address the issue with her later. Meantime, this was a fitting punishment for Latham. He'd answer to the alpha for losing the first batch of prey and have to round up a second one.

A moment later, John lowered the cup. "Your daughter's a lawyer and she knows murder is against the law. Do you really think you're in danger from her?"

"Not unless I threaten her or those she loves." Gunnolf grinned. "She's my true heir and I can't even win an argument with her and that was before I knew she had Corrine on her side."

"One of our new associates gave me a box of fresh maple bars from our town bakery. Your receptionist stored them somewhere." John grimaced. "He wanted me to give them to Corrine, not the officers here, but I didn't realize that was your wolf. My cousin complains constantly about people feeding human food to pets."

"Well, we just won't tell him." Gunnolf wasn't surprised about the doughnuts, not when she loved the cookies his second daughter made. "And I'll make sure Corrine doesn't gorge on them."

"Good luck with that," John said.

Lorena came in the room and opened the cupboard where they kept cleaning supplies. She removed a pink box tied up with multi-colored ribbons. "Rowdy says she can have one of these. Make yourself useful, Gunnolf. Brew her a cup of chamomile tea to calm her nerves. Last time we went shopping, we brought home soup from the bakery."

Gunnolf followed directions, washing out the teakettle. He did his usual protection spell over it so nothing would harm those who used it. He filled it with distilled water before plugging it in, found her favorite cup that read, 'That which doesn't kill me, should run!'

"Where do I find the soup?"

"In your freezer." Lorena placed a maple bar on a saucer.

"Rowdy says two bowls of her favorite, home-style chicken noodle. He'll come tomorrow to check on her and Astra will be here too. And Corrine agreed to sleep in the kennel in the basement because she can't control her actions when she's dreaming."

Fascinated, John asked, "Where does she usually sleep?"

"In my bed with me," Gunnolf said. "She always hogs the pillows and blankets."

## 27

*Eagleville, Washington*
*Saturday, December 1ˢᵗ, 2018*

METEOR CONTEMPLATED SPENDING THE NIGHT IN THE APARTMENT
she shared with Astra at the ranch and then changed her mind. If she
was there, her sister wouldn't be able to sleep with Rowdy. Since
they were headed to Corbettstown, Meteor wanted, no needed, the
night with Jed first. She'd barely pulled into the parking lot behind
the bakery when she spotted the headlights from Jed's truck. She
waited for him to join her. Or was it a different shifter? One who
intended to kill her?

She watched as he and Gard traded places, the bodyguard sliding
behind the wheel. Jed strode toward her rig. She eased out of the
passenger seat, her gloved hand resting on the hilt of the silver
dagger sheathed at her hip. "Why are you here?"

"We wanted to be sure you got home safe." Jed trailed a finger
along the chain of the necklace she still wore to the spokes of the
sun-shaped disc. "I'm surprised you didn't take this off after the
spellcasting last night."

"It wasn't time yet, so I'll keep it a while longer." She felt the sun warm at his touch and knew he meant to reassure her. She smiled up at him, rested a hand on his beard-stubbled cheek. "If you come inside, what happens to Gard?"

"He sleeps in the truck unless he goes back to my place."

"Now, I'm feeling guilty."

"Don't. He said he'd be fine. It's safer than when we were Marines in combat."

"Unless the shifters attack."

"Well, he's got plenty of silver bullets. He'll take out most of the patrol with that and he'll finish off the rest with his new silver KA-BAR. They'll be sorry."

"Okay." Meteor took a deep breath. She ought to send Jed away, but the proposed trip to Corbettstown terrified her. She longed to sleep safely in his strong arms. "What happens if I take you upstairs with me?"

"Nothing you don't want." He lowered his head and his lips brushed hers. "I owe you a *Trilunon Nine-Time Kiss* after the games we played at the bonfire on *Samhain* and you—"

"I owe you three." She managed to smile and took his hand. "Let's help each other through this night since there's no guaranty we'll live to come home tomorrow. We've died together before."

"I want us to live together this time and teach our younglings everything they should know to have good lives."

"Me too." Meteor led him toward the back door of the building. "Me too, Thojedescar."

She led the way upstairs to her apartment. Inside, she turned on the lights and walked into the kitchen, aware he followed. She opened the small refrigerator under one of the counters and removed a bottle of her favorite red wine. He nodded when she held it up, so she put it on the center island while she took two glasses from the cupboard.

"You said that Andi Corbett came to visit today." Meteor opened the Pinot Noir and filled the goblets. "Did she say what she wanted?"

"It was all about the charges filed when you were at my house before *Samhain*."

Meteor passed him a glass, then raised hers to drink. "I thought you told me your uncle arranged to have those dropped."

"That was the story I heard, but apparently there's more to it."

"I'm not sure how to handle that." Meteor frowned, remembering the incident. "It was a full moon, and I had to shift into an animal after the Halloween Party we catered at the cocktail lounge. I was in my cat-form and Junior tried to hit me with his truck."

"I know. I was in the passenger seat." Jed sipped the wine. "I grabbed the steering wheel and yanked it. The pickup veered, crashed into the telephone pole on the opposite side of the street from you. Junior ended up in jail with another DUI ticket. The pole swayed but held…"

"I didn't know that."

Jed shrugged, finished his wine, and put the glass on the counter. "You got hit, a glancing blow. If you'd been totally human, it'd have been a lot worse, but you're the queen of the shifters. You were unconscious when I took you to my house…"

"And I called Astra." Meteor grimaced before she set her empty glass beside his. "Not on my cell phone, but telepathically. She and Freya came to take care of me and of course, you caught hell. She made sure Brigid's cousin arrested you. I'm sorry."

"Nothing to be sorry about, *Laspowima*." Jed stepped toward her, framing her face with his hands. "Rowdy and Hugh hadn't come through the *Time Portal* yet. They couldn't keep my uncle and your father from killing you or stop them from overshadowing me and influencing my actions. You and your sisters had to protect yourselves."

She trembled, staring into the dark *magick* of his eyes. "You're a little too understanding."

"I want to share your bed tonight, Matiranika. To be with you before we face our enemies tomorrow."

She fisted a hand in his shirt, pulled him close and kissed him. She'd make love with him as much as he wanted tonight. She wouldn't get pregnant. Thankfully, it was the wrong time of the month for that. And the only thing that changed it was if she mated in a different shape, as one of the creatures she could become or the time she borrowed her sister's form three and a half years before, so she looked like Venus. The consequence of that choice was Fallyn.

Meteor kissed him again, his mouth warm under hers. She could kiss him forever. She traced his lips with her tongue, then brushed a kiss over his beard-stubbled cheek. She laughed when his arms tightened around her.

He lowered his head. His mouth captured hers and she yielded to the fierce passion. He lifted her into his arms and carried her toward the bedroom. While the kisses continued, she managed to unbutton his flannel shirt. She slid her fingers up his wide chest toward his broad shoulders.

In the bedroom, he lowered her onto the king-size bed. He shrugged the rest of the way out of his shirt, and it landed on the carpet. She unbuttoned her blouse, and it followed his shirt. He unhooked the front closure of her bra, and it went next. He trailed kisses down her throat. She moaned when his tongue teased her nipple. "Please."

"I've barely started." He blew softly, then licked a new path to the other nipple. "Wait until I have my mouth on you."

"I always come too fast when you do that."

"Not for me."

She gasped when he bent his head and drew her nipple into his mouth and sucked. He fondled her other breast, rolling the nipple between his thumb and fingers. She moaned, arching against him, turning her lips into the strong column of his neck, then nipping his ear.

He lifted his head and his mouth claimed hers. Between kisses, they continued to undress each other. Her pants, his jeans and boxers fell to the floor. His hand sought out the curls between her legs, curving over the mound. "I can't believe you went commando."

"I played too long with the kids and then I hurried to dress."

"Good story. Stick to it."

She tensed, wanting the next touch so badly she thought she'd explode. His thumb found the tiny bud nestled between her legs and caressed it.

"You want this, don't you?" He slid one long finger inside her. "You want me. Say it."

"You already know it." She trembled when he started the slow movements, his finger slipping in and out of her. He knew how to drive her to the heavens and beyond. She moved with him, eager to match the strokes. He swirled his tongue around one nipple, then began to suck on it.

She cried out when a second finger joined the first and her hips met the motion of his hand, rising and falling. His thumb added to her pleasure when he rubbed the small bud, rocking into her. His mouth teased her nipples, shifting from one to the other and he continued to suck. His fingers slid in and out of her. He sent her spiraling ever upward until she reached the heights, convulsing until she collapsed into his arms.

This time when he kissed her, she surrendered, aware his hand was still on her, in her. "Not again."

"Oh yes, my shape-shifting queen. I want you hot and begging like you were the first night I had you."

She stared into the rugged features, the dark magick of his gaze. "I didn't know you remembered that."

"How could I forget?" He smiled, his lips a breath away from hers. "I spent hours touching, tasting, teasing you and making you come again and again. At the end, I only had to look at you and I could make you climax."

She bucked against his hand, unable to resist when he moved his fingers and started the pattern, this time varying the strokes, slow and easy, then fast and hard. She met him, motion for motion. "It amused you to drive me into a series of climaxes whether we were alone or in public. You flaunted your *Power*, your expertise in *Sex Magick*. I thought I'd die of pleasure."

"Instead, you lived, cured of the deadly diseases that would have slain you when our world ended. In the nights that followed, you begged me to have you, really have you. And I did."

She twisted her fingers in his thick, dark hair, responded to the wildness of his kiss. She never had been able to deny him or herself when they fell into bed. Kisses, touches, and caresses continued as they explored each other's bodies until they couldn't wait any longer. He eased her legs apart, resting most of his weight on his elbows. His lips captured hers, his tongue laying claim to her mouth as he drove deep inside her.

Dimly, she was aware he didn't use a condom, but she really didn't care. Her hips arched against his. She met each stroke, some fast and shallow, others long and deep. She writhed, twisted under him, gasping and moaning. Their kisses didn't seem to last long enough. She clawed at his back, trying to hurry the pace he set, but it didn't work.

He knew what she liked, what she needed. Nothing altered the steady rhythm of his thrusts. They seemed to go on forever until they climaxed together among the stars. Afterwards, he lay next to her, his hair-roughened thigh between her legs pressing it into the nest of curls. He smoothed her hair away from her face, dropping little butterfly kisses on her forehead, her eyebrows, her cheeks.

She sighed, letting her fingers explore his chest and toy with his nipples. "Aren't we going to sleep tonight?"

"That's vastly overrated." He pulled her closer, his mouth trailing across her cheek toward her ear, then down the side of her neck. "I'll wait until you're ready. Hot, needy, and screaming. Then, I'll have you bucking beneath me while I take you to the moon and back."

She shuddered when his hands slid down to her hips, and he held her still while he rocked his thigh against her core. She groaned, kissed his neck. "Do it now."

"Not yet." He smiled, turned his head so their lips were a whisper apart. "First I'll make you come right here and right now."

---

He'd had her all night long and now she slept in his arms. She didn't wear the entire set of enchanted jewelry he'd made her so long ago, at least not yet. He still enjoyed seeing his gold necklace around her neck, the bracelet on her wrist. The little creatures inlaid on both pieces darted and danced, obviously pleased she'd finally taken them as her own.

She needed to accept the other bracelet and the earrings before *Yule*, a little more than three weeks from now. Somehow it didn't seem like a faraway dream the way it had at *Samhain*. He remembered the advice Rowdy Tall-Deer had given him during the weekend celebration when they worked on the boundary fences at the Rocking J.

"You'll be the next of us to *invoke the talipenlace*," Rowdy had said. "You wait until *Yule* in December when your mate wears the entire set of jewelry you made for her."

"What good will that do?" Jed had demanded. "She has before, and nothing changes."

"Listen to me, Thojedescar. She must wear it of her own free will," Rowdy went on. "You will ask if she wears it as her desire, not that of her mother and aunt. If your soul-match does, she'll admit it in thought and words."

"Like that's going to happen." Jed had glared at the fallen timber surrounding them. "It'd be easier to stand up those trees again or add two more moons to the one in this realm's sky. Now, I'm in the miracle business. Then, what?"

"You repeat your vows together."

Jed had pointed out it'd been three hundred years from the time he'd been bound to Meteor. He'd died four times since then, and now he knew he'd been murdered by his uncle again and again. A month ago, Jed didn't have a clue what the soul-binding spell was. Rowdy informed him that he had nearly two moons to regain those memories.

And surprisingly they were coming. Jed knew he'd begin the spell by announcing the time and place, then calling on the *Lord* and *Lady* as well as the other *Ancient Powers* to witness the spell he crafted. Then he and Meteor had to recite their *real* names and lineage during the first part of the incantation. He wasn't sure what came next, but he still had time to learn the rest.

Meteor stirred against him. "You should sleep before we fight tomorrow, Thojedescar."

"I'll sleep when we return from Corbettstown." He kissed the hollow of her throat below the sun-shaped disc, glancing at the radio-clock on the nightstand. "We still have an hour. It's long enough."

"For what?" She giggled when he pressed her back against the pillows. "You always want more time to have sex."

"True, but I want my mouth on you." He followed her down, his kisses creating a long line from her neck to her breasts to her navel. "I can do that even if I don't have enough time to take you for as long as I like."

She moaned, sighed when his lips teased the inside of her thigh, then roved toward the nest of curls between her legs. "Tell me that you're mine, Matiranika."

"No." She shook her head. "I'm not."

"Oh yes, you are. And you'll admit it before dawn." His lips found her, his tongue driving deep inside her in a long intimate kiss. She writhed against him, moving with each intense stroke. She clutched at his hair, threading her fingers in it. She came in moments. His name escaped on a long moan, "Tho-jed-es-car."

She didn't say she belonged to him, and he didn't stop. He continued lapping at her, softly, gently while she arched against him, begging for more and eventually surrendering as a second orgasm swept through her. He stayed with her, giving in to her and driving her onward. He finally took the bud of flesh into his mouth and sucked. Pleasure engulfed her and she convulsed in delight.

He smiled, moved upward, resting his weight on his elbows. He eased inside her. He shifted, pushed deeper. She rose against him. He lowered his head and his lips claimed hers, his tongue demanding entrance. She yielded, kissing him just as fiercely. He pulled back, then drove into her again, a long deep stroke.

She met his next thrust with her hips, then a third. She caught his mouth with hers, clawing at his back with her nails. He deepened the series of kisses and she surrendered. Her hips met his, matching the pattern of his thrusts. Some were shallow, tiny, barely inside her. Others went deeper.

He increased the pace. She twisted, arching beneath him, their hips meeting as he slid in and out of her. He kept thrusting, deliberately holding back until she spasmed, wildly digging in her nails. She threw her head back against the pillows and called his name, his real name, his wizard name as she convulsed, tight around him.

He moved again, one quick stroke after another. She met his thrusts. His tongue enticed hers into a duel when he kissed her. They whirled through a sensual dance among the stars until they climaxed together. He held her close, still inside her. "Are you going to give me another little girl this time?"

"It's the wrong time of the month for that."

He chuckled. "Oh, sweetheart. You need to listen to your mother occasionally."

"What does that mean?"

"What works with mortal men doesn't always with *mages*, Matiranika." He kissed her slowly, tenderly. He cupped her breast. "I've had you more than enough times tonight for us to create a new wolfling to add to our family."

"I didn't plan on that." She tried to pull away.

"I did." He tangled a hand in her hair, his lips brushing hers. She arched, twisted beneath him and he hardened inside her. "I want a houseful of pups with you. Let's dance, sweetheart."

Her hips met his when he began to move, long deep strokes alternating with slower, gentler ones. "Don't stop now."

"I won't." He kissed her. "Let's go for twins this time."

## 28

*Eagleville, Washington*
*Sunday, December 2<sup>nd</sup>, 2018*

THE BAKERY OPENED LATER ON SUNDAY MORNINGS, SO METEOR HAD time to make breakfast for her, Jed, and Gard before she went downstairs for the day. She served several rashers of bacon, huge slices of ham, a boatload of scrambled eggs and thick slices of sourdough toast from a loaf of homemade bread. When they finished eating, the guys volunteered to clean the kitchen in her apartment while she opened the business.

Brigid was busy at the Silver Lake Pony Ranch on weekends, so she didn't come to Captivating Catering. After partying with her flock of fairies most Saturday nights, Lizzie was usually the last to arrive, which meant Tolliver and Daphne always opened with Meteor. She was frosting the maple bars when the bell over the front door rang in the dining room. She heard voices, a man asking to speak to her and then Daphne arrived with Donald Dawson.

He must still be on duty since he wore a wrinkled uniform and all the usual cop accoutrements. He removed his wide-brimmed hat, revealing short auburn hair and looked at Meteor as if she'd grown a second head. "I'm surprised to see you here, Ms. Jamison. You were barely conscious when the ambulance took you away from the Cross-Cut Tavern last night. The bartender and several patrons wrestled Jed Corbett away from you. He damn near killed you."

Meteor eyed the young deputy. He bore a strong resemblance to her apprentice witch and his cousin, Brigid. Donald was taller, not quite six feet. It must have been a long night for him because he was obviously tired. There were dark circles under his weary blue eyes. He kept more weight on his right leg, compensating for some old injury to his left.

"What are you talking about? I was home all night." Heat swamped her cheeks. "And Jed was with me. We didn't leave my place."

"Ooh, tell me more. I thought you were taking a hiatus from jumping the guy." Daphne filled a cup with black coffee and handed it to the law enforcement officer. "Didn't you go to the ranch to play with the kids because we close early on Saturdays?"

"I did and Jed met me there." Meteor took a deep breath, struggling to ignore the blush still heating her cheeks. She glowered at her friend who knew far too much about what went on between her and Jed, before glancing at Donald Dawson again. "What time did this fight occur?"

"At nine-thirty last night. I've been at the hospital ever since. One of the other officers took Corbett to jail."

"Not this particular Corbett." Jed stood in the doorway, Gard behind him. "It sounds like someone is still stealing our identities."

"I don't understand." Donald frowned at them. "The woman I saw had a concussion, cracked ribs, a fractured leg, and bruises all over her face. The patrons beat the crap out of the man who said he was you before we got there." He scanned Jed. "And you're fine. Both of you are. No bruises or broken bones."

"That's because they were here, safe and sound." Removing his wallet, Gard advanced on the young county cop. "I'm a private detective. Astra Jamison hired me to look after Jed when we learned someone pretended to be him and tried to harm her sister. I spent the night in the parking lot here. If either of them left, I'd have seen them go. I didn't. They stayed here."

"Do you have any idea who the woman was?"

"Not my sisters or cousins." Meteor glanced toward the back door when it opened, and Lizzie entered, ready to cook the morning entrees. "Take a seat in the dining room, Deputy, and we'll fix you breakfast. Jed, could it be Andrel Corbett? You said she came to see you yesterday afternoon and tried to—"

"She claimed to be you, Meteor." Gard replaced the identification in his wallet. "I don't know who the guy was, but it had to be someone she involved in the set-up."

"Could have been one of her ex-boyfriends or a brother or cousin, but I don't know which." Jed led Deputy Dawson toward the dining room and Gard followed. "Meteor, come join us when you can."

"I will." She gestured toward the stack of menus on the counter. "Daphne, would you please take his order?"

"I'm on it." Daphne grinned mischievously. "Afterwards, I want details about last night."

"Me too." Tolliver smirked at both women. "You know how I feel about sex. I like it. I love it and want more of it. The next best thing to having it is talking about it."

Lizzie folded her arms, giving their other two partners a stern look. "It isn't our business who our friend jumps. Her love life is her concern."

"You're just more tactful than they are." Meteor slathered the last maple bar with extra frosting. "You want to know too. Yes, we spent the night together. As the three of you already know, it wasn't the first time, and it won't be the last. He's great in the sack and I never did go for second-best. That's all I'm saying."

"It's not enough but I guess it will have to do for now." Tolliver picked up the large silver tray and carried the maple bars toward the display case.

Laughing, Meteor put the last one on a saucer for her, filled a cup with coffee and started toward the dining room. Daphne came along and Lizzie carried the now empty frosting bowl to the dishwasher. The two women enjoyed healthy sex lives but didn't hold a candle to Tolliver. Being part satyr, he admitted he was half-man and half-beast. When he wasn't working, he liked to spend his time drinking, playing instruments, and chasing willing females.

The three men sat in the corner booth, and she joined them, sliding onto the bench next to Jed. He draped an arm over her shoulders. "Are you planning to share that maple bar?"

"No." She licked the frosting off her fingers. "It's mine, all mine. I made it especially for me."

"Greedy." He brushed her lips with his. "Then, I'll just take a sample from you."

Daphne arrived with two more cups and a carafe of coffee. After she filled the mugs and returned to the kitchen, Meteor eyed Jed. "Any clue who the guy was?"

"When we visit my uncle this afternoon, I'll tell him Andrel is in the hospital. Maybe, we'll find out who else he sent to raise hell while we're there."

"We'll hear back about the fingerprints in a few hours," Donald Dawson said. "I'll let your lawyer know who stole your identity this time and of course, we'll be asking the prosecutor to file charges."

"Works for us." Meteor choked back a gasp when Jed stroked the back of her neck, fingers trailing to the opening of her T-shirt. She discreetly elbowed him.

He smiled, but his attention remained on the deputy. "I'm going to want to press charges against Andrel Corbett too. She's tried this game before but if she's not careful, her next partner may do what you said and kill her."

———

After lunch, Hugh and Trina took the boys off to ride with Hester's children and their young friends from the coven. Ignoring her foster daughter's complaints, Venus put Fallyn down for a nap. Rebekah promised to keep an eye on the little girl, so she'd remain in bed, not change into a wolf pup and race for the indoor arena to join the other younglings.

Venus headed for the bunkhouse to talk to her older sister. The two huge black male dogs rested on the porch and watched her approach. Neither stirred, allowing her passage to the door. When she opened it, she saw Astra sitting at the table, a plate of toast in front of her along with a cup of peppermint tea. The matriarch of the canine trio lay by her sister's chair.

Rowdy stood at the counter, putting small brown packages tied with twine into a box. He glanced at Venus. "Are the Elder Witches ready to ward the ranch and us?"

"They're setting up the circle in the workroom." Venus glanced at her older sister. "When you leave, they'll have the coven protect your car and Jed's truck. Are you meeting Meteor, him, and Gard in town so you can caravan to Corbettstown?"

"That's the plan." Astra eyed Rowdy. "I still don't like it. I've told you more than once it's not safe for you to go there. Despite his promises yesterday, my demon-father is the prince of liars. He will try to turn you over to the shifters and have them tear you to pieces."

"I don't trust his word either, but Lorena Corbett called and asked for my help with her daughter. And from what we've heard, and you remember from your past life, Corrine has done her best to keep her bargain with you."

A memory seeped into her mind and Venus knew it needed to be shared. "She vowed to try and keep our demon-father away from us if we protected her sons and I agreed. I don't know what happened to them. Did they live, grow old, die and are we waiting for them to be born again?"

"No. When I talked to her yesterday afternoon, I remembered what I did with them," Astra said. "Their wetnurse and the other adult shifters who looked after the children wanted to kill them because they were different. The babies started turning into wolf pups before their first birthday. Add in the witch talents from our father and they were challenging authority constantly. I took them with me on the star paths to the *Priest-Mages*. They were special, sons of the *Stalenary* and the *Warrior Guild* promised to raise them until they could return to their mother."

"What's the *Stalenary*?" Venus tucked her hands in her pockets but didn't know what the term signified. "What do they do?"

"They're hereditary, powerful alphas, either male or female, who control all the shapeshifter packs in a region." Rowdy glanced over his shoulder at them. "Trained by the *Mage-Priests* or *Mage-Priestesses* to rule equitably, there is usually one for each were-species and they ensure all the were-groups support each other. They work with the *Trilunon* royal family. However, they're subservient to no one."

"And that's Corrine?" Venus gaped at him. "Why did our mother keep it a secret?"

"Probably because she didn't know. Corrine has successfully hidden it from our demon-father all this time. Everyone seems to think she's just a strong, potential pack leader." Astra finished a piece of dry toast. "I only learned this last night when *Hecate* finally revealed it to me."

"Your father is strongly attached to her even if he doesn't understand that or he wouldn't have promised whatever I wanted to save her."

"What's wrong with her?" Venus demanded. "She's barely out of puppyhood herself."

"She's remembering her lives with our father." Astra picked up her tea. "It won't all be pain, but yesterday, she only had a partial revelation when she was awakened prematurely. She needed to know her pups were safe. Rowindache will see her today to ensure the rest of the dreams went smoothly. I'll make sure nobody harms him while he performs his *High Healer* duties."

"As much as possible, but you'll also look after yourself." Rowdy crossed the room and rested a hand on her shoulder. "As I've said too many times, *Vaslattel*, start taking better care of yourself and stop blaming yourself for what others do. That's a weakness we can't afford. You need to speak to your mother."

"Why would I do something so stupid?" Astra lifted her chin, glaring at him. "Diana and I get along best when we ignore each other."

"Rowdy's right." Venus sat down across from her sister. "Before the five of you travel to Corbettstown and face the alpha and our father, you need to *Heal* the divide between you and the Elder Witches."

"I can't believe you're agreeing with him and telling me that, Katiranika."

Venus took a deep breath. "I'm the war-queen, Satiranika, not you. And if you allow your negative feelings toward them to be used against you, then you won't be the only one who pays the price. You and Rowdy may die. So will our sister and her mate. I'm not sure whether Corrine will be able to continue to try saving the Corbettstown pack without our help. It will devastate Rebekah to lose her soul-match again."

"What are you saying?" Astra demanded. "Rebekah doesn't have one of those."

"Yes, she does." Rowdy kissed the top of her head. "She and Gard Devlin have never been able to fulfill their destinies, but they are meant to be together."

"What stopped them before?" Astra stopped speaking and stared at Venus. "Our father and Latham."

"That's right. Meteor told me Rebekah confided in her at *Samhain*. Jarvesel used his dark powers to tear away her *healers'* talents once he murdered the soldiers who tried to protect them and then he killed those *healers* too. By the time he gutted and disemboweled Gard, our father had already stripped Rebekah of her *magick*. It took more than a day for him to die in agony and Jarvesel raped her in front of him."

A tear slid down Astra's cheek, followed by a second, then a third. "I've seen some of what happened in her past lives and knew it mirrored what he'd done to me, but she didn't share all the details. When he demanded I visit him in Corbettstown after I graduated from high school, I insisted on having her as a maid. And I saw to it that she wasn't sent to share the alpha's bed to see if she'd conceive and bear a wolf pup when she reached puberty. They'd have killed her if she couldn't have shifters for the pack."

"She didn't remember everything about her past life or ours until a month ago. Meteor intervened when our father tried to contact Rebekah at the ranch and blocked the calls on her cell phone." Venus rose to her feet. "Come with me, Astra. You and Rebekah aren't the only ones Jarvesel tortured. Our mother and aunt suffered at his hands too. You need to hear their stories before you leave."

———

Mid-afternoon on Sunday, Cherry arrived at the bakery to help customers. While he waited for Meteor to finish working, Jed gestured for Junior to join him out in the parking lot. Since moving to Eagleville a few days ago, the shorter brown-haired man bore an even stronger resemblance to Jed. After joining the new pack, Junior gave up much of the high-calorie foods he enjoyed and exercised more.

Winter gray clouds filled the sky. The cold rain continued. Ignoring the drizzle dampening his hair and misting across his face, Jed leaned against his pickup. "I didn't have time to tell you Hester and Treyton Corbett moved here on Friday. They're staying out at the Rocking J for a while."

"What? Why? Won't Chief Marvin be looking for them? They're cops. They've been working for him forever."

"Treyton was afraid for his siblings. His sister hasn't been able to change yet. She probably has a different gift."

Junior shuddered. "Then, they'll kill her today and eat her in a few weeks at *Yule*."

"That's why they're here." Jed folded his arms. "You and Cherry go to the ranch after the bakery closes and help guard the younglings. The Elder Witches and the coven will be doing protection rites to keep us safe."

"So, what is your plan? I know you have one."

"I'm going to mark off this end of Liberty Valley for us. Your dad can have the high country around Corbettstown."

"He'll complain about not being able to use the main highways to the larger towns and the county seat."

"Let him. He and his pack can drive around on the back roads." Jed shrugged. "Not our issue, Junior. He sent in Andi Corbett and one of the other wolves to raise hell at the bar last night. He told them to use my identity and Meteor's."

"I didn't know anything about that. Cherry and I spent the evening at home." Junior raked a hand through his hair. "If I'd heard—"

"You'd have called me." Jed glanced toward the bakery door when it opened and Meteor started toward them, followed by Gard. "Meantime, when you get to the ranch, help Orion with his car. It's a mess after he went off the road at *Samhain*. You're a good mechanic and great teacher. Get Holt in on the job."

"Who is he?"

"You'll recognize him when you meet him." Jed met his cousin's dark gaze. "Remember where we came from and who we served on *Trilunon*, Frajunescar."

Junior froze at the sound of the wizard name. "Is that my—"

"Your name," Jed told him. "Your real name. You should remember who and what you are—"

"Why don't I?"

Meteor must have heard the last of the conversation. She shook back her red hair, pity filling her sky-blue eyes. "Your father and mine have a lot to answer for, Junior. They've been blocking our memories not only in this incarnation, but also in most of our past lives. If we remembered why we were sent here, then we'd know what they did to our world."

"And we'd be prepared to fight them," Gard added. "The philosopher, George Santayana wrote, "Those who cannot remember the past are condemned to repeat it." When we arrived, the *dracklegons* had adjusted our lives to fit in with the people who were already here."

"It's why we're born again and again and again in this realm. Memories of our previous lives start to return when we're thirty or when we find our soul-matched mates." Meteor rested a hand on Junior's arm. "We need to go to Corbettstown now, but when you and Cherry are at the ranch, ask the Elder Witches, my mother and aunt to remove the *magickal* obstacles set by your father and mine. They will have the power of the coven and can restore the two of you to yourselves."

"Is that a good idea?" Junior asked. "Don't you need them to protect you first?"

"Having our allies at full strength will aid us even more." Meteor glanced at Jed who nodded agreement. "Do it, Frajunescar!"

## 29

Corbettstown, Washington
Sunday, December 2nd, 2018

TRUE ENOUGH, SHE WAS IN THE BASEMENT KENNEL, BUT CORRINE didn't mind. She remained in her wolf shape. From past experiences, the thick dog bed proved comfortable enough. Rowdy Tall-Deer, the *High Healer* had explained she might attack and kill innocents while she worked through her memories of the past three hundred years. He'd promised to visit tomorrow, well later today, and make sure no residue remained from her dream journeys.

Yes, she was part of the various Corrines who'd come before, but when she saw the past, she looked like herself. Probably a good idea because it'd have been difficult to recognize the different bodies Gunnolf gave her. She still grieved over missing out on her sons' lives, but the witches took good care of them. And they were safe from Latham's machinations.

Rowdy was undoubtedly right about the disgraced *priest-mage* drugging them, so they appeared dead and then taking them away in

1888 Liberty Valley. Another name to add to her 'kill' list. Someday, some way, she'd end him.

Gunnolf brought her a bowl of chicken noodle soup for supper. He'd followed that up with the last two peanut butter cookies from her stash in the cottage. Now that her sentence was finished for wrecking his car, she'd go to the bakery in Eagleville and replenish her supply.

She glanced through the kennel bars and saw him sleeping in the recliner. Since he claimed her last Yule, he always stayed close to her. She wouldn't have blamed him if he'd gone upstairs to the main bedroom, but he worried about her.

She heard the other woman's voice in her mind. *He's mated to you, to us, even if he doesn't realize it. He's part of your pack. It's why I called him your enforcer. You claimed him years ago, back when he united us.*

*'I don't understand.'*

*You bit him and drew blood when he transferred my soul into your body on the road trip from California. He scolded you and you licked the injury, taking his blood. You said you were sorry and cried. He comforted you, called you 'his puppy' when you shifted. You changed back and wanted to know if he was your 'forcer'. And he said he was.*

*'That makes no sense. I couldn't have been so verbal. Not when I was barely two years old.'*

*Mind to mind talking, Corrinadora. You know he hears your wolf. He's a sorcerer.*

Corrine drifted off to sleep again, still learning more about her past and abilities. Dimly, she was aware Gunnolf brought her another bowl of soup. He didn't open the door this time but slid it through the slot in the front. He rarely used it. *'Master?'*

"It's all right, Corrine. Sleep and rest. It may be time for you to travel to *Summerland*. Go, my dear girl."

She shuddered at the endearment. He hadn't used it in years, not since she was a little, bitty, baby shifter. When he called her, 'my dear girl', he wanted her to remember to use her human form. He'd explained she needed to fit into the pack. Changing to her wolf pup form upset the neighbors and then Lorena went all 'mama' wolf on them.

"Eat your soup."

*'Later. Too tired now.'* She pretended to fall asleep and saw him stalk away. When she glanced at the recliner, she saw the *real* Gunnolf. Did he know his executioner had seized *Power* and become the demon in charge. She whimpered softly.

He'd be so hurt by the betrayal, but it hadn't happened in the last few years. From what she'd seen of their shared past, she knew Abahendes, the ruler of the nether regions, what their people referred to as the 'dark realm' and humans called, 'Hell' lied to Gunnolf. He actually believed he was the *Soul-Eating, Demon-Prince of Transgressions and Untruths.*

It wasn't true. What would give Abahendes more pleasure than turning the novice against the master? Latham's ability to create deadly poisons would be a bonus. And lying to a proud, angry *Priest-Mage* determined to wreak revenge when he became a warlock and then a demon would be even more of a diversion.

Of course, Gunnolf's bragging about how strong and mean he was added a new dimension to the issues. She heaved a sigh. Training her enforcer—she'd have her work cut out for her. However, regaining all her memories years earlier than most shifters meant she also would have all her *magick* soon.

Next time she woke, she saw Gunnolf, her Gunnolf unlocking the door. He froze when he spotted the bowl of untouched soup. "Who brought this? When?"

She shifted into her human form. "Latham. Early this morning. Get rid of it." She paused. "Carefully. You should probably check the food upstairs and make sure it's safe to eat before you fix breakfast."

"And what are you planning to do?"

"Go upstairs. Take a shower." She stretched, twisted and saw his gaze fall onto her breasts. He was such an incubus! She paused, patted his morning beard. "If you hurry, I'll let you fuck me before I get dressed. If you dilly-dawdle—"

"I'll still fuck you."

"You wish." She walked past him, ignoring it when he snapped his fingers. Such an incubus! When was he going to learn sex didn't solve everything? She had *Power* of her own, everything earned when she accepted the responsibilities and privileges of her new position as the ruler of the shapeshifter wolf packs. If he wanted her to have a climax, he was going to have to work for it. At least today!

———

Police Chief Gunnolf Marvin sat behind his huge, oak desk, his gaze locked on the male shifter standing in front of him awaiting punishment. Aeric Jonah Corbett, known as A.J. to friends and enemies alike was typical of the adult males in the pack, sturdy, dark-haired, dark-eyed with rugged features. Like several other of Gunnolf's deputies, he enjoyed making trouble when he was off-duty and had a great time raising hell in Eagleville on Saturday night.

"Explain why you disobeyed orders." Gunnolf folded his arms. "Andrel won't be out of the hospital for at least a week. Even when she gets home, it will take too long for her to heal since she can't shift into a wolf, pay-back for failing when she took the witch's form. The earliest she will be able to run with the pack is February."

A.J. shrugged. "I was told to make it look like Jed, the alpha's nephew attacked her. I used his shape and miscalculated his strength."

"Don't lie to me." Gunnolf slammed his fist on the desk and saw a moment of fear enter the younger man's eyes. The gray wolf behind the desk stood, bared her teeth and growled.

"I didn't send a novice to ruin his reputation in the county," Gunnolf rumbled. "You've pretended to be him before, not only in tavern brawls but on other occasions. You knew exactly what you were doing. I saw the report from the county cop. Andrel has a concussion, broken and cracked ribs, a fractured leg, internal injuries, and bruises from head to toe."

"She ran her mouth and insulted me in front of the humans. She's pack. She knows better than to disrespect her betters." A.J. glared at Gunnolf. "I did what was needful."

"There's more than one way to seize *Power*." Gunnolf stood. "You're a true misogynist who enjoys beating women, so you'll appreciate this task."

"What is it?"

"Hester Corbett took her children and fled so we wouldn't test her youngest daughter for *Yule* and eat her if she couldn't shift." Gunnolf pointed toward the door. "Find them. Kill Hester and her sons. I want the girl to see their deaths before you bring her to me."

"They won't die easy." A muscle throbbed in A.J.'s jaw. "It will take a great deal of work for me to slay them, especially in front of the girl. Who goes with me?"

"Nobody." Gunnolf smiled, amusement building. He always enjoyed watching a shifter dreading an upcoming gruesome demise. "You fought alone last night. Fight alone now."

"Hester and her oldest boy are cops. They won't die easy," A.J. repeated. "They'll try to kill me."

"Sounds like a personal problem." Gunnolf narrowed his dark eyes. "Yours. Oh, and I won't give you any different shapes."

"This is a suicide mission."

"Yes. You have a choice." Gunnolf rested large fists on the desk blotter. "Hunt Hester and her younglings. Or face me in a fight."

A.J. turned and stormed toward the door. It was a winning proposition. The shifter probably would die on his quest, or he'd try to ambush Gunnolf in the next few days. Either way, the upcoming battle would be fun to watch. While he was a good disciplinarian, the police chief hated killing and it was why he'd always passed on the task to someone who enjoyed it.

Latham waved his hand and the illusion of the wolf on the dog bed dissolved. He turned to the shelves where the older man stored his bottles of *magick* power. He couldn't get past the wards. It meant

Gunnolf was still alive. Latham hadn't really expected him to die when he discovered his dead pet in the kennel. However, Gunnolf would go crazy and unleash his ferocious temper on all those around him while he tried to find his Corrine again. He'd fail.

Happy times were coming again! At least for him. He melted into smoke as he heard the deputies arrive for the morning shift. Someone commented that the chief was late. Oh, they'd be sorry when he arrived! Death and destruction awaited them and Corbettstown today.

———

Having Corrine in the shower led to another hour of sex in the bedroom before breakfast. Then even more when they dressed. Latham must have thought he'd be heard if he lingered in the house, so he'd contented himself with giving her a bowl of poisoned soup. He hadn't meddled with the rest of the food in the kitchen and pantry, but he didn't want Gunnolf to die quickly. He needed him to suffer. Losing Corrine would do it.

Gunnolf buttoned his shirt. "How did you know about the soup?"

Sitting on the bed, she finished drawing on one stocking, reached for the second. "By what he said. He may have looked like you, but he didn't smell like you. And when he called me by name, then told me to go to *Summerland*, I knew it wasn't you. He's a fool, a dangerous one, but still a fool. You've never allowed me to leave you."

"And I never will. I'm going to kill him."

"I know." She picked up the lacy brown panties next to her. "Besides, he didn't understand you stopped calling me 'your dear girl' when I got old enough to remember not to freak out the old fogies in the pack."

"Don't wear those. They get in the way."

"Silly Grandpa." She waved them at him. "Crotchless. You'll like them. Stop your whining."

"Don't call me that."

"Why not?" Her bra matched the panties. "You are one even if you're too stubborn to make amends with your daughters and meet the kiddoes. Your two-and-a-half-year-old granddaughter is majorly cute, especially when she stomps around demanding to learn how to shift into her wolf."

He couldn't resist. "Has she yet?"

"Nope, but Venus has been teaching her how to use a wooden sword so she can kill monsters." Corrine buttoned her blouse, tucked it into a short, flowered skirt and stepped into her chocolate stilettos. "We better go, or we'll be even later, and you'll keep griping. Who wants to listen to it? Not me."

When they arrived at the police department, she went to unlock the front door while he checked the assigned deputies were making the rounds. He still hadn't come to terms with the idea that Latham was stronger than a mere executioner, but Gunnolf would consider the best, most painful ways to vanquish the younger demon. *I know all his shortcomings. He may be highly intelligent and cruel, but I'm more cunning and I have Corrine on my side.*

He returned to his office, crossing to his desk. Her doggie accoutrements sat on the blotter, and he moved them to the top of the file cabinet. She'd undoubtedly break the rules again soon and he'd need them, so they weren't going into the storage cabinet, at least not yet.

The intercom buzzed. "Two F.B.I. agents are back to see you."

"Bring them here." Gunnolf deliberately sat down behind the desk. "We'll go to lunch after they leave."

A few minutes later, Corrine ushered the two men in dark suits into his office. She pointed out the visitor chairs, but they refused to sit down. So, she did. When she crossed her legs, he glimpsed a hint of her panties. He frowned at her. "Go back to your desk."

"No." She smiled, taunting him. "I'm staying. You're not saying anything I can't hear."

The older one, a tall, stocky man, stepped forward, opening a black billfold, and revealing a badge. "Chief Marvin, we've spoken before. I'm Wardrow Roberts." He gestured to his companion, a handsome, young African American, Native-American, mixed-race man with close-cropped black hair. "This is Agent Fletcher Gaines. We're investigating what happened to Special Agent Newsome and Agent Endicott."

"How are they?" Corrine asked. "I like them, although Newsome should stop drinking so much. It's bad for his liver. Those mints don't hide the smell of vodka."

Special Agent Roberts looked over his shoulder at her, obviously shocked by her assessment. "What else?"

"He's nice. He shares."

"What?" Gunnolf glared at her, furious. "Alcohol is poisonous. You could have died."

"Don't be silly. He gave me some of his peppermints and I'm perfectly fine." She pointed one brilliant pink fingernail at him. "Besides, I prefer wine. Now, listen to these nice men and help them. They want whoever hurt their agents. You better tell them."

Gunnolf leaned back in his chair, hoping he didn't give away his irritation. What was going on with her today? Why was she being so damned helpful to humans? He should have considered himself one, but he didn't. Not when he started life as a *Priest-Mage*, became a warlock, then a demon and finally a member of pack of shifters. No, he didn't change into a wolf, but it didn't mean he couldn't. He didn't see the necessity of wasting his store of *magick* on such silly pursuits.

"We want to know who ran our agents off the highway and abducted Special Agent Newsome." Fletcher Gaines took an angry step forward. "Your daughter, Astra Jamison, was attacked when she tried to help him. Are you looking for the man who stabbed her?"

"What are you talking about? I spoke to her yesterday. Astra's fine."

"You're delusional. She had a sword in her back and was bleeding out barely a week ago." Fletcher Gaines' hands knotted into fists, a concerned frown on his face, dark brown eyes narrowed. "I've seen people die in combat. She was taken away before receiving medical treatment—"

"By whom?" Gunnolf demanded. "Who took her? Who hurt my girl?"

"Latham, of course." Corrine tilted her head. "And Rowdy Tall-Deer took her home. He's her *Chosen* mate. You ought to listen to my mama, Gunnolf. You should give Latham to him for *Yule*. You know what Rowdy says, about *healers*. Good ones can put bodies together and they certainly can take them apart. Latham will die horribly. Won't that be nice?"

"Who is Latham?" Special Agent Roberts demanded through gritted teeth. "Was he the one who attacked our agents?"

"Well, sort of." Corrine heaved a dramatic sigh. "If you're going to come to Corbettstown, you really need to be more broadminded. Now, Gary Smith went after them first. He was tired of being followed so he decided if he did a *blood-magick* rite, he could open a portal in the forest and travel back in time to Liberty Valley in 1888. He made a big mess when he ran your agents off the road. Frank Corbett sent a patrol to do clean-up. Latham was helping them. Astra, her apprentice and Rowdy were in the way. Because she refused to have sex with Latham after he raped her on her fourteenth birthday and passed her around to his friends, she was expendable."

"That's insane."

Gunnolf glared at Corrine. "She never told me it was them. Her mother claimed I did it and used it to keep me from seeing my daughters for years. I knew I hadn't, but a huge public trial would have destroyed my girl, so I—" He stopped. "How do you know that? You were only nine years old at the time."

"Astra's maid, Rebekah, and I went to school together. She heard some of your arguments when Astra started visiting you ten years ago. Rebekah warned me to stay away from you."

"Doesn't appear like it worked," Roberts said. "You're here."

"Gunnolf tends to bluster a lot, but he doesn't assault women. I didn't say Smith's or Latham's or Frank's brains were all there and they do." Corrine twirled her finger in the typical, 'whoo-whoo' motion. "Eating humans will make you nuts. I'm glad Agent Endicott was too badly hurt for him to use, or Smith would have taken her instead. She's a good person, you know, even if she wouldn't let Newsome give me more than two peppermints each time they visited. Nice belly rubs."

Gunnolf glared at her. "You let them in my office and allowed her to touch you? You always attack the deputies if they even cross the threshold."

"I don't like your nasty minions. They're on my 'kill' list right after you." Corrine kicked off her shoes and rose to her feet. "I'm tired of wearing these stilettos. They hurt my toes."

"I like how they look on you."

"Then, you wear them, Gunnolf Marvin. Endicott and Newsome are good, decent humans and they were kind to me when I was being punished. Nobody else was except Hester and you always gave her extra work to do so I didn't get to see her, plus we usually went home before her son came on duty. Trey's still kind to me even though you claimed me as your mate. He brought maple bars some-times for his mom to give me, even if they're not as good as the one your daughter, the kitchen witch makes. And I like belly rubs and peppermints."

Gunnolf stood. "You're a wolf, damn it. You're not a dog—" He stopped, realizing the feds were still there, hearing every word. He sounded crazy.

"It's all these damned, stupid rules with you and you have such a fit when I break them. No, you can't drive my car, Corrine, because you crash it every time. It's fun playing bumper cars with it. It sucks being locked in the dog cage when you drive. I'd shit in it, so you'd have to smell it, but I don't like lying in crap." She tossed her head. "Don't eat humans, Corrine. They're toxic. Don't drink alcohol. It's deadly. No chocolate. It will kill you."

She stomped toward the door. "I'm getting coffee and a maple bar. If you don't piss me off, I'll bring your insipid breakfast tea. Too bad you got rid of my rat poison when I made Trina use it on you. I think you need another dose."

"Coffee is too dangerous. The caffeine will kill—"

"Ma'am, you better stay with us," Special Agent Roberts said. "Were you attacked by the wolf here yesterday? It sounds like you're hallucinating."

"Haven't you ever been grumpy when somebody wakes you up from a good nap? I know you take long ones in your office during the winter. I can smell it." Corrine flipped him off and kept walking. "All this crapfest because I tried to kill Latham yesterday. You and Gunnolf have a lot in common. You probably would have locked me in a kennel last night too."

"It was medical advice so you wouldn't kill me when you were dreaming."

"Don't worry. I'll do it when I'm awake and you are too. I'll enjoy it a lot more."

Gunnolf sank into his chair, eyeing the two agents after she left. "I'm going to have to mind-sweep the pair of you, so you forget everything she just said, or all hell is going to break loose when you file your reports."

"No need for that." Special Agent Roberts chuckled and sat down in one of the visitor chairs. "We actually aren't from the F.B.I. We work for a different agency and our associates will be along soon to help clean up this place."

"Meantime, I'll go help with the coffee." Agent Gaines said. "Maybe, Miss Corrine will let me use silver bullets next time I'm shooting her shifters. Of course, she'll have to give me some. They didn't work on my last assignment and I'm still waiting for our supply people to fill the requisition."

"If any of them are the deputies she hates, that's a given." Gunnolf ran a hand over his jaw. "She never understands I have to keep them close, or I can't control them."

"I'll mention it." Laughing, Agent Gaines sauntered from the office, as graceful as a large cat on the prowl.

# 30

*Eagleville, Washington*
*Sunday, December 2nd, 2018*

METEOR SLID INTO THE PASSENGER SEAT OF THE PICKUP, SCOOTING over until she sat in the middle, next to Jed. She left the side closer to the door for Gard Devlin. Neither guy had dressed up for Sunday dinner at Frank Corbett's and she hoped the lack of respect didn't come back to bite Jed in his wolfish tail. Both men wore work clothes, jeans, flannel shirts and boots.

She was grateful she'd taken time to go upstairs long enough to change into slacks, a light blue sweater that matched her eyes, and ballet slipper style flats. She'd freshened her makeup, braided her hair, and decided against adding the rest of the *talipenlace* set. The bracelet and necklace would provide sufficient protection, especially since she couldn't remove them, and their power seemed even stronger.

Her smart phone buzzed, and she shifted enough to remove it from her purse. She read the text from her sister. "Astra wants us to wait here for her and Rowdy. He made an amulet for you, Jed and apparently there's also one for Gard."

"I don't do jewelry." Gard glanced at Jed. "I figured you were too big a man for that stuff."

"When it comes to my uncle and the way he steals shapes, I'll take all the protection I can get." Jed switched off the truck engine. "We already know he's willing to use someone else to kill me when he doesn't do it himself."

"And if Rebekah is remembering what happened to you in your past lives, Gardersolter, you should be too." Meteor tucked away her phone. "What do you know about how you died the first time?"

"Not much." Shock filled Gard's rugged features and his jaw tightened. "I tried to stop a rapist from assaulting a woman I was assigned to protect. His friends killed me before I could. And it's happened more than once. When I was a kid, someone attacked our neighbors, an old lady whose grand-daughter was visiting. I still have nightmares about it."

"And that's why my brother, Orion, calls you a guard in name and nature. Astra says you seek justice for your dead." Meteor rested a hand on Gard's shoulder. "The same person who keeps hunting you has slain my older sister in her previous lives. Today, we'll face him as well as the alpha, the pack executioner and—"

"Your father." Jed glanced at the black Lexus when it pulled in beside his truck. Astra parked and Rowdy opened the passenger door.

"Okay, let's get this done." Jed eased out of his rig.

Meteor watched and waited as the two men went to meet Rowdy. It didn't take long for them to talk. Jed returned first. He now wore a pendant, a black tourmaline stone on a thick cord around his neck. She met his gaze. "What does it do?"

"Keeps me safe from evil and it will protect me if my uncle tries to shoot me or stab me again." He frowned, ran a thumb over the gleaming rock. "Rowdy reminded me about what happened when we'd just come through the portal to this realm. I found you dead in our chamber the first time. I was devastated. Hugh refused

*Warpathian* justice to me although I begged for it. I wanted to be sent to the stars in your coffin."

"What did you do?" She gripped his hands with hers. "I thought you were the one who brought me a drink to settle my queasy stomach, but it was poison. I really didn't want it, but you seemed so concerned. And agony ripped through me, burning pain—"

She paused. "Whoever it was intended to kill me. While I died, I heard him laughing and I saw the evil gold of his wolf eyes."

"It wasn't me." He tightened his hold on her fingers. "I swear it wasn't. Afterwards, when Hughondear and Rowdy refused to let me die, I went back to our room. My uncle found me there. He brought me a large decanter of brandy-wine. I drank it and the next thing I knew I was with you in *Summerland*."

"He killed you too." Meteor heaved a sigh and pressed close to him. "We've got to destroy him before he comes after us again."

"Rowdy just told me that they thought I committed suicide. I didn't. I wanted vengeance and after I'd found it, I might have sought that solace. I loved you so much and I didn't want to live without you."

"Don't die for me. Not now, not ever. Kill for me instead." She found his lips with hers, a brief, warm kiss. "Avenge me if he succeeds again and look after our wolflings."

"I will." He tipped up her chin. "And you do the same, Matiranika."

She nodded. Some might not understand the bargain they'd just made with one another, but she did, and she'd honor it. The passenger door opened, and Gard joined them in the cab of the truck. He wore a gold chain with a green stone covered in strange designs. She'd have to ask her sister what they meant. *Later,* Meteor thought. *I'll find out later.*

———

The temperature dropped and the misting rain changed to snow. Small flakes drifted down, sticking to the grass, bushes, and trees beside the highway. It hadn't started to accumulate on the roads yet. When he drove into Corbettstown, Jed noticed various law enforcement vehicles parked near the town hall. County sheriff department rigs, Washington State patrol sedans and SUVs, even more sedate cars that must belong to various federal agencies including the FBI. His gaze fell on a row of black Town Cars. He hadn't expected *dracklegons*, the ancestral law-givers to finally come to Corbettstown.

It shouldn't have come as much of a surprise, but it still did. Having several other agencies here was bound to attract their attention. Granted, they were proponents of 'go along to get along' before it was fashionable. While *magick* always had a price, it didn't mean everyone in the area, especially the humans they lived alongside, needed to know it was real and the *Priest-Mages* preferred to be discreet.

Meteor gestured to the luxury vehicles. "Do those belong to who, I think? Are the lawgivers finally here when they've been ignoring us for the past three hundred years?"

"I suspect your father and my uncle had something to do with that." Jed glanced swiftly at her. "Shall we stop and ask or just go to my uncle's house?"

Before she answered, the driver's door of the first vehicle opened. A lean, muscled man stepped out into the street, blocking the truck. Jed recognized the distinctive red and black uniform he wore as one similar to those of the Warrior Guild, the ancient protectors of the *Ethlestial* priests. Snowflakes dusted his shoulder-length, salt and pepper hair as he approached. A close-cropped dark beard framed his jaw and cheeks.

Gard narrowed his eyes. "I feel like I ought to know him, that we've fought together before, but I don't recall his name."

"I don't know the one he uses in this time, but in *Trilunon*, it was Iarvosarvel." Jed shifted the truck into park and opened the driver's door. "He was a trustworthy ally who insisted we preserve the lives of the war-queen's army, rather than killing them when Hugh invaded *Amalodia* to claim his bride."

"And I'm sure you went along with that." Meteor glared at him. "You always had a penchant for looking at other women, especially those in armor."

"They were nearly as lovely as you are." He chuckled and brushed her lips quickly with his, amused at her jealousy. "Let's go see what he wants and then we'll head to my uncle's house."

She slid off the bench seat and followed him out of the pickup. He took her hand as they walked toward the older man, Gard behind them. Jed heard her mutter a few choice words under her breath. Luckily, it wasn't a spell.

Jed inclined his head in greeting. "It's been a long time."

"Ian Velasco. It's good to see the two of you together." He glanced past them to the late model Lexus parked behind the truck. Astra and Rowdy came to join them. "So, you and your *vaslattel* have finally united, Rowindache. It's taken long enough."

"Three hundred years since we arrived, Iarvosarvel." Rowdy shook hands with the older man. "What happened to the *dracklegons*? Why haven't they intervened and stopped Jarvesel from killing so many of us again and again? We've barely been able to find each other in this life and it's taken too long for us to combine our *magick* so we can serve our people as we're meant to serve them."

"*Time Portals* are only large enough to admit a few riders at a time. You and the *Trecesalty* led your people through, but the doorway closed before we could join you. When we managed to open it again, we landed in a different world. We had to fight to protect the priests. The *magick* there was strange to us, and it took two hundred years for us to learn how to control it so we could return to those who'd journeyed from *Trilunon*."

Jed flashed a sideways glance at Rowdy, his long-time friend, the *High Healer*. "That sounds like a curse cast by a sorcerer."

"Or my demon-father," Astra said in even tones. "The last thing he'd want is his grandfather and the other *priest-mages* here insisting we follow the laws set forth by them."

"Precisely." Ian looked over his shoulder when the rest of his patrol, an equal number of male and female warriors filtered out of the vehicles and came toward them. The twelve sword-mates encircled them, providing a secure barrier. "So, what is your plan for this visit?"

"Thojedescar and Matiranika are here to proclaim they are ready to have their own pack and where their territory begins and ends." Rowdy rested a hand on Astra's arm. "I will serve as their *High Healer* and my *vaslattel* is a dark sorceress. She will send those who choose to die, rather than respect the new pack onto *Summerland*."

"A fair decision." Ian gestured toward his group of warriors who protected them. "My guild will support this choice. What else happens today?"

"One of the shifters here, Corrine had a bad reaction to dream-walking through her past yesterday." Rowdy stopped when a priestess stepped forward. "What is it?"

"I'm Isabelle Velasco." Her uniform fit the woman perfectly. High cheekbones, a wide mouth, beautiful light green eyes. "Where is she? I failed her before. I won't again. I should have expected the attack and countered it."

"You and your soldiers died to the last woman, Daughter." Ian put a hand on her shoulder. "Nobody expected you to defeat two demons determined to steal your charge."

"Two?" Meteor stared at him. "My father was—"

"One of them. He saw Corrinadora and wanted her, so he seduced her, enchanted her and took her away while his apprentice who'd become an executioner slew her guards. To be fair, Jarvesel was furious when he learned of their deaths. They were only supposed to be immobilized, not murdered." A faint smile creased Ian's mouth. "When you make a bargain with Abahendes, the *Prince of Lies*, don't trust him. Jarvesel demanded some of the talents of a sex demon. He received them but didn't know the cost."

Astra froze. "How could he be so foolish? Why didn't he read the *grimoires*? Study the *mages* who came before?"

"Explain it to the rest of us who aren't lawyers or judges." Meteor poked her older sister. "I'm baffled."

"Depending on the spellcaster, it means once he chose his partners, either female or male or other, he'd be unable to harm them. The sex would always have to be consensual." Astra stared into the distance but was obviously recalling the past. "If that's true, then our demon-father didn't commit many of the crimes we thought he did. Someone else did that raping and killing. He's been falsely accused."

"And our mother? Did he slay her time and again? Torture her in this life when we were children?"

"I don't know." Astra took a deep breath and met Ian's gaze. "At some point, you and your people must interrogate him. If Latham has been doing all the torturing and killing, we need to know more about him. And Corrine?"

"She had finished her training and was ready to go to the first pack who needed her. She'd signed her contract to serve as *Stalenary* for a thousand years in this realm." Ian explained. "She and Jarvesel had already bonded before he slew Lavarutesel, the killer of my daughter and her soldiers. Corrinadora and Jarvesel have been together ever since. What else?"

Meteor lifted her chin and met his light green gaze. "My mother wants her bond severed to my demon-sire. She sent word to the *Dracklegon Council*, seeking her freedom."

"It's under consideration." Ian held up his hand to quell any protest. "There will be repercussions. Jarvesel may protest because it stops you and your sisters from being reborn into your next lives or having more younglings to carry on our heritage."

"I am willing to have this be my last life," Meteor said. "I can't speak for Thojedescar, but I've died early in my previous incarnations, and he has too."

"Count me in." Astra stepped forward to take Meteor's free hand. "I've been used as a virgin altar too many times for blood sacrifices. If my father was trapped by his choices, it must have been your cousin Lavarutesel who raped me, gave me to his followers to use and then slew me while his minions watched, cheered my death, drank my blood and ate my remains."

"And your sister?" Ian's quick look around his circle of warriors stopped the hisses and furious snarls. "What does she say?"

"If we choose merciful deaths at the end of these lives, she's willing to die with us rather than come around again," Meteor said.

"And you, Thojedescar? What do you say?"

Jed slipped his arm around Meteor's waist. "While I'd rather live with my soul-matched mate and be a true father to our younglings time and again, I'm willing to journey to *Summerland* with her. My uncle has stolen my shape to kill her and our children more than once."

"What about you, Rowindache? As a *High Healer*, you must want the same thing your new *vaslattel* does."

"Her heart leads her to try and protect me." Rowdy folded his arms, jaw set. "The first lesson a *healer* learns when putting a body together is how to take one apart. I offered mercy to Lavarutesel when he stole my mate on our first soul-matched night and your grandsire granted it."

"I remember that well." Ian turned to Astra. "You have accepted this wizard as your true mate. My grandsire says he hears your vows in the winds."

Jed saw a blush seep into his sister-by-marriage's cheeks before she spoke. "Rowindache enjoys that spell far too much and sees I do as well. I won't have him seek vengeance for anything that's happened to me. It will cost him too much. Since we are merely bedmates, he will not die when I do and he can find another, a true soul-match, not one so damaged."

"I asked the Council for the right to slay Lavarutesel before he mortally injured you ten days ago. A lesser *healer* couldn't have saved you, my own."

"I witnessed the attack," Jed told the warrior-priest. "As did my *laspowima*. We helped get Astra and her familiar to safe grounds. I will stand as Rowindache's second at the duel."

"Not needful. I demand that honor," Ian nodded to Rowdy. "If we find him today, I will have him brought to the alpha's house. After the shapeshifter battle, you may meet my cousin and treat him as he so richly deserves. He certainly knows what's expected of my *relkinam* and chose dishonor instead. If not today, you'll have him when we capture him."

"I appreciate your support," Rowdy said.

"My grandsire says it pleases the *mages* to see Satiranika determined to save you as she did almost a fortnight ago. Still, the cost is too high for her to pay it especially now."

Jed eyed the others in the circle. Gard looked as baffled as he did, but Meteor and Rowdy seemed to accept the words at face value. Only Astra appeared ready to dispute the point. Despite her bond with Rowdy, she hadn't changed much since his arrival at *Samhain*.

Two deputies came out of the town hall and stared at them. Jed gestured toward his truck. "I'm ready. Let's move to the alpha's house."

Ian eyed one of his senior warriors. The man inclined his head in acceptance of the unspoken order. "Most of my patrol travels with you. The others come with me. Wait until my arrival to start the clash between the alphas. Choosing a new leader must be done according to the rules of the pack and *Ethlestial* protocol."

"Fair enough," Jed said. "I've never broken our laws."

A youngling's yip startled all of them and he turned to see two youngsters, a black and then a brown wolf pup tumbling out of the lead Town Car. "What are they doing? Why bring those to a battle? They're babies."

"We didn't have a choice," Ian said. "If we left them, the barracks would be destroyed when we returned. They're very mischievous. They're your mate's half-brothers and between having Corrine for a mother and a sorcerer for a father, we didn't dare let them grow beyond two years of age."

"It's hard enough handling them now," Isabelle agreed. "When they're teenagers—"

Ian shuddered. "It was bad enough raising you and your sisters. These two— You better catch them before they're run over. That will only annoy them."

Isabelle nodded and hurried off, followed by three other guards. The pups seemed to think this was a great game. They proceeded to dash back and forth, running under the various vehicles. Then, they'd dart into the street and race around the warriors who failed to capture them.

———

"Are you serious?" Meteor planted her hands on her hips and looked the *dracklegons* up and down. "What is wrong with you people?" She didn't wait for an answer. "Come along, Astra."

"Me? Why me?"

"Because I can smell it. You're pregnant and you don't know what talents your child will have. What will you do with a shifter?"

"Give it to you until it's old enough to reason."

"Good luck with that." Meteor walked to the closest rig and waited. When one of the pups ran by, she snatched him up by the scruff of the neck. *'Bad boy.'*

He twisted in her hold and snapped at her. A quick shake elicited a ki-yi and the second, bigger pup attacked her, determined to protect his sibling. Meteor bent, grabbed his neck fur and shook him. A yelp. She turned and started toward Jed's truck where he waited and watched.

Typical male. What did he think was going to happen if they had two more of the little furballs? She'd raise them and he'd strut around town telling the whole pack about his wonderful pups?

Out of breath, Isabelle arrived with her companions. "Don't hurt them. I'll put them back in the car. Maybe, they'll stay this time."

"I'm not hurting them. They need to learn to behave appropriately." Meteor kept walking. "Astra, be ready."

"For what?"

The pups attempted to wriggle free. Meteor didn't release them. Instead, she growled and shook them again. *'Be good.'*

*'No! You bad!'* The larger male glared. *'Go now!'* He shot an energy ball at her.

"What the—" Astra lifted her hand, blocked it and sent it back to the youngster. It struck his nose, then his head.

Startled, he barked, then whimpered.

Meteor plunked the pair in the back of the truck. *'You stay, bad boys. You stay!'* She glowered up at Jed. "Are you sure you want two more?"

"Ours are much better behaved. Of course, they have a mean mama and when she's not happy, everyone's sorry." He tipped up her chin and kissed her. He grinned at the pups. They sat on their little furry butts and looked back at him. The smaller one curled his lips, revealing tiny white fangs and snarled.

Meteor elbowed him. "Correct them."

"What?"

She sighed. "Remember when Edwin had a tantrum and bit you back in the day? Do that alpha wolf thing you do. Papa up!"

# 31

*Corbettstown, Washington*
*Sunday, December 2ⁿᵈ, 2018*

ALONE IN THE BREAKROOM, CORRINE ADDED WATER TO THE COFFEE machine and selected a pod of decaf coffee, then one of breakfast tea. She glanced at the door when Fletcher Gaines strolled into the room. "So, what does a cat drink? I have tea—valerian, peppermint, apple, apricot, blueberry and chamomile."

He blinked, then smiled. "How did you know?"

"No offense, but I learned to recognize the smell of different were-species when I was in training." She propped a hip against the counter. "And your partner? He's a bear, isn't he?"

"Yes. A grizzly." Fletcher scanned the selection of teas, then chose a mixed berry pod. He followed that with a cranberry-apple one. "Amazing you recall that class after so much time, Miss Corrine."

"Just Corrine. It helps I was doing a dream journey all the way back to when we arrived last night." Tears stung and she blinked hard. "I'm so sorry my teachers were slaughtered. Even watching

Gunnolf kill their murderer the first time only helped a little since he was resurrected a few days later."

Fletcher rested a hand on her arm, bumped her head gently with his. "How long did it take you to forgive him?"

"Mostly it was forgiving myself for letting a handsome wizard seduce me. I started feeling sorry for him when we found the queen dead, their daughters stolen, and he was arrested. I knew he hadn't killed her because it happened when he was charming me in the gardens at the school and we were—" She paused, trying to find another word for 'fucking' under the stars and the light from the three moons. "Being intimate for the first time. After he was convicted and sentenced to die in the *Fires of Eternity*, I helped him escape. Then, the plague struck, and he worked day and night trying to find a spell to counteract it. None of them lasted for long. The disease kept mutating and he blamed himself when so many died."

Her cup finished filling and she switched out the mugs, starting one for Gunnolf. "I didn't know why until I saw it last night. A poisoner and executioner, Latham sabotaged everything Jarvesel did, and he didn't have enough *Power* to save *Trilunon*."

"He's going to have to be questioned by the Warrior Guild, Corrine. If you stand as a witness for him and he's cleared, we'll return him to you."

She studied Fletcher's face, trying to read the truth. "Is that a promise you can keep?"

"Yes, but you'll have to keep taking responsibility for him. You're alpha."

"Yes, I am." She managed a smile as she changed the cups again. "His alpha too."

"That's right." Fletcher wrapped an arm around her shoulders to give a quick sideways hug. "You'll need your enforcer when you come to the meeting for all the *Stalenary* in March."

She nodded. "If everything is functioning well here, I'll look forward to the opportunity."

Footsteps, male laughter and voices preceded four deputies coming into the breakroom. Three of them always cheered, laughed and made bets on how many climaxes she'd have when Gunnolf fucked her. The fourth, Jasper Alan Corbett had reformed when she claimed him at the beginning of November.

The biggest, a burly dark-haired shifter smiled and grabbed his crotch. "If the boss is going to share you, I'm going first. My turn to make you scream."

"In a minute." She put the last cup on the tray, cut one of the two maple bars in half. "Gunnolf doesn't care for sweets. Leave mine alone."

"How long is this going to take?" Fletcher asked, picking up the tray. "Five minutes. Ten?"

"Come when you hear them screaming and crying." She ignored the hoots and laughter, pointing at Jasper. "You sit. Be quiet."

Jasper frowned, shaking his head. "I'll fight with my alpha."

"Soon. But not today." She waited until he obeyed, taking a chair to the corner of the room and sitting down, out of the way.

Oh, this was going to be great! She walked to the center of the room and waited while the other three circled around her, recalling everything her teacher taught about hand-to-hand combat. When one of them reached for her, she laughed. Time for the party to start!

———

Fletcher Gaines returned to the office, carrying a ceramic tray with four cups and two maple bars. "Corrine will join you soon."

"Don't you mean us?" Gunnolf asked.

"No. I mean what I said." Fletcher passed him a cup of tea. "No rat poison. I promise."

A loud thump sounded down the hall, followed by a second and then a third. Wardrow Roberts accepted his tea and half the doughnut. "How many are there?"

"Three, so I'll need to borrow a pair of your handcuffs." Fletcher sipped his own tea. "Unless one of them accepts her as the alpha."

"Think that's likely?"

"No."

Bangs and crashes followed. Gunnolf half rose to his feet, but the other two officers blocked his path. "Move."

"She said to wait until I heard screams and crying." Fletcher finished his part of the maple bar. "Pretty sure she doesn't want you to interfere. I just hope she doesn't tear off the big one's balls. Ian never brings along a *Healer* until the second wave."

———

Corrine straightened her blouse and tucked the knife back in the sheath under her skirt. The three injured shifters lay crumpled against the wall. The biggest was still unconscious. The other two slowly stirred, one wrapping an arm around his cracked ribs. If she allowed it, the trio would heal as soon as they shifted to their wolf forms.

She shook her head. Nope, she'd make them remain human. Healing slowly would teach more manners than she could. They certainly needed to learn who was in charge. And it wasn't them, not anymore!

She glanced at Jasper. "Cuff them. They go with the E.W.G."

"The what?"

Before she answered, she heard the steady clomping of marching boots. A cluster of warriors entered a tall, muscled man in the lead. She stared at the distinctive red and black uniform he wore. Snowflakes melted on his shoulder-length, salt and pepper hair as he approached. A close-cropped dark beard framed his jaw and cheeks. Five other officers followed him, two women and three men. All of them were in similar attire.

One of the women came closer. A friendly smile warmed her strong features and green eyes. "Hello, Corrine. I'm Isabelle."

"It's so good to see you again." Corrine hugged the woman. "I mourned you for years."

"I know. I heard you in *Summerland*." Isabelle kissed her cheek. "Child, it was never your fault an incubus seduced you at your graduation party and a second demon massacred us. We were meant to guard you, not the other way around."

"What demons?" Jasper glanced up from where he fastened silver handcuffs on his former comrades. "These shifters? I grew up with them."

"Oh, no. Not them. They're just stupid, mean and lazy." Isabelle wrapped an arm around Corrine's waist. "A lifetime or two in one of our prisons may redeem them. If not, they'll go to the fires. We prefer our meat roasted and that way, they'll never return to bother you or your pack leader."

Her words prompted moans and pleas for mercy from the injured shifters until Ian waved a hand and silenced them. "Instead of fighting your new alpha, you should have bound yourselves to her for the good of the pack. Now, we'll ask the *Priest-Mages* to see what the future holds for all of you and if you even have one."

If they'd been halfway decent to her, she might have intervened. Since they hadn't been, Corrine watched as the men were taken away by some of the lawgivers. More footsteps. This time it was Gunnolf Marvin and the other two officers.

Fletcher carried her coffee and maple bar. "Next time, you say there will be screaming, make sure it happens."

"All right." She sat at the table and waited while he brewed more tea for the new arrivals. When he pointed to the supply cupboard, she nodded, and he sliced the three remaining maple bars into pieces, putting them on a plate for his companions.

Gunnolf came and picked up her hand, eyeing the two broken nails. "The salon is closed today. And you know I like it when you look like a pretty puppy."

She sighed, drove her elbow into his ribs, then back-fisted him in the throat. He went to his knees. She picked up the knife off the table. She dropped to her knees, held it to his neck. "No more, Gunnolf."

He struggled to speak, barely able to croak. "What?"

"Call me a puppy one more time in public. You die. Got it?"

He stared into her face, and she let him see her true self. Not just the primal alpha female or dominatrix, but the *Stalenary*, the ruler of all the wolf shifters from Canada to Mexico, from the Rockies to the Pacific Ocean. True, she wasn't in charge of the native packs who'd been here before her people came from *Trilunon*, but she had enough responsibility controlling their people. Granted, Gunnolf kept her safe from Frank Corbett, the alpha and the executioner for almost a year when she was sentenced to death, but enough was enough!

Blood trickled down his throat and she met his gaze. "I've served my time. You ask and I'll consider it. I'm alpha. From now on, I tell my pack what to do."

He blinked, then nodded. He didn't bow his head. Good. She liked him large and in charge at certain times in certain places, especially when they were together at home.

She leaned forward, kissed him. "My enforcer. All mine. You see to it my wolves do what I say. Yes?"

"Your enforcer. All yours." He smiled, caught her wrist and moved away the knife. "May I heal your injuries?"

"Please." She rested her hand on his cheek, staring into his rugged features and dark eyes. She hadn't admitted it to anyone but a few of the blows had landed. Her ribs hurt, bruised not broken. "I have more shifters to fight today."

"I know." He stood and helped her rise, drawing her into his arms. "After you teach them who their pack leader is, I will battle for my alpha."

"I know." She clung to him for a moment. "And you'd better win."

"I will."

———

Meteor dreaded the visit to Frank Corbett's house. Her fears slowly dissipated when they were accompanied by six members of the fierce *Ethlestial* Warrior Guild. She frowned when Jed stopped in the driveway of a large three-story, brick Colonial. Obviously, the alpha had company for Sunday dinner because several cars and trucks were parked along the verge of the road.

"I don't remember this house being here before. It wasn't where Frank lived a hundred years ago or where we did."

"No. Your sisters had fits and fell in them after we were killed. They rounded up several allies and attacked the town, destroying it and the adult shifters." Jed switched off the motor, removing the keys from the ignition. "Since most of the buildings were made of wood, they were decimated when the town burned. This time, the shifters were determined not to have the same thing happen again. I don't know if it will work for them or not."

"Oddly enough, that makes perfect sense." Meteor let him help her out of the pickup. Gard stood nearby while they waited for Astra and Rowdy to join them.

Meteor walked to where she could view the truck bed. The two wolf pups eyed her warily from where they curled up on one blanket, a second over them. '*You stay. Be quiet. Hide.*'

'*Yes, Mama,*' the little one said.

'*Yes, Mama,*' his larger litter-mate echoed.

'*Not Mama. Big sister. Your mama comes soon. Be good boys.*'

'*Yes, Sister,*' the pair chorused.

Meteor took a deep breath, concerned about leaving them but more concerned about taking them into Frank's house where they could be eaten. Surrounded by the guards, the five of them started up the sidewalk to the front porch. The senior warrior rang the bell.

Lorena, an older shifter female in black leggings and a matching tunic answered the door. Her light brown eyes widened when she saw the members of the *Warrior Guild.* "What does this mean, Jed?"

"A challenge." He took Meteor's hand. "My mate and I are here to announce the forming of our own pack. We will hold western Liberty Valley for those law-abiding members who choose to obey our rules. Others may stay with my uncle. However, be warned the *dracklegons* will be imposing the traditional customs and mores. They are sending the Guild to ensure it."

Lorena hesitated, tears filling her eyes. "The enforcer is mated to my daughter. I can't leave without them. She was dream-walking through her past yesterday. Has the *High Healer* seen her?"

"Not yet." Rowdy stepped forward, taking her hands. "I will. I was checking on their pups."

"What?" Lorena gaped at him. "She had them in her last life. Not now."

"And I took them to the *Warrior Guild* to keep them safe." Astra glanced toward the living-room, then added tactfully, "They overwhelm the soldiers because they're like the others in Corrine's family and shift early before their first birthday. It's hard to handle two-legged babies, but four-legged ones—"

The lead warrior nodded agreement. "They hurl toys at us, refuse to eat vegetables and set fires in the barracks. They even burn our uniforms. When Ian wants to punish us, we're assigned to bath and bedtime. That's horrendous. We couldn't believe it when you witches were able to stop them from running into traffic."

A smile slowly dawned on Lorena's face. "Where are my grandsons?"

"In my truck." Jed handed her the set of keys. "Do you have somewhere safe to take them?"

"Of course. We'll go to Corrine's house. She's their mama."

"Won't Frank's people be able to find you there?" Meteor glanced toward the Great Room, hearing voices for the first time. "Will he miss you?"

"Oh, he'll forget I was ever here. I'm like the enforcer. Corrine marked me as hers years ago. He has warded the house against the deputies. They can only enter when he's there to protect her. Since he's working, we'll be safe."

Three of the warriors, Astra, Rowdy and Gard accompanied Meteor and Jed when they went into the Great Room. Couches lined the walls; a bar took up the corner and about twenty people waited for the sorting of the children to start in the adjoining dining area. A few of the women cried softly while their mates paced and cursed. Silence fell as the group of shifters turned to face them. Three deputies stood between them and the hallway to the front door.

Frank Corbett took an angry step forward. "How dare you bring witches into my house?"

"I've brought my mate, Matiranika, the shape-shifting queen of the *Trecesalty*." Jed kept his gaze and tone even. "And our sister, Satiranika, a dark sorceress who serves *Hecate, the Goddess of Death*, Rowindache, the *High Healer* who saved her when you sent a patrol to kill them."

"There was a mess that needed to be cleaned up and they shouldn't have been there or intervened."

"We serve the *Goddess* and her consort, now and always. We protect the innocent, human and *Trilunon* alike." Rowdy stood next to Jed. "Today, we are here to witness the separation of the packs. I will heal the damaged wolves who wish to join the Eagleville shifters. My mate will send any ready to die to *Summerland*. And..."

"We will take the lawbreakers with us." Ian Velasco spoke from the doorway. "We have seized three of them already. They go to our safehold to face judgement. Lavarutesel, known as Latham Sellers in this life, has been promised to Rowindache who will teach that a *healer* can take apart a body as well as put one together."

Frank scowled at the cluster of guards and the young blonde woman who stood close by one of them, a black and red cloak around her shoulders. His gaze narrowed on her. "Corrine is ours. She belongs to our enforcer and is his favorite pet. Come here, shifter."

"Are you sure you want that? You ordered him to kill me more than once after he announced I was his mate. And he refused to do it. He wouldn't let anyone else slay me or collect the bounty you promised." Corrine lifted her chin. "His good deputies, the ones I claimed, and many other shifters helped hide me from you."

Frank glanced over his shoulder. "They brought these traitors for meat. They serve me, not you."

"The choice is yours." Corrine gazed at the deputies. "Lay down the weapons, surrender and I will grant you a merciful trial by the law-keepers. Refuse and I won't stop them from killing you."

Silence fell as the rest of the shifters eyed the officers and their automatic rifles. Meteor looked at her uncle who signaled his warriors. They circled around the alpha and started toward the cops.

One raised his rifle and Ian shook his head. "Don't do that. Shooting my dracks just angers them and we'll roast you for our dinner."

Silence while the deputies considered their options and then the weapons were placed on the floor. They knelt and waited to be handcuffed by the warriors.

"What are you doing?" Frank glared at Corrine. "They serve me."

"Not anymore." Corrine didn't raise her voice. "This pack is mine."

"Not yet," Frank said. "You'll have to fight me."

"Not a problem." Jed rumbled. "You've killed too many including my parents. I challenge—"

"No, Thojedescar. He's mine to kill." Corrine stepped out from under the cloak. "If he ever returns, you can have him."

She didn't wear a typical cop uniform. She'd opted for a scoop-necked beige blouse, a very short, flowered skirt that barely covered her butt and brown thigh-high stockings. Her chocolate-brown stilettos shone. Sunshine blonde hair was neatly coiled into a bun at the nape of her neck. She kept her makeup discreet, highlighting the golden-brown eyes and long lashes, bright pink polish on her artificial nails.

Corrine walked into the room, facing not only Frank but the rest of the shifters. "In one of my past lives, he conspired with a demon to take my babies for meat. In this life, he refused me a trial by combat when I was falsely accused. He beat and raped me when the enforcer claimed me as his mate. I am the *Stalenary*. He dishonored me."

"I'm the alpha. You disobeyed me. I sentenced you to death. I had to—"

"I am the *Stalenary*," Corrine repeated. "I agreed to serve as ruler of the wolf shifters from our realm, to guard and protect them for a thousand years. The enforcer is my mate. It is our law that mate-bonds must be honored by all, including you."

The law-keepers opened the French doors. They ushered the children outside onto the patio to wait for their parents. The former deputies were led away.

Frank looked wildly from Corrine to the guild to the muttering members of the pack. "Who says I haven't?"

"Thojedescar and his mate, the second queen of the *Trecesalty*." Meteor stepped up. "I bear witness to you killing me in my last four lives, killing the child I carried and murdering your nephew time and again."

"As a *High Healer*, I bear witness to you having your shifters disembowel me, rip me to shreds, and eat me alive while I heard the shifters quarrel over my bones more than once to keep me from my mate," Rowdy said.

"I am a high priestess of *Hecate, the Goddess of the Crossroads and of Death*." It was Astra's turn. "I bear witness as an advocate for my half-sister, an obedient member of the pack. You promised her to Lavarutesel who tortured and murdered her in past lives in the guise of my father."

"I am the *Stalenary*. For these and other crimes, your sentence is death." Corrine shimmered in an aurora of light. From woman to a giant female wolf in moments.

Then she was across the room.

She leaped. Frank slammed onto the floor.

She didn't hesitate. Her fangs slashed his throat. Blood sprayed.

She jumped away before it covered her. Ian took her place. A sword thrust to Frank's heart. A second to behead him.

Shocked, the adult shifters stared at the large gray timber wolf. When she stalked toward them, they dropped to their knees. One by one, each of them swore their allegiance to her. Afterwards, they exited through the glass doors to join their younglings.

The new alpha turned, circled around Frank's body and paced toward Meteor and the others. Corrine started to shimmer, and Meteor hastily covered the wolf with the red and black cloak as she changed to her human shape. "We remain allies as we were in the past, as we are today, and for the next thousand years. What is your choice?"

"He does not return, my queen." Corrine tucked her hand in the crook of Meteor's arm. "Make it so. Please."

"Very well." Meteor met Ian's gaze. "The *Trecesalty* requests the *Priest-Mages* prevent him from journeying to *Summerland* and keep him from *Rebirth*."

"Agreed." Ian met their gazes. "Anything else?"

"He's been eating humans," Corrine said. "I don't know about *dracklegons*, but his meat would be toxic to us. I suggest you burn it to ashes and scatter those to the four winds so he never returns."

"Agreed," Ian promised.

## 32

*Corbettstown, Washington*
*Sunday, December 2nd, 2018*

HE'D SPENT THE AFTERNOON HELPING WARDROW ROBERTS TRACK down errant shifters the *Warrior Guild* wanted to question. Thankfully, Gunnolf was glad to be rid of the worst troublemakers. Life would be much more peaceful without them, especially since he'd be short of deputies until he trained more. They hadn't found any trace of A.J. Corbett, high on the list of wanted shifters, and Forest Gaines went to collect Andrel from the hospital. He said it'd be a little while before he returned because Corrine texted him a shopping list.

Several vehicles parked in front of his house made it a bit tricky to find a place for the Crown Victoria, but Gunnolf finally managed. Wondering who'd come to visit, he headed into the living room. Two wolf pups rolled and tumbled on the carpet in the middle of the room, under Lorena's watchful gaze.

Gunnolf glanced across the room at Corrine sitting in his recliner. "Where did they come from?"

"Really, Father." His lawyer daughter didn't move from her seat on the couch. Astra shook her head. In black leggings and a matching dark tunic, her gold *talipenlace* set drew attention. "After being around more than three hundred and fifty years, becoming an incubus and siring five children, one would think you'd know."

"What?" Gunnolf stared at her. "They're—"

Looking over the rim of a wineglass, Meteor took obvious pity on him. "Your sons. Our half-brothers. Astra took them to the *Warrior Guild* a hundred years ago but they're like you, too tough for mere *dracklegons* to raise. You have them back. Good luck. You'll need it."

"What does that mean?"

"Remy shoots lightning bolts when he's angry." Lorena pointed to the larger pup when she held up her scorched boot. "They didn't like it when I put them down for naps after snack time. Rom threw fireballs at me. They can do it as humans or wolves."

"No more being rude to Grandma or guests. Even if they're half sorcerer like their father, no fires in the house or Mama spank," Corrine said firmly. "Gunnolf, I'm glad you're home. Take the boys outside to pee. Forest should be back soon with diapers and other things. Your sons by marriage are reorganizing the guestroom into a nursery. They'll probably kick the crap out of you later."

"I don't know what I've done to deserve that." Gunnolf strode across the room and picked up his boys. He held them tight. The smaller one, Rom, licked his cheek. "I haven't seen you for so long. I've missed you," Gunnolf said.

*'Us too.'* Remy, the larger one growled and nipped at his shirt. *'Gramma mean. Mama kisses too much.'*

"And I'm glad to have both of them." Gunnolf left the room, clutching his sons. "And you. I never thought I'd be glad to see the *dracklegons*."

---

Meteor laughed. "I never thought I'd be glad to see my father or be comfortable in his house." She lifted her glass in salute to Corrine. "Welcome to the family. What's next on your list as the new alpha of the Corbettstown pack?"

"Let's see. Isabelle is moving her patrol into Frank's house, so we'll have a permanent Guild station here." Corrine filled a glass with red wine and passed it to her mother who promptly took a seat in the rocking chair. "It will make it easier for them to help the shifters who need it. Gunnolf will be busy finding new deputies. I'm talking to the principal at the high school and arranging for girls to return to class after *Yule*. And we will not be hunting or eating humans so don't send your criminals here, Astra."

"That all makes sense." Meteor studied the golden-haired, young girl in jeans and a T-shirt. *Until I look in those eyes, it's hard to believe she's been my father's mate for three hundred and thirty years.* "What are you going to do about my father being part incubus?"

"Enjoy him." Heat seeped into Corrine's cheeks. "Cover your ears, Mama. I happen to love long slow fucks all night."

"Corrinadora! Watch your potty mouth. What will your step-daughters think?"

"We enjoy them too, although my *capastrol* prefers to hold me against the door or a wall." Astra lifted her cup of raspberry tea. "Has anyone seen Latham or is he least in sight?"

"Gone for the moment." Corrine gazed into the distance. "I'm going to block him from coming to Corbettstown and my region. I suggest Thojedescar do the same for his area."

"And the shifters you sent us? Do you wish them to return?" Meteor saw Jed coming to join them, Rowdy behind him. "Or are they permitted to remain with us?"

"Ask them. It's their choice. Nobody owns a shifter. Alphas lead their packs. They don't enslave their wolves. Be aware. I want mine to visit your area." Corrine grinned mischievously. "Nobody should miss out on your bakery or your sister's fighting classes."

"You also should visit the Elder Witches when you're in

Eagleville. Bring your wolflings and they can play with Thojedescar's." Rowdy came across the room and sat next to Astra. "Diana and Estelle need to know the truth about Jarvesel, and they won't believe him. And he's been with your people too long to only be a sorcerer. Even if he doesn't do it often, he can change into a wolf like you and your sons. Shifters are different. Not one ever picks reason over feeling."

"He's been saying the same thing about shifters since we fought together on *Trilunon*." Jed took Meteor's glass, finished the last of her wine. "Cousin, where is your mate?"

"Outside." Corrine glanced at her mother, then deliberately added. "He's teaching the boys to pee on the grass and mark their territory."

"Corrinadora! What will the neighbors say? Why do I bother? You younger wolves are enough to turn my fur gray." Lorena sighed, before rising to her feet and bringing over her glass for a refill. "To help raise those boys to adult shifters, Gunnolf will have to do something about his age. Talk to the *Warrior Guild* about it."

"I'll tell him to handle it. He's a sorcerer too. He can take off a few years, but really, he's going to stay around and be my enforcer while I serve out my term for the next thousand years, so it's not a big deal. Meanwhile, with a kitchen witch in my house, I shouldn't have to cook supper. Will you help me, Meteor?"

"Always. Come on, Astra. We'll make it a community affair. Jed, bring in the boys before you attack their father."

"I will." He stopped. "Rowdy, are you helping teach a lesson in manners to him?"

"After you, *siblerbro*. Then, I'll heal all of us before supper."

———

Hours later after their company was gone, Corrine walked into the new nursery. She saw Gunnolf standing between the cribs where their sons slept. She'd told them that bedtime was human time, and they could be their little wolfy selves tomorrow when she took them to the park.

Remy squabbled about it but gave up when she reminded him that baths were much more fun when he didn't have to worry about wet fur. Sure enough, he and Rom happily splashed and played with their toys in the tub. Their father helped dry them, put on jammies and even read an improbable story about a popsicle dragon to them before they put the pair into their beds.

Gunnolf weaved a spell to keep the boys safe, but she didn't mention it. She walked over and tucked her hand in his. "It was a good day. I never thought I'd have them back, be able to raise them myself."

He tipped up her chin. His mouth claimed hers for a moment. "Ourselves, my pet. We raise our sons together."

"When I dream-journeyed last night, I saw what happened after you took the defrocked priest's body and fled Corbettstown."

"After you and Morgan killed me?"

"Yes. You thought I was dead too. You hated the witches for setting the fire, but I told them to do it. To burn the building and the dead shifters. Our sons and I were safe. You didn't know that. You cried for us."

"Demons don't cry, my wolf."

"You're a warlock, a sorcerer who is part incubus. You're not truly all demon. You cried." She slid an arm around his waist. "And then, you went back to the town to see if anything remained of us. You found my necklace."

"Two nights later, you appeared and tried to kill me." He framed her face with his hands. "Such a vicious puppy. You never spoke of our sons, and I thought you knew they were gone, accepted their loss."

"I did because I was the one who gave them to the witches to keep them safe. You fought me, took the knife away and then—" She couldn't say he'd had her, fucked her for hours, not where their sons might hear, even if they were too young to understand. "I should have trusted you. Latham fooled me."

"And me." Gunnolf kissed her. "Now, let's go to bed. Tomorrow, the hunt begins."

"This time, we'll kill him for good and always. We won't let him return. We'll do it together."

"Yes." Gunnolf held her close. "Together."

———

Meteor dozed with her head on his shoulder as they headed home to Eagleville. Jed flicked a look at Gard on the far side of the truck. "Well, today didn't turn out like I expected. I thought I'd be the one to slay my uncle. Instead, it was my long-lost cousin."

"She may look sweet and dainty, but I'm glad she's on our side in the upcoming war. I couldn't believe how quickly she wasted Frank. The woman's lethal. I like that. We still haven't heard about Latham. A.J. has disappeared on some secret mission according to his brother."

"Andrel vanished from the hospital too." Jed focused on the highway. "The nurse said Gunnolf came for her, but we know that isn't true. He was either with the Guild or us all day."

"Identity theft takes on a whole new meaning when it comes to those from *Trilunon*." Gard frowned thoughtfully. "Astra says we may not have all the proof we need to convince the *dracklegons* yet, but she thinks Latham's been using her father's shape for years."

"At least three hundred or more."

"We have to stop him this time around, Jed."

"You know it."

After a quick stop at his house, Jed drove to the bakery. Gard said he intended to sleep in his own bed tonight. They wouldn't have to worry about Frank sending a patrol of shifters to attack them. For now, all of them were safe.

Upstairs in her apartment, it was his turn to pour the wine. Meteor sat at the center island, caressing her bracelet. "Corrine suggested we renew our vows at *Yule*. Do you have the rest of my *talipenlace* set?"

He nodded. "I carry it with me everywhere now. What changed? Why do you want the other bracelet and earrings?"

"Corrine told us that Latham took my father's shape last night and tried to poison her. The necklace he gave her for protection is with her always. When she's a wolf, it becomes a collar. It's her necklace when she's a woman."

"Your *amunecdant* remains the same always. It will shift when you do, but I'd never ask you to wear a collar."

"Yes, but my father is an extremely skilled sorcerer and uses darker elements. You're much more civilized. I will never call you my master or owner, like my stepmother does him. I wouldn't have even if I was under a death sentence for a year like Corrine was."

"Nobody owns a shifter. I should have killed him tonight, not granted him mercy because she wanted it."

"No." Meteor held up her hand, the bracelet shining in the moonlight from the windows. "Even if she doesn't say it, she loves him. And he loves her. Leave their kinky sex thing between them."

"Oh no. Tell me you didn't say that."

"Sex, sex, sex! Okay, now we're done with their sex lives. Back to what I was saying. Corrine recognized the threat for what it was and didn't allow Latham's favorite *Vensonxic* syrup to kill her. I couldn't do that when your uncle or Latham came for me in my last four lives."

"And you think the entire *talipenlace* set will protect you?"

"Between it and the vows at *Yule*, Corrine says we'll both be protected. Rowdy was able to save Astra when Latham murdered her. I want that, Jed. I want us to be together for the rest of our lives."

"I want it too." He reached for the small jewelry box in his pocket. "I've always wanted it."

"I want a big ceremony at *Yule* with our family and friends. On our first soul-matching night, I was near death. I couldn't say my own vows. This time, I want to be the one to speak for myself."

He put the box on the counter. He leaned across and kissed her.

"You speak for you, and I'll speak for me. Our powers will mesh and make us stronger."

"Strong enough to defeat evil?"

"Love will always conquer hate." He trailed a finger over her lips. "Now, about those twins?"

"You still want them after meeting my baby brothers who are half demon and half shifter?"

"Definitely. And I'll always want you."

"Good. Right answer." She added the second bracelet next to the first on her wrist, then the earrings. She heard the little inlaid creatures begin to sing. And so, it finally started for them.

They had a whole life ahead of them, so many lives to live, laugh, love. "Let's go see what we can do about those twins."

# EPILOGUE

*Everett, Washington*
*Sunday, December 2<sup>nd</sup>, 2018*

MOONLIGHT SHONE THROUGH THE WINDOW. IT WASN'T FULL. Andrel couldn't shift, couldn't heal like a wolf. She whimpered softly, still trapped in the form that looked like the witch's. The nurses had been kind enough. They didn't understand why the painkillers barely worked and constantly asked the doctors what more could be done. One threatened to cut her open tomorrow. More torture, but he called it surgery and said it'd fix her.

Her leg, fractured in two places, throbbed and ached. They told her not to move because she had cracked and broken ribs. Her head pounded from the concussion. The bed was so uncomfortable, and she hated the catheter. When a person had to pee, she wanted to pee either in a toilet like a human or else in the woods like a wolf.

Footsteps. Was it the nurse again? They constantly woke her up.

She felt a hand on her forehead and yelped softly. Surprisingly, the pain eased, and she opened her eyes. She saw the Corbettstown police chief standing by her bed. "Sorry, sir. I, I failed."

"Hush. We don't want them to hear." He leaned over, kissed her forehead. "You did your best, my little one. I'm going to heal you from head to toe and then we'll leave."

"How? You're the enforcer, not a *healer*."

"No questions." He tapped her bruised cheekbone.

Andrel almost screamed in agony, then remembered she was a shifter. A cop. She didn't show pain.

She faded in and out of consciousness as he mended her body during the next hour. A *healer* would have stopped the pain too, but she understood he couldn't. He was doing his best. Bones knit, bruises faded. She stirred when he slid a flowered top over her head, guided her arms into the sleeves. She smelled blood and knew he'd killed the person who'd originally worn the scrubs.

Strange. He usually refused to do the executioner's job, leaving the gruesome work to his associate. He brought over a wheelchair, lifted her into it. The cold vinyl seat chilled her bottom.

"Pants," she murmured. "I need pants."

"No, you don't." He slid his hands over her knees, up her thighs. One cupped the mound between them. "Nobody will see these lovely parts but me."

She trembled when he leaned closer. His lips brushed hers. And two fingers went inside her. Her body still ached. Not as bad as before, but she wasn't a hundred-percent normal, not yet. "I can't."

"You will." His mouth found the hollow of her throat. "I'm going to have you screaming for me. But not now. Not yet. For now, show me how well you're going to fuck me."

She squirmed on the seat, began to move back and forth with the steady thrusts of his fingers. His thumb sought out her clitoris. He wasn't particularly gentle with the way he rubbed it. He kissed her when she came, his tongue claiming her mouth, so no one heard her soft cry. Why did her best friend, Corrine act as though he was the best lay around?

*I've had better. Hell, A.J. is better when he's half drunk.*

He covered her legs with the blanket off the bed and then pushed the chair down the hall to the elevator. Oddly enough, none of the nurses or doctors appeared to see them. He stopped outside, picked her up. The blanket fell on the ground, and she shivered in the night air. "I'm cold."

"You'll be warm in a minute." He carried her to the waiting K-9 cop car. He opened the back door. "In you go. *Change*, Andrel. *Change* to your wolf and heal."

Lying on the seat, she stared at him. She began to see through the illusion. A younger, stronger version of the man she lusted for, but he belonged to her best friend, the alpha of the rebel shadow pack in Corbettstown. Six foot tall, sun-bronzed and muscular in his three-piece, pinstriped suit, Latham Sellers tried so hard to look like his mentor, even shaving his skull.

"You're not the chief."

"No. I'm better than him." He smiled but it didn't touch his pale green eyes. "And now I have another wolf-girl to add to my collection. *Change*, Andrel. Heal. You need to be strong when we get to the hotel."

"I'll try. I'll do my best." She pretended it took more of an effort than it really did.

Granted, she couldn't do it like her bestie who always looked as if she danced in an aurora of light. Still, Andrel gathered enough shifter *magick* to make the transition easier on her than it sounded to onlookers. She'd learned a long time ago to give the audience what they expected.

So, while she went through what looked like the normal gyrations of a woman changing to a wolf, she watched Latham start the SUV. He drove well but not aggressively, determined not to cause attention. It didn't take long to reach the waterfront hotel.

When they arrived, he opened her door, collar, harness and leash at the ready. "Your costume, my pretty. Let's make them think you're a cop."

*'I am a cop, you fool!'*

A shock of what felt like electricity lanced through her. She dropped onto the ground, belly in the dirt, panting.

"Did I forget to say I can hear you, Andrel?" He led her toward a basement unit. "We'll have dinner. I'm sure you're hungry after that hospital food. Then, we'll make plans. The war starts tomorrow, but tonight is for fun."

Andrel dreaded the sound of that, but she was a fast learner. She didn't admit it. He was going down! She loved her job, and she was good at it. *'Whatever you say.'*

"Master. Call me, Master."

She whimpered, struggled for a minute and silently repeated her mantra of giving the audience what they wanted. She yelped when he jerked on the collar. Another magickal shock, a third.

She surrendered, remembering what Corrine always said. Nobody truly owned a shifter. This was all an act. *'Master. Please, Master.'*

"That's a good girl."

***THE END***
(Or is it?)

**Don't miss out on your next favorite book!**
**Join the Melange Books mailing list at**
www.melange-books.com/mail.html

———

**THANK YOU FOR READING**

———

Did you enjoy this book?

We invite you to leave a review at your favorite book site, such as
Goodreads, Amazon, Barnes & Noble, etc.

**DID YOU KNOW THAT LEAVING A REVIEW...**

- Helps other readers find books they may enjoy.
- Gives you a chance to let your voice be heard.
- Gives authors recognition for their hard work.
- Doesn't have to be long. A sentence or two about why
  you liked the book will do.

# ABOUT THE AUTHOR

**Josie Malone** lives at a riding stable in the Cascade foothills in Washington State where she organizes riding programs, teaches horsemanship now that she's retired from teaching school, and takes care of sixteen horses. Her life experiences also include dealing cards in a casino, attending graduate school to get her master's in teaching degree, and serving in the Army Reserve - all leading to her second career as a published author.

Visit her at her website
www.josiemalone.com
to learn about her books.

Subscribe to Josie's Newsletter:
https://sendfox.com/josiemaloneauthor

*Contact Josie at:*
josiemaloneauthor@outlook.com

facebook.com/JosieMaloneAuthor

x.com/josmaloneauthor

instagram.com/josiemaloneauthor

amazon.com/Josie-Malone/e/B006HC9VMI

# ALSO BY JOSIE MALONE

**Seattle's Lost Lovers**

Rainy Day Rescue (Coming Soon)

―――

**Baker City Hearts and Haunts**

My Sweet Haunt

More Than A Spirit

Family Skeletons

Ghost of the Past

Kindred Spirits

Merry Ghostmas

Ghost Writer's Inn (Coming Soon)

Summer's Last Call (Coming Soon)

―――

**Liberty Valley Love**

A Man's World

Cowboy Spell

The Marshal's Lady

Hero Spell

A Trail Through Time

Time In Between

Kitchen Witch

Yuletide Magick (Coming Soon)

War Witch (Coming Soon)

www.ingramcontent.com/pod-product-compliance
Lightning Source LLC
Chambersburg PA
CBHW050029030726
47506CB00001B/182